In conjunction

PRAISE FOR

CELING SMASHERS: BOOK 1

THE CLOSER

Beverly Hills Book Award Finalist

Selected as one of Bustle's *"9 Fall Book Debuts By Women You're Going to Want to Read Immediately"*

"*Unreservedly recommended...An original and compelling novel about a woman who must compete in what has traditionally been a 'man's world', The Closer reveals author Shaz Kahng as an impressively skilled storyteller who is able to entertainingly engage her readers from cover to cover.*" - **Midwest Book Review**

"*The Closer is an inspiring and fun take on women in business, with plenty of ceiling smashing along the way. Shaz Kahng's fast-paced, sports-focused The Closer is timely and refreshing, a novel that exposes the difficulties that women face in industries that are dominated by men. Vivien Lee is a thoroughly likable lead...even faced with manipulation and outright lies, Vivien typically picks the higher road. The story takes some inspiring turns, including Vivien's participation in a Wharton-founded secret club, the Ceiling Smashers, which functions as a place to maintain alliances with other women in business. Anecdotes about women's experiences at those meetings read as realistic and give credence to the bonds of sisterhood highlighted throughout.*" - **Foreword Reviews**

"*The Closer gives women the heroine for whom they have been looking.*"
- **BOSS Magazine**

"*From the first page of The Closer, readers are thrown into Vivien's world...We really don't see many female characters like Vivien. It's not until you read Vivien's story that you begin to feel inspired by the type of female role model she is: a strong businesswoman who side steps any "stereotypes" placed on women in positions of power...Shaz's creation of Vivien as a strong character capable of weathering brutal situations speaks volumes--not just about the person she's loosely based on, but also about the deeply ingrained stereotypes that persist today, both in fictional constructs of female characters and real women.*"
 - **Women's Running Magazine**

"*The book is the first in a series designed to keep the momentum going in destroying stereotypes that nice women finish last.*"
- **Good Sports Magazine**

"*Insightful and inspirational.*" - **Renowned Silicon Valley Entrepreneur and Venture Capitalist**

"*Exciting and relevant narrative- Kahng has a gift for storytelling.*"
- **Hollywood Producer**

"*Couldn't put it down.*" - **Former Nike Female Senior Executive**

"*Business savvy and entertaining all in one... I am definitely recommending this book to all of the women in my life who are smashing the ceilings themselves.*" - **Amazon Reviewer**

CEILING SMASHERS: BOOK 2

SMASHERS SYNCHED

SHAZ KAHNG

CEILINGSMASHERS.COM

OLOM
PRESS

~

For Bill
Throughout our incredible adventure of marriage,
parenthood, and life - with all its twists and turns-
to have you by my side has been one of my greatest joys.

~

PROLOGUE

Vivien Lee spent her entire consulting career helping CEOs look good by showing them how to solve problems and improve their businesses. But she walked away from all that to go after her dream of running a business. A lifelong athlete, Vivien accepted a job as the first female president at the Smart Sports company in Portland, Oregon. Having already said goodbye to Coop, her best friend from college and graduate school, Vivien bid an emotional farewell to her Ceiling Smasher friends.

The Ceiling Smashers are a secret society of professional women that four friends—Vivien Lee, Grace King, Sofia LaForte, and Andi Andiamo—founded during their first year as MBA students at Wharton. Vivien envisioned that the Ceiling Smashers would serve as a personal board of directors for its network of talented women in their future careers. The Smashers were optimists but pragmatic; they knew there would be times when they'd need each other for counsel, support, and empathy. Vivien incorporated her father's advice, "Be great and be good," into her founding philosophy for the Smashers: their aim would be not only to achieve success, but to motivate others by conducting themselves with honor. Membership was kept to twenty women, a mix of MBAs and women from other University of Pennsylvania graduate schools. Every other month they got together for dinner in New York, and they would hold strategizing conference calls whenever a member needed focused advice to solve a problem.

While Andi, Grace, and Sofia were generally supportive of Vivien's big move, she knew they were concerned about her being on her own out on the West Coast facing a tough challenge. Vivien loved and respected her friends and she likewise was worried about them.

Grace was taking a yearlong sabbatical from her position as the chief marketing officer of Burberry to write a book about branding, and that was a completely foreign venture for her—how would she fare?

Andi, who had been a highly successful private banker for years in addition to juggling her twin toddler sons, was about to encounter major changes at work—how might that affect her career trajectory?

Sofia, a financial analyst and reporter for CNBC, had been pitching an idea for a new show to her boss for nearly a year—would she finally be given her big chance?

Last, their Wharton classmate and friend Coop was determined to make partner at his accounting firm and yearning to find a life partner—as a gay man, would he find his fit, professionally and personally?

*

Book number one in the *Ceiling Smashers* series, *The Closer,* follows Vivien Lee on her journey as she moves from New York to Portland, Oregon, to take on a daunting role at Smart Sports. Book number two in the *Ceiling Smashers* series, *Smashers Synched*, shares the stories of the other Ceiling Smashers founders—Andi, Grace, and Sofia—and Vivien's best friend Coop and what's happening in their lives while Vivien's story is unfolding. Get ready to dive in.

PART ONE

CHAPTER 1

Late August

GRACE

"Move your butt," a voice behind her said.

The sound of burbled words drifted by Grace's ears, then vanished in the breeze like dandelion seeds scattering in the wind. She tapped the console to adjust the mechanical tee, raising it a bit, and then lined up again to take a swing with her driver. There was nothing more satisfying than watching the flight of a well-struck golf ball.

"You need to move your butt." She spun around and realized that the tall, lanky man at the next stall was talking to her. Grace's first reaction was annoyance. Why was it that men always felt an irrepressible urge to offer unsolicited advice to female golfers? This was the first day of her sabbatical from a high-powered executive role and she wasn't keen on taking orders from anyone.

She half turned. "Thanks, but I'm not looking for any tips." Grace flicked her blond ponytail back and concentrated on her game with a new sense of determination.

The man waited until she swung and then came around to the console, resting one arm on it in a relaxed, confident manner. Still looking down at her ball, Grace could see the guy was wearing dark gray shorts and black golf shoes. With a slight Midwestern accent, he said, "I meant no disrespect, miss. You have a beautiful swing, but I think you could get a lot more distance on the ball if you bend over slightly."

Why couldn't the guy leave her alone? She looked up, ready to give him a menacing glare like Medusa turning a victim to stone. His chin was lowered and he looked up at her, doe-eyed. Though his face was partially hidden by his ball cap, Grace instantly recognized him.

Flummoxed, Grace said, "Wh-what did you say?"

"If you stick your butt out a little you'll generate more power from your core as you swing through, like this…" He turned sideways to her and demonstrated. Then he flashed his high-wattage smile. "By the way, I'm Winston Wyatt, but everyone calls me Win." He stuck out his hand. This was unreal. Of course Grace knew who Win Wyatt was; she'd just seen his face on a thirty-foot-wide movie screen last night, in addition to his many other films. Win was stunningly handsome in person, with brilliant blue movie-star eyes and perfect gleaming teeth. His flawless, slightly tanned skin was glowing, and he exuded vitality.

Grace shook his hand. "Hi, I'm Grace. Grace King. A pleasure to meet you, Win."

"You know who I am?"

Despite her shallow breathing she kept her cool "Of course, I don't live under a rock. In fact I just saw your latest sci-fi movie last night." She brushed some lint from her white golf shirt and was happy she'd chosen to wear a navy blue golf skort that flattered her long legs. "Great story and well acted, but the title of the movie was just awful. I bet that film would have broader appeal with a better title." Although Grace hailed from the Midwest she'd long ago acquired the New Yorker's habit of speaking her mind.

"Right?" Win's eyes were wide. "I tried to get them to change it! The film was adapted from a Japanese movie and I wanted them to just translate the original title, but the producers thought it was too edgy. They wouldn't even listen to my opinion." He let out a breath.

Grace had to suppress a smile. Apparently even Hollywood leading men had to handle work frustrations and political footballs. "Well, if it makes you feel any better, Win, I'll listen to your opinion now and try out your golf tip, though I don't usually accept unsolicited advice." Summoning all of her self-control to remain calm, Grace turned around and practiced hitting balls with that slight adjustment. In her role as Burberry's chief marketing officer she'd often dealt with celebrities and prided herself on treating them like normal people while others fawned incessantly. A soft breeze came in from over the water, providing some natural air-conditioning.

Thwack. The unrelenting sound of golf balls being struck at the Chelsea Piers driving range wasn't doing much to alleviate Grace's pounding head. She'd had a weekend of late nights with her Ceiling Smasher friends. On Saturday night they had thrown a sentimental send-off dinner for their dear friend Vivien Lee, who was moving to Portland, Oregon, to take an executive job at Smart Sports. Sunday night she'd taken in a movie with Andi and Sofia, and they'd grabbed a late dinner with a little too much wine. Grace's brain was moving at a slower pace this Monday morning.

After hitting all of the balls allotted on the card she'd purchased, Grace relaxed her shoulders and packed up her clubs to leave. Win walked over and renewed the conversation. "So, Grace, what do you like most about living in Manhattan? I'm new here—recently moved from LA."

"First of all, New Yorkers don't call it 'Manhattan,' we say 'the city.'" She chuckled. "I love the energy, the arts, the diversity, the great restaurants—everything's super convenient. Even hopping in a cab to come here to Chelsea Piers was easy."

"Do you live close by?"

Grace nodded. "Actually, I do. I live in Chelsea, which is a really fun neighborhood. And Harrison Ford lives in the building across the street from me." She groaned internally. Now she sounded like a groupie—her cheeks reddened, and she wished she hadn't offered up that tidbit.

Win cocked his head. "I didn't know Harry lives in Chelsea, I'll have to give him a call."

Guess all the big stars have each other on speed dial. Grace smirked. She picked up her golf bag and threw the backpack straps over her shoulders. "Well, good to meet you, Win. Have fun living in the city, I'm sure you'll love it."

He paused and wrinkled his forehead slightly, then bowed his head. "I enjoyed meeting you too, Grace King. Have a fantastic day." Win gave her his movie-star smile.

Grace grinned, and as she walked away, she shook her head. *Stuff like this only happens in the city.*

*

The next morning, after sleeping in and squeezing in a workout, Grace scrolled through her emails while she ate a healthy breakfast. Although she was on a sabbatical from her marketing role, that didn't mean she was going to lounge around. No, Grace was about to embark upon a career-defining project. One item grabbed her attention—a message from her literary agent saying he'd lined up a meeting with a potential publisher for the next week. This was big news.

Grace's plan was to write the definitive book on how to turn around a brand, and prior to leaving her job she'd outlined the book and created a nonfiction book proposal. A friend had connected her to a literary agent, who agreed to take her on and said they'd iron out the details later. It didn't make sense to write the entire book until she'd signed on with a publisher, so Grace had decided to take a couple of weeks off to just relax and think about what she'd write. She was thrilled to get a meeting with a publisher this quickly.

Today her plan was to run some errands and enjoy her freedom. The first item on Grace's list was getting new bath towels at Bed Bath & Beyond on Sixth Avenue in Chelsea. Smack-dab in the midst of the massive sea of towels, Grace was weighing the benefits of organic

Turkish cotton over MicroCotton when she heard someone say, "Move your butt…you're blocking the best towels." *Huh? Win Wyatt? Again?*

"You need a new line, Win," Grace quipped. She turned and squinted at him. "Are you stalking me? Ryan Reynolds did the same thing and it took ages to shake him off."

Win ran his hand through his thick, short sandy blond hair and smiled, revealing his perfect teeth. His slightly rumpled aquamarine T-shirt perfectly matched his eyes and was clingy enough to show off his pecs. He wore jeans that had just the right amount of wear, and he sported cool slip-on sneakers. With his chin tilted down, he fixed his eyes upon her. "Wow, Grace, two days in a row. This is some coincidence. Both of us hitting the driving range at the same time and now buying towels together—" He was interrupted by some loud squeals of delight from a couple of female shoppers gaping at them.

Grace nodded in their direction and said dryly, "I get that excited when I see Turkish cotton towels on sale, too."

That elicited a big belly laugh from the film star, and his eyes crinkled slightly at their corners. "I like your style, Grace." He waved good-naturedly at the women. "So what type of work do you do that lets you golf and shop on a weekday?" Win's eyes scanned her outfit of skinny jeans and ballet flats topped off with a drapey blouse.

Grace put aside the teal bath towels she was considering buying. "Well, I spent many years traveling the world as chief marketing officer for Burberry and helping turn around the business and the brand. But now I'm taking a yearlong sabbatical from work to write a book on branding." She wrinkled her forehead. "Actually this is the first time I've taken a break from work in my entire professional career."

"Impressive experience, boss lady." Win whistled. "How's the writing going?"

"Oh, I haven't started yet," Grace explained. "I'm taking a staycation and giving myself two weeks to do anything I want, and then I'll start writing." Her eyes drifted upward. "You know, I used to think people who took time off were slackers, but after only a couple of days I'm definitely starting to see the appeal." She chuckled.

Win rubbed his chiseled chin. "So you're allowing yourself to do anything for the next little bit? Would you be interested in grabbing coffee with an aspiring Broadway actor?"

Puzzled, Grace asked, "Who would that be?"

A rosy color came to Win's cheeks. "Um, that would be me. I'm starting rehearsals for a Broadway show next week." He gave a little shrug. "So how about it, Grace? You can tell me your favorite hangouts in Manhattan—I mean, 'the city'—over a cup of coffee."

Was he for real? The most bankable star in Hollywood, Win Wyatt, was asking Grace out for coffee? Why? For a second she felt a thrill but then quickly started wondering if hanging out with a movie star was her cup of tea (or coffee). From the magazine covers at the grocery checkout, Grace knew that Win had last dated Jessica Dylan, an actress known for her edgy fashion sense. His world seemed so foreign to her.

"I…I don't know, Win."

"You're not married, are you? Or do you have a boyfriend?" He looked a little apprehensive.

She shook her head. "No, nothing like that. I just had a nice solo day planned out. I'm going to have lunch at my favorite little Greek place in SoHo and then go to see a video art installation by a Korean artist at the Whitney Museum. Then I was going to finish the day watching the sunset over a glass of champagne on the roof deck of the Peninsula Hotel."

That sounds awesome. Mind if I tag along with you for lunch?" There was a pleading look in his eyes, and suddenly Grace realized that although Win Wyatt was a world-famous movie star, he was also a new guy in town, and maybe—just maybe—he was a little lonely. Anyway, it was just lunch, right?

*

Grace and Win hopped the subway down to SoHo, getting off at Spring Street. As they walked the few blocks to the restaurant, Grace was aware of the excited glances they were catching from others on the street. Some pedestrians stopped in their tracks, pointing in their direction, while others whipped out their smartphones to snap a few photos of them. You'd think a famous person might wear a disguise, or at least a hat and sunglasses, but her companion was unadorned. Win walked and talked naturally, appearing not to notice the attention, but for Grace it was a completely unfamiliar and unsettling experience.

The Greek restaurant was the size of a postage stamp with only five tiny wooden tables. When Grace walked in they greeted her as usual, but when the waitress caught a glimpse of Win, she froze. Then she turned around and hustled over to the two people seated at the best table next to the window and asked them to move over one table. With a flourish the waitress seated Grace and Win at the newly vacated table. The displaced couple was grumbling a bit, and Grace and Win leaned over to say thank you. When they realized they were sitting next to Win Wyatt, their mood suddenly improved and they were all smiles. Grace advised Win on what was good on the menu, and immediately after they ordered the waitress brought over some complimentary sparkling lemonade. Grace had been to the restaurant many times but this was a first.

Win smiled at the waitress. "Oh, you're spoiling us. Thank you so much."

Grace chuckled, shaking her head. "Must be good to be you, Win."

Her dining companion winked.

He must get treated this way all the time. What that's like? "So how did you get into acting in the first place?" she asked.

"It was a total accident. I've been practicing martial arts since I was a little guy, and when I was in graduate school a sparring buddy of mine told me about—"

Grace interjected, "Did you say graduate school? I didn't know you went to graduate school. What were you studying?"

Win said in a quiet voice, "Um, I was getting my PhD in chemical engineering at MIT."

"No way! You were *chem E?* At *MIT?* You mean you're actually smart?" Grace waited a beat, then caught herself. Her eyes widened. "Oh gosh, that came out sounding so rude. I'm sorry, that's not what I meant. It's just that I'm an engineer by training as well and I remember chem E was the toughest major. Seeing you in movies and on the magazine covers, I would never have guessed you were such a brainiac." Win raised one eyebrow. Grace's shoulders tensed up and she flushed. "Okay, I'm just going to stop talking now." It was hard to believe that this gorgeous, talented man was also that smart.

Win threw his head back and laughed. "Don't worry about it, Grace, I understand. In fact my agent told me to keep that part of my background quiet. He thought it might affect my appeal by making me seem too nerdy."

Grace nodded as she munched on a crostini spread thick with taramosalata.

"Anyway, a sparring buddy of mine told me they were casting extras for an action movie they were shooting in Boston and they wanted guys who knew martial arts. I was trying to save up for a new laptop and needed the money, so I figured I'd try out. We went to the audition and both got cast as extras."

"That's cool. And that got you interested in making movies?"

Win swallowed his bite of crostini. "Yeah, well, there's more to the story. We started rehearsals and the guy who was playing the bad guy injured his back and had to drop out of the movie. So, to my complete and utter shock, the director asked me to step in and play the role. The film starred Tom Cruise as the good guy and I played this character called Milo."

Grace tilted her head to the side. "Milo the Maniac? You're talking about *Countdown,* where Tom Cruise plays a nuclear scientist whose family gets kidnapped and in exchange for their freedom he has to build a nuclear weapon for the bad guys? That was a huge hit. That was your first movie?"

"Yes. That's what got me started in the business, although I'd still love to go back and finish my degree at some point. But the great thing was that I was finally able to afford that high-tech laptop." Win had a faraway look in his eyes as he tucked into his juicy lamb burger. Grace had to wonder: was it the memory of the snazzy laptop or his first acting job that was making him misty-eyed?

This day was not unfolding as Grace had expected. She was having lunch with a megastar and had just learned that he'd gotten his start in Hollywood simply because he was a geek who wanted a new computer. Who knew? She cut into her chicken boureki and took in the warm aroma of béchamel cheese and herbs. As they talked she discovered that Win grew up in a modest home in Michigan (something they had in common) and spent most of his free time playing hockey and practicing martial arts.

"Enough about me," Win said. "Tell me about you, Grace King." He spent the rest of the meal focused on her, and then the conversation drifted to Grace's tips for city living.

They wrapped up lunch and Win asked for the check. "Please, Grace, let me treat you since I intruded on your lunch plans." But when he signaled for the check the waitress just shook her head. Win put his palms together in a pleading gesture and she finally placed a check on the table. When he turned it over it was a blank bill with a big smiley face scrawled on it. He laughed and motioned the waitress over to thank her, and when she shyly asked for a selfie with him he graciously complied and surreptitiously slipped her a Benjamin. Grace liked how easily Win laughed—his laughter reminded her of the joyous sound of bronze church bells ringing clear and bright.

Grace and Win walked out of the restaurant together, but he didn't seem ready to part ways. "How about some ice cream?" he asked with bright sparkling eyes.

"Okay, there's actually a great ice-cream shop a couple of blocks from here." Grace led the way.

The funky little ice-cream shop was clean and bright, and every yummy whiff probably contained a thousand calories. It was empty inside except for one other customer, a well-dressed middle-aged woman. When Win sauntered up to the counter to peruse the ice-cream flavors on the board, the woman stepped back a little and gave him a wide-eyed stare. He gave her a good-natured nod and the woman ordered her ice-cream cone from the clerk, her eyes never leaving Win's face. Even while she retrieved money from her oversized Gucci bag, the woman's eyes remained glued to him. He asked Grace for her ice-cream choice and ordered for them both. The two of them got their cones and were standing next to the Gucci woman, who had paid but was still standing there, immovable.

Grace took out her wallet and said to Gucci woman, "Excuse me, do you mind if we pay?" She was hoping the woman would move away from the cash register and stop her ogling.

Gucci woman said snippily, "I happen to be waiting for my ice cream."

"But, lady, I already gave it to you," said the young male clerk behind the counter.

"Oh? If that's true, then where is it? Where is my ice cream?" Gucci woman demanded, hands on hips.

Win leaned toward her and said softly, "Excuse me, ma'am, but I believe your ice cream is in your purse."

Gucci woman's eyes grew wide with mortification and she turned quickly, hightailing it out of the ice-cream shop while Grace, Win, and the store clerk doubled over in laughter.

*

Out on the street, Grace and Win were still giggling as they ate their ice cream. Finally Grace caught her breath and turned to Win. "Well, I'd better get going now. Thank you for a highly entertaining lunch, Win. It was an experience I won't forget." She held out her hand to say goodbye.

Win took her hand and enclosed it with both of his. "Is that it, Grace?"

"I'm not sure what you mean."

He looked down and scuffed his shoe on the sidewalk. "I was kind of hoping we could do it again sometime." Win's chin was tucked and he gave her a doe-eyed look—was that his signature move?

Grace wrinkled her brow. "You mean get Greek food again?"

"I mean I'd like to take you out on a real date sometime. If you're up for it."

This was too much. Hollywood's hottest actor wanted to go out with her? "You know I'm not an actress, right? I'm just a regular person. And oh, by the way, I'm super fun and interesting, but still I'm a normal person."

His sparkling blue eyes bored straight into hers and for a brief, glorious moment she felt a thrill tingling down her spine while all the noise from the city street evaporated like steam. "Grace, I like normal. In fact, I crave normal. That's why I moved from LA—too much craziness and superficiality there. Too many boob jobs—sorry, that was a joke. I'm a little nervous." That was endearing. "I think you're smart and funny and gorgeous. And a good golfer. What do you say?"

"I like you, Win, you're very genuine, interesting, and seem like a good person."

Confidence was swimming in his eyes.

But then Grace thought about it a moment longer. "I'm sure any woman would love to go out with you, but I don't think I'd be comfortable with all the peculiarities that come with celebrity. You're used to it by now, but it's kind of odd to me to have everyone staring at you and taking your photo. I'm flattered, Win. Really. So thank you, but I'm going to say no." *No* was a word that many women didn't seem to have in their vocabulary, but for Grace that was not a problem.

Win drew back, eyes wide and mouth agape. From his astonished reaction Grace realized that no woman had ever turned him down until now. Confused, but recovering his senses, the actor reddened a bit. He mumbled, "Uh, right. I understand, Grace. I appreciate your honesty. Well, thanks for today, and if the city is full of people like you I'm sure I'll love it here."

They smiled and parted ways. Halfway down the block Grace turned and saw Win standing there with his arms crossed and shaking his head a little, as if he was still in disbelief.

*

ANDI

Andi, half asleep, heard the sound of her children giggling, or was she dreaming? She felt cozy in her warm bed, her brain about to sink back into the delicious heaviness of her dream. Then an extended eerie silence jolted her awake. Her instinct as a mother told her something wasn't right, and the cold chill of alarm caused her to bolt upright. Struggling to get out of bed with her broken foot, she grabbed her crutches off the bedroom floor. Andi hobbled down the hallway of her expansive Upper West Side apartment to her sons' bedroom. She opened the door silently and slowly using the rubber tip of her right crutch and scanned the room for her twin boys. When she flicked on the teddy bear lamp on the dresser, Andi was greeted by a grotesque sight.

A strange sheen glistened on the light blue walls of the bedroom and on every piece of furniture—it was as if an alien creature had deposited some clear biological goo everywhere. Her three-year-old boys, huddled in the corner, were in even worse shape than the room. Their space-explorer pajamas were covered with clear slime, and both had the sticky substance on their faces and smeared all over their hair, which was packed down like glossy robotic helmets. Both boys smiled devilishly. "Antonio, Francesco, what have you boys done? Look at you!" Then the answer became abundantly clear…there was an enormous jar of Vaseline sitting in between the boys and it was completely empty. Her twin toddlers had enjoyed spreading the gooey substance all over the room and each other, and they looked so proud of their work.

"Good grief! Luca, get in here. I need your help!" she shouted down the hallway to her husband, who was preparing the family's breakfast in the kitchen. Andi could smell the coffee brewing.

Luca raced in. "Andi, darling, what's the matter? Boys? *Oddio!*" From her husband's Italian expression for "Oh my god," Andi could see he'd quickly grasped the problem. Luca was a very tall, slender man who towered over her and the boys. He crouched down to examine his sons more closely. "Such a mess, eh?" Both parents let out a grunt of frustration. But a few moments later they somehow managed to see the humor in the situation and burst out laughing, which delighted the boys, who giggled and slithered around excitedly on the hardwood floor. "Please, Andi, I don't want to you fall down in here. You go eat breakfast and get ready for work and I'll clean up this mess. Okay?"

Andi looked up at her spouse and hugged him. "Thanks, honey, you're the best." Her boss at the investment bank had called an all-hands meeting for that morning and she had to get a move on. She wagged a finger at her boys, who both scampered over for a kiss. Andi's lips slid across their cheeks frictionlessly from the greasy substance. Then she headed down the hall to wolf down a quick breakfast, shower, and head to work.

*

The elevator doors were closing when someone jammed a beefy arm through the shrinking gap and wrestled them back open. Andi backed up a bit to give the person some room, wincing from the pain

17

in her broken foot. Though she loved her three-year-old twin boys, their recent antic of dropping a ten-pound dumbbell on her bare foot had only added to the complexities of her life. She tossed back her shoulder-length dark hair.

"Morning, Andi." Mike smiled broadly as he entered and brushed the wrinkles from his suit coat. Though he was easily the size of the Incredible Hulk, Mike was friendly, easygoing, and always maintained a calm demeanor. His ability to handle just about anything that was thrown his way was probably due to his having five boisterous kids, all under the age of seven. Andi noticed a smear of what appeared to be dried oatmeal on the shoulder of his light gray suit coat—food shrapnel from a child's goodbye hug. They were kindred spirits who knew the unspoken secret shared by parents of multiple young children—going to work, even to an intensely high-pressure occupation, was sometimes a welcome sanctuary from the strength-sapping job of parenting.

"Hey, Mikey, how's it going?" Andi had a petite, athletic build and felt like a dwarf standing next to him.

"Fantastic. How's the foot feeling, my friend?"

"It's okay," Andi said, and shifted her weight on her crutches. "The doc said to give it another week and I can switch to a walking cast. I'll be glad to get rid of these darn things." She held up one crutch.

Mike shook his head. "I'll bet. Hope you're taking it easy." He gave her a friendly pat on the shoulder. "Say, what do you think this morning's meeting is about?"

Their boss Ed had sent out an email the night before asking everyone in the private banking department to report to the all-hands meeting first thing.

She scrunched up her face. "No clue." In fact Andi had a good idea of what the meeting was about. A few months ago Ed had approached her about taking over their department. When she'd first come to Goldman Sachs, being one of the few women in the testosterone-laden bastion of investment banking was tough—the men were cordial but not always welcoming. But, Andi was clever and quick, and could trade bawdy jokes with the best of them, so eventually she'd won them all over. Her boss had appealed to her: "It's not just that you're the top-performing private banker, Andi, it's that the guys really like and respect you. You're also one of the few female partners at the firm. I think this role could be great for you and for the firm. Think about your career development, Andi," Ed had advised her. But she had declined. Sure, she got on well with the guys, but would they really want to take their marching orders from a female leader? Anyway, with her twin toddlers and full slate of work, she felt like things were already jam-packed. Leading a banking department had never been on her career to-do list.

Mike squinted at her. "Andi Andiamo! Come on, I know when you give short answers like that you've got more intel. You can't keep a secret from me." He wagged a finger at her.

Andi chuckled and shrugged. After all their years working together, it still surprised her that Mike could read her so well.

He nudged her gently. "It better not be another announcement about some record-breaking deal of yours. I'm getting a little tired of those." Mike feigned a yawn.

Private banking was all about acquiring new high-net-worth individuals (people with over twenty million dollars to invest) and institutional accounts. Andi's client base had steadily grown and added to the bank's asset base. Though it was only late August, Andi was close to making her numbers for the year. Even though she was consistently the top-performing senior banker in her department at the venerable banking firm, Andi always maintained her humility. The last thing the guys would tolerate was a show-off. This was something Ed had coached her on early in her career—Andi's boss was always looking out for her.

Wanting to throw a bone to her friend, Andi said, "Okay, Mikey, okay. It may have something to do with a change in the leadership of the department. That's all I know, really."

All the bankers in their dark slacks, crisply starched shirts, and suit jackets were packed into the boardroom, waiting for the head of the department, Ed, to arrive. Andi wore a magenta silk tunic over black pants. Outside the conference room, the tranquil view of the sunlit Hudson River and boats sailing by stretched across the windows. Some of the guys engaged in snappy banter, some were hunched over their smartphones, and others looked around apprehensively. Ed walked in, punctual as ever. Though he was in his early fifties, Ed had boyish good looks, a runner's physique, and a youthful glow about him. His bright eyes perfectly matched his light blue Barba Napoli shirt. "Good morning, all. I trust everyone had a good weekend?" He gave his trademark dimpled smile, but there was a wistful look in his eyes. "I have two announcements, one small and one big. First, as you know, I've been at Goldman for twenty-five years, and it's been a great ride. But I wanted to let you all know that I've decided to retire."

"Retire? Who retires at fifty-two years old?" Mike whispered, eyes wide, and elbowed Andi, who shrugged. "I've got five college tuitions to pay—I'm gonna be breaking rocks until I'm seventy." Andi knew the truth to his statement and smiled.

It was obvious that Ed had made a boatload of money over the length of his banking career, but he was still young, with many years to live. Andi wondered what he was going to do with all his free time. And was that the small announcement or the big one?

Ed chuckled at the many shocked expressions around the room. "After years of traveling and late nights at the office, I really need to take a break and spend more quality time with my family." Andi caught some guilty looks on the faces of the dads in the room, Mike included. "It's been wonderful working with all of you but it's time for me to start the next chapter." Ed paused. "The next piece of news affects all of you. Goldman has agreed to split off our private banking unit and sell it to Kaneshiro Bank, since private banking is really their forte. Kaneshiro Bank plans to run this department in the US as a stand-alone unit, so not much will change—you'll keep your clients, current titles, pay packages, and benefits. The biggest change in this acquisition is that you'll be moving to the Kaneshiro Bank offices in midtown, and a new leader will be in charge of the business. Your new boss will be taking over next week, and I'll be wrapping up then. I wish you all the best and want to thank you for all the tremendous experiences we've shared." Everyone rushed up to wish their boss well.

So for the first time in years, the private banking department would operate under a different bank and be headed up by a new leader. Ed had been Andi's boss and career champion for her entire tenure at the bank; she had to admit she'd really miss him. What would this mean for her career?

*

Later that week, on Friday morning, Andi was wrapping up a series of client conference calls when she felt telltale cramping in her lower abdomen. She hightailed it to the bathroom on her crutches and was chagrined to discover that her period had arrived. She was even more miffed to discover that the tampon machine was empty.

"Damn it!" Andi muttered under her breath. It was almost lunchtime and despite her jam-packed schedule, she'd have to hobble out to get some tampons.

Andi visited the local drugstore for a box of tampons, ripped it open, then stopped at a nearby deli to use their restroom. She grabbed a takeaway turkey panini, paid for it, and shoved the well-wrapped sandwich into her purse. Moving as quickly as she could she hustled back to her office, the drugstore bag dangling where she gripped her crutches. The lobby of her building was bustling with the lunchtime crowd. As she rushed to get into the elevator with four men, Andi's crutch got tangled up in someone's dangling computer bag strap, bringing the crutch to a stop. Her momentum propelled her forward and she tripped into the elevator, tossing her drugstore bag high into the air. The bag hit the floor with such force it exploded like a water balloon, its contents splayed out across the elevator floor. Immediately all the male occupants came to Andi's aid by getting down on their hands and knees to pick up her belongings. It took a few seconds for her helpers to realize, horrified, that they were all clutching tampons. An attractive older man with light brown hair and the face of a Boy Scout handed Andi her plastic bag, then deposited his batch into it. She held open the drugstore bag while the other guys filled it up with the tampons they had collected, like some sort of nightmare version of trick-or-treating.

Andi said quietly, "Uh, thanks."

Ernesto, a jovial colleague from the Latin American private banking division, gave her a friendly wink. "*Cómo está*, Andrea?" He then asked her in Spanish what had happened to her foot. Andi responded in a rapid burst of Spanish, sharing the story of her injury and how her young twins had caused it. They both chuckled and mercifully the elevator ride came to its conclusion.

*

Andi was packing up her things at the end of the day when Myron Burry stuck his head in her office door. "Say, Andi, got a minute?"

"My husband has to work late so I'm heading home to relieve the nanny, Myron. I'm kind of in a rush to head uptown." Andi knew Myron was coming to ask her for a favor. He was a smarmy character who was only nice to her when he needed something.

"Oh, too bad. I was wondering if you could join me and the guys for a drink." Myron gave a smirk that irritated Andi to no end. He was an average-height guy with dark hair, pale blue eyes, and came from a family with lots of connections.

*

Years ago, at the end of her first week on the job, she had been walking out of the building with Myron, Mike, and Ken, who were all going for a beer together. Mike and Ken were ahead of them, and Myron made small talk with Andi until he reached the bar, where the others had already entered. Andi paused for a moment. Though she was a newbie, she had hoped for an invitation to join them, but Myron said abruptly, "I've gotta meet the guys inside. See you on Monday, Andi." He turned and left her standing out on the street. She remembered feeling hurt to be excluded like that, but she shook it off and started walking to the subway. At the end of the block she heard someone shouting her name…it was Mike, and he was running after her.

Breathless he said, "Man, you walk fast! I thought you were joining us for Friday drinks. We were surprised Myron didn't invite you in, the dope. You're part of the team now, so how about it?" Andi vacillated, unsure that the guys even wanted her there. "Come on, Andi, I insist!" Mike gently took her by the shoulders and steered her in the direction of the bar. She couldn't help but smile.

Myron Burry was the type of guy who was obsequious with his clients—who ate up his kowtowing—and a master at managing up. But he was a jerk to some colleagues, particularly the women. He often made annoying and sexist remarks, and Andi didn't consider him to be a friend.

*

"Nope, can't do drinks today," Andi said.

He lingered at her door a moment and then came into her office, closing the door behind him. "Look, Andi, I need your help." Bingo; she'd known this was coming.

In the next sixty seconds Myron spilled his guts nonstop. "Maybe

I've been a bit jealous of you all these years, Andi. Maybe that's where some of my aggression has come from. It's just that you're so great at what you do and you make it look so easy. I'll admit that it's embarrassing to get my ass kicked by a woman every day at work, especially when I've been here a lot longer than you. I really need to supercharge my performance now that we're being acquired and have a new boss coming in. My wife is pregnant with our fourth kid and we just bought another home in Quogue—the mortgage is insane. Plus we've got our town house and our place in Aspen on top of that. How am I going to afford all that without a ginormous bonus, which I can't get unless I have a kick-ass year? Christ, what do you think the new boss is going to demand of me? Right now I'm in the middle of the pack. Average just isn't going to cut it. So I'm begging you, Andi, please help me. Did I mention my wife is pregnant again?" The words were flying out of his mouth so fast that Andi wasn't even sure he'd taken a breath during his diatribe. He was also sweating profusely, and Andi noticed the dark stains forming in the armpits of Myron's shirt.

She looked him straight in the eye and exercised her trademark bluntness. "Myron, you haven't been particularly decent to me over the years, and as you've probably figured out I don't even like you. Why, out of all the people in the department, are you asking me for help?"

Myron looked sheepish. "Because I think you hate me less than everyone else does. Plus you're the best senior banker in the department and, well, I think I could learn a lot from you." It seemed to be a struggle for him to admit it, but Myron was a guy desperate to secure his standing in the firm.

When Andi heard him say those words she felt a small sense of victory. In dealing with so many men in the workplace, Andi knew that some guys were only jerks until someone helped them stop being jerks. Perhaps there was some hope for Myron.

"I'll tell you what, Myron. I will help you. But are you familiar with the term *quid pro quo*?"

He gave her a blank look.

"It means 'something for something' in Latin. So I will help you, but you will owe me. And when it comes time for me to collect on the favor you owe me, I expect you to deliver. Got it?"

Myron swallowed and nodded. "Got it," he said.

"Okay, we have a deal. Why don't you get on my calendar next week for lunch and we can hash out a plan?"

Myron clasped his hands together. "Thanks, Andi. You're the best! You better get home to your nanny, and have a great weekend!" He practically skipped out of her office and down the hall.

Andi cast her eyes upward as she weighed which was tougher: wrangling three-year-old twin boys or dealing with needy coworkers. It was a toss-up.

*

SOFIA

"Sofia! Where have you been? I've been searching all over for you!"

Sofia LaForte had just walked through the doors of the CNBC news studio early on Monday morning when her petite assistant Chloe ran up to her with an excited expression on her face. Chloe was breathing hard.

"Good morning, Chloe." Sofia took a moment to enjoy the cool air-conditioning of the office and wipe the small beads of perspiration from her brow. Her normal half-hour commute from the Upper West Side to Englewood Cliffs, New Jersey, had taken a lot longer that morning. "There was a huge accident on the GW Bridge and traffic was a nightmare. What's up?"

"Randolph wants to speak with you right away."

Sofia set her travel coffee mug down on the receptionist's countertop. "Did he say what about?"

Chloe beamed. "Well, it must be good news, because Randolph said it was something you'd want to hear about. And he even sort of smiled!" Randolph Millar, the head of the news network, was infamous for being a no-nonsense media executive with a fairly stern personality. In fact, Sofia had only seen a show of emotion from Randolph a handful of times, one of which was when their financial news show won a couple of Emmy awards, causing the slightest trace of a grin to appear on her boss's face.

Sofia pulled a notebook from her bag and handed the bag to her assistant. "Chloe, would you mind putting this in my office, please? I'd better go see what Randolph wants." A mentor of Sofia's had instructed her to always carry a notebook and to walk with a purpose. *You never know when you'll need to write something down, plus it will make you look like a serious reporter, Sofia.* It was sound advice that she followed to this day.

Randolph's executive assistant waved her in. "Go ahead, Sofia, he's expecting you."

The media mogul's massive office would have been nirvana for someone with OCD—it was sparsely but tastefully decorated, and the few small stacks of paper on his glass desk were arranged precisely. Even his pens were lined up just so, and the binder clips in his leather box were stacked in an alternating pattern, allowing them to nest flat. Randolph wore a dark pinstripe suit, and not a single hair on his salt-and-pepper head was out of place.

"Good morning, Sofia. Please, have a seat."

Sofia smoothed her canary-yellow sheath dress, which highlighted her glowing chestnut-brown skin, and quickly moved to sit in a chair in front of his desk. "Good morning, Randolph, how are you?"

"Fine, thanks. It looks like today's your lucky day, kiddo. You know the idea you've been pitching me? I've decided to give you the green light."

Was she hearing correctly? For over nine months Sofia had been trying to convince her boss to pilot a new financial program where she'd interview prominent entrepreneurs of consumer-oriented businesses and delve into their struggles and their career advice for others. She had tentatively called it *Moguls and Their Mistakes*.

Sofia looked straight at him. "Really, Randolph? That's great, thank you!" She practically jumped right out of her seat. She'd finally have her own show! Sofia couldn't believe it.

"Hang on a second. I do have a couple of conditions. First, I think *Moguls and Their Mistakes* will work better as sort of a roundtable discussion versus a one-on-one interview format. So in addition to you, I'd like to add Graham to the team."

Sofia thought for a moment and nodded. Graham was a solid reporter with an enthusiastic personality and they meshed well together. "Sounds good," she said.

Randolph intertwined his fingers, and with his elbows resting on his desk, he leaned forward. Sofia had seen him do that before when he was about to deliver news he didn't think would be well received. She braced herself. "The second condition is that we bring in another female reporter, someone a bit more seasoned than you, to complement the team. Now, I don't want you to think this means I lack confidence in you, Sofia, but my instincts tell me this show will be a hit if we can present greater diversity to our viewers."

Huh? Sofia LaForte's ethnic makeup was Nigerian, French, and Spanish—wasn't that diverse enough?

Her boss continued, "And by 'diversity' I mean diversity of approach and experience."

Sofia's heart sank a little. This was her idea that she'd pitched as her chance to have her own show. She was already sharing the spotlight with Graham and now there would be another, more senior female on board? Still, Randolph was giving her this opportunity, so she couldn't appear ungrateful.

She kept the tone of her voice bright. "Okay, Randolph. And the other female reporter would be whom?"

"Kate Frost from CBS. She's a hardball reporter with a sharp mind and I think she'll add an interesting dimension to the program. I've been trying to recruit her for some time now."

Kate Frost? The name made ice run down Sofia's spine. Kate was a prominent reporter all right, but known for being exacting and prickly to work with.

Sofia tried to hide her disappointment. "I see. And when is Kate coming on board?"

Randolph leaned back in his chair. "She starts tomorrow, eight a.m. My assistant will set up a time tomorrow morning for you, Kate, Graham, and I to discuss the details of the show and start getting the ideas into production. Listen, Sofia, I know this isn't exactly how you may have envisioned the show, but I think it will be stronger with these changes. Let's work together to make *Moguls and Their Mistakes* a success for the network, all right?"

Mustering a smile, Sofia said, "Yes, of course. And thank you for this opportunity, Randolph. I appreciate it and I won't let you down." This was a slight setback, but Sofia knew she'd figure out a way to rise above it and show Randolph that his trust in her was well placed. Who knew, maybe working with Kate Frost would end up being a good thing.

*

"Congrats, Sof, that's awesome!" Andi's voice sounded particularly cheerful over the phone. "You've been trying get this new program going for a while so you must be pumped to show those numbskulls what you can do, eh?"

Sofia chuckled. Andi had always had a blunt, refreshing way of talking, even back in their graduate school days. "I'm not too psyched about having to share the spotlight, though. And working with Kate Frost may not be a cakewalk."

"Hey, it's probably not going to be as bad as you think. Anyway, just focus on your ideas and show everyone what you can do. It'll all work out, don't sweat it, Sofia. You're gonna be great." Andi covered the mouthpiece of the phone to respond to someone talking to her in her office. "Look, I've gotta get going soon. We can talk more later. Let's touch base this weekend on the Smashers portfolio, okay? I have a few ideas for some new equity investments."

The portfolio idea had been Sofia's, which she gave birth to upon the Smashers' graduation from Wharton. She'd convinced the other three founders of the Ceiling Smashers society—Vivien, Grace, and Andi—to put in an equal amount of money to invest, which she and Andi would manage. The objective was to create a nest egg for each of them. The Smashers were pragmatic enough to realize that none of them would stay with the same employer for their entire career (knowing that the average MBA works for at least seven companies in their lifetime) and they wanted to proactively ensure their financial future. "You never know when you'll be in a horrible work situation and will want to quit your job," Sofia had warned the others, "so having financial freedom gives you control over your career."

"Sure thing, let's review the portfolio this weekend over coffee," Sofia replied.

Andi hesitated for a minute. "Have you given any thought to Luca's suggestion?" Her husband worked at the Educational Testing Service and wanted to fix Sofia up on a blind date with a colleague. It was in Luca's romantic nature to want everyone to find happiness with a life partner.

Truth be told, Sofia had been in a dating rut for a while, but she felt too exhausted for another awful blind date. As her friend Vivien said, "Better to be happy on your own than miserable in a bad relationship." Sofia bit her lip and thought for a few seconds. There was no shortage of cute guys asking her out, but she hadn't truly enjoyed a date in a long time. Maybe she needed a new strategy? "I don't know, Andi, after going on so many bad dates in a row I need a breather. Maybe another time, okay?"

With that the friends wrapped up their conversation and Sofia got up from her desk in search of coffee.

*

The smell of gourmet coffee coming from the CNBC break room wafted through the hallway, beckoning her. Sofia grabbed a mug and went over to select a blend of coffee to sample.

A shrill voice behind her startled her. "Oh, Sofia, there you are. Did you have a good weekend?" As she turned to see the pair of women she referred to as LoCo, her back stiffened. Lorrie and Cordelia were the unremitting cause of headaches at the office, always making catty comments about others and sticking their noses where they didn't belong. Lorrie worked in the graphics department as a title designer and Cordelia was a production assistant. Sofia had tried multiple tactics—being kind to them, avoiding them, and simply ignoring their remarks—but now they had her cornered. Lorrie was the one who had asked her the question and she was still studying Sofia through her cat-eye glasses, her arms akimbo. The two of them almost always wore matching black outfits and stiletto pumps.

She forced a smile. "Hello, Lorrie. Hi, Cordelia. Yes, I had an enjoyable weekend, thanks. And you?"

"Any hot dates?" Lorrie arched her brow.

Sofia shook her head. "Nope. I spent time with girlfriends and had a farewell dinner for my friend Vivien, who's moving to Portland, Oregon. Saw a movie with Andi and Grace."

Cordelia squealed, "Ooh, Andy? Is he your boyfriend?" Why were these two so interested in Sofia's personal life and why were they always prying?

Chuckling, Sofia placed one hand on her hip and noticed the two women checking out her toned arms. "Andi is short for Andrea, and she's a friend from business school," she said.

"Sounds like fun—an *all girls* weekend, eh?" Cordelia gave a sideways glance to her friend Lorrie and they both smirked. "What ever happened to that cute guy you brought to the Christmas party?"

*

Earlier in Sofia's career she'd made a mistake that she refused to repeat, one that completely changed how she behaved at work when it came to sharing her personal life. Sofia had thought things were going well with her then boyfriend when he abruptly suggested they take a two-week break from each other. He'd had a lot going on and needed to decide if he even wanted to be in a relationship. The normally composed Sofia was beside herself when the break hit the three-month mark without a single word from her so-called boyfriend. She was so upset about things that she confided in a colleague, Dorothy, about the agonizing breakup.

Sofia was scheduled to conduct her first big CEO interview that week, and when she showed up on set she was shocked to see Dorothy sitting in her seat. A production assistant rushed up to Sofia and said apologetically, "I hate to tell you this, Sofia, but you've been switched out. Apparently the news producer heard from Dorothy that you were going through a really rough time with your personal life and he didn't think you could handle the pressure of this interview. So he made the call to have Dorothy conduct the interview instead. I'm sorry no one told you earlier."

Sofia was stunned. She'd been preparing for weeks for this interview and it was supposed to be her big chance. Now she'd been betrayed by a coworker and shut out of an important career opportunity. She was beside herself. In that moment Sofia resolved to make it her practice to never talk about her private life to colleagues and keep personal things to herself.

31

LoCo were staring at her as Sofia's thoughts had drifted to the past. "Oh, that guy?" Sofia struggled to remember his name and was about to call her Christmas party date by his nickname, Boron. Boron was an incredibly handsome mergers and acquisitions banker whom her friend Andi had fixed her up with for that party. While Sofia had enjoyed looking at him, it turned out Boron was exceptionally dull and they had almost nothing to talk about. Sofia had nicknamed him Boron because he could bore people to death with his supernatural boring powers. "I haven't seen him in ages."

Cordelia said, "So you'd rather spend your free time with girlfriends? I get it." She nudged Lorrie and they laughed.

Sofia nodded stiffly, unsure why her choice of weekend companions was a source of amusement to LoCo. "Yeah, well, I'd better get over to the set." As she started to move away from them Lorrie said, "Sofia, I think there's something stuck on the bottom of your shoe." The two women watched intently as Sofia gave a glance back over her shoulder and lifted up the bottom of her pump to check for debris. Nothing. Puzzled, she looked at LoCo, who shrugged at each other with a distinct look of disappointment on their faces. "Never mind," Lorrie said.

*

"Ten minutes until showtime!" the assistant director called out to Sofia, who was sitting in the makeup chair getting her lipstick touched up. Sofia reviewed her questions for that day's CEO interview and made some notes with a silver pen. For the past five years she had been co-anchoring *On the Ball Investing,* one of CNBC's top news shows, where they shared daily financial highlights, discussed the hot-or-not business sectors, and did an in-depth profile of one company with an interview with the CEO. Last year, when Sofia's co-anchor retired, the network had replaced him with a younger, more attractive man named Josh Hanson who hailed from Australia. Her boss, Randolph, had recruited Josh from *E! News*, hoping that he'd draw a younger, hipper audience to their broadcast. Sofia had to admit Josh was easy on the eyes, but the problem was he didn't have a financial background, so the meatier parts of the discussions fell to Sofia. That was fine with her; she could hold her own by now, though the beginning of her broadcast career had been a bit rocky. She'd had trouble keeping her eyes centered on the teleprompter and avoiding "ping-pong eyes"— moving her gaze back and forth across the screen as she was reading. Sofia had also found it distracting to speak at the same time she was receiving updates and instructions through her earpiece, but now she was a pro and comfortable in front of the camera.

Sofia took her seat behind the desk on set, and Josh settled in beside her. They shared exactly sixteen seconds of small talk and then they were live on *On the Ball Investing*. Josh did a capable job reading off the financial updates in his charming Aussie accent, and he and Sofia traded some witty banter before she launched into the "What's Hot/What's Not" portion of the program.

Today's focus was the apparel retail sector, and Sofia shared key insights that investors would surely find valuable. Next up was an interview with VFU Corporation's new CEO, Stanley Dingle, who had come up through the organization on the sales side. A year ago he'd beaten out a highly talented female peer for the top spot and so far was doing a mediocre job. Also, instead of cultivating the talented women in the organization, Stanley had cleaned house, replacing many of the female executives with men, which resulted in talented women leaving the corporation in droves. That didn't sit well with Sofia, who knew how tough it was for women in business.

Josh pitched some softball questions to Stanley to get him warmed up and then got into a discussion of company performance. "And it looks like your stock price is up quite a bit lately, so congratulations on that accomplishment, Stanley," Josh said supportively.

Stanley sat up straighter. "Thanks, Josh. Don't mind if I do take some credit there." He smiled broadly. "As I always say, with better leadership you get better results. And we've been making wise business decisions, so all that effort is reflected in the stock appreciation."

Sofia never liked deception, so she went in for the kill. "Stanley, didn't you just execute a massive share repurchase program for VFU Corp.?"

"Yes, Sofia. Why do you ask?"

"The reason the stock price is up is because you bought back shares. The stock appreciation isn't due to an improvement in the business. Buying back shares has falsely propped up the stock price—at least for the short term. Isn't that correct?" Sofia glanced over at Josh, whose eyes widened at this revelation.

Stanley coughed. "Well now, Sofia, the buyback was just part of the reason for the stock being up. We've made other changes to positively impact the business..." He trailed off.

"Okay, Stanley, we've discussed a number of companies in the VFU corporate portfolio that are doing reasonably well. I'd like to shift gears now and ask you about Vidya Activewear."

At the mention of the women's brand, Stanley stiffened up.

Sofia leaned forward. "In the previous segment of our show, we talked about the growth in the apparel sector and how women's activewear has driven that growth for years—high double digits, in fact. You had quite a bit of success with Vidya Activewear with the female CEO who reinvigorated the product, marketing, and retail execution. But about ten months ago you replaced her with a male CEO from the luggage industry and since that time Vidya Activewear's performance has plummeted. I'm curious, what prompted the change-out of the female CEO when she was generating such successful results?" Sofia had done her homework. Plus her friend Vivien was about to run a sportswear business and had given her great insights about the sector.

Stanley pulled the collar of his shirt away from his neck as if it were a noose. "We had vastly different views on the strategy for the business." His response was curt and it was apparent that he was hoping this line of questioning would stop soon.

"I see," Sofia said. "And were you able to execute your desired strategy?"

"Absolutely, Sofia. I wanted to get the product into wholesale in a big way. For example, a big win for us was getting the Vidya Activewear line into Kohl's, among other retailers we've also added."

"Congratulations on that," Josh piped up, trying to make a contribution. "Certainly a great retail partner like Kohl's will expand your customer base."

Sofia held up her index finger. "But your margins selling Vidya Activewear in their specialty stores are much higher. Now your margins are getting killed since you've shifted to selling more volume through wholesale. And there's a price point mismatch—Vidya's starting price point for yoga pants is seventy-nine dollars, while the average price for a pant at Kohl's is twenty-nine dollars. So sales in the wholesale channel are quite soft compared to your owned stores. Is that what has caused the overall decline in the business?"

"It's hard to pinpoint exactly, Sofia. There's certainly more competition in the sector now."

Sofia continued. "But the activewear sector is booming and your brand is one of the only ones that isn't participating in the upside. I wonder if the new male CEO has the *vidya* to run Vidya Activewear."

A frown came across Stanley's face. "I don't catch your drift."

"The word *vidya* is Sanskrit for *knowledge*, so I'm asking if a man from the luggage industry has the knowledge to run a women's activewear business." Sofia gave him an inquisitive look.

The CEO smiled confidently. "Our plan is to expand our offering of Vidya tanks and workout tops at Kohl's, to help drive sales of our yoga pants. That's the magic formula, you see."

Sofia tilted her head to the side. "Why would you follow that strategy? I understand that in the activewear industry the main purchase women make is pants, and that drives other purchases, like tops. What you're suggesting is counter to consumer purchase behavior."

Stanley sat in silence for a moment. Perhaps he was realizing for the first time the huge mistakes he'd made. Fortunately for him it was time to wrap up the program.

"Well, we'll be watching with interest to see how things turn out for your activewear business." Sofia turned back to the cameras. "Thanks to Stanley Dingle, CEO of VFU Corporation, for joining us today on *On the Ball Investing.*"

*

"Great interview today, Sofia," Randolph said as he passed her in the hallway. "Let's see what kind of ideas you bring to the meeting tomorrow when we discuss your new show."

Sofia gave Randolph the thumbs-up and planned to spend that evening refining her ideas about how to make the show a success.

*

COOP

When Gary Cooper met Vivien Lee it was magic...and the beginning of a lifelong friendship. Coop, as he was better known, picked up a framed photo from among the many resting on the glass shelf of his étagère and gazed at his favorite picture. It was a photo of himself and Vivien taken their sophomore year at Cornell, not long after he'd transferred from Rutgers. God, they looked like kids in the photo, their arms wrapped around each other, standing in front of the clock tower in the center of campus. Coop still recalled the adrenaline rush of his first day at the pristine Ivy League campus. At new-student orientation Vivien had read his name off the list of students in her group. "Gary Cooper?"

Coop had said, "What can I say? My mom loved his movies. But everyone calls me Coop."

A smiling Vivien commiserated with him. "Nice to meet you, Coop. I'm Vivien Lee—different spelling than the movie star, though. My parents were crazy about *Gone with the Wind*." She winked. "We celebs ought to stick together." An instant bond was formed that day.

Looking tenderly at the picture, Coop's bright blue eyes misted up. He said in a whisper, "I miss you, sweetie. I sure hope you're okay out there." Vivien was starting her first day as president of a sports company in Oregon. While Coop was proud of his dear friend, there was also a tinge of envy not uncommon among competitive, accomplished people. While Coop was slaving away to make partner at his firm, Vivien had become a consulting partner years ago and was now a senior executive at a cool company. When would it be Coop's time to shine? *Well, all that's about to change.* He put the picture back in its place. "Wish me luck, sweetie!" With that he grabbed his computer bag, clicked off the lights, and shut the door of his apartment.

*

The sunshine outside buoyed his spirits and Coop had a spring in his step as he walked to his subway stop. He was wearing his favorite ensemble of medium blue suit, crisp white shirt, and turquoise tie, and that boosted his confidence further. During his last run together with Vivien he had told her about his upcoming Monday meeting with the Promotion Council. Vivien had said, "You deserve to be made partner, Coop. And having the meeting on a Monday is a good sign."

"Why do you say that?"

Vivien had given him a pat on the shoulder. "Because important business news, like a promotion, is given early in the week so employees are happy and motivated all week. Bad news, like someone getting sacked, is usually delivered on Fridays so people have the weekend to cool off and recover. The fact that they called the meeting for a Monday bodes well for you, my friend." Her optimistic tone made him feel like his promotion would finally happen and today was the big day.

*

Coop had spent the better part of the last two weeks working on a special accounting project for a senior partner named Felix Culo. In his earlier days Felix had been known for his creative ideas for saving clients' tax dollars, but he hadn't come up with any new ideas for years. These days Felix Culo was like the Paris Hilton of accountants—famous for being famous. Still, that change in his currency hadn't rendered any reduction in the size of his ego.

Felix was on an extended vacation and had asked Coop to do a cursory review of his client's books and sign off on the audit so the client could close out the quarter. Being his usual meticulous self, Coop had gathered all the data on the account and plunged into analysis mode. Unfortunately, he spotted some discrepancies that he couldn't quite reconcile. Felix, who had prepared the client's books, was enjoying his trip to Rio de Janeiro and wasn't easy to reach. He was notorious at Coop's firm for being a "toxic boss," expecting people to jump through hoops when he barked orders at them in his clipped New England accent. The deadline to close the books was looming and the client was waiting on Coop's sign-off. After many attempts by Coop, his assistant, and Felix's assistant to track Felix down, Coop was finally able to reach Felix on his mobile phone.

With dreaded anticipation Coop started talking. "Hi, Felix, are you enjoying your vacation?"

In his gruff voice Felix said, "It's effing beautiful down here, fantastic. Great food, great wine, and the women are babes. You should see the bikinis these chicks are wearing." Coop could just imagine the salacious grin on Felix's face, his pale complexion dotted with reddish-purple splotches, a manifestation of drinking much red wine. "What's up?"

"Felix, I…I'm calling to let you know that I can't sign off on the audit." Coop drew in a deep breath and continued. "There are some unusual—or should I say, creative—accounting practices your client has used. For instance, in digging into the numbers I found that some of their long-term debt isn't showing up on their balance sheet. I also noticed that they've extended the depreciation time for plant and equipment beyond GAAP practices. Revenues appear to be overstated, which means their earnings are falsely inflated."

"Listen, Coop, I've been dealing with this telecom client for a long time and you're just filling in temporarily. I'm familiar with what you call their 'creative accounting practices' and I assure you they're legit and typical of the industry. You just don't understand this industry sector and these advanced accounting methods."

Coop swallowed hard. "That may be, but I have some serious concerns."

Felix's voice got slightly sterner but he appeared to be trying to keep things light. "Let's not overcomplicate the situation. I just need you to give your stamp of approval so the client has clearance from our firm to close their quarter, okay, buddy? You're going to make our firm look bad if we cause unnecessary delays, so let's just put this one to bed."

Coop gripped the phone tightly. "But, Felix, Hello TelCo is a public company and they need to follow proper accounting standards. If these numbers are released, then the stock price will go up based on numbers that don't reflect the true financial health of this company." Coop said all this calmly but with conviction.

Felix muttered a string of expletives under his breath and shot back, "You know what your problem is, Coop? You ask too many questions."

"I have to ask questions in order to arrive at the truth. Even Einstein said, 'The main thing is not to stop questioning.'"

"Damn it, Coop, I'm down here in Brazil and you're up there talking some nonsense about Einstein while you're not getting the job done. Do you have any idea of the annual fees we take in from this client? Do you want to piss these guys off so we lose their business? That would not be good for your career, my friend." Felix articulated the word *friend* as if he meant the polar opposite. Coop pictured Felix's mottled face turning a more sinister shade of purple.

"I'm sorry, Felix, I'm just trying to do the right thing."

"Christ, I can't even enjoy a simple vacation! Aren't you supposed to have an MBA and a CPA? What a waste of money, since you obviously don't understand accounting at all." Felix knew precisely where to thrust the dagger, and Coop flinched at the insult. "These guys are preparing to do an acquisition and can't afford a delay. You know what, Coop? Just forget about it. I'll take care of it myself; you've wasted enough of my time. All I'm seeing from you is poor judgment and a serious lack of awareness of the situation. But you know what I'm going to do first?"

"Uh, what's that, Felix?" Coop asked with trepidation.

"I'm going to go and have myself a great meal and enjoy an obscenely expensive bottle of red wine. Then I'm gonna figure out how to deal with this effing mess."

"Well, um, have a good—" Coop managed to say just before he heard the click on the other end. He began to second-guess himself— should he just have done as he was told? It was a toss-up for Coop: on the one hand he was up for a promotion for the second time and didn't want to jeopardize his career; on the other hand he wasn't comfortable approving financials that were clearly wrong. Hopefully Felix would recognize that Coop was only acting in the best interests of the firm. Surely that would earn him some points, right? Just to be safe, Coop fired off an email to Walter, the CEO of the accounting firm, explaining that he'd discovered issues with the client's numbers. Walter was getting up there in age and had been somewhat detached from the day-to-day operations for a while. Coop never received a response.

*

When Felix had returned, Coop had learned that he had contacted another senior partner while he was still in Brazil and convinced the partner to sign off on the client's books, probably badmouthing Coop in the process. The partner had done what Felix advised and the audit was closed without further issue. The whole situation didn't sit right with Coop, but he was up for promotion and knew better than to make any more waves.

*

That Monday afternoon, Coop waited patiently in his office. This was his big day, the day that would bring the reward he'd labored toward for the past ten years. This was the day that Coop would enter the ranks of the firm's partners. He sat at his desk rereading the same paragraph of a client's annual report again and again until the clock on his computer finally clicked to three p.m.

Martin, punctual as ever, tapped on his office door. "We're ready for you, Coop." Martin was one of the partners and was head of the Promotion Council. He was a small, fastidious man who carried a compact umbrella attached to the outside his briefcase at all times.

Coop nodded and stood up quickly. His heart was pounding and he picked up his notebook with trembling hands. As he reached for a pen Coop knocked over his pencil cup, sending an assortment of writing implements flying across his desk and onto the floor. He left the mess splayed out everywhere and followed Martin out the door.

As he walked down the long corridor to Martin's corner office, Coop took a deep breath and did his best to visualize a positive outcome, just as he had read in a bestselling self-help book. He pictured himself post-meeting coming down the hall feeling elated…and promoted.

Coop settled into the empty chair across the gleaming mahogany table from Martin and Barry, who sat huddled close together on the opposite side. While Martin had the typical accountant's look—slight build, sparse hair, wire-rimmed glasses, and an air of orderliness about him—Barry was six feet four and built like a refrigerator. Coop felt the jittery anticipation of a sprinter waiting for the gunshot to start the race, the adrenaline coursing through his veins, but he maintained a relaxed look on his face.

Martin leaned forward. "As you know the Promotion Council met this morning to make our decisions about partner promotions." He shuffled some papers and then looked up. "Coop, you've contributed so much to the firm over the past ten years. You've built a solid reputation and consistently turned in stellar work. We greatly appreciate all your efforts."

Okay, okay. Let's get to the details of the promotion.

"But, on a more somber note…," Martin started. The hair on the back of Coop's neck stood up as he fixed on the word *somber*. Did this mean something serious or something bad? He intertwined his fingers and squeezed hard.

Barry blurted out indelicately, "Coop, the Promotion Council has decided not to promote you to partner at this time."

Coop's mind went numb. His heart spiraled down to the pit of his stomach. So many words in that sentence didn't make sense to him: *not, you, this, time.* It was as if he were watching a foreign movie dubbed with the wrong dialogue—this was not what they were supposed to be saying to him right now. He struggled to muster a response and felt like his necktie was strangling him.

"Again?" he said finally and incomprehensibly. "I don't understand. This is the second time I've been turned down for a partner promotion. How could this happen given my performance?"

"I'm sorry you didn't make it this time, Coop. In fact, we're both very disappointed by this outcome, aren't we, Barry?" Martin said, beseeching his colleague to contribute to the discussion.

Barry piped up. "This isn't necessarily a bad thing, Coop. The council believes you have partner potential. And no one is arguing with your performance. You've brought in loads of business, your clients are impressed with your work, and your teams love working with you. Your expertise is highly regarded. And that speech you gave at the annual AICPA conference was pure genius."

"And so prescient." Martin nodded his head in admiration. "The American Institute of CPAs is the biggest stage for those of us in the business, Coop, and you made our firm look great."

Coop looked at the pair in silence. He was in shock. "So what was the issue?"

Martin took off his glasses and placed them on top of his papers. "It's just that, well, there was some feedback that you could be a better team player." He made air quotation marks with his fingers as he said *team player.*

"What? I've never gotten feedback like that before. Where did that comment come from?" Coop demanded, knowing full well they couldn't tell him. The comment could only have come from Felix Culo, who also sat on the Promotion Council and was probably still fuming about Coop's refusal to sign off on the questionable client numbers. Coop secretly wondered if Felix also hated him because he was smarter and had better hair. "Forget it," he said, "let me ask you a question. How can one comment from one person, which is absolutely false, undermine my ten years of consistent, exceptional performance at this firm? Both of you have worked with me, so you know firsthand that comment about me not being a 'team player'"—Coop mimicked the air quotes—"is completely untrue. Is there some other reason I didn't get the promotion?"

"The vote for partner promotion has to be unanimous—if one

partner on the council strongly disagrees about a candidate, he has the right to stop or postpone the promotion," Martin said.

"The right to do something does not mean that doing it is right. William Safire said that," Coop shot back. Both men looked at him, puzzled, probably trying to recall if there was a Bill Safire who worked in the forensic accounting practice. "I believe it's my right to see the paperwork," said Coop. "The 'Recommended Actions' that highlight what I'm supposed to do differently."

With a tentative look on his face, Martin pushed the paper across the table.

Coop pulled the page in front of him and scanned it quickly. There was a single comment at the bottom of the page, a comment that really set Coop off. "Wile E. Coyote? What the hell is that supposed to mean?" he snapped, stabbing at the paper with his index finger.

"Uh, I'm not sure. Do you remember, Barry?" Martin looked flustered.

Barry's face turned crimson, and as he shifted in his seat the chair creaked loudly. "I think it's that character from the Bugs Bunny cartoon, you know, that coyote that keeps on trying to blow up the rabbit? Or is it the Road Runner he's always trying to get?"

"Oh, yes," chortled Martin, "I believe it is the Road Runner. Remember the one where the coyote is on that cliff with the case of dynamite and he pushes—"

Running both hands through his brown hair, Coop interjected, "Excuse me, but I'd like to understand what this feedback means for me."

"I think the message here is to just keep on trying like the coyote and you'll get the promotion," said Martin in a sympathetic voice.

Coop smacked his fist on the table as the rage bubbled up inside him. "Wile E. Coyote? You call that professional feedback? This coyote comment is the worst, most idiotic feedback I've received in my entire career. And for your information the coyote in the cartoon never succeeds in killing the Road Runner. He tries but never succeeds. Is that the message I should be taking away? That I can try and try and— since it looks like a third time is required—try again and still not get promoted?" Coop's voice rose in both pitch and volume.

Martin sat back and held up his hands. "Please, Coop, don't overreact. You're an incredibly valuable asset to us and we want to make sure you're happy here. I've already submitted a special request that we review your case again within six months. I feel confident that you'll earn the promotion then."

"Martin, Barry, I appreciate your help, but here's the thing. I've already earned this promotion. In fact, I earned this promotion a while ago. The question is whether I want to stick around and wait for the firm to finally recognize that fact so I can get what I deserve," Coop said wearily. "Will Rogers said, 'Even if you're on the right track, you'll get run over if you just sit there.' I don't want to keep sitting here and getting run over. Maybe I should just leave the firm."

"Please be patient, Coop. We're on top of this and we'll do everything in our power to make it happen in six months," Martin assured him. "In the mean time, to show our appreciation for all your hard work, we're raising your salary 10 percent effective this week."

"Gee, thanks," Coop mumbled. His face reddened with indignation.

"It's the best we can do for now, Coop. We hope you can see that we have faith in you," Martin said.

"Gentlemen, I need to get on a client conference call now. I can assure you I'll be watching with interest what happens within the next six months." Coop left the room. He walked down the hall in a daze. How could this have happened again?

Coop prided himself on his loyalty, both personally and professionally, but when did it stop making sense to be loyal to his firm? Did they assume he would continue to put in eighty-hour workweeks and not be rewarded? How many times had he canceled vacation plans? How many family gatherings and friends' parties had he missed because of business travel? After years of sacrifice and hard work, how could one comment from the despicable Felix Culo completely halt his career advancement? Coop's stomach churned and his head pounded. He was supposed to go to a family dinner on Friday to celebrate his big promotion…now he'd have to call the whole thing off. He just wanted to go to his apartment, curl up on the sofa, and not speak to anyone.

CHAPTER 2

Later That Week, September

COOP

By the end of the week Coop had finally come to accept that the promotion he'd had his heart set on was not going to materialize. That Friday afternoon the senior leaders of the accounting firm— partners and managers—were attending a mandatory workshop on diversity and inclusion. It would be the first time Coop would see all the partners from the Promotion Council since hearing his negative news. The firm's CEO, Walter, welcomed everyone to the meeting, explained the importance of the workshop, and then left the room.

The workshop kicked off with a lecture from the diversity and inclusion consultant, and then the group would split into small teams for a breakout session. Despite the tough week, Coop was actually looking forward to the workshop and took it as a good sign that the firm was conducting it. The conference room was set up theater style. Coop took a seat and set his notebook on his lap, looking up to see Felix Culo sitting directly in front of him. Felix was a smallish man with pale skin and visible red spider veins crawling across his nose and plain face. Still stewing over Felix's part in getting his promotion shot down, Coop glowered at the back of Felix's head. Through Felix's thinning brown Brillo-like hair, a purplish raised mass was visible on his scalp. *Grow, melanoma, grow,* Coop chanted silently. Ever the good Catholic boy, Coop immediately felt guilty for thinking evil thoughts about Felix. That guilt was quickly replaced by repugnance when, as the lecturer was speaking, Felix, in his sharp New England accent, said to another partner, "Bet that guy's a fruitcake, eh?" The other partner chuckled.

Suddenly Coop recalled a question Vivien had asked him a while ago. "Is it possible that your firm is holding you back because of your sexual orientation? The partners there are über conservative." Coop had laughed it off as preposterous, but now he began to wonder if there might be some truth to it. He shivered, from both the thought and the strong air-conditioning in the room.

The lecturer passed a basket around and instructed everyone to take a slip of paper. On each piece of paper was the name of a color, which assigned them to a four-person team for the breakout session. "The breakout teams have two tasks. The first task is for each of you to share with your teammates an experience in which you've encountered discrimination. The second task is for your team to discuss how discrimination shows up in the workplace. Let's get into our teams."

Coop's team color was aubergine. Some of the other colors were chartreuse, fuchsia, azure—Coop was fairly sure that the lecturer was gay based on his fancy color choices. He went to find his team and came face-to-face with Felix Culo. *Oh great.*

"What the hell kind of color is this *owbergeen*?" Felix said in his grating intonation.

Coop glared at him. "It's pronounced oh-behr-zheen," he said with a perfect French accent, "and it's purple." He left off the last two words he was thinking—*you dummy.*

Natalie, another senior manager, kicked things off by recapping their assignment and asking if anyone minded if she went first. As Natalie started to speak, Coop noticed that her hands were shaking. "I was the project manager for a client in Atlanta and was only getting highly positive feedback. In fact, I was told I was doing a fantastic job." Her look darkened. "So you can imagine my shock when I was abruptly pulled off the project. I asked why and found out that the client CFO demanded that I be replaced with a white male. Can you believe it?" Natalie, who was African American, shook her head in disgust.

Coop sucked in a breath in horror.

Natalie gave an uncomfortable glance in Felix's direction. "It was one of the worst professional experiences I've ever had—to learn that our firm accommodated that client's request." Her indignation was unmistakable, her eyes filled with tears of torment. Coop couldn't believe what he'd just heard. He had worked with Natalie, and she was a superstar. What client wouldn't want her on their account? Even more disturbing was the realization that his firm would respond to such a request and not stand up for their employee—was this a reflection of the firm's values?

Adam was next to speak, and he shared a painful story from his youth. He'd had a summer job working as a caddy for a private golf club and was the recipient of many insults and dirty tricks from others because his heritage was Jewish.

Next it was Felix's turn. "The only thing someone might try and give me a hard time about is for being a hard-core Patriots fan. Tom Brady? Love that guy." He chortled. "This exercise is irrelevant for me. I'm a strong guy, so no one messes with me. I'll pass." Felix sniffed and turned his attention to cracking open nuts from his ever-present bag of pistachios.

Imagine never having encountered discrimination—I can't even wrap my head around that. Now it was Coop's turn. While the others were talking, Coop had mentally prepared a safe, funny story to share about feeling discriminated against for not being tall (he stood at five feet nine inches). He was cautious by nature, and while he didn't hide the fact that he was gay, it wasn't his practice to speak about it at work either. Maybe he had a sense deep down that it might hurt his career. Maybe the smart thing was to continue to play it safe. Or perhaps this was his chance to test the waters and determine if he really belonged at this firm.

Coop's mouth felt dry and he wrapped his arms around his midsection. He chose to tell a different story. "In college I came out first to my best friend, Vivien. I remember being so nervous to tell her I was gay, but she handled it beautifully, telling me she understood this was an important part of my life and loved me no matter what." He paused ever so slightly to gauge Felix's bemused reaction, and he couldn't quite place the emotion on his face.

Coop continued. "Anyway, senior year I was playing singles on the varsity tennis team and the team captain was named Cash Collingsworth." What Coop didn't share was his secret infatuation with the chisel-jawed team captain, an athletic, handsome, and outgoing frat boy. Although Coop had tried to keep his crush under wraps, his stolen glances in the locker room at the lean, muscular team captain sometimes lingered a few moments too long.

"We were playing in the NCAA title tournament. It was my last year on the team and my final singles tennis match would determine the winner of the tournament. My opponent was a skillful player and the match came down to a tiebreaker. On my match point in the tiebreaker, my opponent's return of serve was called out by the line judge. I saw that the ball had actually bounced on the line, so I went over to the chair ump and said, 'Sir, that was a bad call. The ball was on the line.' The chair umpire looked at me incredulously and said, 'Son, you just won the match and the tournament with that point. What is it that you want me to do?' I told him I couldn't win on a point that wasn't fair. The chair umpire called a time-out to confer with the line judge and then the team coaches came over to join the debate. During the break I sat down in a chair on the sidelines. When I looked up Cash Collingsworth was jogging over to me."

Coop dreamily remembered the sunlight glancing off Cash's glossy chestnut-brown hair, his sparkling hazel eyes fixed upon him. He felt the warmth of his anticipation that Cash would share some words of admiration for Coop's sportsmanship or wish him luck on replaying the match point.

"Cash gripped my arm a little too tightly and hissed in my ear, 'Don't choke, you little faggot.'" Coop remembered flinching at Cash's brutal command as if he'd been slapped. "Then he turned and stomped away." Two emotions had risen up inside Coop at that moment—the first was utter heartbreak. Although Coop knew that Cash was as straight as they come, he'd foolishly fantasized that they'd somehow end up together and eventually open up a quaint little bed-and-breakfast in Vermont. Clearly that scenario was not in the cards. The second emotion Coop experienced was humiliation. Cash knew his secret, but did that give him the right to treat Coop with such cruelty?

The pain of the memory caused Coop to falter, and suddenly the air inside the sterile conference room felt devoid of oxygen. He looked at Felix Culo, whose cold, dark eyes glistened like a shark's right before it gobbles up its prey. Now Coop recognized the emotion Felix was feeling…triumph. Felix must have suspected Coop was gay and was contemptuous now that he knew the truth. *Crack.* Felix continued mechanically opening his pistachios and popping them into his mouth.

Natalie placed her hand on his arm. "That's terrible, Coop. What happened next?"

Coop took a deep breath. "I double faulted on my serve, which brought the game back to deuce. Then I lost the next point, so it was advantage to my opponent. It was his turn to serve, but I could see my opponent was tiring so I felt confident I could convert the next couple of points. As the ball flew over the net toward me I drew back my racquet and caught a glimpse of Cash standing there glaring at me. I connected with the ball and flicked my wrist just a touch more than necessary. The ball sailed across the court deep into my opponent's zone and was called out." Coop had lost the point, the match, and the title for his team. He remembered flashing a look of defiance at Cash, then proceeding to the net to congratulate his opponent.

"As I was gathering up my belongings Cash rushed over and said, 'You blew it.' I shot back, 'Maybe next time you should give a better pep talk.' Cash started to walk away but then turned around hauled back and punched me in the eye. I finished the day with a black eye." And—he neglected to say—a broken heart. A tear rolled down Coop's cheek.

Natalie and Adam gave him sympathetic looks.

Felix took a break from cracking nuts and frowned. "So, Coop, let me get this straight." *Interesting word choice.* "You threw the match and the tournament because you didn't like what Cash said to you? Maybe I was right about you not being a team player." With his New England accent, that last word came out like "play-yah."

Coop gasped. Felix had just inadvertently confirmed that he was the one who'd torpedoed Coop's promotion. Before Coop could respond Felix realized his error, got up, and hustled over to the refreshment table.

"That was really brave of you to share that story, Coop. Especially in front of Felix," Natalie said. Adam nodded in agreement, confirming that they knew Felix was a treacherous character.

Coop gave her a feeble smile and then excused himself to the men's room. Inside a stall Coop dropped his head in his hands as the memories flooded back.

*

After that tennis match Coop had made his way to the locker room, waited until it was empty, and broke down in heaving sobs. That night, over a sausage-and-mushroom pizza and a bottle of sauvignon blanc, he poured out his heart to Vivien in her Collegetown apartment.

Vivien handed him another ice pack for his black eye and said, "Coop, you know this stays between us, but you did hit that last shot out intentionally, didn't you? I saw the look you gave Cash and now, knowing what he said to you, I completely understand."

Coop looked at his friend. "He had no right, Vivi. No one calls me a faggot, I don't care how dreamy they are. I wanted him to teach him a lesson."

His black eye eventually went away, but the guilt about throwing the game lingered, and since that day Coop had never picked up another tennis racquet. In fact, until that day's diversity workshop he had never shared that story. Now Coop regretted telling it. What was he thinking, that Felix would demonstrate some humanity?

*

Coop heard two men enter the restroom, and he immediately recognized the blustery, sharp tone of one of them: Felix Culo. "This damn workshop is so painful. Why do we have to sit through this? Did you see Coop crying in my group? What a wuss. You'd never catch me doing that." The other guy gave a cold laugh in response. The two men finished up and left the restroom without washing their hands.

Coop, who had remained silent until then, let out a heavy sigh. He cleaned up and headed back to the workshop.

*

Relieved to be back in the privacy of his office, Coop dialed Vivien's number and tried his best to sound upbeat. As Coop listened to Vivien speak excitedly about her first week as a president at Smart Sports, he felt a pang of jealousy. Then he felt guilty about being jealous of his friend. After waiting an appropriate amount of time she cautiously asked Coop about his promotion.

"I didn't get it." It was torturous for him to say. "Again."

*

Vivien fell into a shocked silence when she heard the news from Coop. "Oh, Coop. I'm so sorry. Maybe it's time to switch firms. Or do something on your own even." She knew how much he'd wanted and expected that promotion.

Then Coop told her the details about the meeting to discuss his promotion. He scoffed at the looks of utter bewilderment from Martin and Barry when he quoted the famed *New York Times* columnist.

Vivien said supportively, "Coop, you are the Jedi master of pulling out the appropriate quote at the right time."

He told her how his suspicions about Felix Culo's sabotaging his promotion had been confirmed that very afternoon at the diversity and inclusion workshop. Coop let out a sigh that sounded like it weighed ten pounds when he explained he'd have to wait a little longer for his promotion. "Sweetie, I'm just so traumatized by all this…it's maddening and frustrating to work so hard and not get rewarded. Maybe I should just leave."

"Hang on a sec, Coop, didn't you just say they promised to promote you in a matter of months? You've made it this far. What's another few months?"

"It could be as long as six months."

"Well, you've put in ten years of stellar work; don't throw it all away now, especially if you only have to wait a little while longer. Get the partner title first and then you can decide if you want to leave. When you move on to something else, leaving as a partner will be a huge plus." There had to be a way to get his firm to give him what he deserved. "What about leveraging your clients? They love you. Some words of support from your clients to the CEO of your firm might sway things in your favor." Vivien wanted the promotion so badly for her dear friend. "Or move things along faster."

"Yeah, you're right, you're right. I should stick it out a bit more until I make partner. And maybe see if my clients can influence things a little."

Vivien continued. "But in the meantime I would do two things. First of all, you need to protect yourself. You could have your accounting license revoked if anyone thinks you were involved in fraud." An idea popped into her head. They actually had a contact in the US Securities and Exchange Commission—their Wharton friend Patrick Ellis had joined the SEC out of B-school. As a member of the SEC, Patrick's job was to protect investors, so it was possible he could help Coop navigate this mess. "Maybe you should talk to Patrick Ellis and get his advice. Second, you may want to share your concerns with HR about your experience at the diversity workshop with Felix. That might give you a hint if your firm is holding you back because of your sexual orientation."

*

Coop could always count on his friend for sound advice. "Good call. Anything else?" He tossed his pen on the desk and leaned back in his chair.

She seemed to hesitate. "Now might be a good time to think about what you'd want to do next. It's always wise to have a backup plan, you know?"

He was silent for a long time. "This wasn't the way things were supposed to turn out, Vivi." Tears started to well up in Coop's eyes. "This is not what I dreamed of. My whole family is counting on me to do something great. I'm just…" He choked on his words, unable to continue.

Gently, Vivien said, "You're just what, Coop?"

He sobbed and blurted, "I'm just terrified of being ordinary." There, he'd said it. The feeling that had been nagging at him for years—Coop finally had the guts to put it out there to his closest friend.

He heard Vivien draw in a breath. "Listen to me, Coop, you're one of the most extraordinary people I've ever met. I don't know anyone else who is so universally well liked. Also, you're incredibly smart, funny, loyal, hardworking, and talented. Don't let a small career setback or a title get in the way of you realizing just how special you are. You have so much to offer and you're capable of doing anything you set your mind to." Vivien's voice was forceful. "On top of all that, you're a good person with a great heart. Coop, please, don't let this get you down, okay?"

Coop mumbled an okay.

Vivien said, "Good things are coming your way, Coop, I just know it."

Just then, Coop had no idea what the future held.

*

GRACE

"Looks like you've won the lottery, Grace." Her literary agent, Bob, sat next to her at the large glass conference room table and gave her an encouraging smile.

"What do you mean?"

He adjusted his black rectangular glasses and pulled out a folder from his leather satchel, worn soft with time. He buckled it shut. "Do you have any idea how hard it is to get a book proposal in front of a major publisher these days? The fact that they took this meeting is unbelievable, especially for a first-time author." Bob had worked in the book business for decades and was in his fifties, but his rumpled suit and deliberate movements telegraphed the weariness of an octogenarian. "Are you ready for this meeting, Grace?"

She nodded. Despite giving countless business presentations in her marketing career, this was a first for Grace, because this time she was essentially selling herself. She took a deep breath to settle her nerves. Today's meeting with the publisher would set the direction for her branding book and give her a go-or-no-go decision on whether they would publish it. For the occasion she wore a crepe V-neck dress in forest green with contrasting pale blue topstitching from Burberry's new summer collection. She knew the importance of color and had selected a green dress to subliminally influence the publishing team to give her the green light on her book.

When the team from the publishing house started to file into the brightly lit room, Grace stood up and walked over to each one, introducing herself. Her literary agent followed suit. The team greeted her warmly and everyone sat down, ready to talk.

"We've been looking forward to meeting you, Grace," said Henry, the most senior member of the team. "We reviewed your book proposal and found it intriguing. So why don't we dive in? I'd like to hear what inspired you to write a book on branding and how this book will be different from others."

Grace brushed a wisp of her blond hair behind her ear and smiled confidently. It was her chance to shine, and she intended to win them over. "As you know, over one million books are published every year. Sales of books at bookstores have been on the decline. And the average nonfiction book sells fewer than two hundred fifty copies per year and under two thousand copies over the book's lifetime. If you ask me, those numbers aren't so great." Grim looks on the faces of the publishing executives and their nods indicated they agreed with the stats that Grace had shared.

"So, why on earth would anyone want to publish a book these days?" Grace looked around the room and then leaned closer. "I think I may have the answer, and it's pretty simple. The answer is to publish a book that people are actually excited to read. One that can change their lives. That's why I'm here today. I don't want to write another book that's going to end up on the junk pile. I want to write the bible on rebranding, because that book doesn't exist today. This is the type of book that can help anyone. The absence of something so essential is what inspired me to want to write the book."

A female member of the publishing team chimed in. "I couldn't agree more, Grace. Can you tell us what would differentiate your book from other books on branding?"

Grace sat up straighter. "There are three unique aspects to my book. Many business books are theoretical and don't either give practical advice or show how things work. The first point of difference is that I'm going to explain the specific steps you must take to resurrect a brand. The second point of difference is that I'm providing a POC."

Henry, the head honcho, said, "POC?"

"Proof of concept," Grace replied. "In my book I'm going to prove my approach works and will apply my rebranding steps to a couple of real-life case studies: I'll take readers through a case study on rebranding a product and I'll offer readers a personal rebranding case study. In the first case study I'll demonstrate how to turn around the brand for a product that has run into major difficulties and how to reignite sales. Then I'll show the success of my approach by actually helping a real person turn around their personal brand." She noted the looks of approval on the faces of the publishing team. "The third unique aspect to this book is the emotional hook. I'm going straight for the heart, which is unusual for a business book. Who doesn't love a comeback story? How many times have you seen a situation where a business or a person completely screws up and their brand is so damaged they have no shot at a comeback? My book will show people how you can resurrect a brand that has been obliterated. My book will pull at people's heartstrings by demonstrating that it is possible to triumph after disaster. My book will give people hope."

"Sounds like the magic formula, Grace," Henry said.

She continued. "I also have a lot of creative ideas on how to market the book."

Henry looked around the table at his team, who were nodding in the affirmative. "And we'd love to hear your ideas, Grace. I think we're all in agreement that we'd like to move forward with this project and publish your book."

Bob had a glint of victory in his eye. He smiled approvingly at Grace.

Grace's stomach did a flip and she could barely contain her excitement. "That's great, Henry. Thank you." She was a little shocked— this was easier than she'd expected. "So what are the next steps?"

Henry made some notes. "We'll send you a contract to review and we can meet again to dig into the details of how we envision bringing the book to life. We're prepared to offer you an advance against royalties of ten thousand dollars."

That sounded like a decent advance to Grace based on the research she had done so far.

Bob, her literary agent, perked up at the discussion of money. "So you'll get ten thousand dollars up front, Grace, and then once your book sales exceed ten thousand dollars you'll start earning royalties."

Grace tilted her head. "And what would the royalties be for my book?"

"Our publishing house is known for our generosity to authors in terms of royalty percentage, and we're prepared to offer you the same deal. At the expected price point for your book, the royalty would work out to about a dollar per book," Henry replied.

"So, I would make only one dollar per book?" *That sounds like peanuts.*

Bob said, "That's correct, Grace. But I'm sure the team anticipates selling many copies of your book, so it will all add up in the end."

Grace rubbed her chin. "Since I'm new to this would you mind going over the economics of bookselling so I can gain a better understanding?"

Henry paused as if he was nervous to share the information and looked to a young woman on his team. "Peggy, why don't you share the basics with Grace?"

Peggy seemed to be the most junior member of the publishing team and she beamed at the opportunity to share her knowledge. "To start with, Grace, we distribute our books mainly through bookstores. In order to get them to carry the title we offer a standard 50 percent discount off list price. So if your book is priced at thirty dollars, we sell it to bookstores at fifteen dollars. The royalty is paid on the money we make, so you'd have to sell, let's see…"

Grace interjected, "Six hundred and sixty-seven books to get to the ten-thousand-dollar advance threshold."

A pleased look came across Peggy's face as she looked up from her calculator. "Yes, that's exactly right. And once we hit that ten-thousand-dollar sales mark, you will start earning your one dollar per book."

"So if I sell ten thousand books, the publishing house makes a hundred fifty thousand dollars and I make ten thousand dollars."

"That's correct," Peggy said. "You should also know that bookstores are allowed to return books. They have up to nine months to return any books they've purchased. The returned books will be deducted from your sales numbers. And the average return rate for the book industry can be anywhere from 30 to 50 percent, but we anticipate it being around 35 percent."

"That means that my ten-thousand-dollar sales number could shrink to around six thousand with returns factored in?" As Grace learned more about the harsh economics of the book business, her initial enthusiasm started to dwindle.

"Correct," said Peggy.

A serious look came across Grace's face as she did some mental calculations. If a typical nonfiction book sold two thousand copies, as she'd shared earlier in the meeting, and her book performed at the average level, then she could potentially end up owing the publishing house $8667 from the advance. While she was excited about the prospect of publishing a book, the book business wasn't looking so attractive from a financial standpoint. Grace sat back feeling a little deflated, like someone who'd just won first place in a contest only to find the prize was a year's supply of canned sardines.

Henry seemed eager to move things along. "Listen, Grace, we're excited about the potential for your book. Why don't you look over the contract we'll send you later today, and we'll be happy to answer any questions you may have."

Grace snapped out of her rumination and forced herself to brighten her expression. "Sure, Henry, sounds good. Thanks to you and your team for this opportunity." She stood up and shook everyone's hand as they filed out.

Bob put his folder away in his ancient satchel and said, "Congratulations, Grace, wonderful job. It's fortunate that they want to move forward with the project. I'm pleased that I was able to find you a publisher so quickly."

"Yes, thank you, Bob," Grace responded, remembering that Bob had told her he'd get her the publisher meeting first and then they would discuss the specifics of their business relationship.

"Easiest fifteen hundred dollars I ever made," he cackled.

"What?" Grace drew back in surprise.

"Oh, I thought you knew—your literary agent gets 15 percent of everything you make on your book, so 15 percent of your ten-thousand-dollar advance check is fifteen hundred dollars. The publisher will be cutting a check for you and another for me that reflects my percentage. Pretty straightforward." He smiled.

"I wasn't aware of that detail, Bob. So you would get 15 percent of all my book sales in perpetuity?"

"Yes. That's the standard for literary agents. Of course I'll be assisting you in the publishing process and would be the go-between for you and the publishing house. I'd smooth out any issues you might have."

"I see." *Wait a second, I'm doing all the work and because Bob got me this meeting he gets 15 percent of the take forever? What a racket.* Grace had to stop herself from guffawing. So in the sales scenario she had discussed with the publishing team, her sales number after Bob's cut would shrink to $5156.48. *That's about the cost of this Burberry dress*

I'm wearing right now. Well, at least she was on a paid sabbatical, so she wouldn't starve.

Bob said he'd send over his standard literary agent contract and they said their goodbyes. Grace walked out of the midtown office building slowly and with mixed emotions. It was a huge win to get the go-ahead on her book and thrilling to have a strong start out of the gate. But it was eye-opening to learn how paltry the payout was for all that work. *Is it worth all the effort?* But Grace had already started down a path and said yes to the project, so she'd just have to make sure it was a success.

*

Grace left the building and walked along the sidewalk, deep in thought, and when she got to the street corner she looked up. Win Wyatt was staring her in the face...or at least a picture of him. The MTA bus shelter had a huge poster advertising the Broadway show *Cat on a Hot Tin Roof,* featuring a shirtless Win Wyatt. Good god, he sure was something to behold. Plus he seemed like a genuinely nice, smart person. Perhaps she had been too hasty when she turned Win down. Had she lost that chance?

*

ANDI

On Tuesday morning of the following week, Andi fidgeted with a paper clip on her desk—she felt uncharacteristically on edge. She was about to meet with her new boss, Lester Labosky, who had scheduled meetings with all his direct reports that day. Prior to joining Kaneshiro Bank a few years ago, Lester had spent most of his career at a bank with the reputation of fostering a fairly barbaric corporate culture. Andi was used to the more genteel culture at Goldman Sachs and was curious to see how Lester's style would mesh.

Andi was moving a bit faster now that she had a "boot," or walking cast, for her broken foot. She made her way down the long hallway of posh offices to Ed's old office, where Lester was camping out until their office move. Lester's assistant was nowhere in sight so Andi poked her head in the doorway. She felt a pang of sadness seeing the office devoid of Ed's belongings especially the framed photos from his exotic travels. A man sat at Ed's old desk completely hidden by the *Wall Street Journal* he was holding up.

"Hello, Lester?" Andi adjusted her belted blouse. "Are you ready to meet?"

Upon hearing her voice the man behind the newspaper lowered it and peered over his bifocals at her.

Good lord, Lester is the Boy Scout-looking guy from the elevator the other day. This is my new boss?

A look of recognition came across his face. "Oh, you're the tampon girl!"

Andi's olive complexion instantly turned crimson, matching her rosy lips.

Upon seeing Andi cringe at his remark Lester waved his hand away. "Sorry, bad joke." He cleared his throat and consulted his printed-out daily schedule. "Let's see, I'm supposed to be meeting with Andy Andiamo, the top banker in the department. Could you send in your boss, honey? Oh, and would you get me a cup of coffee? Black." He pushed his bifocals up to the bridge of his nose and continued reading his paper.

Andi straightened up and stood proudly. She said in a strong, clear voice, "Actually, I am here for our eight o'clock meeting."

Slowly, Lester let his newspaper drop onto his desk.

"My name is Andi Andiamo. That's Andi with an 'i,' short for Andrea." She had a steely look of resolve in her eyes.

His brow wrinkled up and he took off his glasses and tossed them aside. Rubbing his face he mumbled, "Um, I'm confused. I heard you speaking Spanish in the elevator the other day so I assumed you were someone's executive assistant."

Andi snorted and gave a slight smirk. "Nope, not an assistant. However I am the top performer in our department. Good to meet you, Lester." She moved forward and stuck out her hand. One of Andi's trademarks was her firm handshake, and that only seemed to bewilder Lester further.

He said, "You mean the number one performer here is a woman? Holy shit." He sat stunned into immobility like a little kid who has just learned that there is no Santa Claus.

Andi gave him a stern look, precisely the kind she gave her toddler twin boys when they were doing something undesirable. Ed would never have spoken to her in this manner.

Finally Lester recovered his senses and broke the silence. "I'm sorry. Sit down, sit down. I've been reviewing your performance stats, Andi, and I have to say they're not bad...not bad at all."

Andi gave him a confident smile. "Come on now, Lester, I think you and I both know that my numbers aren't just 'not bad.' All comparative data indicates my performance numbers are pretty damn great. I work extremely hard and extremely smart, and that's how I've achieved such a strong track record over the years."

He stared at her for a bit longer than was comfortable with an odd smile on his face. "I see. So you're a partner as well—impressive." Though Lester was her boss, as a managing director he was technically at a lower level than Andi. His head nodded in her direction. "What happened to your foot?"

"My twin three-year-old boys tossed a ten-pound dumbbell on it and accidentally broke it," Andi said wryly. She gave a little shrug.

Lester sat back. "You've got three-year-old twins at home and you're still turning in these kinds of numbers?" He whistled. "That's mind blowing!" He leaned forward, hiking up the French cuffs of his shirt, his platinum cufflinks catching the morning sunlight. "I have two boys as well, although mine are a bit older than yours. Kids are such a joy, aren't they?" He gave her a conspiratorial smile and motioned to the family photo sitting on his credenza. His wife was a statuesque brunette and his boys were strapping teenagers—they sat together and smiled happily, like they were posing for a health insurance commercial. So Lester was a family man—that was a good sign. They had something in common.

Andi nodded.

"It doesn't look like I'll need to worry about you, Andi, but I'd like for you to keep me in the loop on your client base and any major deals you're working on." He lowered his voice. "Just between us girls, I'm planning on shaking up the department—you know, bringing in some of my guys and taking action on the guys here who are not performing as well as they should. I think the whole private banking department could be doing better."

So Myron was right to be concerned and come begging for my help. What Myron Burry lacked in business skill and social grace he certainly made up for in his political savvy. He was prescient to see that more would be expected of him. "I understand," said Andi. "You're running the show now, Lester, so you've gotta do what you gotta do."

They chatted a bit more about the department and what was on Andi's docket, and then Lester's look brightened. "Say, Andi, I want to let you know that I'm planning a terrific team offsite to Bermuda in a couple of weeks for the senior bankers in the department. We have to move the team to Kaneshiro's midtown offices anyway, so that's a perfect time for an offsite. We can all get to know each other, get in some golf, and kick back a little while we discuss the future direction of the business. Sound good?" He ran a hand through his light brown hair.

"Sure, sounds good." Andi was already mentally plunging into mom mode to strategize about how she'd arrange for extra childcare while she was away on the trip. Because Andi and Luca both worked full time, it was always a juggling act to ensure their boys were well taken care of when one of them was traveling, although usually Luca picked up the slack without complaint. She stood up. "Thanks, Lester, I'm looking forward to working with you."

"Me too, Andi." He gave her a broad smile.

Andi walked out his office feeling a sense of relief. Her new boss seemed like a respectable guy and things were off to a good start. Even though she'd miss her family, she was tickled about taking a trip to sunny Bermuda and the chance to play some golf.

Andi had been the one who'd encouraged her Ceiling Smasher friends to take golf lessons shortly after they graduated from B-school. "It's an essential business tool and something we actually might enjoy," Andi had declared. "I can't tell you how many stories I've heard about women getting cut out of business deals or losing out on career decisions that were made on the golf course." So, the four Smashers had spent a week at a Palm Springs golf camp together and ended up enjoying the game and the strategy behind it. Ever the gifted athlete, Andi effortlessly picked up the game and now sported a seven handicap.

*

When she arrived home from work that evening Andi thanked their nanny for her help, sent her on her way, and set about preparing some frozen chicken nuggets and french fries for her boys, Antonio and Francesco. The life of a private banker was highly social, and typically Andi would have to attend dinners or special events with clients two or three nights a week while Luca looked after the boys. Between the two of them Luca was the better cook and housekeeper, but Andi always made her time with the boys fun. She scrutinized their dinner plates and then threw a bowl of frozen peas into the microwave to add some green to their meal.

She and her sons were giggling over dinner when Luca rushed in the door of their apartment and gave everyone big kisses. He set down his bags of groceries, laid her dry cleaning over the back of a chair, and scooped up Andi in his strong embrace kissing her for a long time while the boys made silly smooching noises. "I missed you, *cara mia*," he whispered in his still-strong Italian accent. Luca ran his fingers through his head of dark curly hair and looked at Andi with his hazel eyes. Her heart swelled when he looked at her in such a gentle, loving way.

"I met my new boss today, honey. A guy named Lester Labosky." She gave him a recap of her day.

Her husband's face lit up. "Wonderful, Andi, wonderful. This Lester, he sounds like a nice family man. I know you'll miss Ed, but maybe Lester will also be a good boss, no?"

"I think so. The only thing is he's planning an offsite to Bermuda for week after next. Do you think your parents would mind staying over and helping with the boys that week?"

Luca threw his hands up. "Are you kidding? Mamma and Papa would love to spend the time with their grandkids. I will call them tonight to arrange it."

Andi breathed a sigh of relief that she could go on her trip without any worries. Usually Luca handled the boys on his own if Andi was away on a short trip, but when she was gone for a week he might need reinforcements.

"What about your friend Sofia, did she agree to go on a blind date with my colleague?"

Andi shook her head. "I tried to convince her, Luca, but Sofia said she's taking a break from dating right now."

"Too bad." Luca puckered his lips. "Sofia is such a beautiful person inside and out. She deserves to be with someone who will make her happy."

"But you know she's said many times that she doesn't want to get married. She just wants to focus on her career without any 'distractions.'"

Luca's gaze dropped to the floor. "Such a pity, eh?"

Andi moved closer to her husband and put her arms around his waist. She smiled. "Oh, honey, you just want everyone to be happy, don't you?" She gave him a hug and took in his scent, which was a blend of his cologne and a slight lemony scent. Andi pawed through the grocery bags. "Hey, did you get those organic rice crackers I like? I usually snack on them at work."

Her husband shook his head. "Oh, no, Andi, I'm so sorry. I forgot."

Andi gave him a pouty look. Luca sighed in exasperation. "Okay, okay." He grabbed his keys and cell phone, "I will run out and get them for you, darling." He gave her a wink, waved to the boys, and ran out the door.

Andi paused for a moment. Her marriage and family life were going smoothly and work was great. What more could she ask?

*

SOFIA

Today was the day Sofia would meet her future co-anchor, the infamous Kate Frost. The woman was a smart, seasoned broadcaster but had a reputation for not being the easiest to work with. Sofia took a deep breath, steeled herself, and pushed open the door to Randolph's office. His office always smelled of peppermint and leather. Randolph, Graham (her other co-anchor), and Kate were already seated around the large marble conference table. Kate stood to meet Sofia.

Kate Frost was about ten years older than Sofia and was a woman of jaw-dropping beauty, her slim figure clad in her trademark sleeveless body-skimming dress. Her light brown hair was parted in the middle and fell in a sensible layered cut that just grazed her shoulders. Kate removed her serious looking black-rimmed glasses and gave Sofia a big smile. A whisper of wrinkles appeared at the corner of her eyes. It was almost as if Kate wore the severe-looking glasses to distract people from her winsomeness. "Sofia, I'm a big fan of your work. I'm looking forward to working with you." She held out her hand.

Sofia blushed and shook Kate's hand. She hadn't expected Kate to be this friendly. "Thank you, Kate, but the pleasure's mine. I've admired you for some time. I'm sure I'll learn a lot from you." She said hello to Randolph and Graham and took a seat. As she sat down Sofia disturbed a stack of magazines that were neatly laid out in a precise fan on the table and Randolph quickly tidied them back up.

Randolph sat back. "Now that we have the niceties out of the way, let's get down to brass tacks. I'd like to do some brainstorming on our new show *Moguls and Their Mistakes*, talk about format and content, and then come up with a short list for our first few interviewees who have founded consumer-oriented businesses. Sound good?"

Everyone nodded.

"So, let's discuss show format to start."

Kate held up her index finger. "Excuse me, Randolph, I have a question."

"Of course, Kate, please." He gestured for her to continue.

She tilted her head to the side. "I was wondering how wedded you are to the show's title. I mean, *Moguls and Their Mistakes*? Well, it's just not a good title, is it? I hope I'm not stepping on anyone's toes here." Kate gave a little shrug.

Randolph paused. "What's your take on it, Kate?"

She crossed her arms. "I was just thinking if you're a smart, powerful CEO, would you feel compelled to appear on a show called *Moguls and Their Mistakes*? Probably not."

Sofia's back stiffened. "But the show is supposed to be about leaders revealing their struggles on the road to success, warts and all."

Kate said, "I get that, Sofia, I do. But don't you think a title like

Titans Tell All would be more inviting?"

Sofia's pride deflated like a leaky balloon. The title had been her idea. And now, listening to Kate Frost scrutinize it, she realized that Kate's instincts were on the mark. Randolph and Graham looked at the two women expectantly. Sofia's cheeks reddened. "You're right, Kate. I think *Titans Tell All* would work better. Let's go with that." Randolph nodded. It was Sofia's first meeting about the show that was her idea and she felt like she'd made a huge blunder. Maybe she wasn't ready to host her own show after all. Sofia forced herself to stay positive and focus on their brainstorming.

The four of them talked about format and content and agreed that one person would take the lead on interviewing their guest and then open it up for a broader discussion with the other co-anchors. The content would cover key successes, greatest challenges, biggest mistakes, and regrets.

"I love it," Graham said. "I think it will make for a rich and interesting program." He was always so positive and upbeat; Sofia liked that about him. "But what about our starting lineup? Who could we get on the program that would give it the most exciting kickoff?"

Sofia piped up. "How about Elon Musk and Tory Burch?"

"Hmm, those aren't bad. But they've already done tons of interviews. Why not pick some executives that no one has heard from before?" Kate put her elbow on the marble table and leaned closer to Randolph. "What if we could land Bryce Stewart?"

"The founder of the Scottish jam company? I adore their products!" Graham practically jumped out of his seat. "That would be fantastic, but I understand Bryce doesn't normally grant interviews. How would we swing that?"

"That might be shooting for the moon, Kate, though I'd love to have Bryce Stewart on our show." Randolph looked wistful.

Kate grinned. "I met Bryce last year when I was doing a story on the fastest-growing food companies. I just might be able to persuade him. Rumor has it he's looking to sell his company, so being on our show could be an enticement for him to get more traction in the sales process."

Randolph raised an eyebrow. "Really? Now, that would be a good get. Any thoughts about our second interviewee, Kate?"

"How about Hideyoshi Sakamoto, the founder of Deki?"

Sofia said, "The Japanese fast-fashion retailer that's entering the US market this year? That would be awesome. Randolph, does the network have any contacts we can leverage to court him?"

"If it would help I can reach out to Yoshi. I met him when I was covering the Olympics and Deki was the official sponsor for the uniforms for the Japanese athletes," Kate said.

"My gosh, Kate, I do believe you're going to be a tremendous asset for *Titans Tell All*. This is just wonderful." Randolph gave her a nod of respect and shot a knowing look over to Sofia. She had to admit her boss was right to bring in a more experienced person, but Sofia was starting to worry about Kate's overshadowing her. Would this become the Kate Frost show, also featuring Sofia LaForte?

Kate sat back and set her glasses down on her notebook. "Look, I know I'm the new kid on the block here and this show was Sofia's idea. So why don't we have Sofia and Graham take the first two interviews? Graham can take Bryce Stewart and Sofia can interview Hideyoshi Sakamoto, if I can get them both on the show."

What? Kate Frost was taking a backseat and giving Sofia and Graham the opportunity to shine? This didn't sound at all like the woman whose reputation preceded her—perhaps Sofia had been wrong to put so much stock in what she'd heard about her new colleague. "Kate, are you sure you want to do that?"

"You don't even want to take the lead on one of the interviews? Especially since you're landing them both for us?" Graham raised an eyebrow.

There was a glint of confidence in Kate's eyes. "Listen, we're a team, right? You guys take the spotlight this time and I'll have my chance later. No issues here."

"Why, thank you, Kate. That's really big of you." Sofia smiled in appreciation. Graham nodded enthusiastically. Randolph clearly had the correct instincts in bringing Kate on board—in just the first meeting she'd already added a lot of value. And she seemed like a true team player. Kate Frost could turn out to be a great colleague and things were starting off better than Sofia could ever have imagined.

*

Sofia was finishing up lunch and a conversation with Graham in the CNBC cafeteria when LoCo started approaching them. "Oh god, not those two," Graham muttered. "Sorry, Sofia, I'm outta here." Graham grabbed his food tray and swiftly got up from the table, maneuvering around LoCo while Sofia remained trapped with them. One or possibly both of the women was wearing a strong floral perfume with a cloying scent, and as the cloud of fragrance engulfed her it gave Sofia an instant migraine.

Lorrie always spoke first. "Congrats on the new show, Sofia. So exciting!"

"Thank you," Sofia responded, dreading what they were going to say next. They were always asking bizarre questions of her.

"That Kate Frost, she's pretty amazing, right?" Cordelia said. "And so attractive, to boot. I'll bet you'll really enjoy working with her."

Sofia took a sip of her bottled water. "Sure, she seems really great. And she is actually even more stunning in person. Anyway, I'm sure I'll enjoy doing the show with her."

Lorrie said, "Interesting that she never married, isn't it?"

Sofia shrugged, not sure where the conversation was heading.

Not so subtly, Cordelia elbowed her friend and then eyed Sofia's hands. "Say, do you know of a good manicurist around here? I really need to get my nails done. Let's see yours, Sofia."

Sofia held up her hand like a fan with the back of her hand toward her and made a mental note to get a mani-pedi over the weekend. "Sadly, Cordelia, I don't know of anyone around here. I could use a manicure myself." Disappointment came over LoCo's faces. What was that all about anyway?

Just then, thankfully, her assistant, Chloe, came up. "Ladies, are you harassing my boss? Beat it," Chloe said playfully, but with an undertone of protectiveness. LoCo skulked away.

"Ugh, thank you, Chloe. I find talking to those two so uncomfortable—they're like the grade school bullies who rove around the cafeteria dumping lunch trays on the laps of weaker kids."

Chloe shook her head in disgust and slid into a seat next to her boss. "You know what they're doing, Sofia, right?"

Sofia sat back, confused. "No, what are you talking about?"

"Lorrie and Cordelia are doing all these stupid tests to confirm their suspicions about you."

"Suspicions? About what, Chloe?"

Chloe rolled her eyes and said, "They think you're a lesbian. That's why they do the tests."

"Tests? Like what?" Sofia wracked her brain trying to remember all their strange requests.

"I've seen them do it to others in the building. Like they'll tell someone they have something stuck on their shoe and they watch to see how the person looks at the sole of their foot. If they lift up their foot and look back over their shoulder, then they're straight; if they bend their knee, grab their foot, and look at it in front of their body then they're supposedly gay. I just saw them doing the nail test with you." Chloe made a spitting noise.

Sofia slapped both hands on her lap and laughed. "Is *that* what that was about?"

"Absolutely, if you fan out your nails and look at the back of your hand you're straight, if you turn the inside of your hand toward you and curl your fingers over that means you're gay."

"That's the silliest thing I've ever heard. Just because I'm a single woman in my thirties, that means I'm gay?" Sofia chuckled. "Those two really do act like they're still in grade school."

Chloe leaned closer. "I know they're ridiculous, but just watch your six. Those two are notorious for spreading damaging rumors about people."

Sofia let out a sigh and nodded. She'd do her best to avoid LoCo and would listen to Chloe about watching her back.

"Oh, and don't forget you have your big speech coming up soon. Just let me know if you need any help with it." Chloe smiled at her boss.

"Will do, thanks," Sofia said. Yet another thing she'd have to work on over the weekend.

*

Relaxing in her Upper West Side apartment that Saturday night, Sofia set the evening in motion and dialed a number that she'd committed to memory. Then she eagerly awaited the person's arrival. In preparation Sofia placed a freshly pressed linen tablecloth on her dining table and laid out silverware that was polished to a fine glow. The pink peonies in the center of the table gave off a subtle sweet scent. She poured chilled sparkling water into a crystal goblet and put a generous pour of a spicy cabernet sauvignon into a wineglass. Breathing a sigh of contentment, Sofia played some jazz music in the background—she loved listening to something beautiful while she was dining, a habit from when she was growing up with her jazz musician father. As she lit the tapered candles on the table, her door buzzer rang. Sofia took one look back at the table and sighed again—everything was perfect.

Sofia opened the door to a familiar face. "What took you so long?" she teased. "I was beginning to worry."

They smiled at each other.

The man replied, "I'm sorry, things were a little backed up at work tonight. It took me longer than usual to get here."

"Well, I'm glad you made it," she said as she opened the door to let him in.

"How are you, Sofia?" he asked eagerly. "I saw your show earlier in the week when you were talking about the Gap. I see those stores everywhere and was wondering if they were doing well."

"Don't buy the stock. I think their executive team has weak spots and their strategy of being on every corner is about to implode," Sofia responded.

Conversation flowed so easily with this man, whom she often saw twice a week. After a bit more chitchat, Sofia said, "Well, what do I owe you?"

"It's forty-two eighty-five tonight."

"Okay, here's a fifty. Keep the change. Thanks, and have a great evening," Sofia said to the delivery guy.

She brought the food from her favorite Thai takeout restaurant into the kitchen and put it into green crackled ceramic serving bowls that she'd bought on a trip to Italy.

While she was enjoying her delectable meal, Sofia realized that recently her most frequent contact on a Saturday night was with the food delivery guy. *The headline? That is just wrong.*

Last night at her regular Friday night Smashers get-together with Andi and Grace they had chided her for not getting out there and going on dates. Though she enjoyed her solitude and the chance to catch up on her favorite cooking shows on TV, Sofia had to admit she was in a romance rut. She was fine with being on her own, but at times she longed for some quality male company. And the fact that LoCo from the office were spreading rumors that she was gay didn't help matters. Perhaps it was time to put herself back out there. Before she sat down to her meal she fired off a quick text to Andi—maybe it was time to try again.

CHAPTER 3

One Week Later, September

GRACE

The alarm clock beeped at six a.m. Grace switched it off and sat up, wiping the sleep from her eyes. Her staycation had come to a close, and now it was time to start writing her branding book. She planned to attack her project with the same gusto and discipline that she'd applied to her marketing role. She climbed out of bed, did some quick stretches, and hopped into the shower. In her mind she was now in the business of writing, and Grace prepared for the day as she would a normal workday.

After getting dressed and having a healthy breakfast of hard-boiled eggs, avocado toast, and coffee, Grace was ready to roll. She made the short commute to her office, her second bedroom on the other side of the living room. Her fridge was stocked with snacks and refreshments, and the plan was to lock herself in her Chelsea apartment for at least the next few days to write. Grace took a seat at her desk in front of her computer and felt the energy flowing out of her brain, through her fingers, and onto her computer screen. She'd already settled on the title of her book: *Rise: Six Steps to Resuscitate Your Brand After a Fiasco.* The budding author rubbed her chin. First she'd outline the steps to resurrecting a brand, and then she'd fill in all the details and examples for each step:

- **Step 1: Own Your Mistakes**. Take responsibility for your mistakes and own up to them. This includes being a good sport when people make fun of you and taking things in stride.
- **Step 2: Say Sorry.** Provide a genuine and public apology to everyone you've negatively impacted and reach out to individuals for an in-person apology. Be sincere, be humble.
- **Step 3: Show Your Humanity.** Find a cause that you can contribute to, one that you authentically believe in. Support that cause, speak out about it, and do something concrete to advance it. It's important to be known for helping others.
- **Step 4: Stand for Something.** Decide what you want to show the world you're great at and become known for that, along with your desire to do good.
- **Step 5: Amplify Your Brand.** Find ways to tell the world about what you do best and about your positive impact. In this step, grand gestures that show you're going above and beyond for your selected cause go a long way in restoring your brand and reestablishing people's faith in you.
- **Step 6: Live It.** Once you've successfully achieved steps 1 through 5, make sure you reinforce your new brand image and continue to live it. Remember that folks will often give brands (and people) a second chance, so don't squander the goodwill you've regained.

*

Grace sat back and reviewed her ideas. Her plan had been to write a short chapter for each step and add in examples later. After a few more hours she'd completed the first chapter. *Okay, so far so good.* She'd been at it for four hours and took a break to retrieve a grapefruit sparkling water from the fridge, along with some almonds. She was about to sit back down in front of her computer when her intercom buzzed.

Her doorman Khemraj had an excited tone to his Indian lilt. "Miss Grace, you have a special delivery in the lobby!"

"Okay, thanks, Khemraj. I'm actually working on something right now. Would you mind keeping it at the front desk for me, please?"

Her doorman was silent for a moment. "I think you will want to come down for this delivery…it is very special indeed. You will see, Miss Grace." His tone was insistent, not at all like his usual relaxed style.

Grace said she'd be right down. When the elevator doors opened, Khemraj was waiting for her wearing a huge smile. "Come. Come see!" He beckoned her to follow, and as they turned the corner Grace stopped in her tracks. Harrison Ford was holding a huge basket with a big white bow. He gave a slightly crooked smile at her wide-eyed look.

"Hi there. Are you Grace King?" Harrison Ford's familiar voice filled the lobby, and the handful of other residents milling about froze and stared at the famous actor.

Grace smiled stiffly. "Yes, hello, I'm Grace. Nice to meet you. I'm a big fan, Harrison."

He gave her a wink. "Please, call me Harry. I live across the street from you and a good friend of mine called in a favor. Win Wyatt. Guess he's smitten with you and wanted me to deliver this—it's kind of a weird gift if you ask me, but here you go." He handed the basket to Grace and she peeked through the clear cellophane wrap to see a collection of cerulean Turkish bath towels.

Grace threw her head back and laughed in delight. She detached the envelope from the basket and read the note: *Dear Grace, I'd be honored if you'd come to my show (feel free to bring a girlfriend). Afterward I'd like to spend some time with you—perhaps a drink? Looking forward. Yours, Win. PS: Enjoy the towels!*

Enclosed were two tickets for the opening night of *A Streetcar Named Desire*, just a week away. Grace's heart did a happy dance.

"He'd really like for you to come to his show, Grace. He's a good guy," Harrison said, "you should give him a chance. Well, I'd better get going. See you around, neighbor."

Grace smiled shyly and thanked him again. As she turned back toward the elevators Khemraj gave her a big smile and a thumbs-up, and Grace giggled. She returned to her apartment and placed the basket on the large coffee table in the living room, where it was visible from her desk. She knocked out some emails to potential brand case studies to find one product company and one personal brand example, taking advantage of her Ceiling Smashers network of twenty high-powered female professionals. Then she took a quick break for lunch, wolfing down a chicken Caesar salad and daydreaming about seeing Win Wyatt again. She stole a few glances at the gift basket as she continued to work.

*

Grace was pounding away at her laptop when the phone rang. She looked up and couldn't believe it was already three o'clock. She answered it and pushed herself back from the desk.

"Hi, Grace? It's Andi. How's the writing going?"

"Hey, Andi, I've been writing all day and I can't believe it's gone by so fast. And oh, by the way, I'm making great progress! Once I get the brand turnaround examples set it should be a fast writing process." She glanced at the clock. "Think I'll take a quick break and run over to the gym while it's still empty."

"Sounds like a productive day. Did you figure out what to do with the publisher and literary agent contracts?"

Grace put a hand to the back of her neck and massaged it. "Well, I added the clause you suggested about being able to cancel the contract at any time. I have another meeting with them soon to talk through details of the book and marketing approaches. What's up with you? How's everything going with the acquisition and the new boss?" She leaned back and stretched.

"So far so good. At first I wasn't too sure if Lester would fit in with our department from a culture perspective, but he seems like a good guy. In fact, he invited me for lunch today in the executive dining room and we had a pleasant conversation. Oh, that reminds me, Lester organized an off-site for our department next week....to Bermuda. Can I borrow your travel golf bag? The wheels fell off of mine and I don't have time to shop for another one before my trip."

"Darn it, Andi, I was going to invite you along with me to see *A Streetcar Named Desire* next week when it opens."

"Really? How'd you score those tickets, Grace? That's the hottest show in town!"

Grace's face reddened. She'd told her friends about meeting Win Wyatt at the driving range but hadn't mentioned their lunch together since she figured it was a one-off. "Oh, a PR contact gave me the tickets. But you'll be out of town anyway. Guess I'll ask Sofia instead."

"Bummed I'll miss it, but I'll be soaking up the rays in Bermuda. Can I swing by on the way home for the golf bag, Grace?"

"Sure. I'll leave it for you with the doorman so he can run it out to you." They said goodbye and Grace texted an invite to Sofia for the show. Seconds later Sofia texted back, *You've got a date, my dear! Thanks.*

*

A couple of days later Grace sat and studied the other patrons inside the funky coffee shop near Union Square. It was bustling and full of hipsters and students grabbing a late breakfast. Grace glanced at her watch, wondering how long she'd have to wait—actresses were notoriously tardy. She was meeting with Simone Everett and hoping the actress would respond well to their discussion. Simone had been friendly enough over email when she'd agreed to meet, but in person it might be another situation. Was she still harboring any ill will?

Promptly at ten a.m. Simone appeared in front of Grace. "Grace, it's so good to see you again." They air-kissed and Simone slid into the booth across from Grace.

The actress was in her late twenties and looked vastly different than she had the last time Grace had seen her. Simone Everett had been an adorable, energetic girl who became a teen movie star with a trilogy of hit films in which she played a princess who is secretly a scientist and inventor. In her early twenties Simone had fallen in with the wrong crowd. She'd had a brutal breakup with her boyfriend in the lobby of a posh hotel where she hoisted a suitcase and launched it at his head— which was captured on video and went viral on social media, along with whispers about alcohol-induced rage. Simone's low point had been getting arrested for shoplifting a Louis Vuitton bag at a Saks Fifth Avenue, although formal charges were never filed. Burberry had been about to sign Simone Everett for their next big marketing campaign, but when the shoplifting incident occurred they dropped their plans. Grace was the one who'd had to break the bad news to Simone, and she remembered a glum, gaunt girl with dark circles under her eyes and heavy makeup.

The young woman sitting in front of her now looked vibrant and healthy. Her ivory skin glowed and her dark hair cascaded in thick, long waves around her oval face. Her brown eyes were clear and bright, fringed with lush eyelashes. She had an interesting, exotic look, a stunning blend of her Japanese mother and German father. Simone's face was one of the rare ones that looked beautiful without a trace of makeup. She wore a simple T-shirt and distressed jeans— the ripped-up jeans were a look that Grace had never been able to fathom.

"How long have you been living in the city, Simone?" Grace asked.

Simone pushed the menu aside and said, "Over four years now. I'm sure you remember the last time we met I was going through some difficulties. I decided to ditch the LA scene and moved here to attend NYU. Actually I just graduated with a major in finance."

Grace straightened up. "Wow, that's impressive. Good for you!" She signaled the waitress over and Simone ordered a green tea and steel-cut oatmeal with blueberries. "You're not going to become an investment banker, are you?" she half-joked.

Simone laughed and shook her head. "Going to college was a wonderful and grounding experience. I learned a lot, especially about finance and investing. But I realized that I miss acting, although at this point it seems impossible to try and break back into it. I've been gone so long, and..." She trailed off.

"Actually, Simone, that's what I wanted to talk to you about. I'm writing a book about resurrecting a brand, and I'd like to help you get your brand back on track. You know, move it from tarnished to terrific. And I'd write about your journey as a case study, if you agree."

Simone's hand stopped in midair and she put down her spoonful of oatmeal. "You want to help me and possibly get me back into acting?" She sat back. "What's it going to cost me?" Her voice sounded wary, like she'd been taken advantage of too many times in her youth.

Grace chuckled. "Not a cent. I'd like to apply my rebranding steps to your case and show how well they work. So, what do you think?"

The actress bowed her head for a moment and then grasped Grace's hand with her trembling one. "That sounds...amazing. I can't remember the last time anyone offered me something without wanting anything in return. Thank you, really." Her sparkling brown eyes locked on to Grace's face. "Getting help from a marketing guru like you would be incredible, Grace. I'm totally on board."

"Well, all right, then let's get started. I've outlined the steps to brand resurrection on this page, so we can go through them and then start brainstorming on ideas for your case study."

They had such a productive discussion that by the time Grace glanced at her watch again nearly two hours had passed. The two women set out a plan and timeline, Grace gave Simone a few homework assignments, and they figured out their next time to meet.

The personal rebranding case was off to a good start; now Grace had to focus on the product rebranding case.

*

The next day Grace was set for a walking meeting in Central Park with the two cofounders of a startup—a hair-care company called Flip Style. She'd sent a message out to her Ceiling Smashers network asking for suggestions on product brands in need of turnaround help. Flip Style had risen to the top due to its unique situation. The founders of Flip Style, Tom and Venkatesh, had been roommates at Columbia business school, and after graduating they'd launched Flip Style. One of their angel investors was a former colleague of Grace's who was happy to make the introduction.

Flip Style had a unique concept—it offered a line of concentrated natural shampoos and conditioners that would work for any type of hair, leaving it soft, shiny, and healthy. The formulas were packaged under pressure and foamed up when the user dispensed them. Flip Style had started off strong but then crashed and burned due to some recent problems. Grace wanted to meet Tom and Venkatesh to assess the situation and decide if she wanted to help them rescue their brand.

At the appointed time and at the west entrance of the park, Grace saw two young men—a taller, slim Indian man and a shorter, stockier Caucasian man. Both wore the entrepreneur's uniform of sneakers, jeans, and untucked button-down shirts. They greeted her enthusiastically.

"Good to meet you, Venkatesh and Tom." She shook their hands.

The Indian man pumped her hand. "Please, call me Venky. We're grateful for your reaching out to us and would really love the opportunity to work with you, Grace."

"Great, why don't we walk and talk. Maybe you can fill me in on the start of your business, what happened, and where things stand now."

As they wandered through Central Park that lovely fall morning, Venky did most of the talking and Tom filled in the blanks. They were smart, articulate young men. The two of them had done their homework looking for a category in need of innovation and they'd settled on hair care. They'd worked to create a superior product from natural ingredients, with a distinct brand. Venky had also hired a well-known industrial designer to develop beautiful but functional packaging. They did all the right things in launching the brand and got a foot in the door with Sephora, who tested the brand in thirty "doors," or stores. The Flip Style brand generated buzz and initial sales were brisk. Both men slowed to a halt as they got to the next part of their story.

The pained look on Venky's face spoke volumes. "Then disaster struck. Our packaging had a special pressure valve on top to help foam up the product when it was dispensed. There were some faulty parts installed during the packaging process and, well, the bottles started exploding."

Tom chimed in. "Literally there were bottles of shampoo and conditioner exploding in all the Sephora stores that carried our product—it was like a beauty minefield with sales associates and customers running out of the stores screaming. Total nightmare."

Grace's eyes widened. "Wow."

Venky crossed his arms. "Needless to say, Sephora kicked us out of their stores. That was two months ago and we've been trying to regroup. It's frustrating because we know we have a great product, but now the business is a mess. This brand resuscitation project of yours comes at an opportune time for us." He gave a hopeful smile.

The three of them picked up the pace again and Grace asked a number of questions about the Flip Style product, the packaging, the strategy for the company, their unit economics, their marketing plans, what success looked like for the founders, and where they were from a cash flow perspective.

The three of them returned to the park entrance and Venky paused. "So, Grace, do you think you can help us fix our marketing?"

Grace studied the faces of the two founders. "Venky, Tom, I can not only fix your brand, but I can help you fix your company. I'll explain what's involved and tell you my ask. Then I'll give you two time to think it over. I just ask that you get back to me within a week because I need to select the brand turnaround case study for my book quickly and I'm scheduled to speak with some other companies over the next few days." She explained everything to Venky and Tom and informed them that because of the amount of work involved and the value she could add, she would be asking them for a 3-to-5 percent equity stake in the company.

They shook hands and Grace started to walk away. She hadn't made it more than about thirty feet when the two entrepreneurs called out her name and ran after her. They agreed to a 5 percent equity stake and asked if she could start working with them the following Monday. Now Grace had the two brand case studies she'd need to complete her book—all she had to do was resurrect two dead brands.

*

ANDI

The warm tropical breeze blew through Andi's thick dark brown locks like delicate fingers gently massaging her scalp. She inhaled the sweet scent of butterfly jasmine. Just a few hours ago she had been in a noisy, bustling city, and now she was standing on a private balcony in a tranquil paradise taking in the incredible view of the beach, with waves lapping at the shore just thirty feet away. The offsite was being held at Pink Beach Resort in Bermuda. In the meantime the private banking department's offices were being moved up to the midtown building that housed Kaneshiro Bank.

After quickly unpacking and getting dressed in more tropical attire, the group of twenty senior private bankers met in the lobby, ready to play some golf. As usual, Andi was the only woman in the group, and she wore a fiery-red collared golf shirt and black golf shorts. She was glad to be out of her walking cast now; her broken foot had completely healed.

Mike was organizing people into their assigned foursomes for golf, and he just happened to include their new boss, Lester Labosky, in their group. Rob, a guy with a quick wit and a penchant for dirty jokes, was the fourth player in their group, and he'd be riding with Lester. Air-conditioned vans shuttled them the short drive over to the lush Tucker's Point Beach, Golf, and Tennis Club, located on a panoramic hilltop with stunning views of the water.

"Now, this is what I call a golf course," Mike said, winking at Andi, as he loaded both golf bags onto the back of the golf cart.

"What a gorgeous site," Lester said, but his pale blue eyes were fixed on Andi instead of the golf course. She blushed and Lester smiled.

Andi was itching to get out on the course to try out her new TaylorMade driver. She walked briskly to the golf cart and took out her club, ready to take a few practice swings.

Lester sauntered over. "Been playing long, Andi?" He tugged a ball cap down over his light brown hair.

"I learned to play golf after B-school, but with little kids I don't get out on the course very often," she said.

"I hear you. Well, don't be nervous, little lady."

Andi didn't take kindly to being called "little lady" but she let it slide. "Lester, it takes a lot more than a golf game to make me nervous." She laughed it off.

Then Lester started to give her some of his "expert pointers." Andi noted with annoyance that he wasn't giving any tips to the two male golfers. Mike observed all this and was clearly trying to suppress a smile. Finally he said to Lester, "You're up."

Their boss walked over to the tee and took three practice swings. He lined up to the ball and his jerky swing yielded a drive that went way left. He muttered a few expletives as he slashed his driver through the air.

Rob sliced his ball over to the adjacent fairway. Mike hit a nice long drive that hugged the right side of the fairway. He said, "Your turn, Andi. Sure you don't want to play from the forward tees?" He freely teased his friend, having golfed with her before and knowing her better than anyone else in their department. Mike also knew that as a former Olympian, Andi was a great athlete.

Responding to Mike's joke of a question, Andi said casually, "Aww, you know what? I think I'll try playing from these little old white tees with you guys."

Rob and Lester looked surprised at her response.

Andi teed up her ball, took one practice swing, and then got ready to hit the ball. Her swing felt good—smooth and swift. Her club made impact with the ball and it exploded off the tee like a gunshot with a lovely metallic ping from her titanium-head driver. She knew it was a good drive, so she didn't even bother to watch the flight of the ball as she leisurely bent down to retrieve her tee, then looked to see where it landed.

"Nice ball, Andi. Looks like you outdrove me again," said Mike. Her drive was long and straight down the fairway.

"Um, nice one," mumbled Lester. That day, playing from the white tees, Andi shot an excellent 75. Mike finished with a respectable 86. Rob's score was a 98, and Lester finished with a "102," although Andi did note that Lester failed to count all his strokes.

*

They returned to the hotel to get dressed for dinner. Though Andi didn't typically wear dresses, given the warm weather she made an exception and put on a dark blue body-skimming dress that celebrated her curves. By the time she got down to the bar, many of her colleagues had already had a few drinks, including Lester. Andi got a beer and joined a small group. They were recounting highlights of their golf games when Lester came up behind Andi and stood close enough that she could feel his body heat.

"Turns out that Andi here is quite the amazing golfer…especially for a girl!" Lester rested both hands on her shoulders, rubbing his thumbs along her shoulder blades. She could smell the cloud of scotch coming from his breath, and her body tensed up at the unwanted physical contact from her boss. His touch gave her the sensation of spiders crawling all over her bare skin. She shot a look of alarm at Mike, who, seeing her discomfort, extricated her from the awkward situation by asking her a feigned work question and pulling her over to the hors d'oeuvres table.

They had a festive team dinner at the resort that night and Lester outlined the agenda for the next day. He promised that if they got an early start and accomplished the day's objectives, they'd be back out on the golf course in the afternoon. Everyone agreed.

Andi was looking forward to getting a full, uninterrupted night's sleep without the pitter-patter of little feet coming into their bedroom. After calling her husband and kids to say goodnight, she was tucked in bed early. *This trip is just what I needed.* She let out a sigh of contentment and drifted off into a peaceful sleep.

The following two days were filled with meetings, golf, more meetings, and more golf. Andi felt good about her contributions and Lester encouraged her to share her insights with the rest of the private banking team, even complimenting her ideas. She felt valued and integral to the business discussions. At one of the dinners she and Lester even had a heartfelt conversation about the challenges of working full-time and raising kids. So far the offsite was going well for Andi, while Luca and his parents were managing just fine at home with their twin boys.

On the last evening at the offsite, following an extravagant dinner, everyone moved to the hospitality suite reserved for their firm, which had a terrace with a picturesque view of the ocean waves. Many guys were engaged in the usual male bonding with tequila shots and games of billiards and darts. Andi had a craving for a chocolate bar and asked if anyone wanted anything before she sauntered down the hall to the vending machines. She perused the candy options in the machine.

"Tempting, isn't it?" a voice hissed behind Andi.

She whirled around, dropping her money in the process, only to find herself uncomfortably close to a grinning Lester Labosky. He seemed to be eyeing her as if she were one of the scrumptious treats.

"Yeah, just grabbing a chocolate bar." Andi nodded nonchalantly toward the candy machine as she backed away from him and picked up her bills from the floor.

"Why don't you forget about the candy and come over to my suite? We can share a nice bottle of chilled champagne and have a chat." Lester seemed sloshed, and the stale, acrid odor of scotch on his breath invaded Andi's nostrils.

The situation was confounding. On the one hand, Lester seemed to value her as an employee and had championed her ideas in the meetings. He'd expressed a desire to work collaboratively with Andi. Plus he was a family man, so maybe he meant no harm by the invitation. On the other hand, she was getting strange vibes from her new boss at that moment. Flummoxed, Andi simply said, "Uh, no thanks, I'm good."

Lester was undaunted. "Come on, Andi, you need to relax a little. Don't you think we should get to know each other better? We're going to be working together closely." He moved toward her and slowly ran his fingers through his hair.

Feeling uneasy but maintaining her composure, Andi replied,

"Lester, I'm sure we'll get to know each other better as we work together—just like I did with my previous boss." She put her two dollars in the machine and quickly selected her candy bar.

Now Lester was slurring his words. "Aww, I juss wanna talk wis you, Andi." Going to her boss's suite when he was drunk? Bad idea.

Andi snatched the bar as soon as it dropped. She forced a smile. "Sure, Lester, that sounds great. Let's head back to the hospitality suite and we can chat in there." She hightailed it back to where the other guys were congregated.

After a while Andi ended up shooting pool with the other guys and Lester was nowhere in sight. Maybe he'd decided to call it a night or found some other source of entertainment for the evening. She took a final gulp of her drink. "Okay, guys, time for me to turn in. See you mañana!" As she sauntered back to her room Andi ruminated on how best to cultivate her professional relationship with Lester while keeping a safe distance. Or was she being paranoid?

*

COOP

Coop arrived for his scheduled sit-down with the human resources person, Barbara Pat Kelly, a serious-looking woman with a helmet of heavily hair-sprayed blond hair. Most of the time Barbara Pat had a dour expression, and Coop wondered if it was because she didn't like being an HR professional or because she was cross about having three first names. Today she was wearing her normal outfit of a conservative wool-blend dress and a button-up cardigan along with sensible Ferragamo heels with little bows near the toes. Sitting in close proximity, Coop remembered too late that Barbara Pat's hair spray gave off a strong chemical smell, and he tried his best to take shallow, infrequent breaths to avoid the toxic fumes. She listened to Coop as he shared his experiences with the client audit with Felix, his delayed promotion, and the diversity workshop. Barbara Pat nodded all the while with a look of neutrality on her face.

Finally she said, "I'm sorry all that happened to you, Coop. It does indeed sound taxing." Appropriate choice of words as this was an accounting firm. "But what you're saying about being held back due to your sexual orientation, frankly I find that hard to believe in a firm of this caliber. That just isn't the firm I know. And our CEO has always cultivated a culture of inclusivity."

Coop wasn't too surprised at her response. After all, the head of HR reported to the senior partners, so why would she ever question their actions or be anything but supportive of them? He asked, "Just out of curiosity, Barbara Pat, *are* there any gay partners in this firm?"

"Oh, I think not," Barbara Pat scoffed, then caught herself. That was a dead giveaway. So it was true…being gay at this firm meant his career was limited. "Of course, one can't be certain. We are an open and welcoming firm with a proud heritage."

"I see." For the first time in ten years, Coop looked at his employer with fresh eyes and a sickening sense of remorse. He'd sacrificed so much, only to discover that he would not be allowed to go any further if he stayed with the firm.

Barbara Pat placed some papers into a manila folder and said in a cool tone, "Coop, I think the message from the Promotion Council was pretty clear: just keep working hard and things will happen for you. In the meantime, I think you'd be well served to develop a thicker skin. So are we good here?"

"Yup, we're good, Barbara Pat. Thanks for your time." Coop couldn't wait to get out of her office and inhale some fresh unscented air. Now he knew that it was up to him to make things happen…but how?

*

"Great to see you, Coop!" Patrick Ellis got up from his barstool. "I can't believe it's been ten years since Wharton. Man, time really flies, doesn't it?" He had a medium build, neat and trim, with thinning dark hair and light brown eyes. Patrick had such a pleasant demeanor it was hard to believe that in his work at the Securities and Exchange Commission he sent people to jail for a living, although the people that he'd sent to prison really did deserve it.

Coop gave him a man hug—basically bumping chests and slapping each other on the shoulder. "Wow, Patrick, you look exactly the same. Great to see you, too. How are things in DC?" Taking Vivien's advice to call their classmate, Coop had learned that Patrick was in town for a conference that week, so they'd arranged to meet. Patrick wore a custom-tailored dark blue suit with a tasteful reddish Hermès necktie. Although he clearly had grown up with money (his family owned a chain of high-end jewelry stores), he was unpretentious and humble. Coop glanced down at Patrick's designer shoes, which were polished to a high gleam, and started mentally tallying up the cost of his friend's outfit, stopping when the number exceeded his monthly mortgage payment. Even though Coop was earning a good living, he was exceedingly cautious about spending money on himself and would only occasionally allow himself to splurge on a nice suit at Nordstrom Rack.

Coop surveyed the room and then hopped onto one of the barstools at the Monkey Bar in the Hotel Elysée in midtown. It wasn't a bar that his colleagues frequented, which was why Coop had picked it, and he liked that the drinks were served with a tiny colorful plastic monkey on the lip of the glass. The lighting glowed dimly, creating a seductive atmosphere, and the cartoonish mural covering the wall was meant to be studied.

The two men caught up for a bit over vodka martinis, and Patrick proudly shared some photos of his wife and kids. "So, Coop, you mentioned over the phone that you had a tricky situation you wanted to discuss. How can I be of help?"

Choosing his words cautiously, Coop narrowed his eyes. "Hypothetical situation. What if a person—say, an accountant—

suspected that a client, which was a large public company, was engaged in questionable accounting practices sanctioned by their accounting firm? So essentially the public company and the accounting firm were in cahoots. What might happen in that kind of situation, hypothetically?" He felt his cell phone vibrate in his pocket and checked the number. It was his mom. Coop let it roll to voice mail.

Patrick had a trace of a smile on his face. "If the accounting fraud is obvious, then hopefully the SEC would catch it on their own. However, in some 'hypothetical' cases like this there could be an internal whistleblower who shares documents and the like with the SEC to get the ball rolling. An investigation would get started and ultimately the guilty parties would be prosecuted and incarcerated."

"And what would happen to the whistleblower?" Coop's knotted brow telegraphed his apprehension.

"That's a little more involved. Typically the whistleblower testifies in court about the wrongdoing, so their name is publicly known." Patrick's face grew serious. "They can expect to not ever work in that industry again—or at least not for another large accounting firm. But...it all depends on the specifics of the situation. I'm just trying to give it to you straight, Coop."

Coop leaned back from the bar and nodded solemnly, his lips pressed tightly together. So if he did the right thing he'd never be able to work for another accounting firm. But if he was implicated in the scandal he could end up in jail. Of course, there was always the option of doing nothing and hoping for the best. He mentally wrestled with these options and his cell phone buzzed again. "Sorry, Patrick, it's my mom. I'd better make sure she's okay. Do you mind?"

Patrick shooed him off. "Take your time, Coop. I'll order us another round."

*

Outside the Monkey Bar, where it was much quieter, Coop answered his phone. "Hi, Mom, is everything okay?"

"Oh, Gary, it's terrible news, just terrible." Only his family and a handful of close relatives called him by his first name. Coop was the oldest of nine brothers and sisters, and he said a silent prayer that they were all okay. His mom sounded ready to burst into tears. "It's Alma. Her husband has been romantically involved with someone else and he's left her—after thirty years of marriage!"

His brain took a second to process the information. "Oh, you mean Mrs. Jankowski? I'm sorry to hear that, Mom."

"She doesn't even know who the other woman is, Gary, though she suspects it's his trainer from the gym." Coop was a little relieved that the bad news wasn't about anyone in his immediate family. Alma Jankowski was his mom's best friend and lived down the street. She was a kind, efficient woman (stemming from her experience as an executive admin) who loved to bake and often dropped off a fresh loaf of banana bread or sugar cookies for the Cooper family.

"It's awful, Gary, he's leaving her with nothing. She may even lose the house. Her husband has been in charge of their finances all these years and everything is under his name. Alma doesn't even have her own credit card."

Coop frowned. "So she doesn't have any credit history? Wow, that's going to make it tough to get a new credit card or a loan or whatever."

"Honey, I need you to help Alma. Just like you helped me when your dad left us. Can you do that, Gary? Please?" It was not like his mom to beg, but she'd been in the same situation years ago, and judging from the anguish in her voice those painful memories were still vivid.

"Of course, Mom, I'm happy to help her." Coop shifted his weight. "I'm just meeting with someone now for work, though. Why don't you tell her to give me a call and I'll see what I can do, okay?"

She let out a big sigh. "Oh, what a relief. Thank you, Gary. I already gave Alma your number so she'll probably call you later tonight. Bye, sweetheart."

"Okay, bye, Mom."

*

Coop returned to the bar, where Patrick had two chilled vodka martinis sitting at the ready. "Everything okay, Coop?"

Coop nodded and took a sip of his drink. "Yes, everything's fine. My mom's friend just needs my accounting help." He was already starting to feel a nice buzz. Better get something into his stomach—he reached over for the bowl of bar nuts.

"So, did you want to discuss your hypothetical situation further?" Patrick raised an eyebrow as he drank his martini.

He thought about it a minute. "Patrick, I think I need to gather some information first. Can I call you when I'm ready to talk in more detail?"

Patrick waved one hand and said, "Sure, sure. Whenever you're ready." He leaned a little closer. "By the way, are you seeing anyone these days?"

Coop assumed that Patrick knew he was gay and was hoping to avoid an awkward situation where Coop would have to decline being fixed up with some woman. He shook his head slowly.

"Well, there's this woman I work with—"

Uh-oh, not again. Coop was about to protest when he heard the rest of Patrick's sentence.

"—whose brother is in the Secret Service. He's supposed to be a great catch. Would you like me to connect you two?"

Now, that's more like it. Coop's love life hadn't been the greatest and he could have used some help. He smiled shyly and agreed. Who knew that straitlaced Patrick could both be a source of help in the accounting fraud matter and provide a gay dating service?

In the comfort of his cozy apartment, Coop kicked off his shoes at the door and simultaneously dropped his computer bag under the front table, tossing his keys into the silver bowl on top. It was way past dinnertime and he needed to put something substantial in his stomach. Hunting through his kitchen drawer full of takeout menus, he selected one and phoned in his burrito delivery order. New York City was the best—it was the only city in the world where you could order food at any hour. He plopped on the sofa and was about to switch on the TV when he heard his cell phone buzzing.

"Hello?"

"Oh, hello, Gary? This is Alma Jankowski. Your mother gave me your number. I hope it isn't too late to call—did I wake you?"

Coop laughed, "No, Mrs. Jankowski, it's only nine o'clock. I just got home from work and ordered dinner."

"Goodness gracious," she remarked, "you youngsters have so much energy. I don't know how much your mother told you, Gary, but I need your advice."

"Sure thing. Can you share with me what's going on?"

Tentatively and tearfully, Alma Jankowski gave Coop the rundown on her husband's extramarital escapade and told him the story of how he'd packed his belongings and left her. He'd already frozen their bank account and changed the passwords on their investment accounts, so she was cut off from any access. Mrs. Jankowski wailed, "I can't believe my husband is tossing me out like a pair of old shoes. I feel like a piece of rubbish."

Coop felt for her. "Mrs. Jankowski, remember what Eleanor Roosevelt once said: 'No one can make you feel inferior without your consent.' Don't let your husband make you feel that way."

She chuckled gratefully.

"What's your financial situation looking like?"

"I have some income from my work as an executive assistant, but it's not enough to retire on. I'm worried about my future, Gary. I can't believe that my husband has left me with nothing. After doing everything for him for thirty years, this is what I get?" She was starting to sound angry, and that was a good sign—Coop knew it meant she'd be willing to fight for what she deserved.

Coop expressed his sympathies to Mrs. Jankowski and assured her he'd do his best to help sort out the situation. He told her to gather every computer file, financial record, checkbook receipt, property title, and investment statement she could find. "Your husband may have abandoned you, Mrs. Jankowski, but I will make sure he doesn't swindle you as well. I'll come over there on Saturday afternoon and have a look at all the paperwork. We'll figure this out together, okay?"

Alma broke down in tears. "Oh, Gary, I'm so grateful to you. You're such a dear. Thank you, and I'll see you on Saturday."

The moment he hung up, Coop felt knots the size of boulders taking up residence in his neck. Between the politics at work, his struggles to become a partner, and now Mrs. Jankowski's situation, was he taking on more stress than he could handle?

*

SOFIA

Her shoulders ached as if she'd been balancing a heavy barbell on them, a signal that Sofia had been hunched over her computer for far too long. She was engrossed in her research preparing for her big interview with Hideyoshi Sakamoto, founder of the hot apparel retailer named Deki. "Yoshi" (as he was known in Japan) was the hottest entrepreneur to come out of that country. He had a bold personality, a quick wit, and an unbridled ambition to be the most successful retailer in the world. His drive and enthusiasm had captivated the imagination of the Japanese people and made him a hugely popular figure. Yoshi's classically handsome looks only added to his appeal. The *Asahi Shimbun* newspaper had conducted a poll asking readers who was their favorite Japanese person. Yoshi, of course, had ended up in first place. Akira Kurosawa had come in second, and the emperor of Japan was a distant third.

Sofia decided to stretch her legs and swing by Kate Frost's office to ask her a few questions about her interview subject. When she stepped into Kate's office it was deserted. A lovely floral arrangement sat on her coffee table with a card that had been torn open and left lying there. Sofia glanced at it and then looked back at it again. It read, "Glenda, dear, I'm so proud of you and will be watching you as always. All my love, Mom." *Glenda? Who's Glenda?* Before she could think about it further Kate's personal assistant, Jenny, slipped in between her and the bouquet and cleared away the note and the flowers.

Sofia stepped back. "Hi, Jenny. I was just looking for Kate. I wanted to get a leg up on my interview with Yoshi. Is she around?"

Jenny was typically glued to Kate Frost's side. After working with Kate for years, she was naturally protective of her boss and sparing with the information she shared. Jenny squinted at Sofia. "She's finishing up a meeting and will be along shortly. Do you want to wait?"

"Yes, thanks." Sofia sat on the sofa and looked at her smartphone. There was a text from Andi reminding her of her blind date that evening with Luca's colleague from the ETS, a man with the unfortunate name of Jonathan Bland. Sofia had told Andi she was tired of dating handsome jerks and just wanted a nice, normal guy. Her logic was that an average-looking guy might have more brains and personality and would treat women better. She texted Andi back in the affirmative and also received a playful text from Jonathan confirming their meeting location and time. Sofia let out a hopeful sigh.

Just then Kate walked in and saw Sofia sitting there. She glanced at the coffee table nervously for a moment and then Jenny breezed in.

"Sofia wanted to ask you some questions for her upcoming interview so I let her wait in here. I cleared off your table," Jenny said. Kate gave a nod of approval to her assistant.

"What can I do for you?" Kate stood across from Sofia, leaning against the desk.

"Oh, I was just compiling a list of questions and angles for the interview—thought I'd run them by you. Do you mind?"

"It's your interview, so you should do as you please, Sofia."

"Yes, but since you know Yoshi pretty well I thought you might be able to provide some insights." She asked a few questions and got some tepid responses. Kate glanced at her watch a couple of times and Sofia was getting the sense that her co-anchor was reluctant to help. Maybe she was just trying to subtly encourage Sofia to follow her instincts? Sofia decided to wrap things up. "Is there anything that you think I've missed, Kate?"

Kate shook her head. "I can't think of anything."

Sofia thanked Kate and left her office. *She must think I'm in good shape. Great.*

*

After a self-imposed dating hiatus, Sofia was putting herself out there again. She'd been chased after by good-looking guys who wanted to date someone with a bit of celebrity—men who just wanted to share in the spotlight. All she really wanted was a regular, nice guy with whom she could have an intellectual conversation.

On that Monday evening Sofia and Jonathan Bland were meeting for drinks at a trendy bistro in the Meatpacking District. She knew that he was a tallish blond man but that was about it. When she entered and didn't see anyone matching that description, she took a seat at the bar. As Sofia was about to take a sip of wine someone tapped her on the shoulder. "Excuse me, but are you the world-famous Sofia LaForte?"

She turned to see a tall, pale man standing there. Jonathan Bland had an animated smile but was an ordinary-looking man—the kind of person you could sit next to on the subway every day and never even notice. His nose was a bit long and pinched. His blondish hair was thinning with a network of purplish veins visible at his temples. Sofia smiled as she offered her hand, which he took and kissed ever so lightly. Nice touch.

"I'm Jon, and I am thrilled to meet you." He slid onto the seat next to hers. "In honor of our first date I brought something for you." He reached into his computer bag and pulled out a gift.

Sofia tilted her head in surprise. "Oh, Jon, that's so nice of you. And unexpected."

"It is but a small offering. Andi said that you're constantly scribing notes for your work, so I thought you might find this of use."

Sofia untied the ribbon and opened the box to find a nice leather-bound notebook and pen. It was big enough to take notes with easily but small enough to stash in her purse. "Why thank you, Jon, this will come in handy. How thoughtful."

The pair quickly delved into an engaging conversation. Sofia learned that Jon was intelligent, confident, and could converse on a broad array of topics. His cell phone rang and he said, "Excuse me, a pressing issue requires my attention. I'll be but a moment." Jon hurried outside to take his call and returned about fifteen minutes later.

Taking his seat, Jon looked at Sofia with a concerned expression. "You must be famished after a long day of work, Sofia. Shall we partake of some sustenance?"

"I am hungry, but it's packed in here. I doubt we'll get a table." Sofia scanned the crowded bistro. The smell of grilled meat and truffled french fries was making her stomach grumble.

Jon smiled and said in a self-assured manner, "I have already confabulated with the hostess and our table is at the ready. Allow me to settle the bar bill."

Sofia raised her eyebrows. "How'd you swing that? This restaurant is always booked up weeks in advance."

"I took the liberty of calling ahead of our date and requesting that they hold a table for us. I hope that's agreeable." A man who planned ahead. Jon was scoring some major points.

Once they were seated Sofia got the lowdown on her date. Jon had an undergraduate degree from Brown and two master's degrees from Harvard—an MBA and a master's in linguistics. Sofia shared that she'd majored in mathematics at Tulane and minored in Romance languages. She'd graduated from Wharton's Lauder program and spoke five languages fluently. Although Jon's language skills weren't as advanced as hers, he was able to converse adroitly in French, which delighted Sofia. They shared some jokes and amusing stories in French over their appetizers.

They continued their friendly banter until the waiter stopped by to take their entrée orders. Then Sofia got up from her seat. "Excuse me, I'm just going to the ladies' room." Jon stood up when Sofia rose—he certainly seemed well mannered.

When she returned to the table Jon Bland was nowhere in sight. Odd. She signaled the waiter, who informed her that Jon had stepped outside to take a call. After twenty minutes passed Sofia was irritated. Why the ridiculously long absence? And this was already after a fifteen-minute phone call earlier. If he were a surgeon being consulted on a life-saving operation she could understand, but the guy worked for the Educational Testing Service. What, was there some controversy over an SAT question? Whatever the reason for Jon's absence, Sofia was a practical person and a girl had to eat, so when the waiter served their food she went ahead and started her dinner.

Finally Jon returned to the table. He spoke in French. "Sofia, my dear, did you miss me? Were you worried that I left?" He had an inexplicable impish glint in his pale blue eyes.

Sofia gave a clipped response in French. "I had no idea where you were, Jon. It would have been polite to let me know what was happening," she said, chastising him. "The headline is, I was hungry so I went ahead and started eating after waiting for you for half an hour."

"Oh dear, I've made you unhappy. I humbly apologize, Sofia, but it was a pressing issue. A colleague of mine was on a deadline to finalize some questions on a new exam, so I made haste to the quieter environment of the vestibule to take the call."

"I see." Sofia took another bite of her food.

Jon motioned to the waiter to refill his and Sofia's wineglasses. As he devoured his meal he launched into a discussion about a new segment of questions he was developing for the GMAT. He worked hard at getting back in Sofia's good graces, but she was having doubts. The date had started off well, but after being abandoned twice she was feeling both frustrated and glum. *I could've stayed home and eaten my favorite Thai takeout food in my sweats.* Between her *On the Ball Investing* show and her upcoming *Titans Tell All* debut, her work at CNBC was all-consuming and exhausting. Dating required additional mental energy that Sofia wasn't sure she possessed.

Jon changed his tack and began asking thoughtful questions about Sofia and pouring on the compliments. Eventually they shared a few laughs, and by the time they finished their dinner things seemed to be back on track. Sofia told him it was getting late and she'd need to leave soon, but Jon implored her to stay for dessert.

Once he ordered dessert, he turned to her. "Sofia, I find myself prepared to share my assessment of you."

Sofia raised an eyebrow. "Assessment? What do you mean?"

"My conclusions that I've drawn about you, *ma chérie.*"

She had no idea what was coming next; maybe something clever? "Okay, Jon, go ahead."

"You're definitely marriage material, Sofia. I give you a composite rating of 8.83. The rating is an average of three separate components—education, attractiveness, body—all on a scale of one to ten." His icy blue eyes held a cold, analytical look devoid of mirth.

Sofia drew back. *What was he talking about?*

"I grade every woman on three different elements based on a ten-point scale. For education I give you an eight, because you went to an Ivy League school, but I knocked you down a couple of points since you only have one master's degree. For attractiveness I give you a ten rating, because of your mesmerizing face and glowing complexion. For body I give you an 8.5, since you're slender but still curvy. So that brings us to a composite rating of 8.83." Jon smiled, seemingly pleased to share the news of the high rating with Sofia. The only problem—at least for Sofia—was that he was dead serious.

"Wait a minute, Jon. You're grading me, like a piece of beef?" Sofia's tone was sharp and her eyes flashed with indignation. "Do you do this with all the women you go out with?"

Jon held up both hands and his pale skin flushed as he fumbled an apology. "Really, Sofia, it was just a bit of, um, frivolity. My intent wasn't to offend. It's just a little system that I customarily use to assess women. It's particularly enthralling for me due to the fact that I've never before gone on a date with an 8.83!"

It was like talking to a human spreadsheet. "Jon, do you see me as just a number or do you actually like me as a person?"

He coughed and managed to say, "I like you."

"Why do you like me?" Sofia asked in all seriousness.

"Because you're beautiful. And smart and successful. And famous. And you went to Wharton," Jon responded in a flat, dispassionate voice. It was the same dull tone one might use when reading an ingredient list off a box of cereal or the instructions for assembling a desk from IKEA. Robotically he clasped her hand in his and kissed it. She wasn't happy with Jon's unemotional response or the idea that he was interested in her only for her looks and educational pedigree. Would they even have had a first date if she had attended NYU's business school?

Sofia let out a long breath. By now she felt let down by Jon and the entire date. All she'd been hoping for was to meet a nice guy, someone who would treat her well. But this man was unattractive in both appearance and personality, and she felt nothing for him. So disappointing.

Jon appeared desperate to rectify things. "Please, *ma chérie*, this has been such an enchanting evening. I beg of you, let's continue our discourse over dessert." Then Jon's cell phone went off again. Sofia was exasperated. *Three calls on one date?*

"Please excuse me, it must be another pressing issue." Jon rose and ran off again.

Sofia shook her head in disgust. Despite his intellect and his eloquent phrasing, Jon didn't really have anything meaningful to say. On top of all that, she didn't care for his incivility. Sofia was giving the keynote speech at a conference the following week and needed to get some rest tonight and get up early to work on her speech. This date had been such a drain on her energy. *At least I got this nice notebook.* She ripped out a page from the leather notebook and scribbled *Sorry, Jon, I have a particularly "pressing" engagement…with my bed. Goodbye.*

CHAPTER 4

September-October

SOFIA

Putting the blind date disaster behind her, Sofia focused on her upcoming speech at the Inc. Women's Summit, which was being held at Chelsea Piers. She'd been selected to give a keynote speech on the topic of breaking barriers in broadcast journalism. Sofia was looking forward to sharing her thoughts and potentially helping other women navigate their careers.

An accomplished speaker, Sofia had outlined her speech in her sparse free time—in the shower, on the Pilates reformer, eating her meals—refining what she was going to say and what stories she'd share. On the morning of the conference, Sofia felt a tingling sensation down the back of her neck—the telltale sign that she was primed to give her speech.

Wearing a smart green Tahari dress, Sofia walked briskly out of her Upper West Side building and hailed a cab, greeting the driver and giving him instructions to take her down to Chelsea Piers. The Pakistani cabbie perked up when he recognized his passenger. "Oh, you're Sofia LaForte. I've seen you on CNBC. I can't believe you're in my cab!" He gave her a big smile and then sped downtown, weaving in and out of the cars and leaning liberally on the horn. They were rapidly nearing midtown when he asked her, "Are you interviewing someone at Chelsea Piers?"

Sofia explained that she was giving a speech at a conference.

The cab driver's foot was still flooring the accelerator when he turned to ask her, "You're giving a speech? What's it about?"

"The theme of the conference is—" Then Sofia yelled, "Whoa, look out!"

Too late. By the time the cabbie swiveled back around to see what Sofia was warning him about there was a sound of screeching brakes and crunching metal. Even though her seat belt was fastened, Sofia's head slammed into the Plexiglas partition as the taxi smashed into the back end of a black limousine. The airbag in the steering column deployed, so the cabbie, though shaken, was fine and even appeared excited about the break in his day's monotony. He turned around to look at his passenger.

"Uh-oh." He pointed. "Your head. It is red."

Sofia put her hand up gingerly to her forehead and could feel a gash and warm blood oozing out onto her cool fingertips. The limo driver got out to yell at the cabbie, who jumped out of the cab and yelled back. The limo passenger also got out to check on the situation and Sofia saw him look at her and rush over.

"Excuse me, miss, are you all right?" the stranger asked as he opened the taxi door. A tall man bent over her and Sofia found it hard to focus on his face, his features obscured by the brilliant sunshine coming in the door behind him. "Here, I think you need this." He pulled a freshly pressed handkerchief out of his jacket pocket and handed it to Sofia.

She placed the handkerchief against her forehead, suddenly aware of the sharp throbbing she felt. "Thank you. How bad is it?" Sofia grimaced.

The sympathetic stranger examined the wound carefully. "I think you'll live. But you're probably going to need stitches."

"Oh, no," groaned Sofia, "I don't have time for this. I'm supposed to give a keynote speech at the Inc. Women's Summit in a few hours!"

"The one at Chelsea Piers? I'm going to that conference, too," he said. "Listen, we should head to NYU's emergency room—they're the fastest in the city. A buddy of mine is a doctor there. Let's get your head taken care of, and we can go to the conference together," the stranger suggested. He was coming into focus, and Sofia could see that he had dark hair, a goatee, and gentle brown eyes.

"Sure, sure," Sofia agreed in a daze, her head feeling fuzzy.

The stranger told his limo driver to get things quickly sorted out with the cabbie, paid the cab fare for Sofia, and instructed his driver to speed them safely to Tisch Hospital. Sofia didn't know who the stranger was, but she did notice that he was really cute and stylishly dressed.

*

At the ER, the stranger sat Sofia down and said, "You should definitely have a plastic surgeon take care of that wound. You don't want to jeopardize that beautiful face of yours." He disappeared for a moment, then returned having somehow managed to get the hospital's top plastic surgeon to attend to Sofia's forehead. The stranger spoke with the doctors, who said the patient might have a mild concussion and should take it easy. Her head was pounding and the antiseptic aroma inside the examination room was dizzying. Things were a blur, but the plastic surgeon closed Sofia's laceration with surgical glue to minimize scarring and taped a large white bandage onto her forehead. The stranger, who had stepped out of the room briefly, returned and carefully scrutinized the doctor's work. He said, "Here, have some of these. Your blood sugar is probably low." He handed Sofia a small bottle of fresh-squeezed orange juice and some crackers.

Slowly Sofia felt the vise grip of the headache starting to release its hold. Moving cautiously, the stranger helped her back into the limo and they raced over to Chelsea Piers. The tires screeched when they pulled up, and the conference organizers ran out to greet Sofia.

A woman wearing a headset and carrying a clipboard said, "We received a call that you were in a car accident and were so worried." Sofia looked at the stranger and he winked at her. The woman clasped her hands together. "We're so glad you're okay, Sofia, and still willing to give your speech. We'd better get you onstage now." Before they whisked her away, Sofia turned to the man who had been helping her all this time and said a hasty but heartfelt thank-you. It wasn't until she was inside the venue that she realized she'd never learned his name.

The organizers quickly escorted Sofia to the front of the packed conference room, and with renewed energy Sofia bounded onstage. She pointed to her head and leaned into the mic, "You see, this is what happens when you smash the glass ceiling!" The crowd roared with approval, and Sofia launched into her speech.

*

The next day at work the makeup artist at CNBC shook her head sympathetically at the sight of Sofia's forehead but did an amazing job putting on a skin-colored bandage and blending it in with makeup so it wasn't so obvious. Sofia was marveling at the makeup artist's work when a production assistant ran in and gave her a ten-minute warning.

When she wrapped up her *On the Ball Investing* program and walked off set she noticed Kate Frost standing, arms crossed, next to her assistant, Jenny. Kate said something to Jenny, who nodded and then walked away. "Hi, Kate, how are you?"

Kate gave a quick smile and said, "Well, thank you." Her eyes skimmed Sofia's body and she said, "A red dress for a financial news show. That's an interesting choice." It wasn't quite a slight, but it wasn't a compliment either. In the past couple weeks Sofia had received some uninvited comments from Kate about her style choices. *That bracelet is so ethnic. You're so bold to wear that silhouette.* Her cutting words were always delivered with a sweet smile.

Sofia's typical response was "I chose it because I like it." She was hoping they'd be able to work well together, but she didn't much care for the barbs from Kate—that was conduct more typical of high school mean girls.

"All set for your interview next week with Yoshi?" Kate gave her a tight smile.

"Ready as I'll ever be," Sofia said.

"I'm sure," Kate said, "but you never know what curveballs can be thrown your way, right? That's live broadcasting for you." She cackled and walked away. While Kate's tone was light, there was a slightly menacing undercurrent just beneath the surface.

Sofia watched her go and then her phone buzzed—a text from Grace reminding her to meet at the theater for the Broadway show they were seeing that night.

*

"Oh my gosh, Grace, how'd you score these amazing seats? Thanks so much for bringing me." Sofia marveled at their front-row, center-stage seats at the Broadway premiere of *Cat on a Hot Tin Roof*.

Grace blushed. "Oh, I got them from a PR contact." But when Sofia shot her a dubious look, she confessed in a whisper. "Remember I told you that I met Win Wyatt? Well, he sent over the tickets for me." Her eyes widened.

"What? Is he interested in you or something?" Sofia's voice was rising with excitement. "He's hot. Like, really hot."

"I'm not sure what's going on. But he's really interesting and smart. Did you know he was studying for a PhD in chem E before he got into acting?" Grace glanced around furtively and then changed the subject. "How are things going with your new coworker?"

Sofia looked perplexed. "You know, at first I was nervous about working with Kate based on what I'd heard. But then when I met her she seemed very gracious and smart. I was getting excited about collaborating with her. Lately, though, she's been critical about what I'm wearing, my style choices, etc. I don't get it. And our show hasn't even kicked off yet."

Her friend nodded. "I hear you, Sof. I've had a couple of disastrous experiences working with other senior women, which is kind of silly. I mean, shouldn't we all be helping each other? But some women feel like there's only enough room at the top for one female, so they try to destroy the other women to eliminate the competition."

"But in the end that kind of behavior is just bad for all women in business. Right?" Sofia looked at her friend.

Grace nodded. "All you can do is to be the better person and do your best. If anyone can bring her around, Sofia, you certainly can."

Both of them looked through their *Playbill*s and then the lights dimmed. "Oh, look, the show's starting." Sofia noticed that Grace was eagerly perched on the edge of her seat—she'd never seen her so nervous.

*

At intermission, while Grace went to use the restroom Sofia sauntered over to the bar to get a couple of glasses of champagne for them. Champagne flutes in hand, Sofia turned and spotted in the middle of the crowded lobby the kind stranger who'd helped her during her taxi accident. He wore a dark suit with a pale lavender shirt and a purple paisley pocket square—he looked dashing. She swiftly walked over to him and gave him a shy smile. "Hi there!"

The man turned and gave her a big grin. "Sofia, what a pleasant surprise. Your speech at the conference was fantastic. I was going to try to talk to you afterward but you were being mobbed."

She thanked him and gave a slight shrug. "You were such a huge help the other day, but I didn't have a chance to ask your name. I'm so sorry about that."

He chuckled and his light brown eyes twinkled. "It's Jasper.

Jasper Frank. I'm pleased to officially meet you, Sofia LaForte." He took her hand warmly in his. "How's the head feeling?"

"Oh, it's fine, thanks to you. So is it your job to roam around the city saving damsels in distress?" She winked and then caught herself. *Whoa, am I full-on flirting with this guy?*

"Only the really smart and beautiful damsels."

She liked that he put *smart* ahead of *beautiful*.

Jasper said, "Actually I do have a real job, I'm a startup guy. Working on my second startup—a software company that does cybersecurity."

Sofia was feeling giddy. He smelled good and looked good. This was promising. Just then a tall, thin woman came up and slid her hand through the crook of Jasper's arm. "Hi, I'm back," she said. She was a beautiful and very young thing with cascading dark hair, an extremely short skirt, and long dangly gold earrings.

Startled, Sofia took a step back.

"Sofia, this is Lucy. Lucy, this is Sofia LaForte," Jasper said.

She forced a smile but Sofia felt her heart drop to the floor. Why was it that successful guys always went for much younger women? She said hello to the tall brunette. "Okay, well it was good to see you again, Jasper. I have to find my friend Grace." She spun around and tried to get away from the couple as fast as possible, which was difficult in the crowded lobby. Across the room Grace was waving at her.

Jasper rushed after her. "Wait, Sofia! Would you like to get a coffee after the show?"

She gave him a hard stare. "I don't think you and your date need me as a chaperone. No thank you."

His forehead wrinkled for a moment and then he shook his head and laughed. "Sofia, that's not my date. Lucy is my niece and she's fifteen years old. She's in town with her family. Her mom—my sister— is coming to pick her up after the show. So how about that coffee?"

Sofia beamed. "Oh, well, in that case, why not?"

They made arrangements on where to meet and then Sofia walked over to Grace and handed her the glass of champagne.

"Who was that tall drink of water you were talking to?" Grace said.

Sofia could hardly contain her excitement. "That was the guy who rescued me before my speech yesterday. He's cute, isn't he?" She leaned closer to her friend. "His name is Jasper and he asked me out after the show. I hope that's okay with you, Grace, I didn't know if you wanted to go out afterward." *Please say it's okay, Grace!*

"I think you should definitely go out with Jasper."

They clinked champagne glasses and Sofia said, "To possibilities."

*

GRACE

Grace spotted Sofia waiting outside the Broadway theater where *Cat on a Hot Tin Roof* was playing. She rushed out of the cab and ran over. "Hi, Sofia, sorry I'm late. My meeting ran a little long."

Always composed, Sofia gave her friend a reassuring smile. "No worries, Grace. I'm just happy to see you. Relax, we're going to have a good time, okay?"

"How's your head feeling?" Grace gently examined her friend's injury from her taxi accident. "Since the doctor used surgical glue it probably won't even scar, right?"

Sofia smirked. "Here's hoping."

They went into the theater, handed over their tickets to the usher, and were given *Playbill*s, which Grace promptly dropped on the floor.

"Is everything okay, Grace? You seem a little out of sorts tonight." Sofia looked at her intently.

"Oh, I'm fine, just fine," she lied. "Guess I'm just excited to see the show tonight."

Sofia led the way down the aisle to their front-row, center-stage seats. "Oh my gosh, Grace, how'd you score these amazing seats? Thanks so much for bringing me." Sofia was making conversation and

Grace was trying to focus. She noticed that her hands were trembling as she removed her light suit jacket before taking her seat.

She sat back and flipped through the *Playbill*, stopping at Win's gorgeous black and white headshot and perused his bio. It read, *Win Wyatt (BRICK) is proud to be making his Broadway and stage debut in this production. He started his acting career in films and has worked on a number of diverse projects. After recently making NYC his home, Win is hoping his experience here will be full of mirth and grace.* Grace's heart stopped. Was that a secret message he was sending to her? Would he really have snuck that into his *Playbill* write-up? Naw, couldn't be meant for her. Or could it? She shook her head and chuckled. She was struck by the level of humility in his bio despite the fact he was one of the most bankable stars in Hollywood.

The curtain rose and Grace squeezed Sofia's arm lightly in excitement. Then Win appeared, coming to the lip of the stage and he locked eyes with Grace. The rest of the first act was a blur and all Grace could do was hope that no one else in the theater could hear her heart pounding furiously.

*

At intermission Grace raced to the restroom to just have a quiet moment while Sofia went off to get them refreshments. Win's performance was mesmerizing and powerful, and Grace had to admit she was dazzled. His note with the towel gift basket had said he wanted to meet her for a drink after the show, but how would she swing that? Should she tell Sofia that she had plans after the show? How would Win even contact her? Or maybe he'd be too busy? It was possible that he'd forgotten about the invitation. Grace chided herself for getting her hopes up. She'd just go enjoy a drink at intermission with Sofia and see how things played out.

Back upstairs Grace saw Sofia talking to a tall, handsome man.

She waved and Sofia came over. They huddled together sipping champagne. Might be good to warn Sofia about her potential plans after the show, just in case.

"Who was that tall drink of water you were talking to?" Grace said.

"That was the guy who rescued me before my speech yesterday. He's cute, isn't he?" Sofia leaned closer to her friend. "His name is Jasper and he asked me out after the show. I hope that's okay with you, Grace, I didn't know if you wanted to go out afterward."

Score! "I think you should definitely go out with Jasper." Things were working out perfectly for both of them.

They clinked champagne glasses and Sofia said, "To possibilities."

"I'll drink to that!" Grace smiled.

The double chimes indicated that intermission was about to end.

When they made their way back to their seats there was a small envelope tucked into the *Playbill* on Grace's seat, which she surreptitiously opened. It was a note from Win asking her to come backstage after the show. She was so aflutter she could barely sit still through the second act.

After the show Grace said goodbye to Sofia and headed backstage to Win's dressing room. She knocked and the door immediately swung open. Win stood there with a huge smile on his face. "Grace, I'm so happy that you came. Come on, bring it in." He gave her a warm, strong hug and she melted into him. Drawing back with his chin down and eyes up, he whispered, "Did you see my secret message to you in the *Playbill*?"

Grace grinned. "I did. It was lovely, Win." Then she scowled and joked, "But who's this other woman named Mirth?"

*

This was the second time that month that a celebrity had come to visit Grace's apartment, and she noticed that her neighbors were starting to give her quizzical looks. Simone Everett walked around Grace's two-bedroom condo, taking in the art and the funky modern furniture. "Your apartment is so cool, Grace. What a refreshing change from cramped college apartment living." The actress laughed.

What? Simone Everett in a cramped apartment? That didn't compute. "I've been wondering—why did you choose to major in finance?"

Simone's expression hardened and the words fell out of her mouth slowly. "Because I was an idiot. I lost my entire fortune. The main reason I wanted to study finance was because I wanted to prevent that from ever occurring again."

Grace took a seat on the sofa. "What happened, Simone? Weren't you making millions of dollars per film? Plus you had all those product endorsement contracts."

That opened the floodgates. Simone plopped down on a chair opposite Grace and let out a bitter sigh. "Yeah, sure, at one point I had multimillions in the bank. My manager handled all my finances— poorly, I might add—and I didn't kept track of the money. It was totally my fault and I spent irresponsibly. Whenever a relative or a friend asked me for something, like a Lamborghini or a Birkin bag, I bought it for them. I flew myself and my friends on private jets. I threw lavish parties and went on ridiculously expensive vacations with my entourage, and I paid for everything. It wasn't until I decided to go to college that I learned I had just enough money to cover tuition and living expenses. I wasted so much money, and now I have very little savings left. So you see, Grace, I not only want to get back into acting, I actually need a job in order to survive." There was a heartbreaking tone of desperation in Simone's voice, and her complexion was pale. "Interesting that only a handful of my friends from those days bother to call me now." Her eyes were brimming with sadness.

"As they say, 'prosperity makes friends and adversity tries them.' I'm sorry to hear about all your troubles, Simone." Grace nodded sympathetically. She had found that being a brand coach to Simone, a willing pupil, was quite enjoyable, and now the urgency of the need to get Simone's career back on track was evident. "But it sounds like you learned your lesson and you're starting fresh. Do you think you'd be willing to share your story?"

"Absolutely, if it would help other people."

"How about going even further than that?"

Simone sat up straighter. "What do you have in mind, Grace?"

Grace rubbed her chin. "You've successfully gone through steps one and two of my brand resuscitation approach: own your mistakes and say sorry. Now you're ready for steps three and four: show your humanity and stand for something. In other words, find a cause that you believe in and show how you can help others."

"Okay, I'm tracking with you so far."

"So why not start a blog—or better yet, a podcast series—where you help others avoid the financial mistakes you've made? I'm sure that other celebrities have fallen into the same trap that you did, and even professional athletes would need the same help. You could even be their advisor and we could brand you—something like the Wealth Whisperer."

Simone's eyes lit up. "Oh, Grace, that's brilliant! It would be a great way to combine my industry experience and my degree in finance. I love it! How do we get started?"

The two women hunched over the coffee table and sketched out a plan. When they got to a good stopping point, Grace got up and made a pot of green tea for them. She felt like this was a good time to bring up the topic of appearance.

"Simone, you're a smart, talented, and beautiful young woman, and I think it would be good to revamp your appearance along with the work we're doing on your brand. You know, freshen up and modernize your look."

The actress, who clearly trusted Grace by now, looked up inquisitively. "How so?"

Grace smiled. "Let's professionalize your wardrobe so you look the part of a financial whiz—I can get a stylist I know from Condé Nast to help you with that, and we can do it on a budget."

"You mean lose the ripped jeans? I thought that was the look these days." Simone's cheeks reddened.

"I know it's popular, but we want you to stand out. We should be highlighting your brains, not just your beauty, so a slightly more sophisticated look would be appropriate, I think. After all, we want people to take you seriously. Are you willing to try it, Simone?"

Simone nodded solemnly. "If we're going to do this, let's go all the way."

*

The following day, Grace was ready to get started with helping Flip Style turn around their brand and business. The reception area of the Flip Style downtown offices was a little cramped but typical of a small startup company. Grace gave her name to the young, casually dressed receptionist and told her that Venky and Tom were expecting her. The receptionist spoke into her headset and informed Grace that someone would be right out.

An eager-looking young man with blond hair wearing a well-starched, blue plaid button-down shirt rushed over to her. "You must be Grace King. Hi, I'm Preston Ford." He gave a toothy smile.

"Good to meet you, Preston." Grace shook his hand. She noticed his expensive watch and highly polished shoes. "What do you do for Flip Style?"

Preston looked a little disappointed that Grace had no clue who he was or what he did. "I own strategy at Flip Style. I went to HBS intending to work for a big brand but was heavily recruited by Venky and Tom, so I finally decided to come on board."

This guy is a definitely a megaphone, mentioning Harvard Business School in the first ten seconds. Grace had worked with MBAs from top-tier Ivy League schools and found they often fell into two groups: magnates or megaphones. The magnates got out into the business world and did extraordinary things, often with humility. The megaphones were typically the underperformers whose only glory was the brand of their MBA and who somehow managed to mention their alma mater within minutes of meeting someone.

"The guys are just wrapping up an international phone call, so I'll take you to the conference room and we can wait for them." Preston gestured for Grace to follow him as they navigated their way through the open, airy office space. They passed through a huge kitchen area with a counter piled high with fruit and other snacks and a long white communal table occupying most of the space. Grace spotted a foosball table in the corner and remembered her private equity friend Courtney's quote: "If you see a foosball table in a startup, run. It's a sure sign the company will be a failure." But this wasn't just any foosball table; this high-tech table was made of glass and crystal, and had gold and chrome players. She chuckled.

Preston turned sharply. "What's so funny?"

"I was just noticing your foosball table over there." Grace motioned with her head. "Pretty fancy."

The big smile returned to Preston's face and he proudly said, "Oh, that was my idea. I told Venky and Tom if they wanted me to join, my one condition was that we get a really cool foosball table. That's a limited-edition Teckell Cristallino Gold foosball table. Only fifty in existence."

Good grief, I hope they didn't waste the company's capital on that thing. Grace entered the conference room and sat down.

"So, Grace, I understand you're going to be a brand advisor for the company? Is that going to be a formal role?" He continued with the big smile.

Despite his overly friendly demeanor, something about Preston didn't feel quite right to Grace, so she was guarded in her comments.

"I'll be helping with getting the brand and the company back on track."

Preston tilted his head to the side. "Well, as the chief strategy officer, the company turnaround is really in my realm."

Grace looked him in the eye. "Then I guess we'll be working together, won't we?"

"Something you need to understand is that we're a pretty lean team here. I just want to set expectations up front that the strategy area isn't an area that needs a lot of help. Though we welcome your marketing expertise, for sure."

Aha. Now Grace understood the issue. Preston was threatened by her presence and wanted to protect his turf. He was trying to tell her to just focus on marketing, the twerp. "Let's not be premature, Preston." *Or immature.* "Venky and Tom brought me in to help them right the ship, so I think it's up to them what role I play and where I help out. All right?" She gave him a modest smile but her eyes telegraphed, *Don't mess with me.*

"By all means, Grace. I in no way meant to offend you. Let's just forget we had this conversation," Preston suggested hastily.

"Yes, let's." Grace looked around for the cofounders.

*

Fortunately Venky and Tom entered the room, bringing the one-on-one time with Preston to a close.

"Grace, welcome. We are thrilled to have you here." Venky pumped her hand. Tom followed him in and greeted her. "Thanks for looking after her, Preston. I think we can take it from here." That was the signal for Preston to exit. He looked surprised at the enthusiasm with which the cofounders greeted the newcomer, but he flashed a smile and said, "Sure thing," as he left the room.

Venky smiled broadly. "I have some great news, Grace. We just signed a new angel investor who is going to pump a lot more capital into the business so we can turn it around properly."

Tom nodded. "We were running low on funds and really needed a cash infusion, so the timing is perfect."

Grace leaned forward. "That's great, guys. Who's the angel investor, if you don't mind my asking?"

The look on Venky's face grew serious. "Well, it's actually my dad, Devinder Jain. He's the CEO and chairman of—"

"Triumph Group, one of the most successful Indian business conglomerates, with holdings across multiple industries." Grace nodded. "Your father is well-known for his business savvy and tremendous success. So, it will be good to have his backing, right?" She had done her homework and knew that Venky and his brother Prajeet were competing to determine which one would eventually take their father's place at the head of the conglomerate.

Tom's expression was positive but Venky seemed apprehensive. "Yes and no. My dad is incredibly smart and has deep pockets, but he might want to get more involved in Flip Style, which could be, uh... complicated. But I guess we'll deal with that as it comes." He shrugged. "Ever since my mother passed away four years ago, my father has focused all his time and energy on the business. I think he needs a new hobby...or a new wife." Venky gave a little laugh.

Grace pulled her laptop from her tote bag. "Okay, why don't we dive in. I thought we could talk about my six steps to resurrecting a brand and then we can brainstorm on where we need to take Flip Style from a business standpoint. Sound good?"

The cofounders eagerly jumped into the discussion, and they had a highly interactive working session for the next ninety minutes. They took a break to grab coffee and some snacks from the kitchen and returned to the conference room.

"So, how did you find Preston Ford, your chief strategy officer?" Grace asked innocently.

Tom giggled a little and leaned closer. "It's actually a pretty funny story about Preston. He had graduated from HBS and bounced around at a few different companies. Then he saw me speak about Flip Style at a conference and he basically stalked me and Venky until we gave him a job as our strategic planning director. Don't let this get out, but as a thank-you for giving him a job, Preston bought this crazy-expensive foosball table for the company—I think he dropped, like, twenty-five grand on it!" Tom's eyes widened; he was clearly impressed by the purchase.

"Jeez, that's a lot of dough for a foosball table!" Grace said in horror.

"Foolish waste of money." Venky shook his head disapprovingly.

Tom interjected, "But Preston comes from money. His family is loaded."

"Even people who come from money should know not to squander it," Venky shot back. He was most certainly speaking from experience. "Anyway, the jury is still out on Preston. I find that the comments he makes about strategy always harken back to Porter's five forces model. I don't see a lot of intellectual creativity. Despite all his polish, so far I'm underwhelmed."

Michael Porter's book *Competitive Strategy* was required reading for any B-school student. Grace was learning that Venky was tough as well as highly intelligent. And he seemed like a good judge of people. But the three of them had their work cut out for them if they really wanted to turn around the brand and the business for Flip Style.

*

COOP

A powerful executive vice president at American Express who happened to be Coop's favorite client had invited him to a cocktail party at his home on a Thursday evening in early October. It was a couple of weeks after his fruitless meeting with HR, and Coop was still brooding about not getting the promotion to partner. But he was looking forward to a lively and fun evening. Carlos, his client, had told Coop the gathering was a small celebration but didn't give any more details.

Coop was in awe of Carlos. When they had breaks in between meetings or went to dinner occasionally, Coop was always impressed with Carlos's worldliness, his intellect, and his love of the arts. The two of them could talk for hours about theater, art exhibits, books, etc. And Coop always came away from those conversations enlightened by Carlos's thoughts and ideas. He was 95 percent sure that Carlos was gay, but in the office his client behaved in a conservative, professional manner and didn't share much about his personal life.

He arrived at Carlos's home on the Upper East Side. It was a regal town house on a tree-lined stretch of Fifth Avenue just a couple of blocks up from the Metropolitan Museum of Art. Coop's shoes crunched on a few fallen dry leaves on the walkway. When he rang the doorbell he was greeted by an attractive young man clad in a gray suit. Coop introduced himself and the young man said, "Good evening and welcome. I'm George, the butler. Allow me to take those." He gestured for Coop to give him the flower bouquet he'd brought. This was not something Coop was accustomed to. *Why didn't I think of hiring a cute butler?* He giggled at his own silliness.

They wound their way down the long front hall and George said, "Stairs or elevator?"

Coop indicated he'd prefer the stairs, and they walked up into a grand parlor with a white marble floor that led into a large, brightly lit living room full of gorgeous antiques, tasteful artwork, and rich upholstery in muted tones. It was like walking into a spread from the latest issue of *Architectural Digest*. George took Coop's drink order and then swiftly and silently departed.

Carlos came over and greeted him warmly. "So glad you could make it to our little soirée, Coop. There's someone I'd like you to meet." He motioned to a man with dark curly hair wearing red-framed glasses who was talking to a couple of guys in the corner. As the man approached, Coop thought he recognized him but wasn't quite certain.

Carlos put his hand on the man's shoulder. "Coop, I'd like you to meet Samuel Quinn."

The renowned playwright? Coop could hardly contain his excitement, and he extended his hand. "It's such an honor to meet you, Mr. Quinn. I've read and seen all of your plays. Your work is just wonderful, I'm a huge fan."

"Great to meet you, Coop, and please call me Samuel. I appreciate your good taste." He, Coop, and Carlos laughed. George, the butler, appeared with their drinks and told Carlos he was needed by the caterer. Their host excused himself, leaving Coop alone with the playwright. Samuel sipped his drink and motioned for Coop to sit down on the sofa next to him. "Carlos has told me a lot about you, Coop. He really enjoys working with such a smart and well-rounded executive."

Coop blushed. "Well, Carlos is my favorite client. How do you two know each other?"

Samuel leaned in closer and gave a cryptic smile. "Carlos is my husband. We just tied the knot last weekend. This party is to celebrate our marriage."

Coop gasped. "Wow, fantastic news! May I wish you every happiness in your marriage. You guys are quite the power couple!"

That made Samuel chuckle. Then his look grew serious. "You probably know that Carlos isn't out at work. He's always felt that in a conservative company it would be a career-limiting move to let people know he's gay."

Shaking his head, Coop said, "I completely understand. The accounting firm that I've worked for over the past decade is very conservative as well." His look darkened. "I've been one of the top performers for years, but I've been passed over twice for a promotion to partner—I hate to think that my sexual orientation is holding me back, but it's becoming obvious now that it is." He couldn't help it; his eyes started tearing up. "I'm sorry, it's still so upsetting to me."

Samuel's brow furrowed. "I can't believe I'm hearing that kind of stuff in this day and age. When I was an up-and-coming playwright I considered coming out, but my mentor told me not to limit myself."

"What did he mean?" Coop quickly wiped away a tear.

"He asked me, 'Do you want your work to be judged on its own merit or do you forever want your work to be introduced as "such-and-such play by gay playwright Samuel Quinn"?' I thought he made a good point, so I kept my sexuality hidden for years."

Coop shook his head. "Well, in my case I'm afraid I've made matters even worse. I recently let it be known at work that I'm gay, and one of the partners I work with is definitely uncomfortable with that revelation. I don't know what to do, because at this rate I'll never get the promotion."

"We're just going to have to remedy that situation, won't we?" Samuel set his jaw and had a look of determination in his eyes. When Carlos came back into the room, Samuel excused himself and made a beeline for his husband. Coop saw them speaking to each other with serious expressions.

After a few minutes he forgot about it as the other guests—all men—started introducing themselves and mingling. It was a veritable who's who of the New York business and cultural scene. Coop was even introduced to a couple of executives who were his company's clients and knew the CEO of Coop's firm well. Coop was dazzled to meet so many notable men—this gathering was like a salon of some of the most successful and powerful gay men in Manhattan. He couldn't exactly describe the feeling, but somehow Coop felt he had finally found his tribe.

*

"I'm sorry, Gary, I'm not sure I understand what you're telling me," Alma Jankowski said slowly. She'd always called Coop by his given name since he was a boy.

Mrs. Jankowski had provided Coop with boxes of paper files and all the computer files her husband had left behind. Fortunately, from her years as an executive assistant Alma was a highly organized woman, so the files were all in order. Coop had spent much of his limited free time sorting through the data, analyzing it, and compiling a spreadsheet of all her husband's holdings. It was a feat of pure forensic accounting prowess, and he was pleased to give her the good news.

Coop repeated his findings from his investigation digging into the finances of her ex-husband. "What I'm telling you, Mrs. Jankowski, is that your husband's actual assets are far greater than what he was representing. Among other things, I looked into the state database of LLCs and found one that was formed by your husband years ago. I uncovered several investment accounts, holdings in offshore companies, and real estate investments held in that LLC. His net worth is much greater than what he claimed, so you are entitled to a much larger divorce settlement. In other words, add another zero to the figure you were thinking you would get. And while you're at it, you should negotiate keeping your home and tell your husband you're saving him the hassle of getting sued."

Mrs. Jankowski was silent for a moment, then she started weeping. "Oh, Gary, this is such a weight off my shoulders. Because of all your hard work I will have a better life. I can't thank you enough. Will you be home this weekend? I'd like to bake a special chocolate cake for you."

"I'm happy to help you, Mrs. Jankowski. And thank you for the offer of the cake, but I'm actually heading to Portland, Oregon, today to visit a friend for the weekend. I'm taking the day off and my flight leaves in a couple of hours. Feel free to call if you need any more help, okay?"

She gushed, "Gary, you're wonderful. I wish I'd had a son just like you."

Coop smiled at the compliment. "I appreciate that, Mrs. Jankowski. Now go celebrate, maybe have yourself a glass of champagne!"

*

As the plane descended into Portland, Coop looked out the window and noticed the lushness of the evergreens covering the hillsides, along with the slick blanket of wetness from the rain. He was visiting his friend Vivien and could barely contain his excitement. This weekend his focus was on helping Vivien and her fiancé, Clay, unpack and get their new condo set up and decorated, one of Coop's favorite pastimes.

When the wheels of the plane touched down, Coop turned on his phone and it started buzzing immediately from the number of voicemails he'd gotten during his two flights. He'd had a tight connection through Chicago's O'Hare International Airport and instead of checking voicemails he'd opted for grabbing a Gold Coast Dog—Coop was still savoring the memory of the tasty hot dog. He checked the list of calls and two of them were from Martin, the head of the Promotion Council at his firm. *What the heck, I take one day off of work and these guys can't leave me alone?* He ignored the messages, texted Vivien that he'd landed, and focused on getting to someplace in downtown Portland called the Pearl District, where her condo was located.

Once he was dropped off at the condo building, Coop took the elevator to the penthouse floor and wheeled his bag down the hallway to the last apartment on the right. He knocked and the door flew open. Vivien stood there grinning and gave him a huge hug.

*

When Vivien Lee had moved to Portland, she was thrilled about the opportunity and ready for the challenge of being the lone woman on the Smart Sports executive team. In the six weeks she'd been in her role, she'd already been blindsided, tricked, and challenged by some male colleagues and members of her team. In the predominantly male sports industry, the going had been rougher than Vivien had expected, and her mind was swirling. Having her best friend, Coop, standing there in front of her was like having a warm, fuzzy security blanket back again.

"Oh, Coop, I missed you so much!" Vivien squeezed him tight.

"Missed you, too, sweetie." Coop hugged her. He looked into the condo. "Oh my god, Vivi, this place is unbelievable. Just how big is it?"

She ushered him in and showed him around. The condo was expansive, with a huge curved wall of windows that gave a breathtaking view of a snow-capped Mount Hood. The open-concept kitchen flowed into the living room and dining area, and the condo was bright, modern, and stylish...except for the stacks of boxes spread around the room.

Vivien led Coop into the second bedroom, where he would be staying, and he deposited his bags. "I had the furniture set up in both bedrooms, but as you can see we still have a lot of unpacking and organizing to do. But first, let me pour you a glass of wine. Clay is flying in from London and his flight should be landing pretty soon."

Coop took a seat at one of the high backed stools along the huge blue pearl granite countertop while Vivien opened the box of wineglasses. The kitchen was chockablock with cabinets and sported stainless steel, top-of-the-line appliances. "Wow, a six-burner Viking stove with a grill and double oven—I'm so jealous!"

Vivien was excited to be settling into her condo, and the opulence of this place was far beyond her old apartment in NYC. She handed Coop a glass of wine and felt a surge of pride as she toured him around. "Here's the best thing...our very own laundry room! And it has all this storage space, plus this giant wine refrigerator."

"No, you have your own washer and dryer?" A look of disbelief came across his face. "God, I didn't even imagine that was possible. I'm destined to schlep my loads of dirty clothes down to the dark, musty laundry room in my building's basement forever. Ugh."

She shot him a guilty look and then moved back to the kitchen to get some snacks. She placed a plate of cheese, crackers, nuts, and fruit on the counter. "Come on, Coop, let's check out the wraparound terrace. Looks like the sun has come out." She was just so happy to be back with her best friend. It would be good to have a chance to share with him what her experiences had been so far and to strategize with him on his job situation—maybe later that evening. For now, they both just needed to relax a bit. While they were sipping wine and discussing decorating ideas, Coop's phone buzzed.

*

Coop glanced at his phone. It was a text from his client Carlos that read, *Coop, let me know when you get the news.* What was he talking about? Then his phone rang. It was Martin from the firm calling again.

"Ugh, Vivi, I'd better take this call. It's work." Coop grimaced and answered the phone as they stepped back inside the condo. "Hello, this is Coop," he said in his butchest voice. He stood by the curved windows to take his call. Vivien gave a wave and went into the master bedroom to give Coop some privacy.

"Coop, thank goodness. I've been trying to reach you all day!" Martin's tone sounded urgent.

"I've been on planes all day, Martin. I just landed in Portland, Oregon, a short while ago."

"I see, I see," Martin said hurriedly. "Listen, Coop, I wanted to get in touch with you to share some news. Our CEO called a special meeting with the Promotion Council this morning."

Still frowning, Coop listened to what Martin had to say. Slowly a grin spread across Coop's face. Wrapping up the call, he said, "Thanks for sharing that information, Martin. I'll see you in the office on Monday." It took all his strength to maintain his composure.

He set the phone down on the counter and drew in a deep breath, his pulse racing. Then he picked up the phone with trembling hands and texted Carlos. *Just got the news. How did this happen?*

Carlos texted back, *Gay power, my friend. A number of us called your CEO and said we'd no longer be clients of your firm if they didn't give you the promotion you deserved. Congrats!* This was unbelievable.

Vivien popped her head around the corner. "Done with your call?" Upon seeing his odd expression, she rushed over to him. "What's going on, Coop?"

Coop's heart swelled with pride. "Vivien, you are looking at the newest partner at my firm. I just got promoted, effective immediately!"

They both jumped up and down screaming, hugging each other, and spilling wine all over the hardwood floor.

Though it had taken his firm too many years and two failed chances to promote Coop to partner, any bitterness that Coop had harbored had evaporated the moment he heard the news. *My dream has finally come true!* He even started to soften toward Felix Culo, who must have had to approve the promotion. Like a swimmer breaking the surface of the water, concern over the problematic audit bubbled up to the top of Coop's brain...it was a small stain on this moment of joy.

*

ANDI

Andi was on her way home from a client dinner downtown when she decided to consult with her friend Vivien. She dialed Vivien's number at work.

"Listen, Vivi, I know you're busy with the new gig but I just wanted to run something by you. Got a sec?" Andi settled back into her leather seat in the town car that was driving her home and took a deep breath. The inside of the car smelled like newspaper ink and cinnamon air freshener.

Vivien said, "Sure, Andi, I'm just wrapping up my day. What's up?"

"I'm not sure how to interpret the behavior of my new boss," Andi said. "On the one hand he seems to want to collaborate with me and help my career, but on the other hand I'm getting some weird sexual vibes from him. You know my history, so I just wanted to do a reality check to make sure I'm not overreacting."

"Mmm-hmm," Vivien said. She was all too familiar with Andi's past dealings with this kind of thing.

*

Back in their Wharton days, when they were getting their MBAs, Andi had run into an extremely persistent and amorous teaching assistant in her management class named Ted de la Cruz. Ted was a clean-cut guy with a friendly smile, and he was always checking on Andi, Vivien, Grace, and Sofia to see if they were enjoying the class. The problem for Andi was that Ted kept asking her out on dates... and she kept saying no. This was almost a weekly occurrence for Andi until she was finally fed up and decided to have a sit-down with Ted.

"Ted, listen, you've been asking me out a lot—" Andi began.

"Please, call me Teddy."

She ignored his request. "Ted, I don't understand why you keep asking me out while you're a TA for this class. In fact, I don't think it's appropriate for you to be pressuring me for a date at all."

"Andi, you're the most beautiful woman I've ever met. If I don't date you I'll regret it for the rest of my life."

"How much clearer can I be, Ted? I don't want to go out with you, now or after I'm done with the class. So stop asking me out. Got it?"

Ted looked hurt and he narrowed his eyes as the smile fell from his face. "Are you sure that's how you want to play this, Andi? There could be consequences, you know."

Andi stood up. "I'm sure that I do not want to date you, Ted." She walked away.

The first time she had a paper graded from that class, Andi was shocked to see she'd received a "Pass" while Vivien, Sofia, and Grace had each received a "Distinguished"—two full grades higher than Andi's. She asked her friends to borrow their papers and compared the content—the four of them had made exactly the same points. Andi could only conclude that Ted had marked her paper down as retribution for her not going out with him. Seething, she made an appointment to see the professor of the management class—a man who'd just joined the Wharton faculty that fall. Andi fully expected the professor to fire TA Ted. But even when she showed him the grades on the four papers and explained the disparity in her grade versus the others, the novice professor was tentative about taking action. Andi told him that Ted had been pressuring her for a date and that she'd repeatedly turned him down.

The professor said, "What has that got to do with the grade you received?"

Is this guy thick? "Can't you see, Professor? Ted downgraded my paper even though the quality was the same as the others' because I refused to go on a date with him."

"Maybe you should have said yes." The professor smirked. "At any rate, Ted is my TA and I have to trust in his judgment. If I fired him it would reflect poorly upon me as a Wharton professor, and I need to do my best in my new role."

Andi stood up. "Just have a look at the papers. If you review them in detail you'll clearly see that I should have received the same grade as the others. And then you can correct the grade."

He folded his hands. "No, I won't do that. As I said, I have to trust my TA's judgment."

"Aren't you at least going to talk to Ted? Let him know that it's wrong to pressure a student of his to go on a date?" Andi's ire was increasing, as was her blood pressure.

The professor pushed his chair back from his desk. "What if I did talk to him? He might tell me he never asked you out. It really is your word against his."

Andi leaned over the desk and glared at the professor. She could see the beads of sweat forming on his upper lip. "Professor Freckelton, are you telling me that you're not going to do anything? You won't talk to your misbehaving TA, you won't review the papers, and you won't adjust my grade so it's more equitable?"

The inexperienced professor set his expression like a petulant little boy. "No, I won't."

That response lit the fuse on the Andi bomb, and she exploded with a barrage of fierce words. "This is unbelievable! You're supposed to be a *management* professor teaching *us* how to manage. How can you possibly impart any management wisdom to your students when you clearly can't even manage your own TA? This is the Wharton School, one of the most prestigious business programs in the country. How did you even qualify for this job?"

Professor Freckelton recoiled as if he'd been slapped.

"Here's how we're going to *manage* the situation," Andi said. "Moving forward, I fully expect you to review my grades before they are finalized. If this grade disparity happens one more time I will elevate this situation to the dean of the school. I also will not hesitate to write an article about my experience for the school newspaper. Are we clear?"

He nodded. Andi stormed out of his office.

Although Andi was in the right, sometimes she let her temper get the best of her. But at least she'd had the satisfaction of speaking her mind bluntly. When she shared her conversation with her friends, they were incredulous but supportive. This experience set the stage for how Andi would deal with these kinds of situations in the future… with a level of justified intolerance and a short fuse.

*

"So what do you think of the situation, Vivien?" Andi asked after explaining the Bermuda vending machine incident with Lester Labosky.

"Andi, you've got to trust your instincts. You're usually right on the money. If you sense something weird is going on, and if he's making you feel uncomfortable—well, can you just keep your distance from your boss? I know you have to work with him, but just try to avoid the situations that could become problematic for you."

Andi looked out the window as the car whizzed by the city's buildings. "Like don't go to dinners with him alone, don't go to his office late at night, etc.? Yeah, I know the drill. It's weird; I never had this problem with my old boss. This is such BS."

Vivien's voice was sympathetic. "It's the same hassle we all have to deal with from time to time, Andi. Just take the right opportunity to remind him subtly what a star performer you are and maybe he'll back off. You might also want to loop in another colleague about the situation or maybe talk to HR."

"Nah, I don't know anyone in HR yet. I'll enlist one of my buddies for support, that's a good idea. Thanks, Vivi. Talk to you soon."

"Okay, Andi, keep me posted."

*

Entering the venerable Kaneshiro Bank building the following week, Andi was determined to chart a new course. She took in a deep cleansing breath and walked into the midtown offices confidently, navigating her way to her new office. The Kaneshiro offices were elegant and palatial, with rich dark woods and golden accents inspired by the meaning of *Kaneshiro*, which translated to "golden castle."

After getting settled in, Andi reflected. She was the one who'd been in this private banking department longer than Lester Labosky and she'd have to leverage that experience to get through this period of adjustment with her boss. He'd just have to learn that his actions were not appropriate, and she'd continue to rebuff any advances from her boss until he got the message.

Unfortunately, Lester had brought in two new guys to the department—guys he'd worked with previously. Their names were Percy and Richie, but they might as well have been Beavis and Butthead. In front of the others the two newbies treated Andi with respect, but when they had her cornered they'd give her lascivious looks and make a hissing sound as they touched their index fingers to their rear ends. Sometimes they'd mix it up and say, "Ay, ay, ay," when she passed by. Andi simply ignored their juvenile behavior and tried to steer clear of these bozos.

*

It was almost time to head out on a Tuesday evening and Andi was responding to client emails when there was a knock at her open office door. "Andi, got a minute to chat?" It was Lester, who seemed to have difficulty suppressing a smile. His eyes slowly skimmed over her body as if he were a robot scanning a human life form and processing the data.

Andi leaned back in her chair. "Sure, Lester. What can I help you with?" She stiffened up a little when Lester closed the office door behind him.

Eyes locked on hers, he strode over and took a seat in front of her desk. "Something big. Guess who we have a chance to sign?"

"No idea."

Lester moved closer and lowered his voice to a whisper. "François-

Henri Pinault." He grinned and sat back.

Andi's eyes widened. "The CEO of the French luxury group that owns Gucci, Yves Saint-Laurent, Balenciaga, Alexander McQueen, and Stella McCartney?"

Her boss raised his eyebrows, clearly impressed with Andi's detailed knowledge of their potential client's business. "The very one."

Andi whistled. "Now, that would be a good get!"

"Mr. Pinault has varied holdings and is looking for some international tax-sheltered investments, among other things. I thought we could work together on the pitch—we've got to put our best foot forward with this client, so I'd like for you to take the lead on landing and managing this relationship, Andi."

"Really? Thanks, Lester," Andi said. "I appreciate your confidence in me."

"We'll need to fly to Paris sometime in the coming weeks to meet with Mr. Pinault, pitch him our services, and hopefully start building the relationship. Before the meeting you and I can brainstorm about various options to present. Sound good?"

While Andi was excited about the new client opportunity and the trip to Paris, at the same time she was a little apprehensive about spending all that time alone with Lester. But then he did something to completely disarm her.

Lester held up a large gift bag. The handles of the bag were straining under the weight of what appeared to be a large box. "Here's something that I thought your little ones might enjoy. It's a set of Magna-Tiles—the boys can build all sorts of structures with it. It's a great toy for developing motor coordination and for keeping little hands busy; my boys used to love this kind of stuff." He handed the bag to Andi.

"Wow, Lester. That's so thoughtful of you." Andi was surprised that her boss even remembered that she had twin toddler boys. "Thank you, I really appreciate it." She was perplexed—her boss was sending her signals that he was attracted to her but at the same time he was behaving like a mentor and friend. Which one was he?

His eyes grew misty. "Enjoy this time with your kids while you can, Andi, it goes by so quickly." Lester was an attractive man and could be very charming—he certainly seemed to embrace his family life.

Andi nodded solemnly. Her assistant knocked and opened the door. "Andi, your car is waiting downstairs to take you to the concert."

"Thanks, I'll be down shortly," Andi replied. She turned to Lester. "I've got another client event tonight—box seats at Madison Square Garden for the Sheryl Crow concert. Better head out."

Lester got up and started walking out. "I'll have my assistant touch base with you on schedules for the Paris meeting. Have fun at the concert."

*

"What's up, sis? On your way to some fancy event to schmooze with clients?" Andi's favorite brother, Rene, teased her over the phone. Andi pressed her cell phone closer to her ear as the car taking her to Madison Square Garden crawled uptown through noisy rush hour traffic. Rene was the youngest of her four brothers and the only sibling who lived close by—the rest of Andi's family still lived in Northern California, where she'd grown up.

Their parents hailed from Mexico and their mom was a firm believer in destiny, so she'd chosen names for each of her children that would determine their future. Rene was named for René Laënnec, the French physician responsible for inventing the stethoscope, so naturally Rene had become a doctor. Andi's name was inspired by Andrea Argoli, the Italian mathematician and astronomer, and she, of course, had ended up being brilliant with numbers and chosen a career in banking.

"As a matter of fact, Rene, I'm meeting my clients at the Sheryl Crow concert. You still at the hospital?"

He let out a deep sigh. "Yeah, sis, I'm beat. I had a very complicated case today so I'm just catching up on paperwork and then heading home." Rene was a pediatric neurosurgeon at Weill Cornell Medical Center. "How are you getting on with your new boss? You mentioned in your text that things were a bit awkward."

Andi grunted. "I don't know, I'm still figuring it out. I'm not sure whether to get chummier with my new boss or to give him a throat jab."

At this Rene burst out laughing. "Oh, lord, I thought those days were over! I remember when you used to wrestle me and the rest of us boys—you'd kick our butts, but Mom and Dad would be all over us boys about it and we'd be the ones getting punished."

One of the things Andi loved about her brother was his sense of humor, but it was his charm and easygoing manner that had made him one of the most popular kids in school growing up. He often joked about how a Mexican kid had ended up with a French name. Rene was also smart as a whip. Andi had been a year behind her brother, and when she inevitably got one of his former teachers they would always say, "Oh, you're Rene's sister? He was an exceptional student. I hope you can do as well." Andi would nod, but with her strong competitive streak she'd silently vow, *I'll do even better.*

"So you think you can squeeze me in for dinner one of these nights? I am family, after all," Rene teased his sibling, knowing her busy social schedule with clients.

Andi snorted. "Well, I have some upcoming trips to Portland, Boston, and Paris. Why don't you shoot me some dates that work and we'll synch up schedules? Either way, you're still coming over for Thanksgiving, right?"

"Of course, but it would be great to see you sooner than that. You and Luca can bring Francesco and Antonio over to play with the kids." Rene had three young sons and a lovely wife who enjoyed entertaining.

"Um, you might be asking for the Battle of Thermopylae putting all those boys in the same room together, Rene." Andi knew all too well the level of noise, energy, and destruction possible when all five boys played together.

The easygoing Rene laughed. "Aww, come on, sis. It'll be fun. Well, I'll talk to you later." The call ended just in time as the car pulled up to the concert venue and Andi bounded out of the vehicle and into Madison Square Garden. There were aspects of her job that she loved, but with all of the changes lately she was unsure of her footing.

PART TWO

CHAPTER 5

October

COOP

"Special delivery, Coop!" The singsongy voice came from the middle-aged executive assistant he shared with another partner. She breezed into his new, larger office and deposited two items on his expansive desk. Coop felt a shiver of excitement. The first was a gift box wrapped in matte silver paper with a white satin bow. Tucked under the bow was a small white envelope, which Coop tore open. It read, *Congratulations on the big promotion—so proud of you! Love you lots, Vivien.* He opened the fancy box to find a Montblanc special-edition rollerball pen in shiny black with silver accents. He picked it up, enjoying its significant weight in his hand. It was engraved *G. E. Cooper, Partner.* Coop poised the pen in the air and then smoothly scrawled his signature on his notepad as if it were a multimillion-dollar client contract. With a flourish he clicked the cap back on firmly and set the pen down in a special place on his desk, his heart swelling with pride.

The other item his assistant had delivered was a piece of certified mail. As Coop opened the envelope and took out the letter, a piece of paper fluttered to the carpeted floor. The note was from Alma Jankowski, thanking him profusely for all his forensic accounting work in uncovering her ex-husband's hidden assets. She acknowledged the huge effort and many hours that Coop had spent sleuthing, as well as his determination to help make her life better. He'd recovered about four million dollars for Mrs. Jankowski—a windfall that would keep her comfortable for the rest of her life. In her note she said she was enclosing a check for his services and that she hoped it was enough. Coop chuckled and figured the check would be a couple hundred dollars, just like the ones he'd received from his grandmother for every birthday. He bent down to retrieve the check from the floor, and when he saw the extra zeros he nearly fainted. The check was for $200,000. Two hundred thousand dollars—that was 5 percent of the money he'd recovered for Mrs. Jankowski. Gleeful, Coop clutched the check in both hands.

He dialed up Vivien to thank her for the gift, tell her about the check from Mrs. Jankowski, and gush about the thrill of being a partner. "Vivi, I can't believe this is actually happening. I feel like I've won the lottery twice!" He puffed out his chest in pure elation. "Now I can finally afford that Herman Miller sectional sofa I've been eyeing!"

"Aww, I'm so happy for you, Coop! You deserve all these wonderful things. Enjoy it, my friend."

"Plus, I'm going to my first global partners meeting and dinner this Thursday; I can't wait. Then the following day there's a special new partners' outing at a secret location. I've no idea what to wear!" Coop was breathless. "Do you remember your first partners' meeting, Vivi?"

She chuckled. "I sure do. It was a little eye-opening for me when I realized how different I was from all the other partners. Most of them were men, and I was the youngest partner and the first female minority partner at the firm. I'm sure you'll blend in much better than I did."

"Well, I'm not sure what to expect, but I'm excited to go." Coop knew he wouldn't be able to sleep at all the night before the big meeting.

"Have fun, Coop, but not too much fun," Vivien joked.

Coop retorted, "As Mae West said, 'Too much of a good thing is wonderful.' Oh, sweetie, I have to run to a client meeting now. I'll give you a call over the weekend and let you know how things went."

*

The day of the partners' meeting arrived. This would be the meeting in which Coop would finally be welcomed as a member into the elite leadership circle of the firm. To accommodate the nearly five hundred global partners in his firm, the meeting was being held in the main ballroom of the Grand Hyatt hotel next to Grand Central Terminal—Coop was sure the meeting would also be grand. That Thursday morning, dressed in a medium-blue suit, white shirt, and aquamarine tie, Coop arrived at the hotel early so he could grab some food and a Diet Coke and pick his seat before the meeting started.

At the entrance to the ballroom there was a huge spread of breakfast items, fruit, and beverages. The strong scent of freshly brewed coffee permeated the air. Coop was reaching for a yogurt and fruit cup when he noticed someone standing next to him: Felix Culo, his least-favorite partner.

"Good morning, Felix. How are you?" He did his best to make his tone sound bright.

"Morning," Felix grunted. In his jarring accent it sounded like "*Mawning.*"

Now was the time for Coop to summon his courage. He turned to face Felix, who was about the same height as Coop at five foot nine. He swallowed. "Felix, I know we've had our differences in the past, but I respect your skills and I hope you respect me. We're going to be working together as partners, so what do you say we bury the hatchet and start fresh?" Coop offered his hand for Felix to shake.

Felix looked at him with cold, expressionless eyes and paused a moment, then smiled with only one side of his mouth. "Okay, Coop, agreed. You're all right." Felix swatted Coop on the upper arm, then meandered over to the table with the coffee.

Coop let out a sigh of relief and headed into the ballroom. He took a seat at one of the many long, narrow tables that stretched across the width of the room, split by an aisle in the middle. White linen table cloths covered each table, and at every seat was a Moleskine leather notebook with the firm's logo and *Global Partners' Summit* embossed on the cover. Coop ran his fingers lovingly over the words. He'd cherish that notebook for the rest of his career.

*

The ballroom quickly grew crowded with a vast sea of mostly men in dark suits, white shirts, and yellow or blue ties. Soon the meeting was called to order by the firm's CEO, Walter, who welcomed everyone, especially the new partners, and then ran through the agenda: the general session for the partners would take up most of the morning, and then right before lunch the new partners would be in a separate smaller session for their orientation.

Just like in his Wharton days, Coop listened carefully to what was being presented and took copious notes. During a break, a friendly-looking guy about his age approached him. "Hello, I saw you taking many notes, I may need to consult with you on a few things that I missed. Oh, sorry, I am Maxime, a new partner from the Vancouver office." He smiled proudly. Maxime wore a tasteful gray suit with faint pinstripes, along with a pale pink shirt and a magenta silk pocket square.

Coop shook his hand. "Hi, Maxime, I'm Coop, a new partner from the New York office. Do I detect a French accent?"

"Ah yes, I am Quebecois, born and raised in Montreal but now living in Vancouver."

Coop, having learned French at a young age from his maternal grandmother, replied in Maxime's native tongue, "Vancouver sounds like such a wonderful city—I've always wanted to visit."

Maxime's eyes widened in surprise. "Coop, your accent is superb! You must come see me in Vancouver sometime. The food there is magnificent!"

Coop loved Maxime's enthusiasm and positivity and wondered—was Maxime gay or just Quebecois? The two continued chatting in French and made their way back inside the ballroom. One of the partners stepped up to the microphone and announced that the new-partner session would be starting shortly in a smaller conference room down the hall.

After grabbing their stuff, Coop and his new friend walked down the long hallway until they got to a sign on the wall indicating it was the room for new-partner orientation. There were five round tables with six seats each, and a welcome packet at each seat.

Barbara Pat Kelly, the head of HR for the firm in the US, stood at the front of the room with her heavily hair-sprayed helmet of white-blond hair. Coop waved, and in return she gave a perfunctory smile. "Welcome, new partners. I want to congratulate the thirty of you on your tremendous achievement. I'm sure all of you are excited to learn about the privileges that come with being a partner. I'll give you the highlights, and then you can spend some time reviewing the documents in your orientation packet, which you must sign before you leave this room."

Hmm, sounds ominous. Coop could hardly contain his excitement, and it took all of his self-control to sit there and listen to Barbara Pat Kelly without opening the welcome packet. She spoke about the many benefits of being a partner, and about the responsibilities, as well. Barbara Pat informed them that each new partner would be required to attend certain internal meetings, volunteer to lead an internal committee (such as recruiting), and take on more administrative responsibilities in addition to their client work. There would also be bigger expectations of each of them in the area of business development, meaning that they'd have higher targets for bringing in new client work. But, she added, of course the rewards of partnership were manifold. The head of HR shared all of this information in a flat, unemotional tone, like she was announcing a list of flight delays over an airport PA system. Finally she instructed them to open their welcome packets and pull out the document on top.

"The first piece of required documentation is your resignation. As of today I will need you to resign from the firm." She paused and nodded her head in the affirmative. "Today you are becoming an equity partner. As an equity partner you will no longer be an employee of the firm and you will no longer draw a salary." Barbara Pat made eye contact with each of the new partners and took in their expressions of surprise. "Please sign at the bottom and we'll move on."

This was news to Coop. He gulped and glanced around the room at the twenty-nine other new partners, who were dutifully signing the document as instructed. Maxime looked at Coop with wide eyes but signed the paper like an obedient pupil following a teacher's orders.

"Good." Barbara Pat continued as her assistant collected all the signed papers. "Let's move on to the second document. This document outlines the financial requirements that come with being an equity partner. You are expected to invest capital into the firm, otherwise called a 'buy-in.' You may either make the payment up front in cash or we can assist you with setting up a partnership loan, where we will deduct your repayments of interest and principal from your future partnership drawings. Then a smaller investment amount will be required each subsequent year. Please go ahead and review the details of the buy-in."

Coop's eyes flew over the words as he speed-read through the document. He was astounded to learn that he was required to make an investment of $300,000 in the firm as a new partner. *Buy-in? More like rip-off.* He ruminated forlornly about the sectional sofa he had longed for and whispered to no one in particular, "Goodbye, Herman Miller."

Maxime gave him an inquisitive look and then returned to reading the document. He finally caught up to where Coop was reading and muttered, "Sree-hundred taw-sond dollar, *tabernac!*"

Coop had to stifle a laugh at Maxime's use of the religiously based common Quebecois swear word—as an American the expression seemed far too mild for what this situation warranted.

While the excitement of his promotion hadn't died down yet, Coop was beginning to grasp the reality of what being a partner meant. He'd coveted the partner position for so long but was now learning what it actually entailed. It was like when he was teenager coveting a certain pale blue cashmere sweater and saving up enough money to finally buy it, only to find, crestfallen, that it was actually poly blend. Coop looked down at the embossed Moleskine notebook and rubbed his forehead. Essentially he'd be paying three hundred thousand dollars for the privilege of using this notebook—it was the most expensive notebook in the world.

*

The remainder of the meeting was a blur. During the cocktail hour that followed, Coop mingled with the other partners while he mentally wrestled with the fact that his personal economics were about to change drastically. Being frugally minded, the added financial risk that Coop was now taking on was already giving him a headache. He'd no longer have a steady paycheck, plus he'd have to sign over that check from Mrs. Jankowski and empty out his entire checking account to pay for his partner buy-in. No wonder the older, established partners were so welcoming of the new partners. They'd be seeing an influx of nine million dollars into their coffers.

The sit-down dinner was a little more relaxed, and after a couple of glasses of wine Coop started to loosen up. The rich meal wasn't something Coop would normally eat—foie gras with toast points accompanied by a frisée salad, followed by a veal chop in mushroom sauce, and for dessert a rich molten chocolate lava cake. Toward the end of dinner Felix stood up and asked all the new partners to meet him at the bar along with some senior partners. When everyone was gathered, Felix announced that he, along with some other senior partners, would be taking the new partners to an Orvis shooting camp the next day. The camp was located in Millbrook, New York, about a two-hour drive from the city. Two luxury private vans would pick them up in front of the office and transport them to the camp. Coop began to sweat profusely. This wasn't what he'd been expecting for his first partner outing. Sailing around Manhattan on a yacht while sipping champagne was more his speed. *We're spending the whole day running around in the woods killing small, furry creatures?*

Felix had the bar staff serve generous pours of scotch in crystal glasses on silver trays to all the new partners. When Coop politely declined, Felix said, "Come on, Coop, don't be a wuss. You're a partner now, and partners drink scotch. Let's have a toast, and when you finish that we'll pour you another." He let out a staccato laugh.

Coop had to admit that Felix's carefree demeanor surprised him— wasn't he at all worried about the questionable audit for Hello TelCo? Felix seemed to have forgotten all about it, but it was on Coop's daily list of worries. By the time Coop left the hotel and hailed a cab, his stomach was churning and his head was spinning.

*

Early the next morning, Coop, head still reeling from the night before, stepped into one of the high-end vans transporting the partners to the Orvis shooting camp. His stomach was a Gordian knot and he was fretful about the day ahead. Felix sat in the front row with a few of his close buddies, all wearing hunting attire—heavy-duty boots, jeans, and leather ranger jackets with many pockets. Felix was showing off a new leather satchel to a couple of his buddies. Coop wore what he thought was appropriate attire for the cool mountain air: dark jeans, a

Patagonia T-shirt, and a silk/cashmere-blend zip-up sweater. Most of his colleagues were in jeans and wore flannel checked shirts or ones with hunting motifs. He spotted Maxime at the back of the van, who motioned for him to come sit with him. Coop took a seat and noted that his friend was wearing jeans, a pink button-down shirt with a thin sweater tied around his shoulders, and a suede driving cap placed at a jaunty angle on his head. Again, gay or just Quebecois?

When Maxime started to chat, Coop said apologetically, "I'm still recovering from all the rich food and booze from last night, so I think I'm going to sleep most of the way up, okay?" Maxime shrugged and said, "But of course," and he entertained himself with the view outside the window as the vans pulled away from the curb.

It was a lethal combination for Coop: the churning stomach and aching head, the long drive on winding roads, the smell of diesel exhaust, and the mental picture of bloody dead creatures littering the ground. By the time they reached their destination, Coop couldn't have felt worse. He urged Maxime to go ahead of him, saying he just needed to sit for a minute. Coop was the last one to come off the van, but before he could step down an uncontrollable wave of nausea overtook him. He quickly turned to find some vessel in which to vomit. No trash can. Nothing. Coop eyed a bag lying on the seat and grabbed it in desperation. It wasn't until after he tossed his cookies that he realized he'd gotten sick into Felix's new satchel. He cringed and gingerly placed the satchel on the floor, making a mental note to take the other van on the way home.

The new partners, along with some of the established partners accompanying them, milled about inside the Orvis camp lodge. Coop made a quick stop in the men's room to rinse out his mouth and splash some water on his face. Surprisingly, he felt much better.

The main instructor gathered everyone around and Coop was tremendously relieved to learn they were doing sport clay shooting, where each person had a shotgun and one hundred rounds of ammo to shoot at clay targets flying through the air. Mercifully, small bloody animals would not be a part of the day's recreation.

Six instructors each took a small group and taught them how to use a shotgun, including important tips like keeping the muzzle pointed in a safe direction, keeping their finger off the trigger, and learning how to put on the safety. Although Coop had great hand eye coordination, he'd never fired a shotgun. Each person was given a chance to try a few practice rounds. His instructor released a flying clay target over a large pond and Coop missed it twice. The gun kicked back hard into his shoulder when it recoiled, and the blast was a lot louder than Coop had expected, even with earplugs in his ears.

The senior partner assigned to Coop's group was an athletic man with short gray hair named Robert who hailed from their San Francisco office. Robert put his hand on Coop's shoulder and motioned for him to remove his earplugs.

"Track the flight path of the target," Robert said, "then shoot slightly ahead of the target to account for the time delay for the shot to reach it."

Focused and determined, Coop reloaded the gun and turned back to the shooting range. This time when the target flew he aimed toward where the target was going to be. The whole thing was blasted apart into powder.

"Did you see that? I hit the target!" Coop exclaimed to Robert. "Thanks for the tip, that really helped. You know, I've never done this sort of thing before."

"Well, the only reason I know how to do it is because I've had to come up here for many partner outings over the years." Robert glanced around and crinkled his nose. "It's not really my cup of tea, though," he said softly. "Say, isn't that a Ted Baker sweater? I have the same one in aubergine." Unlike Felix Culo at the diversity workshop, Robert pronounced it correctly, and he gave Coop a little wink.

*

Not only did Coop learn to shoot straight that day, he learned that there was at least one other gay partner at his firm, though this news was obviously kept hush-hush. It turned out to be an interesting outing in more ways than one. Except for the large bruise developing in the front of his shoulder, the day of shooting had turned out to be a lot less painful than Coop had anticipated. However, all the while Coop kept looking around at the other partners—new and old—who all seemed so much alike and so different from Coop. Did he really fit in?

Coop had forgotten about his morning mishap on the van until he heard Felix Culo, who was first on the van, swearing up a storm. Felix held the strap of his soiled leather satchel like he was holding a rotting fish, marched up to the trash bin outside the lodge, and tossed in the satchel. Coop quickly got into the line for the other van. While he felt guilty, there was zero benefit in telling Felix he was the culprit— Coop had learned his lesson that it was better to keep some things to himself.

*

SOFIA

Smack-dab in the middle of a live broadcast is not the time to be hit with a surprise. Sofia was sitting at the table on camera with Graham and Kate Frost for the debut of *Titans Tell All*. It was the beginning of their first interview and they were experiencing a broadcaster's nightmare—dead airtime, not due to any technical difficulty but rather a human one. *This cannot be happening.* Sofia was frozen with alarm. Graham was in worse shape, sporting a slick mustache of sweat on his upper lip. The bright, hot lights in the studio were not helping matters.

Graham was interviewing Bryce Stewart, the founder of the Scottish jam company that consumers were going wild about. Bryce was known for being a cordial fellow with great product savvy but someone who rarely granted interviews. As part of Graham's preparation he had thoroughly researched the jam company and prepared a list of probing questions. There was just one problem... the Scotsman's brogue was as thick as congealed oatmeal on a cold winter morning, and save for the occasional "aye" it was nearly impossible to understand what he was saying. Not helping matters was Bryce's speech pattern of sustained rapid-fire bursts of words, his speed significantly increasing with his enthusiasm. Because Scottish people grew up watching American television programs, Bryce had no problem understanding Graham's accent, which meant that he easily and quickly responded to the interview questions. The Scotsman couldn't seem to fathom why his interviewer was having such difficulty understanding him. When Graham asked his guest to repeat his answer for the third time, it was clear that Bryce's patience was evaporating like the morning mist on a sunny Scottish hillside. Getting creative, Graham tried to understand his interviewee by saying things like, "So in other words you mean...," and "Would you care to elaborate on that further?" The more Bryce's agitation increased, the faster the words shot out of his mouth, which only made things worse. That was when they ran into dead airtime.

Their boss, Randolph, who was monitoring the broadcast in the control room, urged Kate and Sofia to jump in and provide an assist. He hissed in their earpieces, "Help him, for god's sake!" Sofia spoke five languages fluently and had a gift for dissecting accents, but even she was struggling to comprehend Bryce Stewart. Her back felt clammy and the fabric of her dress adhered to the skin in between her shoulder blades like wallpaper paste. What could she do to get Graham out of this jam? She had to stifle a nervous laugh at the bad pun.

Kate, who had the relationship with Bryce, piped up. She had a big smile on her face and said brightly, "Bryce, why don't we shift gears a bit. You've accomplished so much, we thought it would be a fun exercise to give you a little pop quiz on your business and career. But the trick is, you can only give single-word answers. Ready?"

The Scottish entrepreneur's eyes twinkled at the challenge and he nodded. "Aye, let's give it a go, Kate." He genuinely seemed to want to make the interview a success and could sense it had been going south for some time now. While Kate asked her series of questions, Bryce seemed to be slowing down his speaking speed by at least half. Sofia glanced down at the table and saw that Kate was reading from a prepared list of questions. *Hmm, lucky that she prepped those questions in advance.*

Finally the interview reached its conclusion and they collectively gave a big sigh of relief as Graham took the lead in thanking their guest. During the commercial break, Bryce Stewart departed and Graham leaned over to Kate. "Why didn't you tell me the man was impossible to understand?" His eyes flashed with anger. Sofia had never seen Graham lose his cool like that.

"Really, Graham? It was your responsibility as the lead interviewer to do your homework and prepare properly," Kate retorted. "And I didn't hear a thank-you from you for my help with the list of questions."

Graham sputtered. "I read every article I could get my hands on and all the written interviews he's ever conducted. But there were no audiotapes of him available anywhere. You'd met him previously— couldn't you have at least warned me about his accent?"

Kate sat back and looked straight at Graham. "It must have just slipped my mind."

Sofia remained silent during the prickly exchange, although she sided with Graham. But there was no time for further discussion as they were moving on to the next segment of the program. Their next guest arrived on set and they got the cue that the live interview was about to begin. Sofia would be taking the lead on this one, but she had prepared well and prayed things would go smoothly.

*

Back on the air, Sofia welcomed their next guest, Hideyoshi Sakamoto, founder of the Japanese fast-fashion retailer called Deki. Looking at the camera, Sofia rattled off Mr. Sakamoto's many accomplishments and recited some impressive stats on the explosive growth of his business. Sofia turned to her guest. "So, Yoshi—may I call you that? What's your dream for the future of your company, Deki?"

Yoshi was a spry man in his late fifties, taller than the average Japanese man, and slender. He had jet-black hair and perfect posture, and exuded warmth and energy. "Yes, please to call me Yoshi." He smiled and said haltingly, "My dream to make Deki best retail company in the world." He held up his fist in victory.

Sofia smiled back. "That's quite an ambition for your company, Yoshi, though you're already making excellent progress. Can you tell us why you chose the name Deki?"

He looked at her quizzically. "What means *Deki*? That what you ask? I'm sorry, my English not so good."

She nodded. Sofia suddenly realized that her interview subject's limited English was going to be challenging with the list of questions she'd prepared. Graham shot her a sympathetic but worried look. Now that the spotlight was on her, Sofia felt the beads of sweat forming on her back again but she maintained her composure.

Yoshi gave a pensive look. The words trickled slowly out of his mouth, like droplets from a leaky faucet. "*Deki* has two meaning. First means quality. Second means brilliant. *Hai*?" He added the Japanese word for "yes" to confirm that Sofia understood him.

"Yes, I see, Yoshi. I'd like to ask you what made you want to start a fast-fashion company in the first place, and what products will you be focusing on in the future?"

Yoshi's brow furrowed, and unlike the speedy Bryce Stewart, his pace of speaking was halting and painfully slow. "Sorry, I no understand question." He pointed to his nose, as was the Japanese custom when someone pointed to themselves. "English not so good." Yoshi shook his head side to side and gave an apologetic look. He was a good-looking man and gave a charming smile. More dead airtime. This interview was going downhill fast, and with it the future prospects for *Titans Tell All.*

While Yoshi was having difficulty understanding her, Sofia now understood everything. The reason Kate had so generously offered to have Graham and Sofia conduct the first interviews on *Titans Tell All* was becoming abundantly clear. Kate had purposely picked two interview subjects who had not done audio interviews before and did not speak English clearly enough to be understood. This was a classic setup disguised as a selfless teammate trying to help her colleagues. Sofia's back stiffened up and she had to do her best to not show her anger. How was she supposed to conduct the rest of the interview with Yoshi if he couldn't comprehend what she was saying? She wished she had a Japanese translator on hand and glanced briefly skyward as if one might magically appear and save the interview.

In her ear piece Sofia could hear Randolph exhaling in disgust. He muttered, "Good god, not again." Out of the corner of her eye she saw Kate leaning back, watching her squirm. Kate's plan to make Graham and Sofia look like fools was certainly working. What, was Kate now going to swoop in and miraculously save Sofia's interview, just as she'd done with Graham's? Did Kate secretly speak Japanese? The seconds were ticking by in an agonizing fashion. Sofia was determined not to let this interview become a disaster…but how? *Think, Sofia, think.*

All of a sudden something in her mind clicked. Sofia remembered reading that although Yoshi was born in Japan, as a young boy his parents had sent him to live with relatives in Chile for several years to broaden his horizons, and he'd spent many summers there growing up. She took a chance. "Yoshi-san, *podemos hablar en español?*"

Yoshi gave a broad smile. "*Si, por supuesto! Mi español es mejor que mi ingles.*" His words flowed comfortably and rapidly, conveying his command of that language. He giggled in delight. Bingo. Now all Sofia had to do was translate her questions and Yoshi's answers for the audience, and they were good to go. She proceeded with the interview and got some great insights from Yoshi, and they were even able to joke around in their newfound common language. Sofia gave a sideways glance at Kate and noticed that she had an eyebrow arched.

*

Out in the hallway directly after the broadcast, they huddled with their boss. "How would you say that went?" Randolph was not one to yell—instead he was using his scary principal's whisper, and the stern look in his eyes telegraphed his displeasure. He glowered at Sofia, Graham, and Kate, who stared at the floor like schoolkids getting slapped with disciplinary action.

Graham offered, "Honestly, it could have been better." He shrugged apologetically.

Sofia glanced at Kate. How would she respond in this situation?

Kate gave Randolph an innocent smile. "Randolph, I really must apologize. In my enthusiasm to get great interview subjects for *Titans Tell All*, I may have overlooked their communication challenges. But despite running into some difficulties, I think we were able to turn around both interviews. I had no idea that Sofia could speak Spanish fluently and her interview turned out just fine in the end."

Randolph gave her a knowing look. He was a shrewd man and he must have figured out what Kate was attempting to do. But he'd worked hard to woo her to the network, so he probably didn't want to come down too hard on her.

"Listen, *Titans Tell All* is a great concept and I want it to work. The show will live or die based on the teamwork that viewers see—and on content people can actually understand," he admonished them. "It's in all your best interests to work as a team or I'm afraid the show will be short-lived. Now go figure it out." He was like a parent chastising young children for fighting over a toy.

With that the three of them were dismissed and they skulked away.

Further down the hallway, out of earshot of their boss, Graham turned to Kate. "Next time make sure you give us the appropriate intel so we can do our jobs properly."

Kate snapped, "I told you it was an oversight, Graham."

Sofia raised her hands to settle them both. "Look, I'm not sure what happened with the interviewees or why, but like Randolph said, it's up to the three of us to make this show a success. That is what we all want, isn't it?" She looked into the eyes of her colleagues, who nodded. "Then let's just reset and start fresh. Okay? Kate, I know you're leading the next interview, so let us know how we can help." Even though Sofia was furious with Kate over her deception, she chose to take the high road.

Kate removed her glasses and folded them shut. Looking her dead in the eye, she said, "Sofia, I'm a professional seasoned broadcaster. I can handle my interviews on my own." Then she gave a tight smile, turned, and walked away.

Sofia drew back.

"What a wench!" Graham hissed in Sofia's ear.

She shook her head slowly. "Listen, Graham, we still have to work with her whether we like it or not. Come on, let's go grab a coffee and then I need to head off to the airport."

*

As Sofia sat back in the car that was driving her first into the city to pick up her friends and then to LaGuardia Airport, she took a few minutes to recover from the rough broadcast and then reflect on her personal life. She'd always made it clear to her friends that she wasn't interested in marriage, but that didn't mean she wasn't open to romance. In all her prior relationships, Sofia was always the one who had been pursued, and she'd found that playing hard-to-get worked to her advantage. But the situation with Jasper Frank was totally different…and, frankly, frustrating.

They'd had a wonderful first date over coffee and dessert after the Broadway show back in early October and things between them had really seemed to click. But a couple of weeks had passed and she hadn't heard a peep from Jasper. Granted, Sofia had been keeping her head down, working on the launch of her new CNBC show, and she knew Jasper traveled a lot for work. Still, he could have asked her out again, couldn't he? Perhaps he wasn't that interested in her? Maybe he was seeing someone else? Should she call him up and ask him out? She shuddered at the thought.

Then divine intervention struck. Sofia's cell phone rang. Jasper. Her heart jumped. "Well, hello, stranger," she said, guarding her emotions. She felt giddy but wanted to sound cool and collected.

"Hi, Sofia, how are you? I caught your *Titans Tell All* show today," Jasper's voice sounded forcibly cheerful. "Rough start, but you managed to save the interview in the end." He certainly was candid— Sofia liked that about him.

She groaned. "Oh, thanks. It didn't go all that smoothly, I know."

"Listen, I've been out of the country and am just heading back into the city from the airport now. Do you want to grab a bite to eat tonight?" Maybe he was interested in her after all.

"Oh, no! What timing. I'm in a car on the way to the airport right now. A group of us are flying to Portland to visit a friend. I'm sorry I can't make it, Jasper."

"Another time perhaps. Have a good trip. Maybe we'll cross paths at the airport—I'm heading back out of town again on Sunday night." Jasper sounded like he was ready to hang up.

Sofia said, "Wait a minute. What about getting together over

Thanksgiving week? Are you around?" Suddenly she remembered her plans to visit her parents in Spain over the holiday. "Oh shoot, I just remembered that I'll be in Madrid visiting my parents that week." Then she had an idea. "Hey, maybe you should come over there and we can get together."

There was silence on the other end of the phone. "What a coincidence. It just so happens that I'll be in Madrid for a conference then."

Sofia straightened up. "Perfect. We can have our second date in Spain, Jasper. What do you think?"

He chuckled. "I'd love to see you, Sofia. But I'm not sure what my work schedule looks like yet. Let's just play it by ear, okay?"

They said their goodbyes, leaving Sofia even more confused. Jasper seemed interested in her and had just asked her to dinner. And they were both going to be in Madrid at the same time; why wouldn't they get together? Was something holding him back?

The car pulled up to Andi's office in midtown and she ran out with her bags. They had to swing by a downtown location and pick up Grace, then head to LaGuardia.

This trip was a welcome break for Sofia, who wanted to put the disastrous experience of her debut show behind her. She was excited to spend time with her friends, relax and have a little Oregon Pinot, and try to not think about work or men for a little while.

*

GRACE

Devinder Jain held up his index finger. "Now, Grace, I'm most looking forward to hearing your thoughts. What you have accomplished with the Burberry brand was nothing short of amazing. I may steal some of your ideas to use for the other companies in my portfolio." He shook her hand warmly.

"Thank you, Mr. Jain, it's an honor to meet you," Grace said. "At my B-school you're one of the most admired graduates."

"Please, call me Dev. So, you went to Wharton, too, Grace? How wonderful. I tried to convince Venky to go there but he chose Columbia instead." He gave his son a patriarchal scowl. Venky motioned for one of the Flip Style team to bring his father some hot tea.

Preston piped up. "If only my alma mater, HBS, was lucky enough to have you as an alum, Dev." Dev gave him a dismissive look. The more time Grace spent with Preston, the more annoying she found him. He was enthusiastic but a lightweight in the area of business strategy.

It was a big day for Grace and the Flip Style team. Their new angel investor, who also happened to be Venky's father, was there to hear their plans to turn around the business. Devinder was chairman and CEO of Triumph Group—arguably the most successful Indian conglomerate, with a broad reach across a variety of industries.

Grace hoped the meeting would go smoothly. In the course of her work with the Flip Style team, she'd learned that they needed some adult supervision. The cofounders, Venky and Tom, were sharp, hardworking guys who sometimes didn't agree on things, and there was no clear accountability for who was in charge of what. This caused a great deal of confusion to the people on their team, who would get one answer to a question from Venky and a different response from Tom.

Grace had given the cofounders some leadership coaching and helped them clarify and formalize roles so it was clear who owned what. Those small changes had already seemed to help accelerate the pace of work and improve morale. She'd been collaborating with Venky and Tom on the business strategy, brand turnaround, product line, and packaging ideas.

In recent weeks she'd also been working intensively with Kenneth, Flip Style's chief creative officer, to come up with a revolutionary new package design. Kenneth was a seasoned creative chief who came across as a good mentor to his team. Grace felt the brand needed to separate itself from the larger competitors with a distinct strategy and product design that would connect with consumers in a unique way. Venky and Tom had also asked Grace to work closely with Preston to determine if he had the chops for the job.

All the key executives and Devinder Jain were gathered in the large, bright conference room, sitting in orange-upholstered swivel chairs around the long white oval table. Venky and Tom introduced everyone and acknowledged their contributions. Devinder was a tall, lanky man with a handsome, angular face, and except for the graying around his temples, he was the spitting image of Venky. Venky started the presentation by sharing their new business strategy and direction. Then Tom reviewed their updated product line. Grace presented a few slides on where they stood with Flip Style's brand idea.

"First, I want to level-set about the importance of brand and brand strategy. Research shows that companies doing an exceptional job executing their brand have a market value at least 35 percent greater than their peers'. What we do with the Flip Style rebranding can and will translate to real enterprise value. If we improve the brand, we improve the bottom line. And oh, by the way, we'll need to make a significant investment in marketing to accomplish this."

Devinder nodded in agreement.

Grace pressed on. "We think that Flip Style isn't selling hair care products, it's selling confidence. That's our brand idea; it's what the brand stands for and it permeates all aspects of how the brand is executed. People want their hair to look great—silky, soft, manageable—but they also don't want to have to worry about it. If you're happy with your hair, you don't even think about it. So this idea of confidence and calmness is reflected in the products we offer, how we offer them, and how we communicate about them. In keeping with that philosophy, we came up with a new line of products named Zen

Glow, and Kenneth will show you our new packaging concept."

Grace paused to take in Dev's reaction. He was leaning forward with both elbows on the conference table. "This is very well thought out, Grace. Simple but powerful."

Prior to today Grace, Kenneth, and Preston had spent a few days together coming up with innovative ideas, with Grace and Kenneth contributing the bulk of the ideas and capturing them on a flip chart while Preston sat there and gave feedback. On breaks, Kenneth and his design team would sketch up ideas and share them with Grace— she liked his energy and collaborative style. Preston, on the other hand, spent most of his time critiquing others' work and flirting with one of the designers.

Andi had a test to determine if someone was a slacker: *Does he actually write anything down?* Andi's perspective was that if Preston wasn't coming up with ideas or physically producing anything, he wasn't adding any value. Grace tended to agree but was withholding final judgment.

She turned over the presentation to Kenneth, who was to review the new product design and packaging elements. One of the major changes was the packaging—while they kept the idea of having the product concentrated, Grace didn't see the necessity or advantage to having it dispensed as a foam, so they ditched that idea. Kenneth gave some introductory remarks but, being a good mentor, decided to give Preston the sexy part of the presentation—the packaging concept they had come up with. Their idea was to completely redesign the shampoo and conditioner bottles. The bottles were a beautiful yin-and-yang interlocking design and were made of lightweight biodegradable material that had the properties of plastic.

Preston, smiling confidently, held up the mocked-up package like a precious jewel. "Beautiful, isn't it?" He turned on the charm and was a smooth presenter, although the idea was so strong it probably could have sold itself. "The concept is to make it easy for the consumer to use. Out of the dispenser comes what we call 'pearls,' which are pre-measured pods of shampoo and conditioner in the exact amount needed. Once the shell of the pearl gets wet it disintegrates, leaving only the product. Easy, simple, elegant. It also makes the product convenient to take on trips."

Preston straightened his posture, a glint in his eye. "Dev, I think we have an opportunity here to be even more bold." He was going off script. What was Preston up to now? "Our second idea is to offer a whimsical package, shaped like a soda bottle, with small colorful pods that contain the product and resemble carbonated bubbles." Preston had no background in product or packaging design, but that didn't stop him from sharing his opinion. This soda pop idea was from one of the female designers on whom Preston had a crush. He held up a sketch and gushed, "This soda pop bottle would be so hip and cool, totally different than what's on the shelves today."

Dev's brow knotted up. "What about the safety aspect of that packaging?"

"What's that?" Preston said, still smiling big.

"That makes the product look like a sweet treat—what if a small child ingested it? The last thing we want is for Flip Style's product to harm children."

Grace shook her head. She had expressed this exact concern about the soda pop packaging. Flip Style would not survive another PR nightmare. She wasn't sure why Preston was even presenting the idea when they'd all agreed to kill it.

Venky interjected. "That soda pop concept doesn't fit with the Zen element we're going for—we will move forward with the yin-and-yang design."

Brashly, Preston backpedaled. "Of course. You're so right, Dev. Kenneth and I discussed it, and while it wasn't the strongest of the two ideas, we wanted to show it so you could see another option." He turned to the creative chief. "Kenneth, like I said, I think we should scrap this one." *Way to be a team player, Preston.* Venky gave Preston a wary look, while Kenneth just sat there blinking a jumbled Morse code of confusion.

The team finished up the meeting by sharing a timeline for when all the work would be completed, when the products would relaunch, and how they would be allocating their capital. Dev gave his approval. "You've got a solid plan for getting the company back on track. I'm eager to see the results. Very good meeting." He gave a nod of approval to Venky.

Preston piped up, "Dev, I believe we're set for a successful relaunch. It just shows what this team is capable of. But, honestly, I think we can do better."

Preston, what are you doing? Grace eyed him with suspicion.

"What you are saying?" Dev furrowed his brow.

"It's just that I'm so passionate about Flip Style and about making a huge contribution. I think we always need to push ourselves to do better. I, for one, always want to push myself to do great work so I can someday be as successful as you." Preston gave Dev a huge toothy smile and concluded the public service announcement for the advancement of his own career. A casual observer might have thought that Preston was Dev's other son vying for control of the Triumph empire. Or maybe he was fishing for a job with one of Dev's companies?

"Yes, I agree. We must always strive to do better and not be satisfied until we reach that goal," Dev replied. "As your country's Yogi Bear said, 'It is not done until it is done.'" He rose and excused himself to head to another meeting. Venky and Tom escorted him out of the office.

*

"Did you understand what Dev said about Yogi Bear?" Kenneth said, turning to Grace.

Grace thought for a second and then let out a laugh. "I think he meant to say Yogi Berra, the baseball player. The quote he was citing was, 'It ain't over 'til it's over.' Basically, we're still in the first inning of the game, so we need to keep trying hard."

Kenneth gave a soft chuckle and then his face grew serious as he turned to Preston. "Preston, I'm a little confused about why you presented the second packaging concept and what you said about it. That was the idea that you were pushing, not me." Kenneth had a look of concern on his face, like a father patiently trying to understand why his child had just scrawled in crayon all over the living room wall.

"Dude, I apologize about that but I had to make a call. I thought that it was critical that Dev had faith in the senior strategy person, the one driving the direction of the company. Everyone knows that designers come up with lots of ideas that don't end up making the grade. So, I did what I thought it was best for Flip Style," Preston explained. "It's all about the company, right?"

Kenneth cocked his head, looking uneasy with that explanation. Then Preston turned to Grace. "I would have appreciated more support from you, Grace. I felt like you just left me hanging."

Surprised by Preston's temerity, Grace shot back, "Did you? How so?"

"I think we needed to show more teamwork and it would have been good for Dev to hear your support of me as the strategy lead since you clearly have his respect. Also, I hate to mention this, but I believe there was a typo on one of your slides that was quite distracting."

Grace nearly laughed. Who was this twerp and why was he lecturing the more experienced, talented, and senior people? And what was this talk about teamwork? When it came to teamwork Preston showed no capacity for it. Grace was 100 percent certain there were no typos in her presentation—she'd long ago learned a technique of reading every line backward to more easily spot mistakes. The hubris Preston was demonstrating was a bit too much.

Grace maintained her cool. "A typo, huh? Can you point it out to me?"

"Oh, I'll get back to you on that, Grace. Gotta run to another meeting." Preston gave her a nervous glance, picked up his notebook, and scurried out the door.

Kenneth shook his head. "Grace, sometimes I really don't understand that generation. I try to be a good mentor and give them many chances, but some of these kids have such an inflated sense of entitlement and no ability to collaborate. I just don't get it."

Grace snorted. "I don't mind a little cockiness now and then, but if it isn't backed up by a significant level of talent and teamwork, that's a problem. And oh, by the way, I don't know what phantom typo Preston was talking about—he seems too eager to criticize others without adding enough value himself."

"I'm totally with you on that, Grace. In fact, I'm going to share that feedback with Tom and Venky. With everything going at breakneck speed we need all hands on deck working together collaboratively."

"Agreed." Grace checked her watch. "I'd better run, I need to catch a flight."

*

Their hired SUV maneuvered deftly through city traffic and delivered Grace, Sofia, and Andi to the airport. They rushed to check in and stood in the security line together.

Sofia tapped her friend on the shoulder. "So, Grace, how's your book going?"

"Hang on a sec, didn't your *Titans Tell All* show debut today?" Grace perked up for a moment, but then she caught a look of caution from Andi, who was standing behind Sofia and shaking her head. It was obvious Andi had caught the show and it hadn't gone too smoothly.

Grimacing, Sofia gave a flick of her hand. "Oh, let's talk about that later when we're together with Vivien."

Grace gulped down the rest of her water, crushed the plastic bottle, and tossed it in the recycle bin. "Well, I have to say, the writing part of my book is going great, as are the case studies, but the actual publishing process is pretty complicated."

"What's the problem? Say, didn't you have a meeting with your publisher the other day?" Sofia shifted her tote bag to the other shoulder.

"Yes, it was a bunch of people reminding me that I'm a first-time author and giving me advice on what to do with my book. Remember how I came up with the title *Rise: Six Steps to Resuscitate Your Brand After a Fiasco*? Well, the publishing team suggested changing the title to *Brand Rejuvenation: An Essential Guide for How to Bring a Brand Back from Death*."

Andi wrinkled her nose and blurted, "Snoozefest."

"Yeah, I didn't like that suggestion and we had an intense discussion. I was able to leverage my expertise in branding and finally convinced them that my title would be more memorable and easier to market. Then they showed me three choices for the book cover, all of which were not that strong. The first two book covers were very dark: one featured a dead body with the word *brand* on its chest lying on a gurney with someone in scrubs standing in the background; the second featured a defibrillator with two hands holding the paddles over a bloody heart with the word *brand* on it. The third option was a picture of my face surrounded by tombstones that read 'brand' and 'R.I.P.'" Grace looked away to hide her despair.

Wolfing down a protein bar, Andi mumbled, "Maybe go with the defibrillator?"

Grace sighed. "I was hoping for something more eye catching, cleverer, or simpler. I tried to be diplomatic and said I liked the options equally but preferred not to have my face on the cover."

"Grace, a lot of nonfiction books have the author's picture on the cover," Sofia interjected.

"That's what my literary agent, Bob, said. He also said, 'You're a very attractive woman and we've got to capitalize on your looks to sell more copies. If I saw a few books on branding at a bookstore and one had a beautiful blonde on the cover, I'd pick that one.'"

Andi crumpled up her protein bar wrapper. "Yikes, he actually said that? What a dope."

"I asked if we could see more options and was told that they needed to finalize the cover quickly so they could start developing marketing materials. I left the meeting pretty bummed out." Grace shook her head. "But later, I had a flash of inspiration and created a simple, bold cover—white background with a red cross in the middle and my title on top. I emailed it to the publishing team and, fortunately, they liked it. But they also told me that authors don't have final say over their book covers." Grace turned to the TSA person and handed over her ID and ticket.

"Really? But it's your book that you're writing with your name on it," Andi said as she and Sofia had their IDs and tickets checked.

"Apparently the publishing firm has the right to decide on the cover, content, direction—pretty much any aspect of the book. It doesn't seem like I have much control, but they're the experts in the book business and they keep reminding me that I'm a first-time author so I need to trust them."

The three of them piled their bags onto the security belt and deposited their items in the bins that went on the belt. After clearing security they looked up at the digital board to find the gate for their flight to Portland and raced off in that direction. The three women arrived at the gate with a few minutes to spare and picked up their conversation.

"Let me get this straight, Grace," Andi said, placing her hand on her friend's arm. "You're the marketing expert with stellar branding expertise, right? So if the publisher wants your book to be successful, then shouldn't they at least listen to you?"

"You'd think, right? But you know, Andi, I'm learning that isn't necessarily how this process works."

Grace reflected on her situation with the publisher. She desperately wanted her rebranding book to be a success, but somehow the publisher's approach didn't feel quite right. Still, they knew the best way to launch books, didn't they?

*

ANDI

Andi was so lost in thought she didn't realize that the plane ride to Portland was almost over. She'd spent most of the travel time fine-tuning investment strategies for her private banking clients, and now she sat back to ruminate on how to work with Lester Labosky while still keeping him at a comfortable distance. The dry air in the plane had sucked all the moisture out of her body and she rubbed her tired eyes.

From across the aisle Sofia woke up from her nap and noticed her friend's intense look. "Are you okay, Andi? Aww, you must be missing the boys."

"Huh? Oh, yeah." While she knew that many working moms spent their days in the office worrying about their kids, missing them, and wondering what their kids were doing at any particular moment, Andi was not that type of mom. In fact, though she was embarrassed to admit it, Andi could be so focused on work during the day that she didn't even think about Luca or the boys until someone asked about her family. It wasn't that she didn't love them—she truly did— but Andi's intensity and focus were two critical ingredients that had helped propel her to the top of her field. A few years ago Andi had become one of the youngest Goldman partners in history and one of the few female partners there. For the fifth year in a row, Andi had been named a top financial advisor on both *Barron's and Forbes's* lists. Now she was at Kaneshiro Bank with a new boss and she knew she'd have to prove herself all over again. On the flight Andi was so fixated on her work that she didn't give a second thought to her family. Sofia's reminder made her feel a little pang of guilt. "Sure I miss the boys… but Luca's got things covered."

Sofia stretched a bit and yawned. "Looks like we're on our descent."

Raising her head up from her laptop, Grace, who had spent the entire flight writing her book, exclaimed, "Check it out, it's all trees down there! Where are the shopping malls? Where are all the buildings?"

Andi glanced out the window and saw hillsides covered in evergreen trees with a thick mist hanging above the tree line like a watery halo. "We know Vivi lives in a condo, so there's got to be at least one building somewhere!"

Upon landing they grabbed a taxi to Pioneer Courthouse Square downtown, where their hotel was located. The three women checked in, picked up a couple of bottles of champagne, and headed to Vivien's condo. The bright sunlight served as a catalyst to their increasingly boisterous mood.

At the appointed time, Andi, Grace, and Sofia arrived at Vivien's building and knocked on the condo door. As it swung open they shouted, "Surprise!" in unison, holding the champagne bottles aloft.

Vivien stepped back in shock, eyes wide. "What? No way! I can't believe you guys are here!" They exchanged heartfelt hugs. "This is awesome. But wait, is Clay with you?"

Grace explained, "Nope, no fiancé this weekend, it'll just be us girls. We arranged our whole surprise visit with Clay and had him pretend to plan a visit with you so we'd be sure you were home. Oh my gosh, look at this place!" She gazed around and took in the panoramic view.

*

Stunned and tickled by her friends' visit, Vivien gave them a quick tour of the place and then set out champagne glasses and some snacks. "It's such a treat to see you guys, I can't believe you came all the way across the country to visit me. Now I understand why you canceled our regular Friday afternoon Skype call—I was wondering about that. Come sit and relax."

She felt the tension in her neck and shoulders dissipate like a snake uncoiling after a long snooze in the sun. What a relief to be surrounded by her Smasher friends. Vivien couldn't wait to share her experiences at Smart Sports with them and get their advice—and empathy. She'd recently returned from a big trip to Asia with the three other division presidents, and the whole trip had been draining, not to mention dangerous. During their stop in Japan, two of the guys, named Duncan Doric and Johnny O, had slipped something into her sake that made her sick the whole night. Not a picnic. Plus she was dealing with a marginally talented and treacherous character, Rebecca Roche, who headed up product design and development on her Women's Apparel team. Things had been far more challenging at Smart Sports than Vivien ever anticipated, despite her friends' warnings. She was out here on her own—was she crazy to be doing this? Vivien sighed. She was determined to be successful…and had to sound at least a little upbeat about her adventure to her Smasher friends.

Vivien made sure her friends were relaxing comfortably in the living room before she started a discussion about how they'd spend their weekend in Portland. She made a number of suggestions, with a caveat. "Portland is a great place, but it's basically like a small town compared to NYC—there just aren't as many choices here. Although I'm sure we'll find some really fun things to do."

Andi was consuming the snacks ravenously. "Yeah, yeah, sounds great, but where are we going for dinner? I'm starving. Remember, we're still on East Coast time."

Luckily Vivien had just the spot in mind. "There's a terrific Vietnamese fusion restaurant called Silk. It's right downstairs and I know the owners, so I'm sure they can squeeze us in. Let me just give them a ring and let them know we're coming." She excused herself to make the phone call. After all, there were some perks about living in a smallish town where the people knew you.

*

"Do you hear that?" Sofia said.

"Hear what?" Andi cocked her head.

Sofia motioned toward the windows. "Nothing. It's so quiet here. No horns honking, no car alarms, no sirens. I don't even hear any traffic noise."

Andi wrinkled her nose. "Yeah, it's way too quiet. How am I supposed to get any sleep tonight?" Secretly she was relishing the idea of being alone in her hotel room with nothing to disturb her. With twin toddlers, Andi was accustomed to being woken up—either in the middle of the night due to bed wetting, or early in the morning by a son hungry for breakfast. The prospect of getting an entire night's peaceful sleep was a thrill beyond compare.

Vivien returned and told them dinner plans were set. "We've got a break in the weather for tonight and part of tomorrow, but"—she looked apologetic— "we're in for some rain at some point. I can take you guys on a tour of the Smart Sports campus tomorrow morning and then to visit the Japanese Garden, which is just beautiful. Then maybe grab lunch downtown? We should be able to fit all that in before the rain returns."

The four women caught up over drinks and then dinner on the most critical things going on in their lives. Just before midnight, after finishing up their wine, Andi, Grace, and Sofia headed back to their hotel.

At the hotel, Andi quickly got ready for bed and shimmied between the crisp, cool sheets and under the feather-stuffed duvet—this was heaven. She texted Luca to say good night and was surprised when her phone buzzed. It was Luca calling.

"Hi, honey, how's it going?" Andi's question was answered almost immediately when she heard loud wailing in the background.

Her husband's voice sounded strained. "Oh, Andi darling, it's not going so well. Francesco has been crying for hours. I checked his temperature and it's a little high. I tried to give him some juice and he wouldn't drink it. I undressed him completely and then dressed him again twice to check on his body. I can't find anything wrong with him, but the poor dear keeps crying and saying 'Ouchy, ouchy.' I don't know what else to do, eh? Maybe he picked up something from another kid in day care this week?"

Andi glanced at the clock. "I'm so sorry, Luca. Wow, it's after three a.m. there! Well, if you can't find anything wrong with him he must be okay. Maybe just put him back to bed and let him cry it out?"

Luca sighed. "I feel so terrible, Andi, he seems really miserable. Maybe I try rocking him to sleep a little more. Okay, I better go to him now. I miss you, darling."

*

"I can't believe this place, how do you actually get any work done here?" Andi asked Vivien as they toured the Smart Sports campus the next morning. The massive business complex sat on the banks of the Willamette River and offered every type of sport imaginable—a soccer field, running tracks and trails, tennis courts, basketball courts, and beach volleyball, plus a massive fitness center complete with a climbing wall. The campus was dotted with tasteful, modern buildings, and monuments celebrating the greatest moments in sports were sprinkled about the grounds. Andi's eyes were popping out of her head as she looked around incredulously. "This is a sports paradise." They picked up some coffee and breakfast at one of the three campus restaurants and continued their tour.

"Really, Vivi. This is impressive," echoed Sofia, "and so pristine. There's not one piece of garbage on any of the walkways, not even one leaf out of place!"

When Vivien signed them in to the employee store and told them everything was 50 percent off the ticketed price, Andi perked up. "All right, I'm going to town!" She found sneakers for the whole family and some workout clothes for herself. After getting a little retail therapy, they were ready to move on to the Japanese Garden, nestled in the West Hills of Portland. As they hiked through the gorgeous and tranquil twelve acres of the gardens, they enjoyed the simple pleasure of spending time together talking and laughing.

"How are the boys doing, Andi?" Vivien asked, walking beside her friend.

Andi cast her eyes downward. "I talked to Luca late last night and Francesco was having a tough night, the poor guy. Actually I'd better check in on him." Andi hammered out a quick text to her husband.

"You're fortunate to have a husband who takes care of everything at home while you're jetting off for the weekend." Sofia gave her a half smile and nudged her. "Seriously, Andi, I don't think you know how lucky you are having Luca. He's always going above and beyond for you and the boys."

Andi felt a little pang of guilt. "Yeah, I know. I probably take him for granted a bit. Luca does all the cooking, takes care of all the house stuff, even shops for clothes for the boys. Honestly, I don't really have to do all that much, which is great because I can focus on my work." She smiled sheepishly and gave a shrug.

Grace said, "I remember shortly after you guys got married the three of us came over for our Friday night cocktails. We were sitting in your living room drinking wine when Luca came in from work, said a quick hello, and disappeared, only to come out twenty minutes later with a platter of freshly roasted chestnuts. I mean, what a sweetheart."

Andi searched her memory and, recalling that incident, felt bad. When Luca had brought in the chestnuts she'd made it clear it was a girls' gathering and that he should give them some privacy, which he did with a smile. Maybe she didn't deserve him.

"That's true," Vivien laughed. "I can't imagine Clay ever doing something like that, but he's thoughtful in his own way. On my first day of work, when I came back to the hotel he had arranged to have a necklace from Tiffany delivered to my room."

"It's wonderful that he's so supportive, Vivi." Sofia smiled. "Looks like you've finally found your true love."

Andi cleared her throat authoritatively. "Well, ladies, as the only married woman here I can share the secret of true love." Andi was about to impart her wisdom and her Smasher friends waited eagerly to hear what she had to say. "The secret to true love is simply finding someone you can live with." She gave a nod of authority.

"And someone who can live with you, right?" Grace quipped. They shared a chuckle and continued their walk through the gardens.

Andi's phone rang, so she excused herself and took a seat on a nearby bench. "Hi, honey, is everything okay?"

Luca's voice sounded raspy, like sandpaper, and she could hear the exhaustion in the sluggish pace of his speech. "Hello, Andi, we just got back from the doctor. Both boys were crying since early this morning and both had a fever. Plus they had some kind of rash on their faces and the palms of their hands, so I took them in to the emergency pediatric clinic."

"Oh my gosh, Luca. Is it serious?" Spatters of rain started to fall and Andi hunched over her phone.

"The doctor examined them. She even looked inside Francesco's mouth—it was covered with sores. I couldn't believe it! I never thought to look inside his mouth—that was why he was crying all night, the poor dear. I feel so terrible. Fortunately Antonio doesn't have the mouth sores."

Andi massaged her head in her hands. She felt bad that her toddler sons were so miserable. "What's causing all the symptoms?"

"It's something called hand, food, and mouth sickness," Luca started, then corrected himself. "No, no, I mean hand, foot, and mouth disease. It's a virus and highly contagious. She said they probably picked it up at day care, so I already left a message for the director of the day care center to warn her and the other parents."

"So what are we supposed to do? Is there some kind of medicine to fix it?" Andi looked up at her friends, who were huddled in the gift shop out of the rain and signaling for her to join them.

Luca let out a short laugh. "Nothing, we can do nothing. There's no treatment, so the doctor said we just have to manage the symptoms with ibuprofen and keep the boys comfortable. She said it should go away in about a week or so, but the boys should not go to day care or be around other kids during that time. I think I can work mornings from home this week until the nanny arrives, so you don't need to worry."

Andi thought for a moment. This was one of the toughest things about being a mom—kids with an unexpected illness. "Honey, can you handle things or should I fly home early?" She was silently praying he'd give her a pass. The last thing she needed right now was to be exposed to a highly contagious virus. She had a bunch of important client meetings scheduled and couldn't show up with some kind of freakish rash all over her face.

"No, no, Andi. You enjoy your weekend with the girls, darling. Antonio and Francesco are doing much better after I gave them some Advil. Also the pancakes and bacon I made for them seem to be helping. There's really nothing more we can do. The boys will be fine."

Andi breathed a sigh of relief. "Okay, well give the boys a big hug from Mommy. And thanks, Luca. You're an amazing dad." She wasn't sure what she'd be walking into when she got home, but Andi was grateful to have another day to spend with her Smasher friends.

By now it was full-on pouring rain, so she ran to catch up with her friends. The four women hightailed it back to Vivien's car and sought out someplace warm and dry for lunch.

After a leisurely lunch and coffees all around, Andi glanced at the emails on her phone. Travel details for her upcoming meetings in Boston that week—she'd have to fly out on Monday morning. Also Lester had sent her a message saying their potential new Paris client wanted to meet with them in a week's time. Andi would have one more evening to spend in Portland with her friends before she had to jump back into the thick of things.

On Sunday evening, when she returned home to NYC, Andi had a quick visit with Luca and the boys, then unpacked, repacked, and got ready to leave again. The evidence of her children's hand, foot, and mouth disease was apparent—both boys had angry red rashes in a ring around their mouths, on the palms of their hands, and on their feet and ankles. But despite their unsightly physical condition, Luca had done a great job of keeping them entertained and managed their discomfort with children's Advil, so the boys were in surprisingly good spirits.

When Andi left for the airport the next morning, she hugged both of her children while steering clear of any direct contact with their rashes, just as a precaution. She'd get through her Boston meetings, then turn her laser focus to the opportunity with the potential new French client. Andi was looking forward to the Paris trip...and dreading it.

CHAPTER 6

November

SOFIA

Sofia approached the second episode of *Titans Tell All* with the focus, energy, and discipline of a quarterback competing in the Super Bowl. Determined to make the show a success, she watched every recorded interview of their next guest like a football coach reviewing game film of the opposing team. Since there was a two-week break before their next *Titans* episode due to a programming change, there was ample time for Sofia to take copious notes and craft compelling interview questions intended to reveal a new side of the technology business mogul to viewers. Preparation complete, Sofia marched into the team room where Kate Frost was seated with her assistant, Jenny, plus Graham and one of the production assistants.

Sofia tried to project positive energy. "Hi, Kate, you're probably putting the finishing touches on your interview questions for John Brennan. Just wanted to offer my help."

Kate kept her eyes on her laptop screen. "Yup. I'm all set." She tossed her hair back and angled her screen so Sofia could see. "Take a look, Sofia. This is how a seasoned professional does it."

Sofia read the questions and reacted with a start. "Kate, I've watched every single interview that John Brennan has done—a couple of them with you—and taken plenty of notes. It seems like some questions on your list are things he's already been asked before. Several times."

Kate's nostrils flared. "This is my interview and I'll conduct it in the way I see fit." It was an uncomfortable exchange to have in front of the others, but they were airing the show later that afternoon and needed to be in synch.

"I know you have a ton of experience, Kate, but in the interview you conducted two years ago you covered this ground already. For *Titans Tell All* don't we want to offer a fresh take? Maybe ask him some questions about how new technologies like AI will impact his business in the future?" Sofia held out a piece of paper. "I wrote up some new questions that could be intriguing."

Kate stood up and faced Sofia. Graham pretended to check his smartphone while he watched the scene unfold out of the corner of his eye. Jenny kept her head down and the production assistant tapped furiously away at his laptop. Kate swatted the paper in Sofia's hand away as if it were a pesky fruit fly and said a firm, "No thanks."

Sofia was undeterred. "Listen, Kate, we're both professionals here and we both want the show to succeed, don't we? John Brennan is known for his impatience and I don't think he'll take too kindly to being asked repeat questions. Won't you at least look at what I prepared? I'm trying to help you."

Hands on hips, Kate snapped, "Did you not hear me the first time? I'm not interested in your little list. The best way you can help me is to leave the room while I finish getting ready." She flicked her hand toward the door.

Sofia's cheeks flushed. She'd never been treated so disrespectfully by a colleague. Kate Frost had just humiliated her in front of the others. She noticed Graham sitting with his mouth agape and his eyes bugging out. It was a struggle but Sofia maintained her dignity. "I'll let you get back to it then."

*

In the few minutes before the show was about to start Sofia, Kate, and Graham sat around their table preparing for the broadcast. Still smarting from their earlier exchange, Sofia organized her papers and avoided eye contact with Kate.

Jenny, Kate's trusty assistant, breezed in and said sweetly in a hushed voice, "Kate, your evening gown and shoes for tonight's gala are ready to go and waiting in your dressing room when you finish up here."

Kate nodded. "Thanks, Jenny. I've been looking forward to this evening for months." She turned to Graham. "I'm attending a big gala at the Met this evening—it's the social event of the season. All the bigwigs will be there."

Graham replied indifferently, "Sounds great, Kate."

They got the cue that the broadcast was about to start and the three reporters put on big smiles as they faced the cameras. Their guest, John Brennan, a tech mogul known for starting a computer company in his parents' basement, came in and took his seat.

John said, "Kate, wonderful to see you again. Thanks for having me." He smiled at Sofia and Graham.

Kate nodded. "As ever, a pleasure to speak with you, John." She turned expertly to the cameras. "We're thrilled to have John Brennan as our featured guest on this edition of *Titans Tell All*. First, let's get the audience caught up on how you started the company in your parents' basement and built it up into a multibillion-dollar enterprise." She let film roll on John's background and his rise as a tech titan. The film wrapped up and Kate commenced with her questions. "John, can you tell the audience what gave you the idea to start your company?"

The tech titan complied.

"Now, take us back to when you were first starting out. What were the main struggles you faced?" John Brennan frowned a little and gave a curt response.

Kate pressed on, ticking off the questions on her list. "You've had such success in building your business, John. What was the product that really made your company succeed and how did you go about developing it?"

"Really, Kate?" John Brennan sat back in his chair, arms crossed. He had a look on his face like he'd just drunk spoiled, clotted milk. "I came here all the way from Silicon Valley and this is what you're asking me. Seriously?"

Looking confused, Kate replied, "Why, John, I think viewers want to know the background of your thriving enterprise. What's wrong with that?"

"I'll tell you what's wrong with it. You asked me the exact same questions in the same order when you interviewed me two years ago. Just roll tape on that interview if you're going to rehash the same questions. I don't even need to be here." Sofia could swear she saw steam shooting out of John Brennan's ears.

Uncharacteristically flustered, Kate said, "For those members of our audience who aren't familiar with—"

The tech mogul cut her off. "Kate, you're a seasoned professional." Sofia noted he used the exact words Kate had used earlier. "You should know better than to ask me the same questions—questions I've already been asked in other interviews. I thought *Titans Tell All* was supposed to be a fresh take on titans with a vision into their future, not a recap of their company history." Sofia noted that John Brennan also used her exact words. He barked, "Do you have anything new to ask me? Did you actually prepare for this interview?" Kate's eyes grew wide and she drew back with a start.

Sofia and Graham both sat there in shock. This interview was disintegrating before their eyes and with it, perhaps, the future of *Titans Tell All*. In all the years she'd been watching Kate Frost on TV, Sofia had never seen Kate lose her cool or get flustered...until now. She silently prayed that Kate would somehow get things back on track.

As Kate held the printout of her interview questions in her trembling hand, it fluttered like a dying bird trying to flap its wings once more. She stammered, "I, um, John, I must apologize. I certainly didn't mean to…" Her face fell. Kate knew she'd blown the interview. But to her credit she made a stunningly quick recovery. "Of course, you're absolutely right, John. Let's not waste any more time with questions you've already answered. Sofia has prepared some questions that I think truly reflect the tenor of what we want to cover in this interview."

Kate looked pleadingly at Sofia, the tension showing up as a knotted vein on her temple. Tentatively Sofia took her list of interview questions from her stack of papers and pushed it toward Kate, assuming she'd want to continue leading the interview. Kate shook her head. "No, Sofia, you did all the hard work, go ahead." She gave Sofia an encouraging smile.

Sofia paused for a nanosecond—was this another setup? Still, she said, "Okay," obligingly and launched into her questions. "John, how will the proliferation of artificial intelligence impact either the design or manufacturing of your products?"

The tech mogul smiled at the first question. "Now, that's a thought-provoking question, Sofia"—John Brennan nodded—"and something I'd really like to discuss." Sofia proceeded with the interview and at the end of the show they concluded with a conversation among the four of them about the future of the technology business. By then John Brennan was relaxed and all smiles.

*

When the show wrapped the tech titan thanked Sofia for her insightful questions and he turned to Kate. "Great to see you again, Kate. No hard feelings, right?" He seemed to gloss over their uncomfortable on-air exchange. Kate smiled and thanked him again for coming on the show, even managing to joke around with him a little.

Sofia and Graham didn't dare say a word and started to gather up their belongings. As they were about to walk out of the studio, they heard a voice.

"Sofia. Graham. How about getting a coffee together?" Sofia turned to look at Kate, who had a sincere and hopeful expression in her eyes. Was she trying to make amends? "Or a cocktail," she added. "After that interview I could use a drink. My treat. How about it?"

Graham remained silent, waiting to follow Sofia's lead. Sofia replied cautiously, "Okay, Kate. Let me grab my coat and purse and we can meet in the lobby."

Though he seemed reluctant, Graham said, "All right." After all their aggravating interactions with Kate Frost, it was clear he wasn't a big fan.

"Great, I'll get my driver to run us over to the bar." Kate flashed a shy smile.

*

The closest bar to the CNBC studios was about a ten-minute drive away. The three of them entered and found a corner table. The place was clean but had a faint odor of stale beer and fried food. After receiving their drinks, Kate turned to Sofia. "I'd like to say something. I owe you an apology, Sofia. I'm sorry. You were right and I didn't listen to you. I realize now that you were just trying to help me."

Sofia raised her eyebrows in surprise. It must have taken a lot of guts for Kate to say that, and Sofia felt the right thing to do was to make it easier on her. "We all make mistakes sometimes, Kate. Apology accepted, no worries." She gave Kate a genuine smile.

"No, no. It's not that simple." Kate took a sip of her vodka soda and shook her head. "I'm a seasoned broadcaster but I'm still the new kid on the block at this network and on this show. I was eager to show what I could do, but I went about it the wrong way. Completely. Instead of working with you guys as a team I tried to be the one to outshine you.

Maybe it's my insecurity about my age, I don't know. I feel like older women in broadcasting are continually having to prove our worth to the network when we're put up against shiny new faces. I think it just got the better of me. I'd really like to just start fresh, if you'll allow me."

Graham gave her a sympathetic look. "I'll drink to that." He lifted his beer glass.

Sofia raised her glass of red wine. "Here's to a fresh start."

The three reporters clinked glasses and then Kate unexpectedly began to giggle. "Did you see how mad John Brennan got? I thought he was going to blow a gasket. He's famous for his temper, you know." She leaned closer.

"I swear I saw steam coming out of his ears during the interview," Sofia said.

The three of them shared a laugh. Kate called out to the waitress, "Miss, another round, please." People trickled into the pub for Friday-night happy hour and the air was buzzing with the sound of laughter— relief that the work week was over. Kate turned to her colleagues. "Are you guys hungry? Why don't we order some food?"

Sofia knew that Kate had a gala event that evening that she was dying to attend, but here she was sitting in a local pub relaxing and having drinks and nibbles with them. Their former nemesis conversed with them at a leisurely pace. While Kate hadn't been that communicative with her colleagues in the past, the fact that she was giving up an exclusive social event to spend time building a relationship with Sofia and Graham spoke volumes about her. And it was a good message.

*

Days later, Chloe ran into her office. "Sofia, you're needed to help with an emergency."

Sofia looked up from her computer. "What's going on, Chloe?"

"Kate Frost is guesting on another CNBC show and she's on air shortly. But her assistant, Jenny, who normally preps her, is trapped in an elevator that's stuck between floors. The tech guys said Kate is asking for you."

"Me? She's asking for me?" Sofia jumped up. "Okay, where?" Maybe Kate wanted Sofia's ideas on another interview?

"I'm supposed to get you to go to Kate's dressing room pronto," Chloe said.

Sofia rushed out of her office and headed for the stairs. Taking the steps two at a time, she bounded up two flights. She raced down the hall, dodging people like they were gates in a slalom course, and arrived breathless at Kate's dressing room. One of the tech guys stood outside, and he let out a huge sigh of relief.

"Thanks for coming, Sofia." He held up a microphone pack. "We need you to put this mic pack on Kate's bra strap in the back, but she has some kind of complicated dress and only wants help from you."

Sofia's face fell a little. This was what she'd raced up here for? To prep Kate's microphone pack? This hardly seemed like the type of thing that required Sofia's skills or attention. Was Kate back to her old antics? Resignedly, she knocked on the door.

Opening it a crack, Kate peeked out. "Oh, Sofia, you've saved the day. Thanks so much for coming." She opened the door and let Sofia in and then closed it. Kate was wearing a navy blue wrap dress and a pained look on her face. "It's my fault for picking such a complicated dress today, but I need help getting the mic pack on—would you mind?"

Kate turned her back toward Sofia. She untied her dress and hesitated for a moment, then let the fabric drop from her shoulders to down around her waist.

What Sofia saw on her colleague's back was jolting. Kate's back was covered in a horrific network of red, protruding eye-shaped scars. She sucked in a quick breath but said nothing. Sofia quickly grasped that Kate would have been too mortified to let the tech guy see this—that was why her assistant, Jenny, always prepared her boss for broadcasts.

This was probably the first time someone other than Jenny was seeing this aspect of Kate Frost. Sofia snapped back to attention, quickly got the mic pack affixed to Kate's bra strap, and helped pull the fabric of the dress back up over her colleague's shoulders. "All set," she said brightly, and patted Kate's shoulders.

"Thanks for your help, Sofia." Kate retied the dress and turned to face her.

Sofia opened the door and was about to leave when Kate stopped her. "Wait...can I ask you—" Her eyes held a raw look that Sofia would never forget—it was mixture of anguish and helplessness, like someone who'd been hurt too many times.

She gently put a hand on Kate's forearm and squeezed it. "Don't worry, Kate, you can trust me." Sofia gave her a warm smile.

Kate exhaled in relief with a weary look in her eyes. "I appreciate your discretion, Sofia."

As Sofia turned to leave, she bumped into LoCo standing in the hall right outside the open door. They'd just overheard the exchange and seen Kate Frost tying up her dress and closing the door.

Lorrie said, "Oh, Sofia, I see you were just having a little visit with Kate Frost?" She exchanged sneers with Cordelia. Could these two women be any more annoying? Her assistant, Chloe, had warned Sofia that they suspected her of being a lesbian. The encounter they had just witnessed would only add fuel to the fire they were certainly spreading.

"Just helping a friend," Sofia said curtly, and walked away.

*

The following Friday evening Andi and Grace were over at Sofia's place for cocktails and their weekly Smashers Skype call with Vivien. Their friend was slugging it out with men who didn't want an industry outsider, especially a female, in their midst. Vivien shared just some of her recent challenges and the four Smashers commiserated over their trying work experiences, with Andi and Vivien competing for last place. Just the previous night Sofia had been at a work function and happened to see Vivien's fiancé, Clay, having drinks with his ex—she subtly asked Vivien to call her so she could let her know.

After they hung up with Vivien the three of them ordered in food for delivery, opened another bottle of red wine, and hung out. Sofia was leaving for Madrid the next morning. Before getting ready for bed, Sofia texted Jasper and let him know she was arriving on Saturday evening and that she'd be staying at a hotel in the center of town for a few days. Her parents lived in a beautiful home in the suburbs of Madrid and she'd join them for the holiday and the weekend. *Looking forward to seeing you in la villa del Oso y el Madroño.* With the six-hour time difference Sofia didn't expect to hear from him immediately, but surely he'd respond by morning, right?

*

Sofia spent Monday morning shopping, met a friend for *la comida*— the big midday meal—took a stroll, and was heading back to her hotel in the afternoon. She checked her phone again. When she'd landed on Saturday she'd received a noncommittal text from Jasper. *Would be great to see you, Sofia. Let me figure out my schedule.* But since then nothing. Sofia was starting to feel more anxious about seeing Jasper and fretful that this chance would pass them by. For the first time in a long while she was interested in a man, but he wasn't pursuing her like most guys did.

She rounded the corner, and as she was passing an outdoor café two doors down from her hotel she noticed a cute guy sitting there talking on the phone. Jasper Frank! He looked up and saw Sofia standing there and waved, then quickly finished up his call and rushed over to her. He gave her a strong embrace and Sofia felt a delicious tingle down her spine.

"I just finished up my work for the day. Are you free, Sofia?" Jasper winked.

Sofia gave a shy smile. "I am. Actually, I was going to check out the Museo Nacional Centro de Arte Reina Sofía."

He shook his head. "Naw, forget that. I've got somewhere even better. Ready for an adventure?" He held out the crook of his arm for her to take. Sofia sucked in a breath like a balloon filling with the promise of love, and away they went.

*

COOP

Coop was huffing and puffing on the brisk walk back to the office from a client meeting in midtown. He held his cell phone to his ear, careful not to knock any oncoming pedestrians in the head with his elbow. "Being a partner is not all it's cracked up to be," Coop sighed over the phone to Vivien. He stood at a corner on Sixth Avenue waiting for the light to turn.

Vivien gave a little chuckle. "It's a rude awakening when you realize the goal you've been working toward isn't exactly what you expected. So what's the rub?"

"I'm just finding that a lot of the other partners are really closed-minded. At our office partners' meeting yesterday I made a suggestion to increase the frequency of work quality reviews on our accounts. That way we can consistently deliver the high-quality accounting services we tell clients that we deliver. It also gives us a chance to catch any mistakes or problems early."

"Makes sense to me. What was their response?"

Coop let out a puff of air. "Let's just say I went in asking for the world and I came out with Rhode Island. The other partners don't want someone constantly looking over their shoulders."

"Coop, you know if you're unhappy there you can always leave. You're a partner now. Who says you have to stay at that firm?"

This was the dilemma. He knew his friend was always in his corner, but when he complained about his work situation Vivien would actually expect him to take some action.

"Oh god, I can't quit after being a partner for only a couple of months! That would be crazy. Wouldn't it?" Coop entered the revolving doors to his office building and headed to his elevator bank. "But, on the other hand, if this is what it's going to be like for the rest of my career…I don't want to be sixty years old and realize, 'Hey, this sucks!'"

"You've earned the title, Coop, no one can take that away from you. Now you're free to do whatever you want. I always say play by the rules until you reach the point where you can make your own rules. If that firm isn't the right place for you, go do something else with your skills."

He rushed in, made it back to his office, and shut the door. "But, what would I do? I'm not like you, Vivi, you're a risk taker. I'd never quit my job without having something else lined up."

"I'm just saying you need to ask yourself what you'd rather be doing, Coop. We spend too much of our lives working; we might as well choose to do something we're passionate about."

"You're right, you're right. I promise I'll think about it. But first I need to get through all the work that's piled up on my desk before Thanksgiving." Coop surveyed the stacks of files. He prided himself on being a good soldier and a hard worker but he was the first to admit he'd easily let work seep into every unfilled crevice of his free time.

Vivien cautioned him. "Just don't get so caught up in the day-to-day stuff that you let the bigger issues go unresolved. 'Life is like riding a bicycle—in order to keep your balance you have to keep moving.' Albert Einstein said that. You've gotta keep moving forward, making progress, if you want a great life."

Coop chuckled. "It's hard to move forward when you don't know exactly what to do." He rubbed the back of his stiff neck. "I want a great life, I just need to figure out how to get it."

"Coop, life is what you do next."

"I like that quote. Who said that?"

Vivien snorted. "I did, Coop."

"Oh, look at the time. I have a ton of stuff to finish and then I have a hot date tonight. At least I hope he's hot, it's a blind date! Anyway, it's a Monday night, so if it's going terribly I'll just cut it short and say I have an early meeting in the morning."

They said goodbye and Coop turned his attention to finishing his tasks. He grabbed his belongings, stuffed them into his computer bag, and dashed out the door.

*

It had been ages since his last date so Coop was looking forward to meeting the guy Patrick Ellis had mentioned. Coop had tried to do some recon but could find little information on his blind date, Brad, and certainly no pictures. They had had a fun and flirty email exchange and Brad had come across as intelligent and witty. Coop took a deep breath as his fingers closed around the cold iron door handle of the Chelsea restaurant they were meeting in. All he knew was that Brad had dark hair and blue eyes.

It took a moment for Coop's eyes to adjust to the dim light. After scanning the room, he saw a handsome man—probably a male model—sitting way in the back. Coop kept looking around for his date. He decided to take a seat at the bar and wait. He'd just ordered a drink when someone tapped him on the shoulder.

"Hi, are you Gary?" It was the handsome man. Guess he was on a blind date as well.

"I'm Coop, actually," he replied, and turned back to his drink.

"Gary Edward Cooper, like in your email address? Or Coop for short, I guess? It's you, isn't it?"

What? Was this gorgeous man actually his date? *Thank you, god!* "Um, yes, that's me. You're...Brad?" Coop asked tentatively.

A grin broke out across the gorgeous man's chiseled face. "I am. Good to meet you, Coop." He was even more magnificent close up. His skin looked like it was airbrushed, it was so perfect, and he had short, dark hair and incredible violet-blue eyes. *I could crack open a walnut on that strong jawline of his.* Coop had to catch himself from staring with his mouth open.

"Here, let me grab that for you so you can carry your drink." Brad took Coop's heavy computer bag and lifted it in a couple of fingers as if it were a shopping bag full of tissue paper. So chivalrous. Brad's well-defined bicep was visible even in his suit jacket.

As the two men walked back to the table that Brad had procured, Coop's heart skipped a beat. Over a few drinks and then some food, they got acquainted, with plenty of laughing and flirting along the way. Brad was mesmerizing. And he was clearly in fantastic physical shape given his job as a Secret Service agent. Coop had to stop himself from mentally undressing his date. He couldn't believe he was sitting there talking to this beautiful man.

Probably the best thing about their conversation was Brad's many questions about Coop—his job, his promotion to partner, his family, how he came out, etc.

"Tell me, Coop, why did you decide to become an accountant?" Brad put his chin in his palm and leaned forward.

"You really want to know?" Brad nodded sincerely. God, this guy was dreamy. "It was because of my father." Coop made a sour face.

"He inspired you to become an accountant?" Brad jiggled his glass in the air to signal for the waitress to bring him another.

"Indirectly, yes. And my specialty is actually forensic accounting, kind of like being a financial detective." Coop took a breath. "When I was a senior in high school I came home one day and my mom pulled me into the living room. I knew she wanted to talk about something serious because we were never allowed in the living room unless we were having company. She was shaking and her eyes were filled with tears. She told me that my father was having an affair with a woman from his advertising agency and they were running off to Florida to get married. He was abandoning her and our family and leaving us with pretty much nothing, financially, just the house."

"Well, that's just awful," Brad murmured as the waitress brought him another drink.

Coop's jaw was set firmly. "As the oldest of nine kids I had to quickly figure out how to help my mom and to take care of my brothers and sisters. My mom, who was trained as an engineer, had to return to work for a defense company. I and my older siblings got part-time jobs to help out. But I had this unsettling feeling—my father had supposedly accumulated all this wealth over the years working for the ad agency, yet he was giving nothing to his family? He was expecting us to survive on our own? That didn't sit well with me."

He looked at his date, whose intense gaze made Coop feel like the only person in the world.

"To make matters worse, I'd been accepted at Cornell but because of the change in our financial circumstance, I had to do my freshman year of college at Rutgers instead. And I had to live at home. During my first semester, every night when I came home, I dug through all the boxes of my father's files in the basement and scoured all his financial statements, computer files—basically everything I could get my hands on. I put together an updated schedule of all his assets, so when my mom walked into the courtroom for the divorce proceedings she and her lawyer were prepared to ask for a much bigger settlement. And they got it." While attending Rutgers should not have diminished his pride in any way, Coop's lifelong desire to attend an Ivy League school had been put on hold because of his father's stingy nature—it still nagged at him to this day.

Brad took a couple of sips of his tequila and looked pensive. "So, ultimately, it was the experience of your father trying to pull a financial fast one on your family and your ability to solve the problem that attracted you to the field of forensic accounting. Wow, what a story, Coop!" Brad's look of admiration made him feel as if he were over six feet tall.

Coop smiled. The divorce settlement that he'd helped his mother obtain had allowed him to transfer to Cornell his sophomore year and paid for college for all his siblings. In a strange twist of fate that could only happen in real life, his mom had ended up rekindling a romance with her high school sweetheart named Jim Cooper, and when they married she didn't even have to change her last name. With his big heart and joie de vivre, Jim was embraced by the Cooper siblings, who came to call this kind man their true dad.

This date was going great, and the fact that Brad was genuinely interested in getting to know Coop as a person was a refreshing change. Coop had felt jaded by the Chelsea gay dating scene—he'd been in too many clubs where a guy would give him the once-over and then brusquely move on before any conversation. Brad shared that he grew up just outside of Pittsburgh and in the past year he'd come out to his family and friends, but no one at work knew about his personal life. He lived in Washington, DC, and enjoyed his job on the Secret Service detail for Falcon.

"Falcon? Is that some sort of clandestine government agency?" Coop giggled.

Brad's eyes held a look of amusement. "It's the code name for the vice president of the United States." He sat back and seemed to enjoy Coop's bug-eyed expression.

"Does that mean that you're packing heat?"

Brad laughed. "Actually, Coop, no one really says that. I do carry a sidearm, a SIG Sauer P229, when I'm on active duty. My work brings me to New York frequently…which means possibly a chance to spend more time with you?" Brad gave a shy smile. *His dimples are adorable.* Coop nodded in the affirmative.

By the time their conversation wrapped up and he looked at his watch, Coop realized it was nearly midnight—their date had lasted five hours, a first-date record! They exchanged mobile numbers and made plans to get together for dinner on Wednesday night before Thanksgiving. Coop's head was swirling in his excitement and a tiny thought started to bubble up from deep in his brain…could Brad be *the one?*

*

"Coop, how are you, my friend?"

He turned to identify the source of the friendly voice and was stunned to see Felix Culo walking briskly down the hall to catch up with him. "How are you enjoying being a partner so far? Pretty great, eh?" Felix asked and answered his own question.

"Thanks, Felix. So far, so good." Hmm, something was different about Felix. What was it?

"And your big new office, how are you liking that? The view is even better from the upper floors, isn't it?" That was an understatement. Coop's previous office was an internal one with no windows, so he'd never even seen the light of day from inside, like a mole inhabiting a dark tunnel. "Say, do you have a minute? Let's go to my office for a quick chat."

Coop nodded cautiously. Felix had never been this friendly to him. Was he finally accepting of Coop now that he was a partner? Now he realized what was different—Felix was smiling at him for the first time in—well, ever. It was the day before Thanksgiving; maybe Felix was in a festive mood.

This was a maiden voyage for Coop, as he'd never been invited to Felix's office before. He looked around at the many framed photos on the bookshelves of Felix with clients at banquets, golf tournaments, and hunting events. There was even one of Felix with the CEO of Hello TelCo at the Super Bowl—that was certainly chummy. Rumor had it that Felix had been married and divorced twice, so perhaps that explained the absence of any family photos. On his massive desk was a silver bowl full of pistachios, and nut shells were scattered on his desktop. "Have a seat, Coop. Got something I want to show you." Felix gestured to one of the large leather club chairs in the sitting area. From the corner of his office he retrieved a wooden crate that had already been pried open. Felix lifted out one of the bottles and blew off the ancient film of dust coating the bottle.

"Take a look at this beauty." Felix cradled the bottle lovingly, like it was a newborn. "A 1995 Château Petrus Bordeaux blend. Guess what it's worth, Coop. Go on, take a guess."

Coop shrugged, smiling a little. "I don't really know that much about French wine, Felix."

Felix held up three fingers with pursed lips and raised eyebrows.

"Three hundred dollars?" Coop asked feebly.

Felix scoffed. "Try three *thousand*, my friend. Yup, three G's for each one of these babies. But the holy grail for me is a 1947 Cheval Blanc St. Emilion. The price tag on that bottle is one hundred thirty-five thousand big ones."

Good grief, what idiot would waste that much on one bottle of wine? That's more than what I paid for graduate school. Coop just replied, "Wow, Felix." He was starting to wonder why Felix had asked him into his office and why he was showing him this insanely expensive wine.

"So, why am I showing you this, you might be wondering." Felix sat down in one of the club chairs. "This, all this"—he spread his arms wide—"could be yours. You could have an incredible life just like mine, Coop. As partners we're all in this together. We've got to work together, cooperate, do what is asked of each other. Understand what I'm saying?"

Coop didn't really but he nodded anyway.

"Good, good." Felix gave him a look of approval. "Oh, by the way, Coop, there's a little item that the other partners wanted me to follow up on. We haven't received your partner buy-in check yet. In fact, you're the only new partner that hasn't submitted it yet. I'm sure it was just an oversight, but can you get that done today, buddy?"

Aha. So that explained the extra friendly tone in Felix's voice. Coop had not written the $300,000 check to the firm yet and would have to completely empty out his checking account to do so. It wasn't something he felt comfortable doing, but in the past week he'd gotten several email reminders, a text from Martin, and two voice mails from Barbara Pat Kelly in HR about this very topic. Was that what all this was about?

He gave a weary look to Felix. "Sure, I'll submit it by end of day."

"That'd be great, Coop, just great. Maybe we'll have a chance to crack one of these babies open sometime soon." Felix patted him on the shoulder and walked away to store his wine back in the crate, then sat down at his desk to look at his computer screen. That was Coop's signal that their friendly exchange had come to an end.

Before leaving that evening Coop swung by Barbara Pat Kelly's office with the partner buy-in check in his hands. The head of HR was on the phone but saw Coop's check and motioned for him to leave it on her desk. As he did Barbara Pat gave him a trace of a smile. Coop walked out looking back forlornly at the check like a parent leaving their tearful toddler in day care for the first time. He let out a heavy sigh and then straightened his posture. At least he had a dinner date with Brad that evening to brighten his mood.

*

The two met for their date at a fancy seafood restaurant in Union Square. The hostess escorted them to their table with Brad behind her and Coop bringing up the rear. As they walked through the restaurant, something magical happened to Coop—people were turning to look at him, giving smiles of admiration. Were they bestowing their silent approval of them as a dashing gay couple?

Coop studied the situation a little more closely. No, in fact the people weren't smiling at him, they were smiling at his date. As Brad strolled along unawares, women and men turned to gaze at him, and upon seeing that degree of gorgeousness, they beamed instantly, as if Brad were human sunshine. This was a whole new world for Coop—the world of ultra-beautiful people and the special treatment they received. What must it have been like to have people respond to you in such a way everywhere you went? It was a startling revelation for Coop, who often walked into places unnoticed.

They were given a primo corner table on a slightly elevated platform. It was as if the hostess wanted to put Brad's face on display for all to see like a precious jewel in a glass case. Coop and Brad ordered drinks and were toasting each other when a middle-aged woman came over to their table. "Excuse me for interrupting, but I just wanted to tell you that you are a very attractive man. Very attractive." She nodded her blond head in approval. "Are you a model?"

Coop felt invisible. Brad was gracious. He blushed and said, "Thank you, ma'am. No, I'm not a model."

The woman wouldn't leave. "You should model. I mean it, you are such an attractive man."

"Thank you kindly," Brad replied.

By then the waiter had appeared and was tapping his foot impatiently until the woman took the hint and departed. He took Brad's food order carefully and made several suggestions on cuisine, laughing and flirting the whole time. For Coop he just jotted down what he ordered and said he'd be back. Again, Coop felt invisible.

The meal sped by and Coop continued to be mesmerized by Brad's sparkling violet-blue eyes and perfect smile. As they were wrapping up another great conversation, the waiter came by with the check. "How would you like to handle the bill? Split it on two cards?"

Coop said, "No, it's my treat, Brad. You can pick up the tab on our next date."

"Thanks a lot, Coop."

"Date?" the waiter said incredulously. "You're on a date? I assumed it was a business dinner." He stared at Brad as he absentmindedly took the small leather check presenter back with Coop's credit card. "My mistake," he murmured.

As they left the restaurant Coop noticed they walked the same gauntlet of gawkers. The entire waitstaff and the hostess all beseeched them (i.e., Brad), "Please, come again. We hope to see you soon!" It was an alien experience for Coop but he smiled, satisfied in the knowledge that he was the one walking out with Brad. But in the back of his mind a troubling thought was forming. *Am I really comfortable being Mr. Cellophane?*

*

GRACE

It was just like old times. Grace and Andi were sitting in Sofia's living room having their weekly Friday Smashers' gathering, although Vivien was joining virtually via Skype. It was the week before Thanksgiving and the four women recapped their week, listened to each other's struggles, and supported each other. Out of the four of them, Andi had had the worst week.

Trying to lighten the mood a bit, Grace introduced the concept of WAFWOT to the Smashers.

"WAFWOT?" Andi half laughed. "What on earth is that?"

Grace gave a mysterious smile. "When I was a freshman in high school my guidance counselor strongly urged me to try out for the varsity cheerleading squad. He thought it would make me more well-rounded on my college applications. So I did and ended up being the first freshman ever to make the squad."

"Good for you, Grace," Sofia said and gave her friend a pat on the arm.

"At first I was thrilled. But I soon realized that the other cheerleaders, all older than I, were very different from me. My family didn't have a lot of money and, well, I didn't have the right brand of jeans or cute shoes like the other girls. It was obvious I didn't fit in. The other cheerleaders made catty comments about my worn-out clothes and they'd exclude me from the social gatherings they'd have after the games." Grace closed her eyes tightly for a moment, as if she were trying to squeeze the memory out of her brain. "At that time I only owned two pairs of jeans and I'd have to wash them during the week so I could wear them again. One Friday I was standing in front of my locker and a couple of cheerleaders stopped in the hall to speak to me. One of them, Debbie, said loudly in front of everyone, 'Grace, didn't you wear those same exact jeans on Monday? That's so gross!' The other cheerleader, Barb, shrieked, 'Ewww!' I was mortified."

"What a bunch of jerks!" Andi scowled.

Grace continued. "My best friend, Evelyn, was right there, and she slammed my locker shut and dragged me away from those girls. When I told her I was thinking I should quit the squad, Evelyn said, 'Don't let those girls win. Show them you're better than they are.' That was her simple advice. After that I made sure that I was the most energetic, peppy, smiling cheerleader out on the field. But Evelyn also gave me a gift—a pair of sweatpants with the letters WAFWOT emblazoned across the butt. 'For your cheerleading practices.' I said, 'Thanks, Evelyn, but what's WAFWOT?' A sly smile came across her face. She said, 'It stands for "What a F-ing Waste of Time." Those girls have no right to treat you so poorly. This can be your silent protest when you're with those awful girls at practice.'" Grace let out a hearty laugh. "So I wore those WAFWOT sweatpants with defiance to every cheerleading practice."

"Didn't the other cheerleaders wonder what it meant?" Vivien said.

"Sure. But when the other girls asked what it stood for my reply was, 'Without Fail, Win One for the Team.' Those dimwitted cheerleaders blindly accepted my explanation without ever recognizing that the letters didn't quite match up."

The four women hooted with delight. "WAFWOT, that's a good one." Andi snorted.

*

The wooded trail was covered with a thick layer of white powder, and as snowflakes floated down gently around them, Grace and Win strapped on their cross-country skis. Since they were each spending Thanksgiving week with their families near Michigan's Upper Peninsula, they'd made plans to meet up for an active date. It was early in their relationship and they were keeping things under wraps, so this was the perfect venue. Out in the middle of nowhere, Grace was just happy to be outdoors, with Win, and away from prying eyes.

Win pulled his woolen beanie over his head and then held up a handful of loot—granola bars and a couple of blueberry yogurt containers along with plastic spoons. "We've got some sustenance in case we get hungry before dinner." He grinned his trademark high-wattage smile before stuffing the snacks into his backpack on top of their change of clothes. Then he pulled on his ski gloves.

"Thanks, Win." Grace raised an eyebrow at the yogurt containers, which were sealed with only a thin layer of foil on top. "Uh, you think the yogurt will be okay in the bag?" Her frosty breath hung in the frigid air. They were both bundled up in ski pants and jackets, goggles, and hats and gloves.

"Don't worry, darlin', I'm an expert at cross-country skiing." He gave her a wink.

"Alrighty," Grace said skeptically, and then aligned her skis in the tracks to start on the trail.

They started the uphill climb up the trail and managed to have a meaningful conversation despite all the huffing and puffing. They were about to reach the highest part of the trail when Grace's cell phone rang. Seeing it was the Burberry CEO, she shouted out to Win that she needed to take the call. Standing at the top of the hill, Grace chatted for a few minutes on her cell while Win waited patiently.

Gliding over to him after she finished talking, Grace said, "Sorry, Win, that was my boss, the Burberry CEO. She asked me to come in after Thanksgiving weekend to meet with her."

"Everything okay?"

Grace wiped her nose with the back of her ski glove. "Oh yes, I love working with her, she's a fantastic leader. Before my sabbatical we discussed what I wanted to do next, which is to run the Baby & Kids business. My boss set it up for me to move into that role when I come back. She probably wants to discuss the transition details."

Win gave her a nod of approval. "Grace, I had no idea that you wanted to run a business. That's so cool."

"It's been at the back of my mind for a while. And with my friend Vivien running a business at Smart Sports, I feel like my time has come as well. I'm really excited about it."

He moved closer to her. "Grace, is there anything you can't do? You're amazing— writing books, leading businesses, turning around brands." Win embraced her and gave her a sweet kiss.

Grace gazed into his sparkling blue eyes and melted like a dripping icicle in the strong winter sun. "Thanks, Win. You're not too bad yourself." She shifted her weight. "In fact, I think you're...whoa!" One of her skis had started to slip out from under her and she tried to jerk herself upright by grabbing Win's arms. He lurched forward to help her but somehow their skis got tangled up. They started sliding rapidly with Grace facing downhill and Win facing uphill, like a couple of alpine tango dancers racing down the slope. One of Grace's skis caught an edge and they began tumbling first as a single jumbled unit and then as two separate rolling objects. After a thirty-yard-long spill, they both came to a reeling stop.

Win shouted, "Yard sale! You all right, Grace?"

Both her skis were off and she'd lost her hat somewhere up the hill. Grace wiped the snow from her face and rushed over to him. "I'm okay, Win. How about you?" From his prone position he gave a thumbs-up. "Sorry, Win, I lost my balance. I'm just relieved that I didn't kill you!"

Win's laughter emanated from deep in his belly and soon the two of them were lying back in the snow cracking up. It took a while for them to collect their belongings, which were strewn all over the trail, and pull themselves together. By the end of their skiing expedition they were soggy and shivering, and their ski outfits were covered in debris.

*

They arrived for dinner at the fancy hotel restaurant where Grace had made a reservation. Win opened the backpack to pull out their clothes so they could make a quick change in the hotel restroom. But then his face grew ashen.

"What's the matter?"

"Um, have a look." Win tilted the backpack toward Grace so she could see inside the opening. In the course of their wipeout down the hill the yogurt containers had exploded, leaving a thick coating of bluish goo over everything—their clothes were unwearable. Her LBD was now a Little Blue Goo Dress. Win gave her a sheepish look.

"Yikes, must have been from the fall. Oh well, no matter." Grace wrinkled her nose. "I don't know if we can get into the restaurant dressed like this, though."

"Let's give it the old college try." He took her arm. "Anyway, it's the day before Thanksgiving—how busy could the restaurant possibly be?"

Strolling up to the host at the fancy French restaurant, the two of them looked a sorry sight. Grace explained that they had a dinner reservation but their clothes had been damaged, and she asked if they would still honor the reservation.

The host, a fussy-looking older man, gave an imperious look and sniffed. In a fake French accent he said, "We have a strict dress code here which we must enforce for the sake of our esteemed clientele."

"I understand," Grace said, "but you don't seem all that busy." She gestured to the sparsely populated tables. "Maybe we could sit somewhere in the back?"

Win leaned in confidently and flashed his movie star smile, chin down and eyes gazing upward. "Please, could you make an exception? Just this once?"

Either the host didn't recognize Win or he simply didn't care for actors. He puffed up his chest in a show of power. "No. You might find the casual bar off the lobby to be more suitable for your attire." With that the host scratched their reservation off, clicked his pen, and closed the reservation book with an air of finality.

Win blinked, unmoving. It probably wasn't often that he was treated so rudely.

"Come on, Win, let's eat in the bar. A cheeseburger and a beer sound good to me." Grace tugged his sleeve gently.

Inside the lively, dark bar, Grace and Win grabbed a table and ordered some grub. They had a fun, relaxed time and no one disturbed them. Except for the blueberry-yogurt-covered clothing and the attitude from the snooty restaurant host, this had been the perfect date.

*

Stepping back inside the gleaming, modern Burberry offices after the holiday weekend, Grace breathed in the exquisite scent of elegance. She straightened her posture and felt the thrill of walking the halls of such a venerable brand. The tasteful décor consisted of dark oak paneling, white marble floors, and smoked glass. Grace made her way around the office saying a quick hello to friends and colleagues before heading to the CEO's office.

Grace's boss, Celeste, gave her a warm hug and invited her into the sitting area of the office. Celeste was a smart, sophisticated woman who exuded culture and civility. She poured piping-hot tea into two china cups while Grace made herself comfortable on one of the large mouse-gray linen sofas. They sipped tea and caught up on how Grace's sabbatical was going, then Celeste dropped a bombshell. "Grace, I have some news. We are merging with Palazzo."

Grace's eyebrows shot up. "Seriously, Celeste? Oh my gosh." Palazzo was a behemoth combination of many Italian luxury brands and was over twice the size of Burberry.

"I know, it's hard to swallow. Palazzo's global CEO wanted to broaden their portfolio to include other European brands, and apparently Burberry has been on their shopping list for a while." She set down her cup and saucer. "This transaction also means that I will be leaving the CEO role. The board has hired a new CEO to handle the merger and run the combined businesses—a guy who was a rising star at JMC." She shrugged.

JMC? The huge manufacturer of household cleaning products, detergents, personal care products—what did packaged goods have to do with the luxury industry?

"Oh no, Celeste. What are you going to do?"

"I've been asked to join a media startup in Los Angeles as their CEO. It looks very promising, so I'm excited about it."

Grace's heart sank. Celeste was a great mentor and someone whom she'd admired. Who would be her new boss? What would he be like? She caught herself and forced a smile. "That sounds great, Celeste, congratulations."

Celeste's look brightened up. "I thought it would be good for you to meet the new CEO. He officially starts next week when they announce the merger, but he happens to be here today, so I wanted to make the introduction personally. Let me call him in. Would you excuse me?"

Bewildered, Grace nodded as Celeste got up and asked her assistant to call the new CEO.

The man who walked in looked like a packaged goods executive from central casting—he was tall and slim, with dark, short hair graying at the temples, and with oval horn-rimmed glasses. He wore a white-button down shirt, a navy sports coat, and dark slacks. He carried a thick leather portfolio.

Celeste looked up and smiled graciously. "Please, Skip, do come in. I'd like to introduce you to our chief marketing officer, Grace King. Grace, this is Skip Palmer, our new CEO."

Skip said hello, then the three of them sat down to chat. Celeste explained that Grace, who was instrumental in Burberry's turnaround, was on a sabbatical and writing a book on branding. "When Grace returns we plan to have her step into the role of GM of the Baby & Kids business. I know she'll do a marvelous job with the business, just as she's done with marketing. Skip, can we agree to keep to that plan?"

Skip wrinkled his forehead for a nanosecond. "Of course, Celeste. If that's something you already put in place, I'd be happy to honor it. From what I hear about the rebranding work, Grace is a superstar and we want to keep her happy. Right?" He flashed a grin.

Grace sat back in relief. "Thank you, Skip, I'm looking forward to working with you." After a few more minutes of small talk, Grace sensed that the two CEOs wanted to move on to their agenda, so she said a quick goodbye and gave Celeste a hug. They promised to keep in touch.

*

Leaving the midtown headquarters, Grace practically pranced down Madison Avenue despite her high heels and surprise at the merger. She was about to publish a book, and when she returned to work she'd be able to realize her career aspiration of running a business.

Her cell phone buzzed and she saw it was Venky from Flip Style.

He and Tom had been executing the relaunch strategy for their hair-care business that Grace had helped them with, much to the chagrin of their head of strategy, Preston Ford. A big shift was moving from wholesale to direct selling—she'd pushed for this so Flip Style could control their narrative and develop one-to-one relationships with their consumers. So far the plan was yielding better-than-expected results, along with tremendous buzz from the brand relaunch plan Grace had created. Venky and Tom asked her to meet with them so they could review the results and fine-tune the execution. They were effusive with their praise and clearly appreciative of the value she'd added. Elated, Grace wrapped up her call as she entered the coffee shop where she was meeting Simone Everett.

Simone waved her over excitedly. "Grace, you'll never guess what happened."

Grace slid into the booth. "Tell me, tell me."

The actress poured out all of the information in a single enthusiastic breath. "Have you seen the number of hits we've gotten on our *Wealth Whisperer* podcasts? They've gone viral since the launch a couple of weeks ago. Who knew that a video podcast on personal financial health could be that popular!"

Grace laughed and rubbed her hands together in glee. "Simone, this is awesome! I'm sure that getting practical financial tips from a smart and multitalented woman like you is a huge draw. Something that makes the podcasts real is that you talk about the mistakes you've made, so I think that adds a touch of humanity. Besides, who wants to watch some old dudes on CNBC?" Grace joked.

Simone leaned forward and squeezed Grace's forearm. "There's more. I got a call today from a casting director and they want me to audition for a part in a cool new miniseries. It's about a successful, smart female entrepreneur who doubles as a secret agent—and the pilot is slated to start filming in London this spring. Can you believe it, Grace? I mean, after all this time away from the business they're actually considering me for the lead on a series. I have to fly to LA next week for the audition. Isn't it incredible?"

Grace beamed. "Simone, I didn't think my day could get any better, but it just did. You're going to kill it in that audition, I just know it." Both of her rebranding case studies were on a clear path to success—if this continued she'd be able to wrap up writing her rebranding book with pizzazz.

*

ANDI

When the jumbo jet's wheels touched down on the Parisian tarmac and the brakes screeched, Andi sat up, alert and energized for her client meeting. Her boss, Lester, was taking a flight to Paris from a meeting in Tokyo, so the plan was to rendezvous at the hotel and meet for dinner to sketch out their meeting strategy for the next day. That evening they'd be dining with some of their private banking colleagues from Kaneshiro Bank's Paris office to get the lay of the land and generate ideas for their new client.

Over dinner Lester was focused on meeting prep and consulted Andi for her thoughts on investment vehicles for their new client. Their two French colleagues, both with heavily accented but proficient English, added their perspective, and they all enjoyed a delectable meal and fruitful discussion.

The following day was a whirlwind. The meeting with François-Henri Pinault went better than they could have imagined, with Lester letting Andi take the lead on the discussion. She listened carefully to the client's needs and goals and then presented her creative solutions, to which Monsieur Pinault was highly receptive. Then and there he agreed to sign on as a client. Lester was so pleased he suggested they cap off the day with a special team dinner.

Elated with the success of the trip so far, Andi felt her sense of optimism restored when it came to her work situation. She was about to lead a major new client relationship, plus Lester had shown confidence in her and they were working well together. Since she had some free time to kill before dinner, Andi explored the shops and side streets along the Champs-Élysées, stopping at a toy store for some gifts for Antonio and Francesco. Andi made a special stop at Ladurée to purchase an obscenely large box of colorful macarons to satisfy Luca's sweet tooth.

She returned to the hotel to drop off her packages and quickly change for dinner. The team dinner was taking place at the exclusive Guy Savoy restaurant, one of the most coveted dining experiences in Paris. When Andi arrived at the restaurant, she took in the understated but glamorous setting—a dark-paneled dining room with soft, elegant lighting and a spectacular view overlooking the Seine. The hostess led her to a special table near an open window—it was so romantic a setting she could only imagine the number of marriage proposals made there. Lester sat waiting for her. Alone.

"Good evening, Andi," he said, smiling. "Awesome day, eh?"

"Hi, Lester." Andi's eyes scanned around the restaurant. "I thought we were having a team dinner. Where are the other guys?"

Her boss waved his hand. "They couldn't make it tonight so it's just the two of us. This is one of the top restaurants in Paris, so I'm sure we'll manage to have a fine celebration dinner without them. Right?" Lester had dressed up for dinner and looked dashing.

Andi's heart rate sped up but she collected herself and forced a smile. "Of course, Lester."

Lester ordered a bottle of Billecart-Salmon Brut Rosé champagne to kick things off, and they clinked glasses to celebrate acquiring their newest client. Lester kept the conversation light and upbeat, talking about Paris and his favorite places to visit. As the sumptuous meal began, beautifully plated, well-crafted dishes arrived at the table, and Andi allowed herself to relax and enjoy the amazing culinary experience. Lester ordered an exquisite bottle of Bordeaux. During her modest upbringing in a Mexican family, Andi had never imagined she'd be dining at one of the finest restaurants in the world, and she had to pinch herself at this unique experience. The wine and soft jazz music were helping to set Andi at ease.

By the time they finished dessert, Andi had loosened up and was sharing a few laughs with Lester. He gave her an intense look and leaned toward her. She was recounting the story about her twin boys and the jar of Vaseline when she felt a sensation that made her heart thud to a stop. Underneath the table, Lester's hand was on her leg, and he was sliding it up Andi's thigh like a slithering snake. A jolt of alarm ran through her like a thousand-kilowatt electrical current. Andi smacked Lester's hand away and pushed back from the table violently, causing the water and wine glasses to wobble and nearly slosh their contents onto the white linen tablecloth.

"Lester, don't do that! Don't touch me," she hissed.

Lester gave a devilish smile. "You need to just relax, Andi. We're in Paris, the city of lovers. Who says we can't have a little fun together?" His eyes stayed glued to her face as he ran his fingers through his light brown hair and ran his tongue over his lips.

Andi looked around the room and then gave him a stern look. "Look, Lester, I don't want that kind of relationship with you, let's keep things professional." She raised her voice in ire. "I'm married. Happily married."

He leaned toward her and put his hand on hers. "That's okay, I'm married, too. But I'm obsessed with you—you're beautiful and so damn sexy. You've bewitched me, Andi. I can't stop thinking about you, about the two of us together. I always get what I want and I've got to have you, Andi, whatever it takes." The intense expression in Lester's eyes conveyed that he was ready to devour her. "Just tell me we can be together."

Andi trembled, stupefied. "No, Lester. That is never going to happen."

He cocked his head and slumped back in his seat. Finally he gave a nod. "Understood." Lester summoned the waiter for the check and swiftly paid the bill. Andi told him she was going for a walk to clear her head…alone.

"Fine, fine. I've got to get back to the hotel." Lester had an odd expression in his eyes.

The November breeze was picking up a bit and Andi pulled her pashmina wrap tighter around her as she walked onto a bridge overlooking the Seine. She shivered with angst as she stared down at the dark water; the faint sound of accordion music drifted over the river in the wind. The day had gone so well, then Lester had pulled that stunt at dinner. What the heck? But she'd firmly given Lester the ixnay on any chance of an affair, and it seemed like he'd gotten the message. Letting out a sigh, Andi hoped they could put this nonsense behind them and focus on work.

When Andi got back to the hotel her brain felt heavy and dull from the jet lag. She opened the door to her suite, where the lights were dim and music was playing. Probably turn-down service trying to make the room more relaxing. Andi kicked off her heels and sauntered down the hallway. When she rounded the corner to the bedroom, the breath was knocked out of her. Draped across her king-size bed was Lester, wearing nothing but a bathrobe and a mischievous smile. The soft light on his hair gave him an undeserved halo effect. "I thought we could relax together, Andi." His voice was sultry.

It took Andi a moment to recover from the shock. "What the hell are you doing in my room?"

"Come over here, Andi. You look a little tense. Let me give you a massage." He patted the bed nonchalantly. "No one has to know about this."

Things were getting bizarre, and fast. She tossed her purse onto the table. "Lester, this is insane. Get out of my room. Now. I'm tired and I want to go to bed."

Lester cocked his head. "Can I watch you undress?"

"Number one, no. Number two, creepy." She was trying to keep her cool but was starting to panic about having her scantily clad boss in her room. Her heart was pounding out of her chest, while her eyes frantically scanned the room in search of a weapon.

"Stop being so coy, Andi. You know that having a good relationship with me can give your career a boost." He fingered his swelling crotch. She shuddered with revulsion.

"I'm not looking for that kind of boost, Lester. I want you to leave now."

He grinned. "You can't make me." Lester was a clean-cut, good-looking man—lying there on the bed, he could have been posing for a mattress ad.

Why did this kind of situation always happen to her? What should she do? Lester was about eight inches taller than her and certainly weighed a lot more than she did. She considered her options: Call security? Too slow. Call their firm's head of HR? Probably nothing would happen. Call Lester's wife? It was almost as if Lester were reading her mind, because what he said next was chilling. "You know, Andi, whatever happens in this room? It's your word against mine."

Something snapped inside her. That familiar old rage bubbled up like lava and Andi resolved she wasn't going to take this crap a minute longer. She wanted Lester out, no matter that he was her boss. Andi looked Lester straight in the eyes. "You know what, Lester? You're right about that. Give me a sec."

Lester gave her a satisfied smirk of conquest and relaxed back into the bed, expecting a more cooperative Andi to emerge shortly, hopefully sans clothing.

Andi ran into the bathroom and grabbed a garbage can, using it to prop open the door of her suite. Then she quickly moved back to the bedroom. Without a word, she wrapped each of her hands around Lester's ankles in a tight grip.

"Grrr, playing a little rough, eh? I like that." He growled playfully and pawed the air.

Suddenly Andi yanked him hard off the bed onto the carpeted floor. Stunned by Andi's swift action, he didn't have time to resist. She heard him say, "Wow, you're really strong," and "Ouch, I hit my head." Using her formidable strength, she dragged Lester across the slick marble floor, kicked open the door, and deposited him outside the door in a rumpled heap.

She leaned over him. "Never do that again."

He was still looking up at her, bewildered, as she slammed the door shut.

Her heart was racing and she sank to the floor to catch her breath.

Andi was left shaken and exhausted by the whole ordeal in Paris. That night she'd gone down to the hotel's front desk to change the keys to her door, bolted it from the inside, and propped a chair in front of the door for good measure. Still, she hadn't slept at all, somehow sure that Lester would find a way to sneak into her room in the middle of the night.

Thankfully, the next day Lester had a few more meetings in Europe scheduled, so that meant Andi could fly home on her own. She couldn't wait to get out of that city and kept glancing back over her shoulder nervously as she raced through Charles de Gaulle airport to make sure Lester wasn't shadowing her.

*

"Andi, that is crazy…and horrific! You poor thing." Vivien's eyes were wide on the computer screen as the Ceiling Smashers had their regular Friday evening Skype call together. The sheets of rain pelting the windows of Vivien's office in Portland were visible in the background.

Sofia topped off Andi's wineglass and sat down with her friends on the living room sofa. Sofia's laptop was propped up on a stack of art books on her coffee table. She put her arm around Andi. "Are you okay?"

Grace shook her head in disgust. "What a filthy creep. But it sounds like you kicked Lester's ass!"

Andi gulped her wine, then dropped her head back on the edge of the sofa, looking up at the ceiling. "Ugh, I can't believe this is happening to me. *Again.* I was thinking about leaving investment banking at some point, but now I've really gotta get the heck out of Dodge. This is even worse than the Finbar Fiasco."

At the mere mention of Finbar, Andi's three friends fell silent. It had been years since Andi had uttered that name, but the memory of her experience still felt all too fresh.

She was grateful when Grace steered the conversation in another direction. "You know what this is? A classic case of WAFWOT." In response to their quizzical looks, Grace explained the concept and its origin. "In other words, maybe it's time to leave, Andi, especially if you feel like you're wasting your time and your talent there."

Andi sat forward, cupping her chin in her hands. "Yeah, my mind's made up. I'm going to quit right after the holiday. Do you guys think I should tell Luca about all this stuff with Lester? I don't want to freak him out."

"Andi, Thanksgiving's coming up next week," Vivien said from the computer screen. "Maybe when you and Luca have a quiet moment over the break you can share it with him. And let him know you're quitting. If he knows you're going to leave the bank soon, he may not worry too much about the situation with your boss."

"Okay, that makes sense. You're still coming over for Thanksgiving dinner, right, Vivi?" Satisfied that she had a plan of action, Andi strengthened her resolve.

*

"Who wants more gravy? Francesco? Antonio?" Andi held the gravy boat aloft. Her twin boys, dressed in their little holiday suits, looked adorable—she smiled at them lovingly.

Their dining room was festive and packed with family and friends gathering together to celebrate Thanksgiving. The delectable scents of the holiday feast permeated the apartment and welcomed guests like a warm hug. Andi's doctor brother, Rene; his wife; and their three boys were joking around with her sons, who, thankfully, were back to their healthy, happy selves. Rene, dressed in a suit, was of medium height and slim, with short, jet-black hair and warm brown eyes. His ready smile, quick wit, and calming manner made him a favorite among his patients. Rene's wife was a skillful lawyer with a short, dark pixie haircut and a bubbly personality. Their boys were carbon copies of their parents. Also joining the celebration were Vivien and her father, Dr. Lee.

"Please, everyone, eat more turkey. I roasted an extra-large one, so we have plenty of food. Andi, darling, please pass the mashed potatoes," Luca said. From the bright expression in his eyes he was clearly reveling in the cheerful noise and the chaos of the holiday.

The lively banter and festive mood around the table made the meal merrier, and Luca was doing his best to make all the boys laugh with his silly jokes. Since their early days of dating, one of the things Andi had enjoyed about her husband was his goofy sense of humor. He took the huge platter of mashed potatoes from Andi and set it down in front of him to scoop some onto his plate. Luca looked over at Andi and gave her a wink. Then he sat straight up, paused for a moment, and made an "aaaahhh" sound. With that Luca's head flopped facedown into the mashed potato platter.

The five little boys around the table hooted with laughter. Antonio and Francesco could barely contain their giggles as they pointed to their dad.

Exasperated, Andi said, "Honey, what on earth are you doing?"

Her husband continued to lie face down in the potatoes, not moving...for a little too long.

"Stop goofing around, Luca." He remained still. Suddenly Andi sensed something was wrong. "Luca?" She hurried over to her husband. When she slowly pulled him upright, his eyes were closed and his face was covered in a sticky potato mask, which Andi wiped off with her napkin. He was unresponsive.

Her brother Rene jumped up and rushed over. "Luca, can you hear me? Are you okay?" He shook Luca's shoulders firmly.

Luca's eyes opened and he looked around, confused. Then he tried to smile.

Half of Luca's face drooped down like melted wax—it looked like some sort of hallucinatory Salvador Dalí painting. Andi stepped back in shock. "Holy shit, Luca, what happened to your face?"

Antonio whispered, "Ooh, Mama said a bad word."

Luca's hand went up to touch his face and his eyes were wild with confusion. When he tried to speak his voice came out muffled and slow. "My ff-face, it ff-feelf kind of fweird." Only the left half of his lips moved. The left half of his face was normal; the right half seemed frozen and looked about an inch lower—like Luca was wearing a grotesque Halloween mask.

"Daddy!" Francesco screamed, and covered his eyes with his tiny hands. Rene's wife scooped him up and cuddled the frightened child in her lap.

The rest of the people around the table sat in stunned silence.

"It's okay, everyone." Rene's voice was soft and soothing. "Here, Luca, let me take a look." He gave a kind smile to Luca as he examined him carefully.

Andi's heart was pounding, and a wave of panic started to wash over her. She put her hand on her brother's arm. "Why is his face like that, Rene? What's wrong with him?"

Rene's face held a grave expression. "I think Luca has contracted Bell's palsy."

"Bell's palsy? What is that?" Andi demanded.

"It's when the facial muscles on one side of your face are paralyzed," Vivien said in a quiet voice with a worried look in her eyes. "A client of mine had it."

*

Vivien had first heard of Bell's palsy while working on a consulting project years before for a client in Pennsylvania.

A woman on the client's team named Juliet, a former beauty queen a few years older than Vivien, had apparently been struck during her sleep, waking up in the middle of the night to find that half her face was immobile. Her doctor had urged her to continue to work because using the facial muscles regularly would speed the recovery process. It was heart-wrenching to see this beautiful woman with such distorted features struggling to speak, but Vivien was in awe of Juliet's courage. She seemed to ignore people's stares and happily repeated whatever she was trying to say, seemingly undaunted. It took a huge effort, but within a year Juliet recovered fully.

Vivien prayed that Luca's condition wouldn't take that long to improve.

Andi looked at her brother. "Okay, so Bell's palsy. How do we fix it? Can Luca just take a pill or some kind of medicine?"

Her brother shook his head. "It's not like that, Andi. Bell's palsy comes on suddenly and there's no cure for it. It's usually connected with exposure to a virus, like chicken pox, mumps, measles, or the coxsackievirus."

"No cure?" Andi raised an eyebrow. "What did you say,

216

coxsackievirus? Hang on, that sounds familiar. I'm sure I've heard that before."

"It's the virus that causes hand, foot, and mouth disease in kids," her brother explained.

Andi brought her hands up to cover her mouth, her eyes wide in horror. "Oh my god. The boys had that not long ago. And Luca was taking care of them that entire time. He was definitely exposed to the virus."

Vivien sensed that further discussion in front of the children wasn't a good idea. "Um, Andi, why don't we move Luca to the master bedroom so he can rest?" Vivien and her dad stood up to assist Rene in moving Luca down the hall to a more comfortable, quiet place. This was all happening so fast. They got Luca to sit on the bed and Vivien gave his shoulder a gentle, supportive squeeze.

*

Dr. Lee shut the door behind him and Vivien, giving Rene, Andi, and Luca some privacy. Instead of lying on the bed, Luca immediately rushed over to the mirror and stared at his face in bewilderment. When he tried to smile, only half of his face moved. He put one hand up to cover the frozen side. His speech crawled out of his mouth, words slurred. "*Oddio!* I flook like a monfter. Fwhat can I do?" Luca flopped down on the bed in despair.

Rene's look darkened. He sighed. "I'm sorry, Luca, there's nothing you can do. Bell's palsy can last three months, six months, a year. It's caused by a virus, so there's no way to cure it. It just takes time."

"Are you saying his face is going to be freakin' frozen like that for potentially a year?" Andi asked, immediately realizing her insensitivity.

Her brother shot her a look as if to warn her not to get Luca more upset than he clearly was already. "It may not take that long and it usually does resolve itself." Rene put his hand lightly on Luca's back. "I'm so sorry, Luca. Just call me if you need anything."

Andi snorted in disbelief. She let Rene out of the room and then turned and looked tenderly at her husband, who was reclining on the bed. "Honey, why don't you just rest awhile. Let me take care of the boys and our guests and I'll come back and check on you. Okay?" She covered him with a thick bouclé blanket and kissed his forehead. Luca sank down further into the bed and pulled the blanket up over his face.

Andi left the bedroom and closed the door, leaning against it for support. She felt like someone had thrust their fist into her chest and was crushing her heart.

CHAPTER 7

January

GRACE

Tonight was the first time Grace would be going on a public date with Win Wyatt, and her breath was shallow with excitement. Judging from Win's compressed lips and pacing back and forth across her living room, he was a bit nervous as well. He had picked up Grace at her apartment for their dinner date and now he was scrutinizing her outfit. She wore a pale blue merino wool tunic with a silk Hermès scarf, and body-skimming jeans with cute furry boots.

"What's the matter?" Grace asked.

Win squinted. "Some friends of mine are having a cocktail party and I thought we could swing by before dinner. Maybe you could wear something more…sexy?"

The comment struck Grace the wrong way. She'd always been sensitive to remarks about her clothes and didn't appreciate having her attire critiqued by her date. Her stubbornness kicked in. "Win, if you want to go to the party before dinner, then we're running short on time." Then her practicality kicked in. "Also, it's freezing cold January weather outside, so I want to dress warmly. I think my outfit is fine, so let's just go, okay?"

Win seemed deep in thought but he snapped out of it and managed a smile. "Okay, Grace, okay. Let's get going."

They headed downstairs, where Win had a driver waiting for them.

Always the gentleman, Win opened the door for Grace to get in and then went around and got in the other side of the car. He gave the driver the address of the apartment building in TriBeCa where the party was being held. They were having dinner in SoHo, so it was all pretty close.

*

When they pulled up Win asked Grace to sit tight. He got out and ran around the car to open the door for her. She assumed it was kind of his thing and made him feel chivalrous. As Grace exited the car, Win held his hand out to help her. "Whose party is this anyway?" she said.

Win shrugged a little. "Just an old actor friend. Should be fun. We won't stay long." He avoided her gaze. Grace had to admit that he seemed a bit agitated.

The elevator opened up into a sophisticated loft apartment, which took up the entire floor. It was an intimate party and a few clusters of guests were scattered around the room. An efficient-looking young woman with round eyeglasses greeted them and took their coats. As they entered a man and a woman rushed over to hug Win. He quickly said, "Hey, guys. This is Grace; Grace, this is Warren and Tessa."

Grace recognized Warren—he was another actor—and his girlfriend Tessa was a fashion model. "Great to see you, bud! We should all get together sometime, have a double date." Warren winked at Grace.

Win seemed distracted, his eyes darting around the room. "Sure, sure. Give me a call. I'm just going to introduce Grace around." Grace smiled politely at the couple as she was whisked off to the next group.

Three women stood together by the brick fireplace and looked happy to see Win but seemed to view Grace as an intruder. They chatted excitedly to Win while ignoring Grace. After a few minutes one of the women leaned closer to him and said in a low voice, "I didn't think you'd actually come, Win. She's over there." She gestured to the corner of the room with a tilt of her chin.

Win grabbed Grace's hand and led her over with some urgency. He didn't say a word. A woman was sitting with her back toward them, facing the corner, talking in hushed tones to a cute dark-haired man. Win tapped her on the shoulder.

The woman turned, looked up at Win, and stood. She shrieked, "I can't believe you made it! It's so great to see you!" She threw her arms around his neck while Win stood there stiffly. She stepped back. "I heard your Broadway run has been amazing. You totally deserve all the praise, Win." She swatted his chest with her left hand, on which sat an enormous diamond and sapphire engagement ring.

It took a moment, but Grace recognized the petite woman. It was Jessica Dylan, the actress and style maven whose photos graced many fashion magazines; she also happened to be Win's ex-girlfriend. Jessica was wearing a stunning deep V-neck dress made of a diaphanous red silk, along with four-inch heels. She looked gorgeous and sexy with her ample cleavage and her long, dark hair swept to one side.

"Hi, Jess," Win said in a shy voice. "Yeah, the Broadway gig has been fun." His response seemed stilted.

The actress turned her gaze up toward Grace. "Oh, and who do we have here? I'm Jess, by the way. You are…?"

Win cleared his throat. "Jess, this is Grace King, my girlfriend." Grace started—that was the first time she'd heard Win use that term. "Grace is the chief marketing officer for Burberry and she's a soon-to-be-published author, too. Super smart and creative." He waved his hands in front of Grace with a flourish, as if he were unveiling a masterpiece sculpture. "And absolutely stunning on top of all that," he added with a wink and a smile. "She could easily have a career as a model."

Grace stiffened up, not sure how to respond. She felt like a used car that was being pushed upon a hesitant buyer.

Jessica paused for the slightest moment. "Oh. Well welcome,

welcome. There's a full bar near the kitchen and some good things to eat. You know I'd normally be drinking champagne, Win, but I have to avoid it in my condition." She framed her hands around her belly. Judging from the size of the bump, Grace guessed she was about six or seven months pregnant.

Grace looked down at her furry boots and her cheeks reddened—she was acutely underdressed for the occasion. She gave a tight smile and pulled her silk scarf around her neck more closely, like a protective cloak shielding her from any more embarrassment. Grace merely said, "Hello." She felt completely out of her element.

Win took Grace's arm. "Shall we get a glass of champagne, darlin'?" They made their way over to the bar and Win handed her a champagne flute.

She took a big gulp. "What was all that about, Win? Why are we here?" The smile had vanished from her face.

"I thought it would be fun for you to meet some of my old friends." He tilted his head down and gave her puppy-dog eyes.

Just then the cute dark-haired man came over to them. He looked at the floor. "Listen, Win, I'm sorry about how the whole thing went down. No hard feelings, man, right?" He held up his right hand for Win to grasp.

Win didn't move for a second, then raised his arm swiftly. The dark-haired guy flinched as if he expected Win to strike him. Then Win clasped the dark-haired guy's hand in the air. In a voice that sounded almost too casual, he said, "Hey, man, it is what it is." Then Win looked at Grace. "Anyway, how could I be anything but thrilled with life when I have this spectacular woman by my side? I'm on top of the world, man. On top of the world." He grinned broadly and slapped the guy on the back a little too hard. Grace recognized the man as another actor, but she couldn't for the life of her remember his name.

The dark-haired guy sighed with relief. "All right, man." He shrank back to the corner.

Win fixed his gaze on Grace. "Okay, well that's done. You must be famished. How about heading to dinner now?"

Grace drained her glass of champagne. "Yes, let's get out of here," she said coldly.

They retrieved their coats from the greeter with the glasses and headed down in the elevator.

*

Outside the frosty wind whipped about, blowing Grace's long blond hair into her eyes. Win opened the car door for Grace and she shivered as she got in. The toasty interior of the car matched her temper, which was heating up.

Win plopped down on the seat and the driver maneuvered the car away from the curb toward the restaurant. There was absolute silence for an extended period of time, with Grace staring straight ahead, ignoring Win's tentative glances. Her hands trembled as her anger bubbled up inside her. Finally Grace turned to him. "What was the point of all that?"

He started, "I thought—"

"Thought what?" Grace's eyes flashed and her nostrils flared.

Win stiffened up. "I'm not sure why you're upset, Grace. I just wanted to stop by and say hello to some old friends. And introduce you to them."

"No, that's not what happened. You were showing me off like arm candy. I don't like being used like that, Win. What, were you trying to make your ex-girlfriend jealous?"

"Can you blame me for wanting to show you off a little, Grace? You're amazing." Win turned on his Hollywood smile.

The car stopped in front of the restaurant. Grace looked him straight in the eyes. "I thought we were going on a date tonight to be together. I didn't know I was walking into an ambush. I will not be used like that, Win. I'm a person, not a pawn. You should have told me what we were walking into and that your ex was the one throwing the party. Is that why you wanted me to wear something sexy? Well, all of this"—she moved both hands in a wide circle and brought them back together—"is definitely not for me." She jammed down the door handle and threw the car door open.

"Hang on, Grace, please! Let me get the door for you." Win bounded out of the car.

She leapt out and called to him over the roof of the car. "I'll get my own damn door, and oh, by the way, I'll get my own damn dinner, too." Grace stomped away down the street in fury. She heard Win calling after her but she dashed away as fast as her unsteady legs would carry her.

*

Early the next morning Grace was lying on her yoga mat listening to the soothing new age music that was played before class. She closed her eyes and took in deep breaths to clear her mind. When she opened her eyes someone was standing over her. Simone Everett.

"Grace, what a surprise. I didn't know you took this yoga class."

"Hi, Simone. Yeah, it helps me decompress."

"I was actually going to call you today." Simone beamed. "Guess what? I got the part!" The actress's eyes bugged out in disbelief. "I actually got it!"

Grace jumped up and hugged her. "That's awesome! I'm so thrilled for you, Simone."

"They want me to fly to London next week to start pre-production work. I was wondering, would you come with me? They said I could bring a companion along for the first week, all expenses paid. How about it?" Simone laid out her yoga mat next to Grace's and sat cross-legged, clasping her hands together like she was praying. "This could be a great way to end your book, Grace."

Thinking for a minute, Grace said, "The manuscript is being edited now, but I suppose I could always add a bit more to the last chapter. Show the exciting results from the rebranding case studies."

Simone tilted her head and batted her eyelashes. "So you'll come with me?"

Grace laughed. "All right, Simone, I'll be your plus-one to London. Count me in!"

"Cool, let's grab some tea after class and we can coordinate schedules." Simone squeezed Grace's forearm. Then the chimes sounded, indicating the class was about to begin and silence was required.

Grace let out a long exhale. After the drama-filled evening with Win, a change in scenery and some distance might be just what she needed. She had been falling hard for him, but last night was a wake-up call—maybe they didn't belong together. Anyway, accompanying Simone could add an interesting twist to the end of her rebranding book. Flip Style's marketing relaunch campaign that she'd helped execute had been hailed as one of the best brand comeback stories in years. Grace had been working hard. Didn't she deserve a bit of a break?

Before jetting off to London, Grace met up with Sofia for coffee and to update her on the drama with Win. Sofia was the only one who knew they were dating. The four of them—Grace, Win, Sofia, and Jasper—had met for cocktails just after Christmas. While Sofia liked Win, she agreed that a short break might be good. She indicated that things with Jasper were going great, but Grace sensed some hesitation. She'd always known her friend to be skittish about marriage, but she had never seen Sofia this happy in a relationship. Grace didn't want her friend to walk away from something potentially great, so she decided to give Sofia the little push she needed.

"Sofi, do you think Jasper could be the one?" Grace raised an eyebrow.

Sofia shrugged. "I'm still figuring that out. Why?" She sipped her latte.

"Jasper's such a great guy. If you don't want to be with him, then I'm sure Simone Everett would love to meet him. Would you mind if I introduce them?"

The look on Sofia's face spoke volumes. Her forehead wrinkled up and her back stiffened as if she were getting ready for hand-to-hand combat.

Grace knew her friend better than she knew herself, and the prospect of losing Jasper to another woman would make Sofia realize how much she wanted him in her life.

*

From the moment they landed in London and were greeted by the studio's handlers, Grace and Simone's schedule was chock-full of activities: costume consultations and fittings, meetings with the showrunner and producers about the development of her character, and prep work. Grace marveled at how smoothly Simone balanced everything and how she took the time—even as they were running from one meeting to the next—to spend a few moments connecting with each person and thanking them. Simone really was a pro. The pilot was slated to start shooting in a couple of months, so Simone would begin doing three hours of martial arts training each day, as well as shadowing an actual MI5 agent for a couple of weeks, to prepare for her role.

At the end of the week the evening before Grace was returning to New York, they attended a charity event hosted by the British royal family. It was the brainchild of a younger member of the monarchy, Prince Alexander, who'd founded an organization that focused on helping women in need find jobs. The charity helped prepare women for job interviews and also offered access to a huge closet full of free professional attire suitable for interviews. Tonight's event was designed to get more publicity for the charity by exposing it to movers and shakers.

Grace and Simone mingled with the other A-list attendees and sipped champagne in the event space atop a museum with a magnificent view of the Thames. While many women were dripping with jewels and ornate gowns, Simone wore a simple but elegant dark blue gown and tasteful diamond earrings. Her lack of adornment only spotlighted her remarkable beauty and exotic heritage.

The event organizer stepped up to the microphone and introduced Prince Alexander. He was tall, attractive...and happened to be one of the most eligible bachelors in the world. Despite the thirty-four-year-old prince's reputation for being a playboy, when he spoke, it was with a level of gravitas and intelligence that Grace had never seen.

In an intense, articulate voice, Prince Alexander said, "It is indeed a hard fact that women's economic futures are dependent on a number of variables. But sometimes just getting the chance to interview for a job is enough of an impetus to change the course of a person's life. Many of you here this evening represent the top tier organizations in England. My hope is that you will help us find job opportunities for these women who are struggling to simply live a better life." This was a royal with a purpose and he was clearly using his position wisely to help others.

Afterward Prince Alexander mingled with the attendees and was mobbed by most of the women. As he was speaking with a small group, he stared across the room—something, or someone, had caught his eye. Simone was in the middle of telling Grace about her upcoming martial arts training and she missed the prince's gaze, which was not lost on Grace. By then the prince had stopped talking entirely and appeared mesmerized by Simone. Grace nudged Simone slightly with her elbow. "Heads up, I think the prince is coming over here to meet you." Indeed, he was making a beeline toward Simone, keeping his eyes affixed to her face.

"Hello, I don't believe we've met. I'm Alex," he said smoothly, and held his hand out to Simone. He gave the slightest nod to a photographer, who rushed over and snapped photos of the three of them.

Simone didn't seem fazed at all. "Hi, Alex. I'm Simone Everett and this is marketing guru Grace King."

"Well, I'll have to get your advice on marketing this charity more effectively, Grace." He chuckled. "What do you think about the organization?"

Diplomatically, Grace said, "I think it's wonderful that you're helping women achieve a better future. After all, women help drive economic growth."

He turned to Simone. "And you?"

Simone wrinkled her brow thoughtfully. "Your objective is a noble one and it seems like you really want to make a difference. However, I think the approach is flawed." Prince Alexander drew back a bit. It was probably a rare occurrence for anyone to offer criticism to him. "Women don't just need jobs, they need careers. To break the cycle of poverty, they need education and training for a career they can build on over their lifetimes. I'm afraid that your approach may result in short-term solutions for these women instead of a profound difference in how their lives might unfold. So, while it's a good start, I think it needs more refinement." She had a serious look in her eyes. Grace marveled at the insight Simone exhibited.

The prince was quiet for a moment. Then he laughed. "Ho ho! A woman who truly speaks her mind—how formidable. And refreshing. Might I ask about your career experience?"

Simone gave a grin. "I'm an actor but just completed my degree in finance at NYU."

Grace chimed in, "And Simone has launched a series of video podcasts helping people achieve better financial health. The series is called *The Wealth Whisperer* and it's gone viral. You should check it out!" She just had to give her protégé a plug.

"Marvelous, I shall indeed," said the prince. "Are you ladies in London for long?"

Grace said, "I leave tomorrow, but Simone is going to be starring in a miniseries that's filming here."

Prince Alexander furrowed his brow. "Perhaps we can continue our conversation about the charitable organization over a cup of tea, Simone. I'd like to hear your ideas on how to improve our approach."

"Thank you for the invitation." Simone pursed her lips. "However, I'll be starting to shoot the miniseries soon, so my schedule is tight. I do wish you luck in your endeavors. It was nice to meet you." She offered her hand. "Come on, Grace, I have an early call tomorrow and you've got an early flight to catch. Good evening, Alex."

Prince Alexander stood erect and then gave a slight bow. "Good evening, Simone." He took her hand and shook it. "It was a pleasure to make your acquaintance. And you, as well, Grace."

They walked away. Once they exited the building Grace turned and swatted Simone across her shoulder. "I can't believe you! A prince just asked you out and you turned him down?"

Simone shook her head. "I'm not so sure he was asking me out, he just wanted my input on his project. Anyway, as dashing as he is, the guy has a reputation for being a skirt chaser, and I'm not wasting my time on someone like that. I'd like to date a nice, smart guy. So thank you, but next."

Grace threw her head back and laughed. "You really are something, Simone. I think you're going to do some incredible things with all your talent and wisdom. I can't wait to see what's in store for you."

The two women touched heads, linked arms, and walked through the streets of London back toward their hotel.

Grace inhaled the crisp, cold air. She'd finally responded to Win's calls and texts with a message saying she'd taken a last-minute trip to London and was returning tomorrow. While she felt him pulling at her heartstrings, she wasn't sure exactly how to handle the situation with him.

The next morning after her long flight, when Grace's car from the airport pulled up in front of her apartment, the doorman, Khemraj, ran out to greet her. He helped her with her bag and asked about her trip, all the while smiling broadly—he seemed in even better spirits than usual. Khemraj pressed the elevator button for Grace and whispered, "Miss Grace, there's a special delivery waiting for you in your apartment. I personally helped arrange it."

A bit jet-lagged from the travel, Grace was oblivious to her doorman's excitement and headed upstairs. As she swung open the door of her apartment her senses were hit with vibrant color and the perfume of roses...hundreds of them. Roses of every hue were in vases on every surface of her apartment, and red rose petals were scattered on the front hall floor.

"What is this?" Grace remarked aloud as she stepped inside.

Moments later, there was a knock at her door. She opened it to see another large bouquet of roses. The bearer held it aside and showed his face. Win Wyatt. "Grace, I want to apologize and explain my actions. Can we talk, please?" Chin down and eyes up, he had a sincere expression on his face.

"Okay, come in." Grace sighed and opened the door.

Win navigated around her rolling bag and placed the bouquet on her coffee table. They sat together. "I'm sorry I brought you to that ridiculous party, Grace." Win relayed the story of how he'd dated Jessica Dylan for several years. Over the summer she'd had an affair with her costar on a film. She abruptly broke up with Win by text message. It was only when Jessica appeared in an ad campaign for an ice-cream brand—obviously pregnant—and Win started getting congratulatory messages on social media from friends and fans that he learned the news. In addition to the emotional tumult from the breakup, he had to suffer through the public humiliation of his recent ex-girlfriend having someone else's baby. He winced in pain as he shared the story with Grace. Apparently even successful movie stars can succumb to feelings of jealousy and rage, and a strong desire to show up their ex. That was why Win had had Grace accompany him to the party. "I know it was petty of me, and frankly, I'm embarrassed about how I behaved. Will you forgive me, Grace?" He reached for her hand. "I think it's important for you to know that I genuinely want to be with you for the person you are."

Grace's brain was feeling fuzzy from the jet lag and from hearing Win's story. But the soulful look in his eyes was touching. She steadied herself. "I'm really sorry that happened to you, Win. And I accept your apology." Though she let Win take her hand in his, the barricade around her heart was still up. Was all this really right for her?

*

ANDI

Every morning since Thanksgiving when she had woken up, Andi had hoped that Luca's facial paralysis from Bell's palsy had just been a bad dream. But lying in bed, when she'd opened her eyes and seen his distorted face, she'd been brutally brought back to reality as if by a violent punch in the face. Luca had stirred and half-smiled at Andi in his drowsy state, but when he saw her expression and remembered everything, his happiness evaporated.

Things had continued like that, and for a month Luca had been holed up in their apartment. For Christmas they'd spent a relatively quiet holiday at home, just the four of them, mainly so Luca could avoid other people's stares.

With all that had occurred over Thanksgiving, Andi hadn't said a peep to Luca about her work situation—he was certainly stressed out enough. If she mentioned that Lester was sexually harassing her it would just be too much. Although Andi was the first to admit her EQ wasn't the highest, she did at least have the sensitivity not to burden her husband with anything additional at this time.

Soon it was early January and their long vacation break was over. Andi had mostly worked from home over the holidays but finally had to return to the office. Over the breakfast that Luca prepared that morning, Andi sensed a change in his mood. Luca was humming a little and he seemed in slightly better spirits.

"Andi, darling, I decided I am going to work today." His speech was slow and slurred but by now Andi was getting used to it and could mostly understand him.

"Really, honey? Sure you're ready for that?"

He shook his head. "I don't know. But Rene said I have to practice speaking if I want to recover faster, so I have to take the doctor's advice. I have to try."

"Good for you, Luca, that's great news." She moved over to give him a hug but he jerked away from her, so she patted his shoulder instead. They were still trying to deal with this new situation and all its obstacles. Something that became clear to Andi and the boys was that while Luca was suffering from Bell's palsy, he wanted minimal physical contact with his family. Obviously the drastic change in his appearance was making him feel self-conscious.

When this catastrophe had occurred, Andi realized that her choices were limited. She was the primary breadwinner and the one with the best health care plan. No matter how crazy the situation was with her boss and her intense desire to quit her job, she'd have to stick it out and endure the situation until Luca recovered. She just prayed it wouldn't take too long.

"I know it's going to be tough, Luca, but we'll get through this together, okay? I'd better head down to the office. Call me if you need anything, honey." She blew him a kiss, hugged her sons goodbye, and headed out the door.

It was the sharp, rancid odor that hit her nostrils first when Andi walked into her normally pristine new office. Either someone had thrown a wild frat party inside her office or a food delivery truck had crashed inside the room. There were piles of greasy food wrappers, soiled food containers, half-eaten sandwiches, and empty soda cans strewn across her entire desk and conference table, spilling onto the floor. The place was repulsive.

"What the hell is this? Who left this mess in my office?" Andi bellowed in her loud mom voice. She heard some snickers outside her office and saw Percy and Richie, two of Lester's cronies, elbowing each other in the ribs and smirking as they entered the doorway. Andi's buddy Mike happened to be walking by and looked in to see what the commotion was all about.

"Oh, Andi, you weren't around over the holidays so we used your office as a workroom," Percy said.

Richie sneered. "You're Mexican, right? Isn't your family in the housecleaning business? We thought you'd be used to tidying up a mess."

Andi's face turned crimson and her temper reached its boiling point, ready to explode like a faulty pressure cooker. "Listen, you assholes—"

Mike pushed his way in past the two guys and turned to face them. "Really, guys? Grow up. Get the hell out of here." He had the build of an NFL offensive lineman, and Percy and Richie shot him a wary look and backed out of Andi's office. Mike turned to her and spoke in a soft voice. "Andi, you know you were about to give them exactly what they wanted, don't you? They were trying to get you all worked up." He placed a hand on her shoulder. "Next time, my friend, don't give them the satisfaction of knowing that they got to you. Just pretend like you don't care and ignore those guys.

Otherwise they'll never stop the foolishness. Okay?"

Andi's heart was still pumping like mad and it took her a few minutes to calm herself down. She looked gratefully at Mike. "Yeah, you're right, Mikey. Thanks, you're a pal." She let out a deep breath.

He grabbed a garbage can and started sweeping the trash into it with his huge arms. "Come on, Andi, we can get this place cleaned up in no time." As a guy with five little kids at home, Mike was a pro at defusing emotional situations, managing tantrums, and cleaning up messes. Andi had also spoken to Mike over the holidays and told him about the situation with Luca and Lester's crazy behavior, and Mike had promised to watch her back. He was already making good on his commitment.

*

She had a meeting that afternoon with Lester and was praying he'd gotten the clear message that she wasn't interested in having an affair with him and simply wanted to focus on work.

Lester's gaze skimmed her body and he had a sly look in his eye. "Andi, I wanted to share some information. First, let's chat about your compensation. I know you were due for a salary increase but I'm not prepared to give that to you right now. I need to see how well you perform on the new Paris account before I make a decision about a raise."

"But, Lester, I'm the top performer in the department. I have the highest dollars under management of anyone else in the department. I've earned that raise." Andi's voice was calm but she felt her heart skip a beat.

"Well, you're just going to have to be a little patient. In the mean time I wanted to give you your bonus check." He slid an envelope across his desk.

Andi tore it open, dreading to see what was inside. "This is half of what I was expecting. Half of what I deserve. What's going on here, Lester?"

"As you know, we had a department bonus pool, and as the leader of Kaneshiro's private banking department I had to distribute the funds according to how I saw fit. Some guys made a big improvement in their performance and I wanted to reward them—guys like Myron Burry."

Myron Burry? She'd been coaching the guy for months and helping him become a stronger contributor to the department. Now Andi's bonus was getting diminished because she'd helped him do better? Maybe she should have charged him a percentage of his upside.

"It's not like you're going to starve, Andi. You'll still get your partner bonus from the firm, and that's not insignificant." Lester sat back and delivered the final blow. "Oh, and another thing. We're moving your office. Sounds like you've had some challenges in getting along with some of the guys—I heard something from Percy and Richie about an outburst from you this morning. I thought you'd prefer moving down to the end of the hallway in the empty office."

Her eyes bored into him, and she wished she had lasers shooting out of them to blow Lester to smithereens, or at least scorch the hair off his smug little head. "You mean the office next to the executive assistants' pool? You're moving me there?" She felt her temper rise but she forced herself to keep her emotions in check.

Lester tilted his head. "Is that not satisfactory? You seem tense sitting near the other guys so I thought you'd feel safer and more comfortable in the company of other women." He smirked. "Anyway, it's already been arranged and they're moving you as we speak."

Andi felt sick as thoughts flooded her brain. Did working at this new bank mean that all her efforts and great performance would no longer be rewarded? Would Lester continue to decrease her compensation and make her miserable until she succumbed to his advances? What could she do about it? Despite her partner status, she knew that Lester was tight with the US CEO of Kaneshiro Bank, who'd handpicked him for this job. Damn it, if she'd known her office was going to be moved she would have left it a pigsty for Percy and Richie to clean up for themselves. Andi steadied her gaze. "I see. Is that all, Lester?"

He leaned forward. "You know how to make this all go away, don't you, Andi? Why don't you think it over. I'm sure you'll come around." His voice dropped to a whisper—it was even more threatening than his regular tone. "Just remember, Andi, in the end I always get what I want." Sinisterly, he ran his fingers through his hair like he was imagining tracing the curves of her body.

*

After the brutal day at work, Andi dragged herself through the front door of her Upper West Side apartment hoping for a moment of peace and quiet. It was anything but. Francesco and Antonio were fighting over a toy airplane, shouting at each other and wrestling and tumbling over the furniture. The living room looked like it had been tossed by CIA operatives searching for secret microfilm. Andi dropped her stuff on the floor and looked skyward. When it came to raising children she sometimes found that the years went by quickly but certain days dragged on forever. She quickly separated the boys, took away the airplane, and told them to behave. The nanny had already left and Luca was supposed to be looking after the boys, but he was nowhere to be found.

Searching around for her husband, Andi walked down the hall to their master bedroom, where she heard a muffled sound. She knocked and then opened the door. Her husband sat on the floor hunched over and holding his knees. His head was buried and his shoulders were shaking with emotion.

"Luca, what happened? Are you okay?" She went over to hug him and he held up his hand to stop her from getting too close.

His face was wet with tears and he looked into her eyes. "Oh, Andi, it was just too much. Everywhere I went people were pointing at my face like I was a monster. At work I had to repeat myself a dozen times because no one understood me. After work I went to pick up some groceries and a little girl saw my face and started crying—her mother thought I did something to her daughter. I look too horrible to be out in public, Andi, I can't go out. I emailed my boss that I need to work from home for a while and she said okay. What can I do with my face like this?" Luca wailed, and Andi's heart shattered into a million pieces seeing her husband in such agony.

"I'm so sorry, honey. I can't imagine how rough today was for you." She rubbed his shoulder. "Listen, from now on I'll take care of the shopping and run all the errands. Okay?" Her husband nodded slowly. "You stay home and work, but I'd like to hire a speech therapist to come in and help you recover more quickly, okay, Luca?" Her husband managed to give her a half smile of gratitude. "Why don't you rest a bit? I'll wrangle the boys and whip up some dinner. Pasta sound good?"

Luca eked out a response. "Okay. Thank you, Andi."

She looked lovingly at her husband. "Don't you worry about a thing. I've got you covered."

*

By the time they sat down to dinner, Luca was feeling a bit better and created a list of that week's errands. On Tuesday Andi would have to do a big grocery store run after work; he gave Andi the list, put in order of how the store was laid out. She could buy everything and have the store deliver her purchases. On Wednesday the boys had their annual doctor's checkup, so she'd have to leave work early, head uptown, and take them at three o'clock, then they had a repair guy coming to fix the oven, so she needed to be back home by four thirty p.m. Thursday she'd need to shop for an astronaut suit for Francesco and a scientist outfit for Antonio for dress-up day the following week at their preschool. Their nanny had a dentist appointment on Thursday, so Andi would need to pick up the boys from a playdate before dinnertime. On Friday she'd have to drop off and pick up dry cleaning and stop by the tailor to pick up some of her clothing that was being repaired. There were also a couple of prescriptions for Luca waiting to be picked up at the drugstore. Some outfits that he had ordered for the boys didn't fit and would need to be returned to retail stores, as well. Andi had had no clue what she was getting herself into when she promised to take on all the family tasks. Her eyes widened at the long list of errands and internally she grumbled, but she smiled and said, "No problem."

*

Over the course of the next few weeks, as Andi performed all the many tasks that her husband usually took care of, she realized two important things about Luca. The first was that on top of his job, Luca did a multitude of extra, special things for the family. She'd had no idea he did so much because he simply did everything graciously and without complaint. The second was that her husband was quite possibly the most popular man on the island of Manhattan. Everywhere she went— the grocer, the dry cleaner, the tailor, the pharmacist—everyone asked after Luca and said they missed his happy, smiling face and their interesting conversations. It appeared that in every interaction her husband had, he'd really gotten to know these folks and spent time connecting with each one. He also did countless thoughtful things for others, like bringing the mail up to an elderly neighbor. Luca's absence in the community was palpable. The guy could have run for mayor and easily won. The experience only made Andi fall in love with her husband all over again.

*

One night at bedtime, in the comforting cloak of darkness, Andi told her husband how much she loved him and she snuggled up to him for a hug. Luca's body stiffened up and he gently pushed her away from him.

"Please, Andi, I don't want you to get too close to me."

Andi snorted. "Why not, Luca? We haven't made love or even kissed in months. You don't have to be embarrassed about how you look, it doesn't matter to me. Don't push me away."

In a soft voice Luca said, "No, no. It's not that at all, *cara mia*. The doctors don't know how this virus gets passed and I don't want you, Francesco, or Antonio to get this same condition. Do you understand, Andi? I could never forgive myself if I hurt you or the boys. Never."

Andi sat up suddenly, realizing that all this time her husband wasn't being prideful, he was being protective. He was trying to shield her and the boys from this illness. She felt ashamed that she'd assumed his distance was due to his vanity. Her throat tightened as the sobs started to spill out of her. "Oh, Luca," she said tenderly, "even if you stayed exactly the way you are right now, you're still the best husband in the world and the only man I could ever love." She kissed her fingertips and laid her hand on her husband's cheek—he pressed it against his face for a moment, then he told her he loved her and said good night.

*

SOFIA

"Quick, hide me!" Elle gripped Sofia's arm, eyes wide with terror. Elle was a model turned skincare entrepreneur whom they were interviewing on *Titans Tell All* later that day. They were about to enter the CNBC cafeteria to grab lunch when Elle stopped dead in her tracks.

Sofia gave a quizzical look to Kate Frost, but the two women hustled their interview subject around the corner and into a utility closet. The three of them huddled in the confines of the tight space. Elle's pale skin was ghostly white and she was trembling. "Elle, what's wrong?"

"I just saw...him." Elle shuddered.

Kate said, "Who are you talking about?"

"Voss."

"Charley Voss? The denim guy?" Sofia asked. Elle was referring to the unorthodox founder of the denim company called Voss & Co., known for its risqué ad campaigns, usually featuring young girls. "He's being interviewed on another program today about the state of the apparel business."

Elle swallowed hard. "When I started modeling I was featured in a Voss & Co. ad campaign. After we wrapped shooting at the corporate photo studio, Voss invited me up to his office. Then he"—she shut her eyes tightly—"he sexually assaulted me. I was only fifteen; I had no idea what was happening. Afterward he acted like everything was normal and I just ran away from there as fast as I could."

"My god, Elle, you poor thing." Sofia's eyes widened in alarm. "How traumatic."

Kate put her hand on Elle's forearm. "Did you file charges?"

The model shook her head. "No. Voss warned me that if I ever told anyone he'd make sure I never modeled again. For eighteen years I've managed to avoid him—up until now." It was evident that even after all that time, just seeing Voss unnerved her.

"Are you okay, Elle? Is there anything we can do?" Sofia was wondering if Elle would be able to do their interview later in the day.

Elle shook her head. "I just need a minute. Can you make sure that monster is gone before we go inside the cafeteria?"

Sofia and Kate nodded and exchanged looks. It was the first time they'd ever heard such disturbing news about the famous and powerful business mogul.

*

They managed to have an engaging interview with Elle on *Titans Tell All*; she'd made a quick recovery after her near run-in with Charley Voss. The former model talked about the bad condition her skin had been in from all the pore-clogging makeup on her modeling assignments. She'd teamed up with a scientist and created a line of natural and nourishing skin care products, from moisturizers to serums, that improved the quality of the skin. The line was carried in department stores and specialty stores and sold online, and had quickly grown into a successful business; Elle had plans to do an IPO. That day the *Titans* programs was a women-only show since Graham was absent. In broadcasting, reporters were expected to report to the set despite illness…with the exception of pink eye, which was what Graham had contracted.

The three women were saying their goodbyes when Sofia's assistant, Chloe, came into the studio. "Sofia and Kate, I just got a call from Randolph's assistant. He'd like to speak with you both."

"Okay, thanks, Chloe. We'll head up there now." Sofia exchanged quizzical glances with Kate. "What do you think it's about?" Sofia was hoping her co-anchor had some insights so she could mentally prepare for the meeting.

Kate shrugged. "No clue. *Titans* has been going well, so maybe he wants to congratulate us?" Kate looked optimistic, but Sofia had an uneasy feeling and her shoulders tightened up.

*

Two days later Sofia found herself on an early morning flight with Kate Frost bound for Richmond, Virginia. After their last show, Randolph had informed them of two important things: First, he was pleased with the strong ratings of *Titans Tell All* and thought the two women were working well together, so he was moving Graham off the show. Second, he wanted to amp up the show and get the "ungettable" interviews. With that he'd dispatched them to Virginia on an impossible assignment—to convince Pete Wilkins, reclusive billionaire and founder of the sports retail chain called Play Action Sporting Goods, to come on the show. Randolph had set up a meeting at the Play Action headquarters in Charlottesville. Now all Sofia and Kate had to do was get there and land the interview.

Snow was tumbling down hard that frigid January morning as Kate drove their rental car away from the airport in Richmond. Since Kate had attended college at UVA and knew the area well, she'd offered to drive to Charlottesville.

Sofia eyed the snowy roads nervously as the wiper blades furiously swept aside the accumulating snow on the windshield. The hour-plus ride was likely to be much longer in these conditions. "You okay driving in this, Kate?" She pulled her down coat around her more tightly.

Kate kept her eyes on the road and nodded. "Fine, fine. I grew up driving in this kind of weather." She always looked so elegant. Today she was wearing a cream-colored cashmere and wool coat and matching beret, along with a pale pink Chanel scarf. "What's our game plan with Pete Wilkins? We've got about thirty minutes with the guy. I'm interested in your take on how we can convince him to come on our show."

A deep sigh escaped Sofia's lips. "What would entice him, a person who doesn't like giving interviews? From everything I've read he's a practical, humble guy reticent to talk about himself or his accomplishments."

"Which is exactly what we need him to discuss on our show. So what do you think he would be willing to talk about?"

"Easy. What does every parent love talking about? Their kids. He has two sons and a daughter working in the business. We can ask him about how they're contributing to Play Action Sporting Goods and what that means for the future of the company. What do you think?"

Kate gave her a friendly smack on her puffy down forearm. "Brilliant, Sofia. Now all we have to do is make it seem like his idea." She peered out the window. "The roads aren't too bad, we should have plenty of time to grab a bite to eat before our meeting." The roads were slick but Kate kept the car going at a good clip for most of the ride. On the snowy highway, just as they were about to reach Monticello, they heard a loud pop and the car jerked to the side.

Sofia sucked in a sudden breath, but Kate calmly slowed the vehicle, pulling onto the shoulder of the road. The two of them got out of the car to survey the situation.

"Oh crap." Kate studied the side of the rental car. "We've got a flat."

Rubbing her hands together to stay warm, Sofia said, "We'd better get cracking on changing that tire." She opened the trunk and rummaged around to find the spare tire and jack. While her head was buried in the trunk, she heard Kate say, "Look, Sofia, the cavalry is coming!"

Despite their being in the South, the sight of the patrol car's flashing red lights behind them was a huge relief to Sofia. Kate trudged through the snow toward the officer, who had exited his vehicle.

"Hello, officer, we just got a flat tire and could sure use some help."

The brawny policeman moved closer to them, then stopped. He pulled down the scarf that was covering his nose and mouth. "Glenda? Is that you?"

What is he talking about? And where have I heard that name before? Sofia thought.

Kate froze for a moment. "Tony! I can't believe it." She gave the officer a hug. "You're always rescuing me, aren't you? Oh, this is my colleague Sofia." Sofia removed her mittens and shook hands with the policeman.

As the officer changed the flat tire in record time, he and Kate (er, Glenda) caught up, and she shared that she was living in NYC. Tony was married with three kids and life was good; he'd seen Kate often on TV and was happy for her success. Sofia stood off to the side to give them some privacy. After the tire was changed, Sofia thanked the officer and skedaddled back into the car. She turned to see Kate giving

Tony a big hug and putting some bills into his gloved hand—he gently refused but she insisted.

*

Kate was strangely silent as they resumed their drive toward Charlottesville. Sofia's stomach started to grumble. "Hey, Kate, let's stop and get something to eat. Maybe find a café somewhere?" Kate nodded and then slowed the car down. She parked in an abandoned parking lot and hunched over, clutching the steering wheel tightly with her forehead resting on it. Her shoulders were shuddering.

Confused, Sofia put her hand lightly on Kate's shoulder. "Are you okay?"

Kate sat back, her face moist with tears and her eyes ringed with running mascara. Her chest was heaving with sobs. Sofia sensed that she needed to give her colleague a few minutes to collect herself.

Fighting to catch her breath, Kate looked over at Sofia. "That officer, Tony? He saved my life when I was in college." Gulp of air. "Tony was working as a campus police officer at UVA when I was a student and there was an…an incident. It happened when I was a junior." Another gulp. "A guy named Christoph had become obsessed with me freshman year—asking me out, taking the same classes, showing up at the parties I went to. He followed me around for two years."

"He was stalking you?"

Kate's breath was slowly returning to normal. "Yes. My friends protected me and I mostly managed to avoid him. But one night—I've wished so many times I could go back in time and change that night—I was alone in the library studying for an exam. I felt someone's presence behind me. I heard Christoph say, 'If I can't have you, no one will.' As I was about to stand and face him I felt a sharp pain in my back. Christoph had plunged a knife into my upper back. I screamed. Then he pulled it out and stabbed me again. And again. He kept stabbing me. Twenty-seven times. Tony heard the commotion and ran in. Shot the bastard dead. Next thing I remember is waking up in the hospital."

Sofia raised her hands to her mouth in shock. "My god, Kate, how terrifying." Her mind flashed back to Kate's dressing room and the grotesque eye-shaped scars covering the expanse of her back.

"My name was Glenda Barton back then. When I graduated from college I changed my name, my appearance, everything about me. I had to."

"Why?"

Kate's eyes held a look first of sorrow and then of resolve. Her expression turned hard, reflecting her determination to erase that agonizing memory over the years. "Because I didn't want to be forever remembered as the girl who was stabbed twenty-seven times." She shook her head. "That's why I never married. Heck, I never even got past a second date with a man. It would be mortifying to have a guy see the scars all over my body. So that psycho Christoph accomplished his objective after all." Kate let out a bitter laugh.

While Sofia had had her share of mishaps during college, nothing came close to the magnitude of what Kate had suffered. "Oh, Kate." Sofia's eyes brimmed with tears and she leaned over and gave her colleague a hug. "I'm so sorry that happened to you. Would you like to cancel the meeting and just head home?"

"Cancel? Why would we do that?" Kate shook her head as she blew her nose. "No. I'm fine, Sofia, thanks. It's just…all those painful memories came rushing back." She let out a breath and attempted to smile. "Let's go find someplace to eat, okay? I'll feel a lot better if we can land this interview." She flipped down the visor mirror, tidied up her makeup, and started the engine.

Sofia sighed, marveling at Kate's strength. Knowing the backstory gave Sofia a better understanding of her colleague's sometimes tough demeanor and made her appreciate Kate even more. There had to be some way Sofia could help.

Play Action Sporting Goods' headquarters was a gleaming glass and steel structure. Sofia and Kate checked in with the receptionist and then sat in the waiting area.

A tall, fit woman in her thirties came out to greet them. "Hi, I'm Jackie. Welcome to HQ." Jackie wore a light sweater under a blazer with dark slacks and sensible shoes. She wore little makeup and had a pleasant, earnest face. Sofia knew better than to assume that Jackie was the CEO's assistant. The women shook hands. "Would you like a quick tour before the meeting?"

Jackie proceeded to show them around the facility, which was well appointed but not over-the-top and of course featured a world-class gym for employees. Going down a long corridor, Jackie pointed to two modest-looking offices and said, "That's my office, next to my dad's."

Sofia's suspicion was confirmed. Jackie was Pete Wilkins's daughter.

Further along the hallway, Jackie pointed at two doors. "These are my brothers' offices." Sofia and Kate poked their heads inside to take a look. Both offices were huge, lavishly decorated, and filled with sports memorabilia, flat-screen TVs, and a wet bar. Sofia caught a trace of an eye roll from Jackie as she led them to a conference room. "Pete wants to meet in here. I'll let him know you're ready."

Sofia remembered reading that Pete Wilkins insisted that his children call him "Pete" at the office instead of "Dad" so other employees wouldn't constantly be reminded of their family ties. The conference room had a large table that was raised up to about waist height but no chairs. Kate turned her palms up and shrugged.

"I've heard that Pete likes to keep meetings short, so he makes everyone stand up for them. Every meeting room has an adjustable-height conference table," Sofia said as Kate gave a smirk.

Sofia marveled at how quickly Kate had bounced back from her traumatic experience just a little while ago—she sure was one tough cookie.

Standing there for a moment, Sofia and Kate discussed how to sell the benefits of being on *Titans Tell All* to Pete. So it came as a surprise when the energetic, trim seventy-year-old founder bounded in enthusiastically and started peppering them with questions about their show and the format. When all his questions were answered, the white-haired CEO stood legs apart and arms akimbo, like a soccer goalie ready to deflect the next ball kicked at him. Pete's eyes twinkled as he nodded once and said, "Okay, I'll come on your show. However, I do have one condition—I'd like for Jackie to appear with me on the program."

What a simple request. Sofia nearly clapped with glee. She smiled at Kate.

"No problem," Kate said, "we can absolutely make that happen, Pete."

Sofia could barely contain her excitement. "We look forward to having you and Jackie on *Titans Tell All*, Pete. Thank you."

Kate and Sofia had just landed the biggest interview in the retail industry.

*

That Saturday night Sofia was going on another date with Jasper Frank—he'd invited Sofia over to his place and was cooking dinner. Knowing that he was a fan of jazz music, Sofia brought him a jazz CD as a gift and a nice Brunello.

Conveniently, Jasper lived on the Upper West Side just a few blocks from Sofia. His building was a prewar structure with beautiful architectural details. After checking in with the doorman and noting the luxurious marble lobby, Sofia made her way up to Jasper's penthouse apartment.

He opened the door wearing a chef's white apron tied around his waist and gave her a kiss. Jasper was tall and handsome, and casually dressed in a charcoal-gray golf shirt and jeans. "I missed you, Sofia." Sofia handed him the red wine and CD. "This is great, thanks. Jazz is my favorite. Here, let me pour you a glass of wine and show you around."

Jasper's four-bedroom apartment was large enough to have housed an indoor basketball court, especially with its twenty-foot ceilings. As he walked her around his home, Sofia observed that although Jasper had a number of expensive pieces, the most cherished possessions he pointed out were the simplest things: a piece of coral shaped like a heart that he'd found on the beach in Bonaire, a walking stick given to him by a guide in Tibet, and a lopsided ceramic mug his niece had made for him.

"I think the paella needs a little more time to cook. Would you like to see some of my family's pictures in the mean time?"

"Sure, why not." Sofia wondered what Jasper's family looked like. She expected to see exotic vacation photos or a perfect smiling family portrait on a sunset beach in Maui.

"In here." Jasper led her to one of the bedrooms, which had been converted into a library with shelves of books lining two complete walls floor to ceiling. Along each of those walls was a metal railing and a wooden ladder on wheels to make retrieving the books easier. Against another wall was a simple modern desk with a laptop and large monitor on it, and some photos. The other wall was covered with oil paintings.

"This library is fantastic. But where are your family pictures?" asked Sofia.

"Over there." Jasper pointed casually to the paintings.

Upon closer inspection Sofia realized that she was looking at a Kandinsky, a Jackson Pollock, and a Frank Stella, all original works.

She leaned against the wall for support, doubling over with laughter. Jasper looked at her with an eyebrow raised. Sofia was gasping for breath. "I thought you said your 'family pictures' not, 'family's pictures.' What a difference an 's' makes! I was expecting to see family vacation photos or something."

Jasper chuckled, which turned into a rolling laugh. Things were clicking between them.

As he put the finishing touches on an expertly prepared meal, Jasper played the CD from Sofia. "I always like to listen to something beautiful when I have dinner—it makes the food taste better. Don't you agree?" Sofia nodded.

"This music is wonderful, it has so much texture to it. Who's the artist?"

"One of my favorites—Jean LaForte," Sofia replied. "My dad." Sofia described how her half-French, half-Nigerian father and Spanish mother met while working on a documentary together for which they'd won an Academy Award. Too embarrassed to display their Oscar, they kept it in the bathroom closet in their home in Madrid. Sofia used to joke with her parents that their toilet paper kept excellent company.

Sofia switched to interview mode. "I'm curious about something, Jasper. You're a smart, attractive, interesting man and you're still single. Why?"

"I wanted to prove myself before I settled down, Sofia. Also there were a lot of adventures I wanted to experience before I got married. And, honestly, I hadn't been with anyone where there was a strong enough connection to make them my life partner." His eyes bored straight into hers. "All right, let's turn the tables. How could someone as remarkable as you not have been snatched up already?"

"The headline is I just haven't found the right person yet. For a while I wasn't meeting anyone who held my interest or, more importantly, someone whom I just felt comfortable with. So, I decided that I'd rather spend my time with friends or at home reading a book instead of going out on another awful date."

"And how would you rate this date so far?" Jasper had a wry smile.

"Good so far, but I have a book in my purse just in case." Sofia winked.

His face grew serious for a moment. "I have a confession to make. You know when we met up in Madrid?"

She nodded cautiously.

"I actually wasn't planning on being there until you told me you were going. I made up an excuse that I had business there so I could spend time with you, Sofia."

"What? Then why did it take you two days to call me?"

Jasper looked at her coyly. "I was playing hard to get. I knew you wouldn't be interested in a guy who was chasing after you too much, so I played it cool. Thought that would intrigue you more." He grinned.

"You rascal." Sofia swatted him with the back of her hand. "You were driving me crazy!"

Jasper grabbed her and nuzzled her ear, whispering a mock apology. They spent the evening basking in the warm glow of their blossoming love, then he walked her home and kissed her good night. Sofia rated the date as perfect.

*

COOP

Things couldn't have been going any better in Coop's life—he could scarcely believe his luck. Coop was a partner at his accounting firm. He was dating a hunk. And now his friend Vivien had just shared the most exciting news. Coop was all smiles as he slowed the speed on the gym's treadmill. It was early on a Sunday morning, so the Chelsea gym was fairly empty, with most patrons still recovering from the previous night out. The late-January snowstorms had made it too frigid and treacherous for a run outside.

"So, I'm expecting the baby this summer, Coop. And Clay is moving to Portland to be with me."

Coop could just imagine the joy on his friend's face. "Vivi, that's amazing news. I'm going to be an uncle!" Coop said in a singsongy voice.

Vivien laughed. "I'll definitely enlist you for babysitting. How's it going with Brad?"

There was no end to Coop's newfound pleasure in being able to discuss his boyfriend of two months. It was something that had been lacking in his life for years, and he was happy—honestly, more relieved—to be part of a couple once again. "Couldn't be better. My boyfriend Brad is just gorgeous, isn't he?" Coop spoke slightly louder so his voice was audible to the few other guys in the gym. "You got the photos of us that I texted to you, right?" He lowered his voice to a whisper. "Vivi, can you believe someone so attractive and dashing is interested in *me*?"

"Of course I can, Coop. And it shouldn't surprise you either, my friend. But is Brad a nice guy? Does he make you happy?"

Coop wiped the sweat from his brow with his microfiber gym towel. "Yes, he's treating me well, Vivi." Truth be told, Coop was harboring some niggling concerns. He'd noticed that when Brad had had a few too many drinks, his demeanor changed and his temper was short—very short. A steely mask would come over Brad's face and a dark, impenetrable look into his eyes—he'd hold his body like a coiled snake preparing to strike. This concerned Coop, but it didn't happen often and he rationalized that Brad's job as a Secret Service agent was highly stressful. Who would want a job where every day at work you might literally have to take a bullet for your boss? Plus Brad wasn't out at work, to complicate matters. Coop continued walking slowly on the treadmill to prevent his legs from cramping up.

There was another issue that was worrying Coop. Sometimes when they'd go out to a bar or a club, Brad would flirt with other guys right in front of him. It had happened the other night at Splash, a gay dance club. Coop loved Splash's festive atmosphere; the club featured music from the eighties and nineties. An added attraction was that on top of the bar, hot young men dressed in bathing suits that left nothing to the imagination writhed to the music while occasionally getting spritzed with water, their muscles glistening like hard candy.

"I'd say the one small hiccup is that because Brad's so gorgeous he attracts a lot of attention—people are just drawn to him. But it's not really his fault." Coop sighed as he remembered the other night at Splash and dropped his voice. "We're sitting in the lounge area at Splash and this cute guy comes over and sits next to Brad. He strikes up a conversation—a long conversation. In fact, he was like human Velcro and wouldn't peel away from Brad." Coop was a little miffed that Brad hadn't drawn him into their chat while he was laughing it up with the cute guy. It was dark in the club, but Coop had seen Brad place his hand on the cute guy's thigh and rest it there. That bothered Coop, but he didn't bring it up with Brad afterward and dared not mention it now to Vivien—in both cases he wasn't sure how he was supposed to have reacted. "Anyway, finally I hear the guy say, 'Are you here with someone?' and Brad says, 'I'm here with my boyfriend,' and he nods his head in my direction. The cute guy stands up and stares at me. Then he points at me and says, 'You? *You?*' Then he shakes his head and walks away. I mean, it's not like I'm an ogre or something, right? The nerve of that guy." Coop huffed.

*

Vivien was quiet for a moment on the other end of the phone with her friend.

"Listen Coop, I know you're excited about Brad but I…I want to make sure he's treating you well and being respectful." She didn't like the sound of what Coop was telling her. Sure, he was excited to be with an attractive guy, but that didn't mean he should be a doormat.

This was Coop's MO, especially when he was in a new relationship—to avoid making waves he'd sometimes allowed himself to be treated poorly.

Vivien had done the same thing in her younger days—letting a cute guy she'd met in the Hamptons play idiotic hot-and-cold games. Finally Vivien had snapped out of her amorous stupor and told the guy to get lost. She had no desire to be with someone who was unkind to her and she wished the same for her friend Coop.

"Just don't make excuses for his behavior. Okay?"

"I'm not making excuses for him, Vivi. I'm happy with Brad. Why can't you just be happy for me?" Coop's tone sounded defensive. "Things come so easily to you—you've got a handsome fiancé, an exciting job, a beautiful condo. It might surprise you that the rest of us actually have to work for everything. Finding someone and being in a relationship has been such a struggle for me."

Vivien let his comment slide. She wanted Coop to know that she was supportive, but that didn't change the fact that she was concerned about Brad's selfish behavior. "Coop, I just want you to find love and be happy…with someone who deserves you and appreciates you, that's all. I think you're a pretty great catch."

*

Coop finally had everything he wanted; why couldn't Vivien just be supportive of him? Normally they could tell each other anything and everything. But maybe he should have kept the story of Brad's antics at Splash to himself. Coop looked at his watch.

"Oh, sweetie, I'd better finish up my run. I still have to get home, pack my bag, and head to the airport. I'll call you from Miami, okay?"

The two friends said goodbye. As he picked up the pace on the treadmill, Coop scoffed at Vivien's comment. Of course Brad appreciated him. Didn't he?

Later that day, Coop donned his Maui Jim sunglasses as he stepped out of the limo in front of the 1 Hotel in Miami's South Beach. The entrance to the hotel was flanked by enormous potted plants, and stylish twentysomethings with copper-colored skin rushed over to greet him. The warm breeze embraced Coop and he drank in the abundant sunshine. A beaming attendant offered him a chilled glass of cucumber water as he escorted Coop inside to the front desk. He was already starting to relax.

The New York office was holding their partners' retreat in Miami, and this couldn't have been a better time to be away from the cold, bleak weather. The thirty partners would be meeting and having some fun over the next few days. It was the firm's policy to have no more than five partners booked on the same flight, so Coop volunteered to take an early flight in order to soak up the sun and chill out a bit. The rest of the guys would be flying in during that Sunday.

Coop checked in to his tastefully decorated room, all white and taupe contemporary furniture with accents of light wood and floor-to-ceiling windows that offered a spectacular view of the beach. He quickly donned his swim trunks, a T-shirt, and a ball cap and headed down to one of the coveted spots on the property—a cushioned white chaise lounge on the beach. Coop slathered on sunscreen, cracked open his latest book club novel, and promptly fell asleep, lulled by the gentle sounds of the churning surf.

When he awoke, Coop let out a big yawn and stretched his limbs like a cat sunning itself in a cozy window seat. He checked his watch. Just enough time for a quick dip in the pool and a shower, then on to the partners' cocktail party and dinner. Coop knew they'd be announcing the winner of the firm's coveted Client Service Award that evening. The award went to the partner who'd accumulated the highest client ratings over the past year. Even better, the prize included an extra week of vacation and a generous travel budget to a destination of the winner's choosing. Daydreaming, Coop imagined someday winning the award and whisking Brad off to the south of France, where they'd have a romantic getaway at a luxurious boutique hotel along the Côte d'Azur.

The cocktail hour was poolside, and as the sun faded to a pinkish glow, Coop greeted the other partners and mingled, even managing to have a pleasant but abbreviated conversation with Felix Culo, who was in unusually good spirits. How could Coop feel anything but chill watching the sunset with an icy gin and tonic in his hand? He asked his colleague Barry when their CEO would be arriving. "He's not going to make it this time," Barry said cryptically. Coop had heard their CEO loved to announce the Client Service Award winner, so it was unfortunate he'd miss out on that cherished tradition.

Toward the end of the cocktail hour, Martin stood on an elevated platform to make some announcements. First he gave directions to dinner in the private dining room. Then he cleared his throat. "And now, I'm pleased to announce the recipient of the Client Service Award."

Coop looked around, trying to guess which one of the other partners would win.

"Gary Cooper."

Is this really happening?

In a daze, Coop rushed up to Martin to receive the official certificate, which was decorated in gold leaf and nicely framed. He was congratulated by the other partners with handshakes and back slaps as the partners made their way to dinner. All the men assembled in a private dining room where round tables with white linen tablecloths seated groups of six partners. Gleaming china and silverware reflected the soft glow of the candles adorning each table, and the cobalt-blue drinking glasses added a tropical touch. Barry clinked his wineglass with his fork while Martin stood up trying to get everyone's attention.

Waiters moved swiftly and silently placing silver baskets of warm bread and small plates of whipped truffle butter at each table. Coop was feeling a glorious high from the thrill of winning the award and a nice buzz from the cocktails. Famished, he snatched a dinner roll from a basket. Martin had a solemn look on his face as he spoke. "Some of you may be wondering why Walter is not with us tonight. The fact of the matter is that our CEO has decided to retire, effective immediately, due to some health concerns. We want to thank Walter for his many years of strong leadership and dedication to the firm."

That's big news. Coop smeared truffle butter on his dinner roll and took a bite. His mind started to wander as he contemplated how he'd spring the news of an all-expenses-paid French Riviera vacation to Brad. He could just picture the look of absolute delight on Brad's face.

Martin looked around at the partners in the room. "Early this morning we had an emergency conference call with the Promotion Council and extended leadership of the firm to determine who would take the CEO's place. The senior partners put in their votes and I'm pleased to announce our new leader..." Martin paused.

Coop took another bite of the delicious bread, naively anticipating he'd hear the name of a partner he held in high regard, someone deserving of the role.

Martin motioned toward the table to his right. "Our new CEO is none other than Felix Culo. Please join me in congratulating Felix." Coop gagged on the bread, almost necessitating the Heimlich maneuver. A beaming Felix Culo stood up and gave a two-finger salute to the other partners.

Coop had never been on solid footing with the guy, and now, with Felix's rise in power, he had an unsettled feeling in his gut. He had witnessed Felix's questionable ethics with the Hello TelCo audit, and Coop felt sure that in the CEO role Felix would be making some perilous decisions for the firm. The news of Felix's promotion was like an ice pick hacking away at Coop's joy over his award.

The next morning it seemed like Coop awoke in an entirely different world. Instead of seeing a warm and sunlit beach outside, Coop parted the curtains and saw dark skies and a deluge sweeping across the sand. He heard the whistling of gale-force winds rattling the windows. Guess that meant a run on the beach was out of the question. Coop threw on his workout gear and headed down to the hotel gym.

The industrial-looking gym was deserted, so Coop did some quick stretches and then hopped on a treadmill. It wasn't until he had logged about three miles that he heard a noise behind him. Someone else had entered the gym.

A clipped voice called out a greeting. "*Mawning*, Coop."

Coop knew that voice without turning around. He looked up at the mirror and saw Felix Culo giving a wave. Then Coop did a double take. Felix was wearing cycling shorts and a tight-fitting tank top over his soft, pale body. Not an outfit Coop had even remotely ever imagined on Felix.

"Your shoelace is untied, buddy."

Coop was about to respond when suddenly everything whooshed by in an instant—surprise, impact, pain.

His head was spinning. Coop found himself on his backside on the gym floor in a daze. He touched his chin at the source of a searing pain and took his hand away to find it covered in blood. What had just happened?

Felix was standing over Coop and let out a guffaw. "Oh man, that was awesome!" He clapped his hands together and smiled. Felix's reaction to the situation spoke volumes about him. In his youth Felix had probably been the type of boy who'd snatch up a butterfly resting peacefully on a flower, pluck off its wings, and fling its body onto the hot pavement, gleefully watching it writhe in pain. Felix caught the icy look from Coop and the smile dropped away. "Um, you okay, Coop?"

Coop's jaw ached and he felt like he'd just been shot out of a cannon. "What happened? Can you hand me a towel?"

Felix kept his distance and tossed a gym towel to Coop. "You turned to say hello and stepped on your loose shoelace. Lost your footing. When you started falling your chin hit the treadmill rail. Man, you slammed down so hard on that metal rail the bong rang out like the Liberty Bell!" In Felix's grating New England accent it sounded like *Lihbiddy Bell*. "Then you got catapulted off the treadmill. Never seen anything like that. Wicked." Felix had a cold look of amusement in his eyes, as if Coop was a source of cheap entertainment like the dying butterfly.

Coop groaned from both the pain and the humiliation that Felix had just witnessed his stumble. His chin was gushing blood and his jaw was aching. When he slowly got up and walked over to the mirror, he saw a large gash. "Ugh, I think I need stitches. I'm going to get this taken care of, Felix. I'll be a little late to this morning's session, okay?" He pressed the gym towel to his chin.

"Sure, Coop. Take care of yourself." Felix nodded and gave a dismissive wave.

CHAPTER 8

GRACE

The Flip Style executive team was elated about the exceptional results of their business. In the short time since the relaunch of their product and brand, their revenues had skyrocketed. Founders Venky and Tom were thrilled with the outcome and generous in their praise of Grace's contributions. Their biggest investor, Venky's dad, Devinder Jain, piled on with his admiration for Grace. Even the nettlesome head of strategy, Preston Ford, was excited about the big success and managed to pay a compliment to her.

"Grace, we can't thank you enough for sharing your expertise, bringing fresh ideas, and being such a brilliant collaborator." Venky pulled out a gift-wrapped box and placed it in front of her. "Please accept this small token of our appreciation."

"For me? Thank you, guys." Grace pulled the box toward her and opened it. Inside was a luxurious orchid-rose pashmina scarf with delicate golden threads woven through in the shape of vines and small flowers.

Devinder had a twinkle in his eye. "Grace, we had it custom-made for you. The finest pashmina from India. The golden vines symbolize how you've helped the Flip Style business prosper."

Grace was moved. "It's absolutely beautiful. Thank you so much." She caressed the baby-soft scarf against her cheek. "I will treasure it always." One of the things Grace enjoyed most about work was developing strong relationships, and it was icing on the cake to be the recipient of such thoughtfulness.

*

As their meeting drew to a close Devinder mentioned he was heading across the Hudson River to the CNBC studios. The renowned Indian magnate was elegantly dressed in a bespoke suit and was set to appear on *Power Lunch*.

"Good luck with your interview, Dev," Grace said. "While you're there you should say hi to my friend Sofia LaForte. She does a show called *Titans Tell All* with Kate Frost."

Devinder's eyes lit up as if a thousand-volt current had shot through his body. "Really, Grace? Then may I ask you a huge favor? Would you accompany me to the CNBC studios and introduce me to Sofia LaForte and Kate Frost? Please?"

"I'd be happy to, Devinder, but I have an important meeting this afternoon. Not sure if I could make it there and back with the traffic."

The business mogul smiled broadly. "Not to worry, Grace, we will be going very fast."

He wasn't kidding. Soon Grace found herself sitting in a helicopter ready to take off. The roaring noise inside the helicopter felt like someone had thrown an insulated blanket over Grace's senses. She could hear nothing but the chopping sound of the rotor blades slicing through the air. Devinder Jain sat with regal posture in the back of the six-seater helicopter next to Grace and handed her a headset, using sign language to show her how to use the intercom. The headset immediately cut the sound of the rotor blades, and once Grace positioned the microphone properly she could communicate again.

"Grace, thanks again for coming with me to the CNBC studios."

She felt herself being lifted up in the air—a sensation of floating and moving side to side, like being inside an agitating washing machine—and it unnerved her. She gripped the armrests as the helicopter rose quickly over Manhattan and sped off across the river. Devinder, who'd flown many times before, seemed blasé about this mode of transportation.

"I must say the Flip Style team could not have done this turnaround successfully without you. Venky and Tom would love to have you on their executive team—you name the role, anything you want. Eh?" Devinder nudged her with his elbow.

Grace gave a chuckle. "I'm flattered, Dev, thanks. And I've enjoyed working with Venky and Tom. But my goal is to run a business." The announcement of the merger between Palazzo and Burberry had been released recently. "And oh, by the way, I'll be getting that opportunity at Palazzo in the near future. That's what my afternoon meeting is about—the new CEO asked me to come in to discuss the plans for me to run the Baby & Kids business."

"Of course, Grace, of course. I should have known you'd have bigger plans." Devinder laughed. "Once we meet your friend Sofia and Kate Frost I'll have the pilot take you back across the river to the Thirty-Fourth Street heliport so you can make it to your meeting on time. All right?"

"Sure, thanks."

"Grace, I want you to keep something in mind." He raised a finger and tapped the side of his head. "If you should ever need backing for a business venture, I want you to call me first. Okay?" Devinder was known as a collector of talented people and it was clear he wanted to include Grace in that select group. What a stroke of luck for her. She'd enjoyed working with him and admired his amazing skills and warm personality—it was easy to see why he was such a phenomenal success.

Grace gave a grateful nod. "Absolutely, Dev. I'll do just that."

*

A car arranged by Devinder Jain was waiting to whisk Grace over to the Palazzo offices in midtown as soon as she landed at the heliport. She felt like a martini shaken, not stirred, as she stepped off the helicopter, legs wobbly from the flight. As the limo maneuvered smoothly through traffic, Grace mentally rehearsed what she'd say to Skip Palmer. She had big plans for the Baby & Kids business and was eager to take the reins. Grace leaned back in the seat, smoothed out her Burberry silk tie-waist dress, and took a moment to relax. As they pulled up in front of the Palazzo headquarters, Grace took a deep breath to calm her nerves—this would be the start of a new chapter in her career. She checked in and was directed to the CEO's office.

"Grace, good to see you." Skip got up from his desk and walked over to greet her. "Thanks for coming in. Please, sit." He gestured to one of the chairs across from his massive glass desk and returned to his desk chair. His style was notably more formal than that of her previous boss.

"Hi, Skip, how are things going with the merger so far? Are you settling into your new role?" Grace turned on the charm, but her jiggling foot belied her bottled-up tension. She'd done a background check on Skip Palmer, speaking to several people who'd worked with him, and the feedback wasn't that positive. The consensus was that while Skip was intelligent and knew how to grow a business, he was a difficult boss with a hot temper. He was also known for favoring a handful of people and bristled at being challenged.

"Good, good." He absentmindedly shuffled around some manila folders on his desk. "Don told me it would take some time to get up to speed on the business, and I've trusted his opinion since our college days."

"I'm sorry, Don…?"

"Oh," Skip chuckled, "Don Spencer, one of Palazzo's board members. He recruited me for the CEO job. Old fraternity buddy of mine." *Aha, so that's how Skip landed the role.* "Well, let's get down to brass tacks, Grace. I want to speak with you about the Baby & Kids business."

Grace nodded and sat forward. "Great, I have some innovative ideas for how we can supercharge the business as well as some thoughts on revamping the product collection. I also had some interesting design collaborations in mind."

The CEO gave her a sudden stern look, like a grumpy old neighbor staring out the broken window of his home and holding up a baseball she'd thrown—Grace shrank back in silence. "I'm a big believer in not disturbing a winning formula. Take SunShine, for instance—a great laundry detergent that has been consistent since its launch in 1966, and at JMC we didn't mess with success. Now, you've done a bang-up job as the chief marketing officer, Grace. You implemented many great ideas that helped bring Burberry back to life and make the brand cool again. It's clear that's where your talents lie, so why mess with a winning formula? I've thought about this and about where Palazzo really needs you. I've decided that I want you to take the reins again as CMO of the combined businesses."

Sound of screeching brakes. Did he just completely change her career plans? This was not what was agreed. Grace kept her cool. "I understand where you're coming from, Skip, but here's the thing—my desire is to run a business. I can do the marketing side of the business blindfolded and standing on one foot. I've wanted to run a business for some time now and I'm up for the challenge. I thought the plan was for me to run Baby & Kids."

Skip removed his oval horn-rimmed glasses and pinched the bridge of his nose. "Actually, that's not my plan, it was the plan of my predecessor. I'm bringing in a former JMC colleague who ran the baby food business to run Baby & Kids, so that slot has been filled. The job we've got for you is CMO."

Grace spoke slowly. "So, either I step back into the CMO role when I return from my sabbatical or…?" Her gaze met the CEO's. Grace's throat was parched and her stomach churned. After all she'd done for the company, this was how she was being treated? Her old boss Celeste had been grooming her for this role for some time and it was widely known in the company.

Skip gave her a condescending smirk. "Let's not be dramatic, Grace. The CMO role is one of the most coveted jobs in the industry. You'll be doing exciting, meaningful work. And perhaps, after I've had a chance to assess your skill set, we can think about moving you over to run a business." He steepled his hands touching the tips of his fingers together and rested his elbows on top of the manila folder. "Being the head of this business, I need to mitigate risk. I can't put someone in a role that they've never done before. Can't do it."

Grace straightened up in her chair. "I'm not sure I understand, Skip. Isn't this your first role as a CEO? Someone gave you the chance; won't you give me the same consideration? There's always gotta be a first time, right?" She smiled and shrugged, palms up, trying to lighten the mood. "Also, wouldn't running the Baby & Kids business be a first for your colleague from JMC? I know the business, the brand, and the industry, so I believe I'd be in a position to add significant value." As someone who was used to speaking her mind, Grace assumed that laying out the facts might sway her boss's mindset. And she was rarely lacking in confidence.

Skip's expression hardened and he set his lips in a thin line.

Note to self—he doesn't like being challenged. Oops, forgot that one.

"This is my plan, Grace. It's how I intend to run my company." She noticed the phrase "my company" and saw by the cold look on his face that he wasn't open to discussing it further. Her boss sat back and faked a smile—the kind where someone's lips are curved but their eyes are shooting daggers. "Listen, I don't need you to decide right now. Why don't you think it over? Get back to me in a couple of days."

"What's the rush?" Grace said. "You do know that I'm not due back from my sabbatical until July, right? That's four months from now."

Skip grimaced. "Yeah, about that. We're going to need you back earlier, so you'll just need to cut your sabbatical short—start up again in two weeks' time. We really need your superior marketing skills, Grace, that's how you can best add value to Palazzo. I'm counting on you." He scrunched up his face in a seemingly friendly way. "Oh, and I'd like for you to give me your top three ideas for how to build Palazzo's business—you can email those to me by end of week. Thanks so much for coming in, Grace."

*

Her head was reeling as she made her way down in the elevator. Grace's dream of running a business at Palazzo had just been crushed like a city sidewalk cockroach meeting its untimely end beneath a businessman's wingtip shoe. On top of that, her sabbatical would be cut off four months early. The more she interacted with Skip Palmer, the more she wondered about what he'd be like as a boss.

As Grace walked through the lobby, she heard her name. Laura, a talented designer who worked in the Baby & Kids business, rushed over to greet her. The designer had apparently just made a Starbucks run.

"How are you, Grace?" Laura's strawberry blond curly hair was like a halo of happiness around her freckled face—this was a woman full of positivity. Laura was also one of the women at the company whom Grace had been mentoring over the years.

"Hi, Laura, great to see you. I was just in for a meeting with the new CEO." Grace couldn't hide her glumness.

"Is everything okay? We're so excited to have you lead our team."

Grace shrugged and said, "I'm not sure if it will work out. I think Skip may have other ideas." She bit her lip.

In a low voice the designer said, "I know Skip hasn't been here that long, but so far he has ruffled a lot of feathers with his outbursts. In fact, some of the most talented people from our old team are talking about leaving Palazzo. I was hoping we could meet for lunch sometime soon—I'd love to get your career advice."

The two women made tentative plans to meet, gave each other a hug, and said goodbye.

Grace walked slowly out of the building. Skip Palmer had no idea, but he was already impacting the careers of many people and quite possibly the future of the company.

Outside on the city streets, the March winds were swirling. Grace pulled her coat around her and tightened the belt. Just then her cell phone rang. Vivien was calling to say she and Clay were expecting a baby in late summer. Grace was so caught up in the excitement of her friend's news that she nearly forgot about her meeting with Skip. After they chatted about Vivien's pregnancy a bit, Grace let out a deep breath.

"How are things on your end, Grace?"

Grace let out a snort. "Ugh, not good. I met with the new CEO today, and Skip isn't going to let me run Baby & Kids. Instead he's bringing in someone from JMC who led the baby food business."

Vivien gasped. "Oh no, what a huge disappointment! I'm so sorry to hear that. What does he want you to do instead?"

"Stay on as CMO of Palazzo. I guess that not so bad, but I really didn't want to be pigeonholed into just doing marketing. And oh, by the way, he's cutting my sabbatical short—I have to return to work in two weeks."

"Yikes." Vivien huffed. "Are you actually going to do that?"

"Have to," Grace said, "otherwise I won't have a job. I still need to pay the bills, and the proceeds from my book aren't nearly enough to live on."

*

After Grace finished her conversation with Vivien, she ducked into a coffee shop to sit and collect her thoughts. Stirring some sugar into her latte, she sighed. The book launch had been good, the book was being received well, and sales were okay, but it sure wasn't a lucrative endeavor.

The two book signings at bookstores that her publisher had set up had been nothing short of a disaster. Those events, thrown together on short notice, were attended by her faithful Smasher friends and a smattering of retired folks—not her target audience at all. Grace cringed when she remembered Andi and Sofia plus a few other Ceiling Smasher members sitting in the nearly empty audience attentive and smiling at her with encouraging looks. The marketing plan executed by the publisher showed no ingenuity, so Grace had taken it upon herself to market the book the way she saw fit. Recently she'd created an influencer seeding plan, making a list of prominent CEOs leading companies that were in trouble, and she'd sent them a handwritten note along with a copy of *Rise*. If she could get the attention of one of those CEOs, that might give her book more traction.

*

Two short weeks later Grace found herself in a conference room at the Palazzo offices with her marketing team—they were thrilled with the return of their leader. The key agenda item was a discussion about the launch of the Coterie Collection—a unique offering of leather totes designed in collaboration with Japanese contemporary artist Yayoi Kusama. They were deep in execution mode when Skip sauntered in.

"Grace, team," he said and nodded, sliding into a leather conference room chair and making himself comfortable. "Mind if I sit in and see how the brand magic is created?"

The fact that he'd already barged in and sat down irked Grace, but she managed a smile. "Of course, feel free, Skip." Turning to her team she said, "Let's review. The photo and video shoots are completed, so we have visual assets for our campaign. The retail windows will feature the Coterie Collection videos—Skip, have you seen this collection of bags we're launching?" Grace gestured to the photos hanging on the conference room wall. She ticked off the elements on their marketing campaign from her execution plan. "What's interesting about these bags is that each one is unique, but when you put all the bags in the collection together you get a different image depending on the placement of each bag." She turned her laptop toward him, pressing a button to play a time-lapse video accompanied by mesmerizing music. It showed the bags being moved around like puzzle pieces and put back together to create ten different jaw-dropping artistic images.

"Wow, I've never seen anything like this. These bags are amazing!" Skip murmured. "What's the price point?"

"Average retail price is ten thousand dollars per bag. But we only have a limited amount," said a member of the marketing team.

Skip rubbed his chin. "Limited amount? Why limited? Don't we want to sell as many of these as we can? We should be making more!"

Unsure of whether their new CEO was making a joke, the team remained silent, exchanging nervous looks.

"Grace, why aren't we making more of these?" Skip's eyes bored into hers, his voice booming. He was dead serious.

How could she respond to her boss without embarrassing him? "It might be helpful, Skip, for me to take you through this project one on one. Then I can explain what—"

Skip cut her off with a slashing motion of his hand. "No. Explain it to me now. That is, unless there isn't a good reason. We should be making more of these bags so we can sell more. At JMC when we saw a product was performing we'd turn up the sales volume, pump out more units. That's Business 101—that's how you make money, Grace."

She didn't care for his gruff style nor his condescending tone. And it was clear the Skip didn't have a clue about how to run a luxury brand.

Grace spoke in a calm and slow manner, as if she were addressing a classroom full of kindergartners. "Well, Skip, this isn't like selling SunShine laundry detergent. In fact, this industry works in the opposite way. Scarcity of product makes it feel special and creates brand cachet. Customers desire what they can't have. We want to create excitement about this collection and elevate it in the minds of consumers, like the Birkin bag from Hermès. That's why it's offered in a limited quantity for a limited time—we're trying to generate demand. If it sells out, that's the exact outcome we want."

Skip stroked the side of his neck. "Sure, sure. Okay, what about a line extension? We could follow up with a line of handbags in the same design next. We've got to look at revenue-generating opportunities."

Horrified looks came across the faces of the marketing team. Although the new CEO had successfully grown a packaged goods business, he clearly wasn't getting how this business worked. And it seemed that he was only interested in making more money, not building brand cachet.

Grace groaned internally, but she forced herself to put on a neutral expression. "That's something we could consider, Skip, you'll have to consult with the head of the bags division. In my experience I've found that offering newness is what drives people to the brand and what makes it aspirational."

"A line extension would be new, wouldn't it?" He pursed his lips in an obstinate manner and then checked his watch. "I have to get to another meeting. I want to see a plan for a line extension on my desk by next week."

Eyes wide, Grace's team members looked at each other uncertainly. As soon as Skip left the room it seemed like everyone could breathe again.

"At least he didn't throw anything. I was in a meeting with Skip last week where he threw a three-ring binder at someone," a male colleague said dryly.

"Grace," said another colleague fearfully, "are we really doing a line extension of these bags?"

Grace shook her head. "I don't think so, but I'll have to get with the department head and figure out a way to tell Skip it's a bad idea." She grimaced. Based on what she was hearing from the other executives, Skip was making a lot of bad calls already.

*

SOFIA

On a balmy day in late March, Sofia soaked up the abundant sunshine and warm breeze as the sailboat cut through the waters of the Hudson River. Jasper had borrowed a friend's forty-foot yacht, and they were touring around Manhattan in style.

"She's a beauty, isn't she?" Jasper rubbed his goatee. Though he was staring at Sofia, she assumed it was a reference to the boat. He wore a navy blue golf shirt and khaki pants along with sunglasses. With Jasper's windblown dark hair and glorious smile as he steered the boat, it was like a sailing scene straight from one of the Kennedys' home movies at Hyannis Port.

Sofia beamed. "Indeed. We'll have to thank your friend for letting us borrow it."

He tilted his head slightly, then nodded.

They'd had a lovely lunch while the boat was docked, and then Jasper had taken the helm of the sailboat and navigated their way out to the river. Although Sofia had lived on the Upper West Side for years, this was the first time she'd actually ventured onto the Hudson River. She had to say she was impressed with Jasper's seamanship and how utterly relaxed he was maneuvering the vessel.

Over the past five months, their relationship had blossomed, and for the first time in years Sofia felt like she'd found a friend, confidante, intellectual partner, and romantic interest all wrapped up in one. She loved spending time with Jasper. He'd even helped Sofia when she shared the story about Kate Frost's scars (with Kate's permission) by recommending a renowned plastic surgeon.

When they returned the boat to the dock, Jasper asked Sofia to sit for a minute. "I'd like to talk with you about something." His eyes held a serious look. "Sofia, I love you. You make me really happy and I can envision building a life with you. But, you've mentioned that you don't think marriage is in your future and I want to understand why."

Sofia reached out to caress Jasper's face. "I love you, too, Jasper. I guess I've just thought for a while now that marriage isn't for me." She drew back. "It's just that…well, a woman I really admired confided in me that she regretted getting married. I've been afraid to make the same mistake." She bit her lip.

Jasper looked at her with an open expression. "Go on, I'm listening."

*

When Sofia was in graduate school, she had ambitious career plans but also wanted to someday find a life partner and raise a family. All of this changed drastically after a lunch with a former colleague, Martina Perry, a senior reporter who'd taken Sofia under her wing.

Martina was smart, well-rounded, and exceptional at asking incisive interview questions. A striking presence clad in her size-four designer clothes, Martina wore her signature perfume with the faint scent of gardenias—the scent that for Sofia signified the sweet smell of success.

Ultimately Martina's work got noticed by a bigwig at NBC and she soon made history, becoming the first African-American female anchor on a prime-time news broadcast. Her story and success gave hope to many women looking to shatter the glass ceiling. One day Martina's fate changed dramatically. She was interviewing the renowned filmmaker Russell Baker, and the electricity between them was palpable. Russell asked her to dinner, and four months later their glamorous wedding was featured in the "Sunday Styles" section of the *New York Times*. Two months after returning from her honeymoon, Martina became pregnant with twins. Within a year of giving birth to her twin girls—and much to her surprise—Martina became pregnant again.

After her third child, a boy, Martina was eager to get back to being an anchorwoman and met with network executives to discuss her return. The executives looked at Martina and coldly told her she'd have to slim down before they'd put her back on the air. She was then a size ten, the size of an average American woman.

Martina asked bitterly if anyone had ever told Dan Rather to lose a few pounds. "This is what a real woman looks like after she's had three kids," Martina explained to the men.

"That may be true, but it's not what America wants to see. They want to see their beautiful, beloved Martina Perry looking exactly the same as she did before."

After many draconian yet unsuccessful weight loss attempts, Martina realized she couldn't juggle three small children, her husband's travel schedule, and a prime-time news job. She also concluded that even with a strict eating and exercise regimen, she'd never return to that elusive size four. In a few short years, she went from a nationally recognized news anchor to being deep into "mommy and me" time.

Martina relayed all of this to Sofia one day over lunch in midtown—a conversation that Sofia would remember as the most brutally honest she'd ever had with another woman. Martina was still a stunning woman, although thicker around the middle and dressed more casually in clothes that didn't require dry cleaning.

"Women are doing other women a disservice, Sofia," Martina said. "All this talk about work/life balance? I'm telling you, it doesn't exist. It's just not possible to manage a high-powered career and have children." Her look was grim. "Not long ago I was jetting off to interview world leaders. Now I think about all those years I spent toiling away at my career—did I make the right choice by getting off the career track?" Only Martina could respond to her own aching inquiries.

"Martina, we all make different choices. I guess it's up to each individual to figure out what's best for them at different stages in their lives," Sofia offered supportively. "Your kids are lucky to have you as their mom. Surely you're enjoying your children, right?"

"Of course," Martina said reflexively. "My children are a joy, Sofia. I never knew it was possible to love another human being so much." She smiled, but a pained look came to her eyes. "But no one ever told me how mind-numbingly boring it can be to go to the playground day after day. Your kids are running around screaming and you're sitting there surrounded by some highly educated moms who choose not to work, plus their nannies. The conversation centers around organic baby food recipes, getting into the right preschools, and where to buy the cutest baby clothes. I have found myself yearning for an intelligent debate with someone over climate change or US foreign relations," Martina said wistfully. "I have to wait until my husband gets home to have a meaty conversation, but by then I'm just too exhausted and he just wants to relax with me and the kids."

"Couldn't you go back to work part-time? Take freelance assignments?" Sofia asked.

"You know that broadcast journalism is all-consuming. And I'm a serious journalist; I don't want to settle for doing magazine puff pieces about Hollywood hunks. It has to be all or nothing for me."

Sofia braved the question that was plaguing her. "Martina, do you...regret having kids?"

"Being married to Russell is terrific. And I love my children, they mean the world to me..."

"I didn't ask if you loved them, Martina, I can see that you do. I asked you if you regret choosing to stop your career to focus on having kids." Sofia searched Martina's face for the truth.

Martina let out a long sigh and crinkled her eyes. She glanced furtively around the restaurant. "You know what, Sofia? Honestly, I do. I wish I'd had a chance to achieve more before I had kids. But don't ever repeat that to anyone." She closed her eyes from the shame of having made this admission aloud. That might have even been the first time that Martina had admitted the truth to herself. Her familiar fragrance of gardenias lingered in the air, but for Sofia it was now the scent of regret.

Sofia was sorry to see Martina Perry that way. For a woman she'd always admired to be trapped in a lifestyle she didn't seem to embrace was distressing. Sofia prided herself on learning not only from her mistakes but from the mistakes of others. After her lunch with Martina she vowed to not fall into the same trap. Marriage was off the table for her.

While paying the bill for lunch, Martina suddenly brightened up. "My twins did the funniest thing the other day." She relayed an amusing anecdote about her twin girls, a jar of peanut butter, and their pet shih tzu.

Sofia put aside her fears and laughed heartily at the slice of happiness that Martina shared. They parted company, promising to keep in touch. Sofia resolved to focus on her career and get the most out of life without anything to weigh her down.

*

Jasper looked concerned and sat back. Was he starting to question his relationship with Sofia now that he knew how resolute she was about not getting married? "So, marriage and family aren't in the cards for you because your dress size might go up?" He scratched his goatee, then chuckled. "Sorry, just trying to lighten the mood, Sofia, you look so solemn."

"I'm just worried about making a choice I might regret."

"Listen, Sofia, I understand your concerns. I want you to know I'd never ask you to give up who you are or what you do. I know how important your career is to you and I'm a huge supporter." He grasped both her hands. "But I also think you should open yourself up to the opportunity for us to be happy together. Let's just take things one step at a time. I'm not asking you to have a boatload of kids or to be a stay-at-home mom—heck, if we decide to have little ones I might even be able to work from home and look after them."

Sofia's eyes widened. She'd never even considered that option, and the fact that Jasper had offered that up was unexpected and unconventional. Her relationship with Jasper Frank was opening up her mind to new possibilities. And it was the first time in a long time that Sofia had a steady man in her life who didn't deliver food to her apartment for a living.

"I'm just telling you that I love you and want you in my life. So can we revisit the topic of marriage at some point?"

Jasper had a knack for soothing Sofia's jitters. It was good that he understood her. "Of course, Jasper."

*

Sofia was sitting on the sofa in Kate Frost's office discussing something potentially life-changing with her colleague. Since their trip to Virginia, the two of them had really been in synch—working well together and developing a strong friendship. When Kate had shared the story of the stabbing attack, the scars, and how she'd settled for a solitary life, Sofia had resolved to do something about it. It turned out that Jasper's good friend was a top plastic surgeon at NYU who specialized in scar camouflage surgery, and he was eager to take Kate on as a patient.

"I appreciate this, Sofia, but…" Kate hesitated. "Do you really think it will work?"

Sofia pressed the surgeon's business card into Kate's hands. "I do. At any rate it's worth a try, Kate. Will you please just make an appointment with him?"

Clutching the card to her chest, Kate nodded slowly. "Thank you for caring about me, Sofia, I really mean that."

She gave Kate a heartfelt smile. Just then her smartphone buzzed, indicating she'd received a text. Sofia looked at the screen. "Hmm, interesting."

Kate said, "What's up?"

Arching one eyebrow, Sofia said, "My friend Grace is working with Devinder Jain, who's coming over here to appear on *Power Lunch*. Apparently he's made a special request to meet the two of us, and they're headed over to the studio in a helicopter."

She could swear she saw Kate's eyes sparkle with curiosity. "Devinder Jain? I'd love to meet him. He's in possession of all the important S's: smart, sophisticated, successful, and super good-looking."

Sofia giggled. "Then this should be fun. Shall we head down to greet them?"

*

That day's *Titans Tell All* program was a doozy—a two-parter with some major fireworks. The first part of the show featured two executives from the chain of convenience stores located in the Southern US called Git It 'N Go. The retail chain had recently been slapped with a class-action suit from a group of employees claiming years of discriminatory practices against women and people of color— qualified people who for years had been passed over for promotions and raises. Sofia and Kate kicked off the interview with some questions about recent company events for Texan CEO Wally Ingleton. Silver-haired and wearing cowboy boots with his suit, Wally had a swagger in his style.

"Hi, y'all," he said in a twang. "Thank you ladies for having us on your show." He spoke about the fine history of the company and the troubling lawsuit. As he spoke, Sofia noticed that he had turned his body toward Kate and wasn't even looking at her—was he being disrespectful or just nervous given the topic? "Now, y'all can see how these legal issues have been distracting us from our main goal."

"Your main goal?" Sofia asked.

"Delighting our customers, of course," the CEO said. "That's our number one goal. It's the number one goal of any retailer."

"So your objective is to delight customers," Sofia repeated.

Wally looked impatient. "Yep, that's exactly my point."

"But aren't most of your customers women and people of color? How are they responding to the class-action suit?" Sofia's ire was raised, especially after reading all the stories from the employees who'd been blatantly discriminated against.

Trying to soften their approach a bit, Kate said, "Wally, perhaps you can enlighten us on the steps you've taken to correct these problems?"

Wally smiled at Kate. "Well, our biggest step is appointing our new head of diversity." He introduced the older white gentleman sitting beside him.

It took immense self-control for Sofia to avoid scowling. "Wally, you've said a number of high-performing women and minorities in your company were routinely passed over for promotions and raises for decades. And the one major step in addressing those injustices was to appoint a head of diversity?" Sofia nodded to the executive, who sat immobile as a human rock.

The CEO responded, "Yep, that's exactly my point."

Sofia continued. "Perhaps it's just my eyesight, but your head of diversity doesn't appear to be that diverse. If you're trying to address the issue of diversity, why not have a woman or person of color lead the effort?"

"I happen to be one-sixteenth Apache Indian," the head of diversity stated.

Kate stifled a chuckle.

Wally continued. "Well, Sofia, this is just the start." His tone dripped with condescension. "Of course we'll consider expanding the task force in the future, adding some other folks. A major part of fixing things up was to develop a new mission statement, and that's going to help turn the situation around." He turned back toward Kate.

"Now I'd like to tell you about some great things we're doing, like our sponsorship of Little League Baseball."

Sofia pressed on. "That must be one powerful mission statement, if it can bring about all the changes you're expecting and end the years, *the years*, of discriminatory practices."

Wally shot back, "That's *exactly* my point. Once we all get behind the new mission statement, we can resolve the problems and move forward."

In an unfailingly polite tone, Sofia said, "I'm wondering, sir, if you wouldn't mind reciting that mission statement for us. Considering it's such a powerful tool to transform your company, I think we'd really benefit from hearing it."

Responding to that question was Wally's first mistake. "You want me to recite it?"

Kate egged him on. "Yes, please share it."

The CEO tugged on the peaked lapels of his pinstriped suit and leaned forward. "All right, I *will*." This was his second mistake. "It goes like this: Our company is committed to building a culture of empowerment, um, equality that empowers all types of people...we celebrate diversity in order to...uh, wait, let me start over. Our company is committed to celebrating diversity and empowering...and, er, something about achieving equality and creating an environment of, um...well, shoot, I can't remember all of it." He turned to his head of diversity, who sat frozen with terror. "Daryl, help me out here." Despite the time they'd probably spent wordsmithing it, clearly neither of them knew the mission statement.

Silence.

Sofia employed Wally's favorite phrase, saying crisply, "And that's exactly *my* point. A mission statement alone will not bring about the changes your company so desperately needs. Many of your employees' lives and careers were negatively impacted, and they're looking to you to set things right, not to rest all their hopes on a solitary mission statement. From what I've read about you, Wally, you're a strong, action-oriented leader. You have a successful company and a great opportunity in front of you to make real change happen, and to set an example for the entire retail industry. And that's something everyone would like to see you accomplish."

Realizing that he'd just been shown up by a smart black woman on national television, Wally closed his eyes, shook his head side to side, and let out a soft chuckle. Then he looked straight at Sofia. "Damn, you sure do speak your mind. I like that." To his credit, Wally made a bold statement. "I see what you're saying, Sofia, and I think you're onto something. Tell you what, I'm going to set about really solving these problems, and I'd like to come back on your show again sometime and tell you about our results. All right?"

Sofia smiled. "You've got yourself a deal, Wally." She held out her hand to him, and he took it.

*

After a short break, the show resumed with their second set of guests—Pete Wilkins, CEO of Play Action Sporting Goods, and his daughter Jackie. When they'd met in Virginia, Pete had said that as a condition of appearing on *Titans Tell All* he wanted his daughter to accompany him. Kate shared some highlights of the company from when it was founded by Pete up to the present. Then she asked Pete to talk about having his family—two sons and a daughter—working alongside him at the company. With a sly smile, Pete shared that the reason he'd named his daughter Jackie was because he had tremendous respect for baseball player Jackie Robinson.

"Since her namesake was a first in his field, I want to let you know that my Jackie will also be a first—the first female CEO of our company. I am announcing today that my daughter Jackie will be taking over as the CEO of Play Action Sporting Goods next summer. We'll take the next year to make a smooth transition. I have every confidence that she'll lead the company to even greater heights." Pete smiled proudly as he put his hand on his daughter's shoulder.

As Jackie thanked her father for the opportunity and spoke about her plans for the company, Sofia realized that *Titans Tell All* had just revealed blockbuster news in the industry—this was exactly what she'd envisioned for the show.

*

After their *Titans Tell All* show wrapped, Sofia couldn't wait to get back to her office and call Grace, who picked up on the first ring.

"Hi, Sof, what's going on?"

"You would not believe what happened after you left for your meeting. I witnessed one of the most powerful business magnates in the world melt like ice cream on a hot sidewalk when he spoke with Kate Frost. Man, was he smitten!"

"Really?"

Sofia chuckled. "Totally. After they met, Devinder and Kate sat down for a chat and flirted for thirty minutes straight like high school kids with major crushes—laughing, joking, and clearly enjoying each other's company. If I didn't have to drag Kate away to go on air for *Titans Tell All* I think the two of them would still be chatting. I heard him ask her if they could see each other again."

"Aww, how sweet. I had no idea I was playing matchmaker. Anyway you've said Kate's a cool person and Devinder is awesome—whip smart, charming, and handsome to boot. They'd make a great couple."

The wheels in Sofia's mind were already spinning. "I agree. Kate has been hesitant about dating, but I think that is about to change."

SMASHERS SYNCHED

*

COOP

Coop sat there stunned. Felix Culo, the new CEO of his accounting firm, had invited Coop along to a management meeting at his telecom client. Felix had led Coop to believe he was asked to join the meeting just to observe, but standing in front of the entire management of Hello TelCo, Felix had just made a big announcement.

Felix repeated it as if to make sure that Coop had heard it and internalized it. "My fellow partner Gary Cooper, or Coop for short, will now be the lead accountant managing this account. He's a superstar in the firm, and out of all the partners he recently won our prestigious Client Service Award, so I'm sure he'll do a bang-up job for you." Felix smiled and gave Coop a thumbs-up like they were close buddies.

Wait a minute, Felix just put me in charge of our firm's biggest account? The idea shot through Coop's brain as he processed this latest development. He was mildly aware of the applause and looks of approval from the many people in the huge conference room. And Felix had actually called him a superstar? Was this a sign that Felix was welcoming Coop into his inner circle? Had his boss concluded that Coop's forensic accounting skills could add value to this client? Whatever the reason, this was huge step up in Coop's career.

Face flushed with excitement, Coop stood. "Thank you, Felix. I look forward to working with all of you and I'll do my best for you." He smiled.

Felix nodded. He started going over his agenda items, pausing at different times to get Coop's input and seek his opinion, complimenting Coop on his insightful remarks. For Coop this was the beginning of a new day in his professional career. Whatever doubts he'd had about this firm were suddenly wiped away. *This is exactly where I'm supposed to be.*

281

A few days later Coop knocked on the open door to Felix's office. "Hi, Felix, do you have a minute to discuss the Hello TelCo account?"

Felix was studying his computer screen and absentmindedly cracking open pistachios and popping them in his mouth. The CEO said, "Okay. What's on your mind?"

Coop cleared his throat and took a seat. "Well, I'm still coming up to speed on the telecom industry and its accounting standards. However, in doing a thorough forensic analysis of the client's books, I've found some accounting irregularities."

Felix narrowed his eyes. "Irregularities?"

"Yes. It appears that Hello TelCo has eliminated some of their largest expenses from their income statement—they are treating them in a way they shouldn't be treated. This practice is against GAAP principles."

Felix sat back in his chair and folded his hands over his protruding belly. "What are you saying, Coop?"

Coop rubbed his forehead, trying to stave off the impending headache. "Hello TelCo is grossly overstating their earnings. If they are inflating their earnings, their stock price is also getting pumped up...falsely. I—and I'm sure you as CEO—don't want to put the firm at risk by allowing this practice to continue, so we need to get their top executives to redo their books and restate their earnings." This was the very client that had had the questionable audit not long ago.

Nodding his head slowly, Felix said, "I see, I see. This is quite concerning. Tell you what, let me bring on Eugene to take another look. I think we need to proceed with caution here and do things properly. I'll circle back with you once he's done some analysis, all right?"

Eugene was a close buddy of Felix's but also a highly thorough accountant. Feeling like a huge weight had been lifted off his shoulders,

Coop let out a grateful sigh. "Sure, that sounds good, Felix. Another set of eyes could be really helpful."

*

The following Monday, Coop sat in a conference room with Felix and Eugene to discuss the telecom client.

Felix smiled broadly. "Good news, Coop. I had Eugene here take a look at Hello TelCo's books and it appears that there are, in fact, some mistakes happening with their treatment of their expenses. I spoke with the Hello TelCo CEO and CFO and they're going to address these things. I appreciate your bringing this to our attention, but I think we're in good shape now."

"Oh, that's great, Felix. So they are going to restate their earnings? What's the timeline for that?" Coop asked.

Tilting his head, Eugene spoke. "Coop, the client execs are up to their eyeballs with the acquisition they're trying to complete. It's not the best timing for them to focus on correcting some minor accounting errors."

Coop shot him a glare. "I wouldn't call these minor accounting errors, Eugene. I would call this accounting fraud. It's serious stuff, you know. There are grandmothers out there who own this stock and their entire life savings could be wiped out if the stock collapses. We don't want to harm ordinary people, do we? We need to resolve this ASAP."

Felix held up both hands. "We hear you, Coop, and we're on it. I'll talk to the CEO again and urge him to make these corrections."

"I'm wondering, Felix, shouldn't I be on that call with you? After all, I am the lead accountant for this client." It suddenly dawned on Coop that he was not being included in some critical client communications.

Felix's look darkened. "No, Coop, don't worry about it. Better for me to handle it on my own—I've known the CEO for many years. I'll update you once I've had my conversation." His terse tone indicated their discussion about this topic had come to an end.

"Okay. Well, please keep me in the loop." As Coop got up to leave he noticed Felix and Eugene exchanging looks. A couple of steps outside the conference room door, Coop looked down and noticed his shoelace was untied. The memory of his treadmill accident was still fresh, so Coop decided not to risk further injury. He knelt down immediately to tie his shoe.

He heard Felix snort from inside the conference room. "God, that guy just gets under my skin, you know? All his whining about grandmothers losing their life savings. Coop's just going to have to learn that those grandmothers are going to get screwed. People get screwed all the time. Boo hoo." It was as if Felix had ripped off the composed mask of the upstanding CEO he'd been wearing since his appointment, only to reveal his true personality.

Eugene laughed. "Gotta hand it to you, Felix, you sure pulled off a brilliant move making Coop the lead accountant for Hello TelCo. If things come crashing down—well, we know who's going to take the fall."

He could hear Felix clap his hands in glee and return to cracking open pistachios. "Yeah, that's exactly the game plan. Even though I've been advising this client for years, Coop will get blamed for everything if this accounting scandal ever comes to light. As the partner in charge of Hello TelCo he'll be in the hot seat. In one fell swoop I'll get him booted out of the firm and wipe away any problems with this client. It's beautiful—what I'd call a double play." Felix's sinister motivations were finally revealed.

The two men laughed ruthlessly like criminals putting the finishing touches on plans for a bank heist.

Coop felt like he was suffocating. His head was spinning and he stood up slowly, clutching the wall. So that was why Felix had given him that big opportunity? Not because of his skills but because he needed a scapegoat in case of emergency. Clenching his fists, Coop marched down the hallway and directly out of the building.

*

Outside in the corporate garden, Coop paced around, trying to collect his thoughts. One thing was clear—he would not and could not remain a partner in that accounting firm, not when he knew there was illegal activity going on. Coop sat on the steps of the garden, his head pounding with stress, and the tears started to fall. After what seemed like forever, he wiped away his tears and picked up his phone.

Letting out a heavy sigh, his fingers trembled as he dialed a number. With each press of the buttons, Coop knew he was making the call that would end his career. He couldn't believe that everything he'd worked for over the past decade at the firm would be obliterated like a bug smashed into smithereens as it hit the windshield of a speeding car.

He was forced to leave a voicemail. "Patrick, it's Coop. Remember our conversation back in September? Well, things have gotten worse and I need you to tell me what to do to expose this situation. Please call me back immediately." He placed his phone next to him and dropped his head into his hands.

Within seven minutes his phone rang. Patrick. His friend from the SEC told Coop exactly what to do and that he should do it quickly. Coop nodded robotically as he listened to Patrick's instructions.

Then Coop took a minute to call his boyfriend Brad to fill him in on the events of the day. Brad couldn't talk long since he was on duty, but he was sympathetic and promised they'd have a chance to talk over dinner the next night.

Back in the office, Coop jumped into action. He transferred the necessary client computer files from the server to an external hard drive that he'd always kept locked in his desk. Then he looked around his office and gathered the things that were the most meaningful to him to take home that night. As evening fell, Coop crept stealthily into the main file room and pulled all the key client documents he needed to copy. He had compiled a list of the documents to get and worked down the list methodically. It took a while to complete this task, but Coop worked quickly and silently, looking up every few minutes to make sure he wasn't being watched. He retrieved his duplicates from the copy room, double-checked that he had everything, then returned the client documents to their file cabinets. Coop scooped up his stack of copied documents into a large pile, switched off the lights, and proceeded down the quiet hallway to his office.

All of a sudden he felt a giant hand firmly gripping his shoulder. "Hey, what are you up to?" a voice said. Coop nearly screamed in terror. He quickly spun around and some papers flew off the top of his stack from the momentum.

"Coop, it's me." Barry towered over him. Seeing Coop's ashen expression he said, "Sorry, I didn't mean to startle you. I was just heading out." Barry's coat was on and he held up his briefcase.

Coop let out a breath. "Oh, Barry. Hi. I thought you were a burglar or something." They both chuckled.

"Burning the midnight oil, I see. What are you working on so late?" Barry helped pick up the errant papers on the floor and placed them on top of the stack in Coop's arms. "Hello TelCo, eh?"

Coop prayed silently that Barry wouldn't question why he had stacks of Hello TelCo documents in his arms. "Um, yes. You know I'm the lead accountant. Just reviewing some of their financials. The work never ends, does it?" Coop did his best to muster a casual smile.

"Good, good. Well, don't stay too late, Coop. Have a good night." Barry gave a wave and hustled to catch the elevator.

Inside his office, Coop loaded his important belongings into a box and stacked it on top of the box with the client files. He sent an email to his clients that he was leaving the firm effective immediately and shut his laptop, leaving it on his desk. Then he swung by Felix's office and left his letter of resignation and ID badge on Felix's desk.

When he walked out of the building that night with his two boxes,

Coop left behind his career as a partner at his firm and took on a new identity—as a corporate whistleblower.

*

Coop's emotions were swirling when he awoke late the next morning—a mixture of relief to be out of such a toxic work environment and trepidation about his professional future. He lay in bed for a moment, imagining the look of stupefaction on Felix's face when he ripped open Coop's letter of resignation. He let out an impish laugh and rolled out of bed.

Patrick was flying up from Washington, DC, to meet Coop later that morning at the SEC's regional office in TriBeCa. Coop went out for a run to clear his head. The exercise helped him regain his equilibrium.

When Coop arrived at the nondescript office building with the box of files and hard drive, he looked around the lobby. Patrick was waving at him and ran over. Patrick gave Coop a hug and a sincere look of appreciation. "Listen, Coop, I know this took a lot of guts, but you're doing the right thing. Fraudulent activity such as this only ends up hurting regular folks like you and me." He took the box from Coop and ushered him up to the floor of the SEC regional office. They entered a sterile-looking conference room where a man and a woman sat, both wearing serious looks and dark suits.

Patrick said, "Coop, these are my colleagues from the OWB. They'll be working with me on this investigation."

"OWB?" Coop raised an eyebrow. His nerves were a bit on edge.

The woman said, "Office of the Whistleblower. Good to meet you, Coop."

"Is that really what it's called?" The name struck Coop as comical and he had to stop himself from giggling nervously.

The four of them sat down and Patrick got the discussion going. With a camera recording his statement and the others taking copious notes, Coop laid out the history of the client, the fraudulent activity taking place, and how his accounting firm was not only involved but was facilitating these activities under the direction of CEO Felix Culo. Coop also talked about the conversation he'd overheard between Felix and Eugene where they were plotting to set him up to take the blame. Unable to mask his disgust, he also shared Felix's quote about grandmothers getting screwed.

The SEC investigators shook their heads in disapproval. They asked a lot of questions and went through Coop's list of the files he'd provided in both hard copy and on the hard drive. Patrick asked Coop if he had a company ID badge—fortunately Coop had snapped a photo of it before leaving it on Felix's desk the night before. Then they had Coop fill out some forms. An assistant brought in a tray of sandwiches for them and they continued poring over the documents and discussing them.

Finally in the early afternoon after a five-hour meeting with the SEC investigators, Coop was fully briefed on their timeline and expectations of him as a whistleblower. Patrick wrinkled his forehead. "Coop, what you're doing is really brave. But I think you should understand that this means you won't be able to work in this industry again. It's doubtful that any major accounting firm would want to hire you after this comes to light."

Coop swallowed hard. He'd anticipated that, but having Patrick say it aloud made it seem more real…and permanent. What would happen over the coming months, he had no clue. "I understand," he said grimly. With that they wrapped up their meeting and Coop walked out into the bustling Manhattan streets.

*

Brad was on duty across town at the Waldorf Astoria. Coop texted him to ask if he was free. Brad said he'd be available within the hour and to text him then.

Ooh, I know. I'll bring Brad a sweet surprise. Coop hopped in a cab to head over to the East Side and made a beeline for the Baskin-Robbins ice-cream shop just a few blocks away from the hotel. He got two cups of ice cream—mint chocolate chip for himself and cookies and cream for Brad—and walked the short distance. When he was standing outside the Waldorf Astoria he texted Brad to come outside and meet him.

Brad came rushing out of the hotel and upon spying Coop hustled him around the corner to a side entrance. "What are you doing here, Coop?" Brad's violet-blue eyes flashed. He didn't seem pleased.

Feeling wounded, Coop said, "I thought I'd surprise you with some ice cream. Here, cookies and cream, your favorite." He held out the ice cream like a servant proffering a gift to his master. Brad scowled. What was Brad so stressed about anyway? When, in the history of the United States, did anyone ever attempt to assassinate the *vice* president?

Brad took the cup of ice cream and let out an exasperated sigh. "I appreciate it, Coop, but you shouldn't be here. I told you I'm not out at work, so you can't just show up where other members of my team might see us together. Do you understand?"

Coop nodded solemnly. "I'm sorry, Brad, I was just trying to do something nice. I've had a really tough day. I had a grueling meeting over at the SEC office."

"I want to hear all about it, Coop, really I do." Brad put his hand on Coop's shoulder. "It turns out I have to finish up a couple of things inside—details for our return trip. I'll meet you at the restaurant for dinner tonight, okay?" He even managed a little smile, which lifted Coop's heart.

Knowing that giving his boyfriend a goodbye hug in such close proximity to his colleagues was not in the cards, Coop just said, "Okay, see you tonight." He walked away, eating his ice cream. As Coop rounded the corner he turned back to see Brad toss his ice cream into a trash bin on the street and head back inside the hotel. That careless act made Coop flinch as if he'd been struck. Brad had become such a cherished part of Coop's life lately. An electric current of anxiety ran through him as Coop realized just how much this relationship meant.

*

ANDI

How much more could Andi possibly endure? It was late March, and over the past two months Lester had taken away some of her major institutional private banking clients and reassigned them to his cronies, all the while trying to coerce Andi into a sexual relationship with him. Even the Paris account she'd help to win was now gone. She felt like an innocent bystander witnessing a train wreck—all she could do was watch helplessly as everything she'd worked so hard for disintegrated into dust. Luca had made some progress working with the speech therapist but was still suffering from Bell's palsy. Andi had no choice but to endure the injustices at Kaneshiro Bank without complaint so her family would have health care coverage. For a person who thrived on being action oriented, waiting it out was excruciating for Andi.

In order to alleviate her stress, she'd taken to having a regular walk around Bryant Park during lunch, following the same loop every day as if it were a giant a hamster wheel. That Monday, Andi was about twenty minutes into her hamster wheel walk when she froze in alarm; she heard heavy rapid footsteps rushing up behind her. She turned and was relieved to see her buddy Mike.

"Got some great news for you, Andi!" Mike raced up, towering over her. He placed a hand gently on her shoulder. She'd been sharing all her work troubles with him and he felt for her. "I convinced Lester to include you on the team to pitch a new account. He okayed it and we're going to be working on it this week. Cool, huh?"

Andi drew back. "Seriously?" It was good news, but in the back of her mind she wondered why Lester was all of a sudden giving her this chance. Maybe the tides were turning? Maybe he realized he was underutilizing her talents? She shrugged. Whatever the reason, she was grateful for the chance. "Thanks, Mikey, you're the best. Well, what are we standing around for? Let's get started."

The two friends hightailed it back to the office.

*

That week, for the third night in a row the team consisting of Mike, Andi, and Myron Burry were working late at the office, getting ready to pitch a new client. Lester had been reviewing their work and giving direction but hadn't stayed late with them...until tonight. The team had ordered sushi delivery and were taking a break over various rolls, nigiri sushi, and Asahi beer, with Lester joining them, seemingly in good spirits.

By now Myron had significantly improved his performance and managed to ingratiate himself with their boss. He and Lester even shared a couple of private jokes. Laughing a bit too heartily, Myron jumped up to grab another beer for his boss.

Andi threw out a hook. "Lester, I thought it would be interesting to put together a scenario for the new client—show them what they could have accumulated by now if they had started working with us four years ago when they selected the other firm."

Lester looked intrigued. "A compare-and-contrast scenario? Hmm, I like that, Andi. I really like it. Why don't you show me what you've got?"

"Sure. Here's what I've put together, you can scroll through." Andi angled her laptop toward her boss. "I'm just going to the restroom. Back in a sec."

*

Andi studied her reflection as she washed her hands at the bathroom sink. This week had been brutal in terms of work hours, and her exhaustion from the past few months was beginning to show in the form of dark circles under her eyes. She splashed some cold water on her face, then swept her hair back into a ponytail using the hair tie from around her wrist.

As she exited the bathroom into the dark hallway she felt herself being thrown back forcefully like she'd been caught in the blast radius from an explosion. Pinned up against the wall her eyes met Lester's. His shiny eyes held a hungry look.

"I've been dying to do this, Andi." Lester gripped her shoulders and leaned in to kiss her. His wet mouth smothered hers and she could taste the beer in his saliva. Yuck.

"No! Get off me!" Andi pushed him off and turned her head away. Down the dimly lit hallway she caught a glimpse of someone standing there—Myron? She saw him do an about-face and scurry away. She turned back to Lester, who was coming in for a second attempt at a kiss. Andi balled up her right fist and gave Lester a swift jab in the nose, causing him to back away sputtering.

"Stop it, Lester. Enough!"

Andi had started to walk away when she felt her head being tugged back violently. Lester had grabbed her ponytail and was pulling her backward toward him. He yanked her head back so she was staring at the ceiling. Something caught her eye but she snapped back to focus.

"Don't you walk away from me!" Lester's voice was sharp. Andi felt his body smashed up against hers, one arm locked around her throat while his other hand clumsily groped her breasts. Lester kissed her neck and hissed, "Remember, Andi, I always get what I want. And I want you."

She tried to break free but Lester tightened his stranglehold. Her breathing stopped for a few seconds, either from the shock of the moment or from his grip. Then Andi's reflexes took over.

She grabbed Lester's forearm and swiftly bent at the waist, performing a perfect over-the-shoulder judo throw. He let out a bloodcurdling scream as he slammed onto the floor. Lester had no idea that Andi had grown up with three older brothers, so this was a woman who knew how to brawl. She realized with that judo throw she might also be throwing away something else—her career. But she didn't care. After suffering through all her boss's unwanted advances over many months, it felt liberating to finally take control of the situation...and crush Lester like a bug.

Mike came sprinting down the hall with Myron lagging behind. Then he froze, flabbergasted by the spectacle, now clear to see in the bright hallway, where the lights had been activated by the motion sensors. "Andi, are you okay? I thought I heard you scream, but I guess it was..." He looked down at Lester, who was sprawled out on the floor, clutching his back in agony.

Andi stood over Lester, gripping his arm back in a twisting hold. "I told you to get your filthy paws off of me." She released her grip and tossed Lester's arm aside.

Assessing the situation, Mike instantaneously figured out what had happened. He leaned over Lester and said menacingly, "I don't care if you're my boss. If you ever touch Andi again I'll knock your damn teeth out."

Two security guards came running down the hall, having heard all of the commotion. They called out, "What's going on here? Miss, are you all right?"

"I'm good," Andi replied. She turned to Mike. "But I sure could use a shot of tequila. How 'bout it, Mikey?"

Mike nodded, suppressing a smile.

The two of them left Lester lying in a heap on the cold, hard floor, surrounded by Myron and the perplexed security guards.

*

Walking slowly into her office the following morning, Andi let out a sigh of relief. She'd received a message on her BlackBerry early that morning from Kaneshiro Bank's US CEO. Hank asked her to come see him when she got in. She'd finally be able to share the crazy goings-on with Lester with someone in a position to do something about it. Though she'd only met Hank once and she knew that he and Lester were tight, she expected that when he learned the facts, this whole mess would get cleared up. Lester would be booted out of the bank and her work life could resume as normal.

Andi swung by her office, took a minute to collect herself, and then marched down to Hank's office.

"Hank, you wanted to see me?" she said in a strong voice.

"Come in, Andi." He motioned for her to sit. "I want to discuss something with you."

Andi nodded. "Yes, I know exactly what you're referring to and I'm frankly relieved to be able to talk about it. It's been a horrendous experience for me."

Hank pursed his lips. "For you? Are you making some kind of joke? This is serious stuff, Andi. I'm afraid you've put Kaneshiro Bank in a problematic situation here. Lester contacted me last night and told me that you physically assaulted him," Hank said curtly.

"What? He said that?" Andi asked eyes wide. "That's a load of crap."

"Lester informed me that since the acquisition you've been making sexual advances toward him and last night you attacked him. His back is hurt and he's in pretty bad shape. Apparently he needs a neck brace and is going to take a week off to recover."

Andi shot back. "Hank, that's a lie. Lester is not telling you what really happened."

He let out a sigh. "All right, why don't you fill me in, Andi."

"Since Lester became my boss he has behaved inappropriately toward me and has been propositioning me and harassing me. Last night he tried to kiss and grope me. Yes, I used physical force against him, but only to protect myself."

Hank looked at her skeptically, like he was wrestling conflicting thoughts. "Yet, Lester is the one who had to seek medical attention. You, on the other hand, look fine to me, Andi. Not a scratch on you. And you're a lot smaller than he is." He crossed his arms and sat back. "Also, Lester has a witness from last night who can corroborate his account. Do you have anyone who can back up your claims?"

A witness?

Hank sermonized sternly, "The witness didn't see Lester attack you. In fact, they heard a scream, ran down the hall, and found you standing over Lester. They said you even had him in some kind of arm lock."

Andi scowled. So the "witness" must be Myron Burry. That ungrateful, sniveling scumbag. After all she'd done to help him? This is how he repaid her? She practically spat on the floor in disgust. Andi would deal with Myron later.

"I think you should apologize to Lester before he gets it in his head to sue this firm and hold you personally liable, for that matter."

"*Me apologize?* For what?" Steam practically shot out of Andi's nostrils. "I have nothing to apologize for, Hank."

"Look, this situation is a mess. I want you to take the week off just like Lester's doing so everyone can cool off. Consider it a temporary leave from you job. Next week when our chairman, Mr. Okubo, is in town for a visit I want you and Lester to report back here so we can all sit down and solve this problem. Got it?" It was abundantly clear that Hank had already decided what action to take without even getting the facts.

"So, Hank, you believe you've done sufficient due diligence to get to the truth?" Andi's temper was starting to flare up.

"Andi, I can only act based on the facts at hand. You're still new to the firm but you should know that at Kaneshiro Bank we do not tolerate this kind of inappropriate behavior—we conduct ourselves ethically and with professionalism. As a partner, you—of all people—should demonstrate exemplary behavior. I think we're done here." Hank signaled that their discussion was over.

Andi's face reddened with anger as she returned to her desk. "Unbelievable!" she fumed under her breath. "That slime ball Lester sexually harasses me and then thinks he can blame everything on me? I am not letting him get away with it." Andi angrily kicked over her trash can. She packed up a small box with stacks of financial statements and reports she wanted to review that week.

Hearing the commotion, Mike appeared at her door and approached her cautiously to see what was up. Andi shared the highlights of her meeting with Hank. Vowing to get the mess sorted out, she said goodbye to Mike, who told her to call if there was anything he could do to help. She stomped out to the elevator and headed down to the building's reception desk.

*

"Can I leave my box and computer bag here while I check out the cab situation outside?" Andi asked the bored-looking security guard, who barely glanced up from his iPad and nodded.

Outside the office building, Andi was deep in thought about the Lester situation—with each passing moment her ire was rising like the temperature on a sweltering day. Suddenly someone growled, "Gimme that!"

Andi was violently pulled forward as some punk in a dark gray hoodie tried to snatch away her purse. Startled, she lost her balance and nearly tripped. Just moments ago she couldn't have believed that her day could get any worse. The strap of her Prada bag was caught on her arm and she began a dangerous tug-of-war with the mugger—Andi was not going to give up without a fight. The mugger pulled so hard he practically dragged Andi along the sidewalk. Onlookers started calling for help.

"Are you kidding me? You are *not* taking my Prada bag!" Andi yelled.

They continued to struggle fiercely, each pulling with all their strength. In the next instant the hardware holding the leather strap to the purse snapped and Andi fell back—the strap remained in her hands while the mugger clutched the purse in his grimy hands like a trophy. The punk gave her a smug smile of triumph and took off running.

"Don't you give me that look!" Andi jumped up, wrenched off her heels in her hands, and started chasing after the mugger. "I'm gonna get you!" she screamed. "You picked the wrong girl to mess with!" Although it had been years since her Olympic showing, Andi was still an amazingly fast runner.

Moving at a good clip up Park Avenue and dodging the pedestrians on the midtown sidewalk, the mugger shot a fearful glance back and saw a madwoman rapidly closing the gap between them. When Andi was just steps away from the gasping mugger, she launched herself into the air and tackled him. They fell to the ground with a thud. The mugger let out an "Oof!" Andi was extremely strong for her size and she started whaling on the thief with her shoes.

He covered his face with one arm and with the other shoved the purse back at her. "Here, take it! Take it, lady. Don't hurt me!" he rasped, still gulping air from the hard run.

"You better think twice the next time you try to take something from a woman, asshole."

The mugger's eyes widened, and though he didn't say a word it was clear that he'd learned a valuable lesson. By then a crowd had gathered around Andi, cheering her on and, like typical New Yorkers, ridiculing the mugger until the police arrived and rescued him by hauling him off to the station.

"Are you all right, ma'am?" One of the police officers helped Andi up to her feet.

"Yeah, I'm fine. Do you need me to provide a statement or something?"

The officer chuckled. "No, no. I think it's pretty clear what happened. Plus you've got a witness to the whole thing."

"All the people on the street?" Andi wiped the sweat from her face.

"No, up there." The officer pointed toward the top of the light post. "There are cameras on every light post—they captured the whole thing. We just need to play back the recording."

Andi looked up at the cameras perched on each street lamp lining Park Avenue. Something clicked in her head and suddenly Andi beamed. "Thanks, that's helpful." She'd just figured out a way to beat Lester. She rushed back to her office building to retrieve her stuff and called Mike on his mobile phone to enlist his support.

PART THREE

CHAPTER 9

April

ANDI

Much to her surprise, Andi actually enjoyed the weeklong break from work mandated by the bank—as a self-professed workaholic, she took it as a sign of just how miserable she'd been in her job. Flowers and trees were blooming in the April warmth, and Andi enjoyed a few long runs around the loop of Central Park during her week off from work.

The following Monday at seven a.m. sharp, the entire private banking department of Kaneshiro Bank was assembled in the large conference room, waiting for the showdown between Andi Andiamo and Lester Labosky. At exactly 7:02 a.m.—just late enough to be defiant—Andi entered the room to face her accuser. He sat stiffly in a leather chair with a neck brace pushing up the skin under his face, giving him an uncanny resemblance to Jabba the Hutt. His eyes skimmed over Andi's form and held a victorious look. No doubt he was relishing the opportunity to humiliate Andi in return for her rejecting his sexual advances.

The chairman of the bank, Kanichi Okubo, sat erect at the head of the conference table, looking dignified and thoughtful. He was a tall, fit man in his late forties with thick black hair and friendly eyes. He cleared his throat and nodded to Hank to get things going. Hank introduced Chairman Okubo to the group and gave a brief summary of why they were gathered.

Hank said, "Lester, you asked to kick things off?"

Lester had an expression of glee and his Jabba eyes danced excitedly around the room. "It's simple, really. I'm a happily married man, but since the day I started leading the department Andi has made it clear she wanted a sexual relationship with me, perhaps to further her career—I don't really know. She's been relentless, and the other night when I again refused her advances she attacked me, causing significant injury. Myron was there, right?"

Myron stood up and recited as if he were rehearsing for a school play, "Everything Lester has said is true. I've seen Andi coming on to him and on the night in question I saw her attack Lester in the hall. Guess hell hath no fury like a woman scorned, eh?" He smirked.

What a backstabbing rat. Andi wanted to leap across the room and silence Myron with a throat jab.

Hank turned to her. "Andi, I believe an apology is in order. Do you have something to say?"

"I do," said Andi slowly. "I made some mistakes in dealing with Lester over the past eight months, and I think now is a good time to admit what I did wrong."

Hank nodded for her to proceed, and quickly.

"At our Bermuda offsite, when Lester massaged my shoulders in front of everyone and later invited me to his room for champagne, I was wrong to not say 'That will never happen, Lester.'"

Lester looked alarmed.

"Then on our client trip to Paris, when I came back to my hotel room only to find Lester on my bed in his bathrobe, it was wrong of me to yank him off the bed and drag him out of my room. When he took away my biggest client accounts, refused to give me the raise and bonus I deserve, and moved my office down to the secretarial pool— well, you know, wrong, wrong, wrong."

Chairman Okubo furrowed his brow and shot a look at Hank.

Mike had hooked up his laptop to the projector, and Andi walked over and clicked on the video icon on the computer's desktop. Andi looked around the room to see amused looks from her colleagues— they knew her well enough to realize she had a big finale up her sleeve.

"And last week, when Lester ambushed me in a dark hallway outside the ladies' room, got me in a stranglehold, and then groped me, it was wrong of me to throw him to the ground. This video shows exactly what I did wrong." She shot Mike a knowing look and hit Play.

Video from the security camera footage in the hallway came on the large plasma screen. It clearly showed how the scenario had actually played out and that Lester was the attacker. Audible groans of disgust came from most of the guys when they saw Lester grinding his genitals against Andi's backside. The footage showed Andi struggling to get free, setting her stance, and then executing a perfect judo throw that flipped Lester over her shoulder and onto the floor. Upon seeing Andi's judo move, many men in the room clapped.

Hank let out a gasp. Lester started coughing uncontrollably and Myron Burry, his star witness, stood with eyes wide like a raccoon caught rummaging through someone's garbage can in the dead of night.

With steely eyes, Andi turned to Lester, who had tiny glistening beads of sweat forming on his upper lip and seemed to be melting into his chair. "Instead of throwing you onto the floor, Lester, I was wrong to not break your freakin' neck! You're a despicable person. You've tormented and harassed me for months, and I'm sorry that you're such a pig." She looked over at Hank, whose eyes were bulging out of their sockets. The room fell silent.

Then came the most unexpected sound. A giggle…from Chairman Okubo. He pointed at the video screen, covering his mouth with his hand. "Wow. *That's* some apology." Chairman Okubo shook his head and then directed his words to Andi. "It's evident that you triumphed over a terrible situation, Andi. On behalf of the firm, I deeply apologize for your harrowing experience." He turned to Lester. "Shame on you. Your behavior is an embarrassment to Kaneshiro Bank, Lester. You must apologize to Andi at once."

Sheepishly, Lester mumbled, "Um, sorry, Andi."

Chairman Okubo stood with a stern look in his eyes. "Hank, I trust you will handle this properly."

Hank turned angrily to Lester. "You imbecile. How could you put the firm in this position? Get out of my sight. I'll deal with you later."

Lester skulked out of the conference room. Then Hank turned to Andi. "I was wrong about this situation and about you. I'm sorry about everything you had to endure. Please, Andi, come back to work—you'll have your old accounts back and we'll get everything squared away. What do you say?"

Despite emerging victorious, Andi was not sure that the outcome Hank suggested was what she really wanted. "I need some time to think about this and decide what I want to do." Andi shook her head in disgust. "It's disheartening that after a decade in the department, despite all my many contributions, my character could be called into question and my reputation essentially wiped out because of one malicious person."

Mike stood up. "I want to say something on behalf of the team. It's an honor to work with you every day, Andi. You're not only great at what you do, but you're a great leader, collaborator, and coach to others. We all admire you and really want you back." He spread his arms and Andi moved in for a hug. "But first we need to take out the trash." He glared at Myron, Percy, and Richie, who shrank into the background.

One by one, every remaining member of the department lined up, and as Andi walked past them the men gave her a fist bump or a congratulatory pat on the shoulder, as if she were an athlete doing a victory walk down the line after a championship game.

At the door Chairman Okubo stopped her. "Andi, please, take a paid week off to recover from all this and to think about what you want to do. Hopefully we'll see you return to Kaneshiro Bank." He gave her a respectful bow.

Andi returned the bow and met his gaze directly. "Thank you, Mr. Okubo. I'll let you know my decision." She walked down the hall, her heart still racing.

She'd nearly reached the elevator when she heard rapid footsteps and she spun around. Myron Burry. What could he possibly have to say to her now? She gave him the death glare, and he stopped a few feet short of her as if held back by an invisible force field.

"Andi, I'm sorry about this crazy situation with Lester—I only went along with him because I was terrified of losing my job. Will you forgive me? Can we bury the hatchet? You know, go back to the way things were, with you coaching me? You're such an amazing talent and I really—"

"Stop!" Andi held her hand up in front of Myron's face. "What the fuck, Myron? After all I did to help you? You turn against me and back up Lester's lies? And now you have the nerve—the *nerve*—to ask for my help again, spoon-feeding you about how to be a successful private banker? Are you brain-dead?"

Myron's eyes narrowed and his face scrunched up as if he were a toddler about to throw a temper tantrum. "But, but—"

"Despite my reservations, Myron, I gave you a chance and helped you out. But you know what I learned about you? Once a jerk, always a jerk. And if you think that any of the other guys are going to lift a finger to help you out, forget it." Andi turned and scoffed under her breath. "WAFWOT." She punched the elevator button forcefully and got on. Myron stood there, mouth agape.

*

By the end of the week, Andi had thought long and hard about returning to her job. With Lester out of the picture, she felt reasonably unworried about going back to the bank. All that changed with a Friday-afternoon call from her buddy Mike.

Andi saw the number flash on her phone screen and answered. "What's up, Mikey?"

"I just learned something disturbing and thought you should know about it." He paused. "After our meeting on Monday it seemed pretty obvious that Lester would be fired from the bank. That didn't happen."

Andi's heart skipped a beat. "Huh? So what's going on?"

She could hear the disgust dripping from Mike's tone. "He's staying put. They've reassigned him to another department. Since you're a partner and are senior to Lester, the firm decided that his actions couldn't technically be defined as sexual harassment. Apparently his buddy Hank gave him a warning, but he's still an executive here, Andi. I'm sure that impacts your decision on coming back. Heck, it impacts my decision on staying here."

"That's crazy. After seeing what he did they're going to let Lester stick around? Why? He's just going to find another woman to harass and make her life miserable." Something clicked instantly in Andi's head. If the bank would make a decision like that, it meant they weren't really concerned about the welfare of their female employees—it also meant this was a corporate culture that wasn't for her. They'd just made the decision easy for her. "I'm outta there, Mikey. I'll call Hank today and let him know exactly why I decided not to come back."

"Not before you negotiate a kick-ass severance agreement, Andi. I'm sure they'll give you whatever you ask in return for not suing them." Mike was always looking out for her.

"Absolutely, my friend. Thanks for the heads-up, Mikey. You've been a true friend over the years and I want you to know how much I appreciate you. Let's hit the links together sometime soon." Andi was secure in the knowledge that their friendship would remain intact regardless of where they ended up.

*

Sofia's apartment felt like a sanctuary to Andi with its tasteful, comfortable furnishings, cool art on the walls, and soft jazz music playing in the background. Andi sipped some wine and nibbled on mixed nuts while Sofia fired up her laptop for their weekly Skype call with Vivien. Grace rushed in, a bit frazzled. Though they normally had their call and then ate dinner together, tonight Andi would head home to spend time with Luca—he'd texted her that afternoon and asked her to come home for dinner.

Vivien's face popped up on the screen and she smiled, although her bloodshot eyes revealed her exhaustion. Andi, Grace, and Sofia were excited to see Vivien, and she even stood up and showed off her growing baby bump. She definitely had the radiant glow of a pregnant woman.

*

Vivien had been looking forward to the Smashers call all week. She shut her office door and sat in front of her computer.

"Hi, guys. I don't know how you could possibly top last week's call—your story about taking down that purse snatcher was awesome, Andi. You're such a superwoman!" She peered at the screen at her three friends and saw Sofia give Andi a playful nudge. "Hey, Grace, maybe that should be the title of your new book."

She noticed Grace was looking pale and rubbing her temples. Apparently working with her prickly new boss was no picnic. Grace seemed to perk up. On their last call she'd announced that instead of writing another book on branding, she wanted to switch gears and write a book with practical career tips for women. Her tentative title was *The Ceiling Smasher's Guide to Career Success*. "What are you thinking, Vivi?"

"How about *The Superpowers of Ceiling Smashers*? That title has a nice ring."

Grace nodded enthusiastically. "Love it! I'm making a note of that." She typed it into her smartphone. "Although with my crazy work schedule, I can't imagine when I'll find the time to do more writing. Heck, maybe the four of us should write the book together—when things slow down a bit."

Andi sat back. "Well, I'm not feeling like a superwoman today. In fact, my recent experience at work showed me how little control I have over my environment." She let out a groan. "But I did prove that Lester was lying, so at least I got the W on that one."

"Good for you," Vivien said.

"Yeah, and they offered me my job back, but guess what? Instead of firing Lester they transferred him to another department. Can you believe that?" Andi threw her hands up in the air. "It's just like you say, Grace: WAFWOT."

Sofia snorted indignantly. "That's absurd! How can they continue to let someone like that work there and prey on other women?"

"They can and they did," Andi replied, "so I quit today. At least I negotiated a generous severance package and continued health care." It was an abrupt end to Andi's ten-year stint in banking. "Anyway, I'm planning on taking the summer off to spend time with the boys and help out Luca. I think I deserve a break." She gave a little smile.

Vivien leaned closer to the computer screen. "I'm sorry you had to quit, Andi, but on the bright side, you'll be better off away from that toxic environment. And you'll get some quality time with your family. Whenever you're ready to brainstorm about what you want to do next, just let us know, okay?"

Grace and Sofia nodded supportively.

Andi said, "Thanks. Anyway, I'm fed up with even thinking about my work situation. What's going on with you, Vivi?"

"Well, Grace, I have to say you called it—that Steele Hamilton sure is a weasel." Grace had worked with him before and didn't think highly of him. "We had our Smart Sports Games this week—

kind of like a company Olympics—and Steele leaked the news of my pregnancy…to the entire company." Vivien grimaced, then switched gears. "Hey, Sofia, I caught your *Titans Tell All* show—looks like it's going gangbusters, eh?"

Sofia smiled. "Yes, thanks. Kate Frost and I are working well together and the show is taking off. The thing I'm really nervous about is my personal life. Jasper and I have been dating for almost six months and he wants me to meet his family." Her eyes bugged out.

"Oh, Sofia, when something good comes along sometimes you just need to grab hold of it, even if you're a little nervous," Grace said, and gave Vivien a conspiratorial wink. They both knew how skittish Sofia was about marriage, but she and Jasper seemed great together.

The Smashers spent the rest of the hour sharing their victories and frustrations and supporting each other by offering up solutions to various problems. Despite the distance from her friends, it always gave Vivien a sense of strength to know that her Smasher circle was there for her, like a safety net protecting a trapeze artist from a dangerous fall.

*

Andi was looking forward to getting home, playing with the boys a bit, and maybe watching a movie with Luca. Though she wanted to tell her husband every detail from the past week, she also didn't want to add to his already high stress level. The past five months had been hellish for Luca.

When she walked in the door it was unusually quiet in the condo. Why were the boys so silent? Andi placed her purse on the table in the front hall and walked toward the kitchen. It smelled heavenly—like Luca was whipping up something delectable and garlicky.

Andi glanced in the dining room and saw that the table was set beautifully with their wedding china, lit candles, and cloth napkins. A nice bottle of Brunello was open and breathing in a decanter. Uh-oh, had she forgotten their anniversary or Luca's birthday? She entered the kitchen and saw Luca working over the stove. "Luca, honey, I'm home."

Her husband turned around and faced her wearing a huge smile. In that instant Andi's memory of all the dreadful things that happened that day were gone, as if a hypnotist had reset her mind with a quick finger snap. "Oh my god! Luca, you're all better!" Andi ran up and threw her arms around her husband. She stepped back and looked at his face, which had returned to its familiar old form, with twinkling eyes and a glorious smile. "How did that happen?"

Luca laughed for the first time in what seemed like forever. "It was the strangest thing, Andi. I was home alone practicing my speech therapy and the phone rang. As I was talking on the phone to my mama it suddenly felt like I could move my face much better. Later when I looked in the mirror I was back to normal!"

Husband and wife, both overjoyed, hugged each other and had a long, romantic kiss.

"Where are the boys?" Andi looked around.

"I had my parents come and pick them up. The boys were happy to visit with Grandma and Grandpa. I wanted to spend the evening alone with my beautiful wife. Is okay, no?" He winked.

Andi noticed that Luca had prepared *spaghetti alle vongole* and roasted eggplant stuffed with ricotta, along with an *insalata mista*— the dinner he always prepared when he was in an amorous mood. The day had just gone from being the worst day ever to the best day imaginable.

*

GRACE

Laura, the designer, poked her head into Grace's office for a quick chat. "Have you met the new guy? The one that Skip brought over from JMC to run Baby & Kids?"

"No, not yet. What's he like?" Grace asked.

Laura placed her notebook on the corner of the desk and looked skyward. "I don't get it, Grace. This guy Colton is single with no kids and doesn't seem to know the first thing about apparel. I was taking him through the product line and he asked me what a onesie was." She guffawed.

Grace pursed her lips and said wryly, "I guess selling baby food doesn't necessarily translate to running a baby and kids' clothing business. But who knows, maybe he'll get catch on to things soon." She was skeptical that someone with no experience in apparel or a luxury brand could run the business well, combined with the fact that her new boss was also lacking the requisite expertise and could provide no coaching.

Laura shook her head. "I'm not so sure about that."

*

Grace's first few weeks working with Skip had not gone smoothly, but she was hoping to change all that. She intended to win him over as the two of them attended the Global Retail CXO Summit sponsored by the Wharton School, a small invitation-only gathering of C-level retail executives.

Since their last Smashers Skype call, Grace had been turning something over in her mind. When Grace had mentioned the difficulties she had working with the new CEO, Vivien had asked the million-dollar question: *Do you even want that job, Grace?* She remarked that being forced back into the CMO role wasn't advancing Grace's career aspirations. While Grace knew her friend was right, a practical matter was that Grace needed a job. She'd just have to make the best of things.

Skip swung by her office that Tuesday morning. "Ready to go, Grace?" He seemed thrilled to attend the prestigious conference and grateful that Grace had finagled him an invitation. It would be a chance to rub shoulders with other executives from the premier retail companies in the world. The two of them took Skip's limo down to the Rubin Museum of Art in Chelsea, the site of the retail summit. On the way there, despite her nerves Grace turned on the charm, trying to increase Skip's comfort level with her. She wanted to get on his good side.

They walked into the museum, and Grace was immediately greeted by Suzie, a former professor of hers and the leader of the Wharton retail center. Grace introduced Skip Palmer, and after getting registered they mingled with the other seventy-five attendees over a continental breakfast. By the time they took their seats in the cozy auditorium, Skip excitedly showed Grace the business cards of the other CEOs he'd already collected. She realized that this was Skip's first CEO role, and he was still acclimating to the title—that explained his reverence for the other chief executives he'd just met.

Suzie kicked off the program and introduced their first panel of speakers, an elegant Swiss gentleman who was the CEO of Rolex, a tall woman wearing four-inch heels who was the CEO of Chanel, and finally the CEO of a successful startup selling high-end eyeglasses. They spoke about the importance of brand, and at one point Suzie paused. "We actually have a highly talented executive from Palazzo here today." She looked out into the audience and said, "Would you please stand up?"

Skip Palmer looked tickled pink and he started to rise—after all, he was the wunderkind from JMC who was leading Palazzo. Suzie continued, "Grace King is the chief marketing officer and brand steward. Prior to the merger she was instrumental in leading one of the most amazing brand turnaround stories in retail, the revival of Burberry." Looking sheepish, Skip sank down in his seat. Grace stood up, gave a tight smile, and waved. "In fact, Grace has recently published a fascinating branding book called *Rise: Six Steps to Resuscitate Your Brand After a Fiasco*, which I highly recommend." The audience clapped enthusiastically.

It was bad enough that she'd outshined her boss in front of everyone, but during the breaks other leaders sought out Grace to ask her advice on turning around a brand. Some practically trampled over Skip to get to her. This wasn't exactly going the way she'd planned—her intention in bringing Skip to the conference had been to give him the opportunity to shine. Grace could tell from his dour expression that there was some professional jealousy simmering just under the surface.

*

The next morning Grace and a few other executives were meeting with Skip in his office when his executive assistant rushed in. She said breathlessly, "Sir, I have the CEO of Harrods on the line for you."

Skip's face lit up. "Really? Wow. Okay, well patch him through."

Grace and the others sat there while Skip got up from the conference table and rushed over to his desk. Skip took a moment to sit and compose himself, then picked up the receiver. "Hello, Skip Palmer here." He smiled broadly, as if the caller were standing right in front of him. "Yes, yes, hello. What an honor to receive your call. Of course, how could I forget I exchanging business cards with you at the Wharton retail summit?" He listened intently for a few minutes and his eyes darkened. Taking off his glasses, he tossed them onto his desk and pinched the bridge of his nose. Skip said, "I see. No, it's fine, I understand. As a matter of fact she's right here. Can you hold for a moment?" He pressed the hold button and looked across the room at Grace.

Oh no, what is it now?

His face reddened. Skip's voice dripped with sarcasm. "Well, aren't you the popular one, Grace. Turns out the Harrods CEO didn't get your card at the summit and called me in order to reach you." He face hardened like a granite statue of an embattled general on the losing side of a war.

Grace stammered, "I...I'm sorry, Skip. Should I—" She couldn't believe this situation.

Skip stood. Then he picked up the phone and hurled it across the room at Grace. One of the female executives screamed in panic. Grace raised her arm to deflect the blow. Fortunately, the cord attaching the phone to the wall was a couple of feet short, and the phone crashed to the floor close to Grace's feet. Everyone sat in a terrified, hushed silence.

Grace bent down and picked up the phone. She released the hold button, amazed that the phone was still functioning after its violent flight. She made the conversation as short as possible—the Harrods CEO had read her book on the plane ride home and wanted to get her guidance on injecting new life into his brand. She suggested setting up a later time to discuss it further. Then she ended the call.

Skip walked over and looked at her coldly. "From now on, your little book promotion activities will not be done on company time. Got it?"

"Yes, of course." She nodded civilly and left the phone sitting on the floor. The executives quickly wrapped up their meeting with Skip and left his office. They waited until they were well out of earshot before they blurted out their shock over their boss's behavior.

"Can you believe that guy? What a nut job!" said Robin, the head of design.

Grace rolled her eyes. "I've heard he's done worse."

Jaymee from merchandising whispered, "Skip must be bipolar or something."

"Might be a good idea to invest in a helmet!" Grace joked.

Her colleagues laughed, then self-consciously looked around to make sure Skip wasn't listening.

"If he wasn't coming up with such great new ideas for the company, I'd really question why he's in the CEO role." Jaymee shook her head. "But I'm actually really pumped about two of Skip's new programs:

the order from the runway program and the modular bags program."

"What are you talking about?" Grace cocked her head.

Robin leaned in closer to the others, his blue eyes wide. "Totally brilliant ideas! Letting consumers watch our streamed runway shows live and then place an order for a product online. And then his idea about having bags where the interior can be unsnapped, removed, and then inserted into another bag—so unique. Those are winners."

Grace's heart thudded to a stop. Wait a minute—those were *her* ideas to build the Palazzo business. She'd emailed Skip a dozen ideas—not three, as he'd requested—before she returned to work. And now he was implementing them *and* taking credit for them? This was not right.

They saw Skip storming down the hall and they all scattered back to the safety of their offices.

*

COOP

If there was ever a night when Coop needed to relax and have a few cocktails, this was it. He and Brad had had a nice dinner at a cozy Mexican place in Chelsea. Over dinner and margaritas, Coop had explained the whole situation with the SEC and Felix Culo to Brad, including Felix's plan to have Coop take the fall. He'd spent the better part of that day sharing evidence with the SEC team. Brad seemed a bit stiff, but he listened patiently with his violet-blue eyes trained on Coop.

"That is wild, Coop. So you're going to be the star witness." Brad crossed his arms and sat back. "Man, that is going to be big news." He downed his drink.

"Yeah, I can hardly believe it myself," Coop said. "My clients and my team are flipping out over my leaving the firm so suddenly. The SEC is moving really fast with this investigation." He rubbed his forehead. "Oh well, let's just have a fun evening. I don't want to think about it anymore tonight."

They finished up their dinner and headed over to Splash to do some dancing. As soon as they entered the club doors they were transported to a world full of beautiful men and bodies writhing to the pulsating music. They rushed out onto the dance floor and joined the throng of guys. Coop noted the looks of admiration that his boyfriend got from others in the crowd.

After a few songs they got seats at the bar and had some cocktails. Then more dancing and more cocktails. By this time Coop had switched to drinking water, but Brad was still putting away glasses of tequila.

"Brad, maybe you should slow down on the drinks?" Coop slipped his arm through Brad's.

"Why, Coop, do I seem drunk?"

Coop knew that diplomacy meant thinking twice before saying nothing, and he sensed this was a time that called for diplomacy.

"Come on, let's just have some fun!" He patted Coop's arm and polished off another drink. Brad pulled Coop toward the dance floor, moving backward quickly until he stumbled and fell. A few other guys rushed to help pull him up from the floor.

Coop had to admit he was embarrassed. He'd never been with anyone who was falling-down drunk. "It's getting late, Brad. Why don't we call it a night?"

"Okay, after one more drink," Brad said loudly, and ushered Coop over to the bar. Brad nearly fell off the bar stool as he motioned to the bartender to serve him. "Tequila." He slapped his hand on top of the bar, knocking over a cup of cocktail straws in the process.

The bartender looked tentatively at Coop, who shook his head in the negative. Then he said, "Sorry, bud, we just ran out."

"Let's just go." Coop nudged his boyfriend toward the door.

Surprisingly, Brad complied and half-stumbled with Coop out of the club. They made slow progress for a couple of blocks, then Brad stopped. He whirled around with a hardened expression on his face. "What are you trying to do to me? Huh?"

Coop's head was starting to pound. "Brad, what are you talking about?"

His slurred words came out in an angry stream. "You're trying to set me up, aren't you?" Brad's eyes were bloodshot and he had his finger pointed in Coop's face. "I told you I'm not out at work. But you go ahead and just show up at the Waldorf bringing me ice cream so everyone in my detail can see us together. What are you trying to do?" He kicked at the air and staggered.

Coop stepped back. "Of course not, Brad. I care about you. I would never do anything to harm you." He wasn't sure what to do. Coop had an uneasy feeling about what Brad might do next. "It's been a long day. Why don't I get a cab to take you back to your hotel." Coop started to walk toward the street to hail a cab.

"No! I won't let you do it! I won't let you ruin my career!"

Coop felt his arm being wrenched back violently and he heard a snap. He cried out in pain. "Ow, you're hurting me. Stop it, please!" Brad was flailing like a wild animal fighting for survival against an attacking predator. He threw Coop to the ground. Coop hit the cold pavement hard, as if he'd just been knocked down by a heavyweight champ. He held up an arm for protection and cried out for help. A couple rushed over to intervene, the woman helping Coop sit up and the man yanking Brad up and pushing him away.

"I can't believe that drunkard attacked you. Do you know that guy?" the woman asked.

Coop looked down, too ashamed to admit the drunkard was, in fact, his boyfriend. He recalled a quote, *Better to remain silent and be thought a fool than to speak out and remove all doubt.* He shook his head no. That was the truth—the Brad he'd seen that evening was a completely foreign person. Coop felt like he'd been hit by a bus and cradled his rapidly swelling elbow. "Ouch, my arm really hurts. Can you help me into a cab, please? I need to get to the hospital." The kindly couple obliged. As the cab pulled away Coop looked back—Brad was stumbling down the street and punching at the air, battling with some phantom adversary.

*

It was late on a rainy evening, and Vivien had just finished watching a movie with her fiancé, Clay, who'd fallen asleep on the sofa before the movie ended. Amid the sound of the rain slashing against the windows of their Portland condo, she heard her cell phone buzz. Coop.

"Vivi, it's Coop. I've had a little accident."

"Uh-oh, Coop, don't tell me it was another tangle with a dreaded treadmill," Vivien half joked. "No, really, are you okay?"

She could hear him sniffle. "Not really, sweetie. I had to go to the ER. I'm actually waiting for them to look at the MRI and then release me from the hospital." Coop let out a big sigh. "Brad had a few too many drinks and grabbed me—he dislocated my elbow. It hurts a lot."

Hearing her friend's news, Vivien sat up, suddenly alert. "Oh my god, Coop. That's terrible. Why would Brad hurt you like that?" She moved over to the bedroom so she could talk.

She listened as Coop told the story. "I lost count of the drinks, that's how many he had," Coop said. "Anyway, after we left Splash is when the accident happened."

"Coop, that was no accident. You were attacked."

He attempted to make a feeble excuse for his boyfriend: "Maybe it's because of his Secret Service training—I guess it's just reflex. Brad just doesn't realize how strong he is."

Vivien harrumphed. "Oh, so the Secret Service trains their agents to drink a lot and then beat up innocent people? I don't think so. No one should treat you like this, Coop. No one. I refuse to stand by and allow my best friend to get abused by some angry guy with a drinking problem."

"You're right, you're right. I'm a battered boyfriend."

Vivien could tell that Coop was trying to make a weak joke. Was he trying to minimize what had just happened to him? What could she do to protect her friend? "Coop, it sounds like Brad is out of control. How can you be with someone like that? And on top of that, he carries a gun for his job. I know you like him, but I think you need to end things with the guy—quickly. Please. I'm worried about your safety. It can only get worse."

*

When Coop heard those ominous words from Vivien, he knew in his heart what he should do, but he felt paralyzed. Yes, he should stand up for himself, protect himself. But if he broke up with Brad he'd be alone again.

Coop imagined waking up and staring at an empty pillow beside him—and it terrified him. The pain of being lonely was more powerful than the shame of admitting he'd been abused. He played devil's advocate like a defense attorney arguing Brad's case—sure, his boyfriend had his faults, but they'd also shared many moments of bliss. Yet, he sensed that Vivien would not relent until she was assured of his safety.

Sighing, Coop said to his friend, "You're right, you're right, Vivi. I need to end things. I'll talk to him tomorrow." His heart sank as if it had been pumped full of lead.

*

In the morning the doorbell to his apartment rang, jarring Coop from his nap. He gingerly got up from the sofa, careful not to move his arm, which was supported by a sling. He opened the door. Brad had puppy-dog eyes and held out a bouquet of flowers.

"Brad? What are you doing here?" The flowers were gorgeous. Coop had to stop his impulse to give his boyfriend a hug.

Pressing his lips into a thin line, Brad said, "Coop, can I come in? I need to talk with you."

Coop stepped back, opening the door wide. "Sure. You'll have to pardon me, I'm moving a bit slowly. My elbow got dislocated last night." He shot Brad a look of disapproval.

Brad took Coop's good elbow and helped steer him to a seat on the sofa, covering him gently with a blanket. He sat in an armchair across from Coop. Rays of morning sunshine streamed through the slits in the venetian blinds, casting a soft, magical glow around Brad.

"How are you?" Brad's voice was halting. "About last night, Coop. I…I obviously had too much to drink and acted irresponsibly. I'm so sorry I hurt you. I feel terrible about it. Can you ever forgive me?" He looked down at his clasped hands and then looked up at Coop. With his violet-blue eyes, dark hair, and striking features, it was almost like watching an actor in a scene from a movie about star-crossed lovers.

Stiffly, Coop said, "Brad, I forgive you. But that can never happen again."

His boyfriend leaned forward and lightly touched Coop's knee. "It won't, I can promise you that."

What was going to happen next? Would Brad vow to reform—cut back on the drinking and be the best boyfriend imaginable? Seeing that Coop was incapacitated, would Brad offer to run out to pick up some bacon and eggs and whip up a gourmet breakfast? After that, would Coop drift off to a peaceful slumber in Brad's comforting arms?

"There's something else I want to talk to you about, Coop."

"What is it?"

Brad clasped his hands together again and dropped his gaze. "I care for you, Coop, but I'm just not ready to be in a relationship right now. I think it's best for us to break up."

Coop's jaw nearly dropped open in shock. Wait a minute, first Brad beat him up and now *he* was the one breaking up with Coop? Wasn't Coop supposed to be the sensible one who was putting an end to the relationship? "I see. Okay." Coop threw off the blanket and stood up shakily. "I think my painkiller is kicking in. I need to rest."

Brad nodded and stood up. "I'm really sorry, Coop. I hope you'll be okay."

"I'll be fine, Brad. Goodbye." He had barely shut the door when the pent-up tears started streaming down his face, leaving hot, wet streaks on his cheeks. Coop sat sobbing on the sofa for a long time, feeling deserted. Coop's phone rang and he picked it up. Vivien. "Hi, Vivi." He rubbed his forehead. "Well, it's over between Brad and me. He just left."

Vivien audibly breathed a sigh of relief. "I know it must have been tough, Coop, but you did the right thing."

Coop let out a sob. "Well, here's the thing. I'm ashamed to admit it, but Brad actually broke up with me—said he wasn't ready for a relationship. What's wrong with me, Vivi, that I can't even end a bad relationship? Why am I not strong enough to stand up for myself?"

"Oh, Coop, you've been through so much lately. Don't be too hard on yourself. Why don't you get some rest, order some food, and watch a fun movie. Maybe a rom-com? I'll call you later to check in on you, okay, sweetie? I love you."

"Love you, too." Coop hung up miserable and humiliated. The searing pain in his elbow was surpassed only by the devastating pain in his heart. *Will I ever find someone who loves me?*

*

Hours later Coop awoke in a haze to a cacophony of sounds. His television was blaring a home improvement show, his doorbell was ringing, and his cell phone was buzzing. Moving slowly, Coop got up to answer the door—it was a delivery guy holding a beautiful floral arrangement. He placed the large vase of flowers lovingly on his dining table and read the get-well card from Vivien.

Dear Coop, feel better soon. Here's a quote to add to your collection: "The best thing to hold onto in life is each other. (Audrey Hepburn). I'm always here for you. Love you lots, Vivi.

He moved back over to the sofa and picked up his phone. Seeing that Vivien had just called, Coop called her back to say thank you for the flowers. His phone rang again. It was Sofia.

"Coop, have you been watching the news?" Sofia asked.

Still in a painkiller fog, Coop said, "Um, no, I fell asleep watching HGTV."

"Turn on CNBC, Coop. Your firm is on the news. Check it out, and I'll talk to you later."

Coop changed the channel and turned up the volume. Sure enough, the CNBC reporter was announcing news about a huge SEC investigation of Coop's accounting firm and of their client Hello TelCo. All hell had broken loose about the accounting fraud, with major repercussions. There was footage of arrests being made at both companies. Coop gasped as he saw Felix Culo outside their office building in handcuffs being led away by the authorities. Felix's eyes were red and brimming with tears.

Who's the wuss now, Felix? Coop allowed himself a self-satisfied smirk. He sat back, watching in a numb state, until he was jolted alert by his own name, which was being announced on national television. "Gary Edward Cooper, also known as 'Coop' in the firm, is the hero in this scenario, stepping forward to act as the whistleblower to alert authorities of the malfeasance."

Coop's accounting firm ID photo was being flashed up on the screen (thank god it was a cute picture—his dimples were visible and his shirt color complimented his eyes).

A spokesperson from the SEC said, "Mr. Cooper came forward due to his concerns about regular people, like grandmothers, being harmed by the fraudulent activities of both his firm and their client."

As the reporter praised Coop, his cell phone started buzzing with texts and calls from his mom, siblings, friends, and former clients, all expressing their pride in his courage. Coop sighed and recalled a quote by journalist Walter Lippmann: *He has honor if he holds himself to an ideal of conduct though it is inconvenient, unprofitable, or dangerous to do so.* That certainly summed up his situation.

*

SOFIA

"Kate, how are you feeling?" Sofia walked into the hospital room and handed a small brown bag to Kate Frost. "Brought your favorite breakfast—an almond croissant and a steaming hot cappuccino."

"You're the best." Kate was sitting in her hospital bed propped up with pillows. She closed her laptop, removed her glasses, and smiled. "Thanks for breakfast. I'm only here for two days but can't wait to get home and have some real food!" Despite the many bandages covering up the surgical scars all over her body, Kate's face glowed. "Honestly, Sofia, I haven't been this excited since I was a kid waking up on Christmas morning. I can't wait to take off the bandages and see what I look like. The surgeon also gave me a special scar-minimizing gel, and he thinks that all my scars will eventually become invisible." She let out a long audible sigh as if she had been holding it inside her for years. "I can't thank you enough for helping me." Her eyes held a sincere look. "And for caring about me. You've been a true friend, Sofia."

Two nurses walked in, one with a huge floral arrangement and the other with a basket of exotic fruit, chocolates, and nuts. Kate opened the card, read it, and pressed it to her heart. "From Devinder." She beamed. Clearly she had strong feelings for him.

Sofia gave her a smile and then pulled up a chair and sat down. The two of them chatted about their show, which had become a huge hit. Much to their surprise, in recent weeks a number of prominent business moguls had reached out asking to appear on their program. The content of their show was getting significant buzz—it seemed that some CEOs would wait to appear on *Titans* to reveal major news or share an experience they'd never before made public. The pressure was on to keep the show engaging and fresh.

Sofia took her notebook out of her bag and flipped it open. "I have an idea for the show. How about finishing each interview with a Titans Top Ten list of questions?"

"Go ahead, I'm intrigued." Kate listened as she devoured the almond croissant.

"We'll have a standard list of ten intriguing questions that we call the Titans Top Ten and ask the same rapid-fire questions at the end of every interview. It could be really interesting for the audience to hear how different CEOs respond to the same questions. What do you think?"

"I like it. I like it a lot. Let's start hammering out the questions."

The two women spent some time brainstorming until they were satisfied with their Titans Top Ten. They also discussed guests they'd like to have in the future. Kate tossed her glasses on the bed and leaned back on the pillows.

After a while Sofia sat back. "Listen, Kate, I also have to show you something and I hope it doesn't upset you. Yesterday when I walked into my office this was lying face down on my chair." Sofia reached into her bag and pulled out a folded-up piece of paper. "Apparently it was left on the desk chair of every employee in the building." She handed the paper to Kate, who opened it. It was a collage of women—not just any women but pictures of well-known lesbian couples: Ellen DeGeneres and Portia de Rossi, Lily Tomlin and Jane Wagner, Robin Roberts and Amber Laign, Cynthia Nixon and Christine Marinoni—and a photoshopped picture of Sofia LaForte and Kate Frost. On top of the page it said, "Couples you might know about…or should."

Kate put her glasses back on and took a closer look. Then she furrowed her brow. "I don't get it. What is this?"

Sofia explained. "This is the work of Lorrie and Cordelia, I'm sure of it. I call them LoCo for short because they act so crazy. Those two are joined at the hip—they even carpool to work together so they can maximize their gossip time." She pointed to the collage. "They think that you and I are lesbians and that we're in a relationship." Sofia rolled her eyes. "LoCo seem to think it's their civic duty to out anyone at work whom they think might be gay."

Kate threw her head back and laughed. "Really? Now, there's a couple of dunderheads who have too much time on their hands. Just ignore it, Sof, it's not even worth stressing over."

Leaning back in her chair, Sofia crossed her arms and tapped her foot on the ground. "You know, Kate, I was going to let it slide. But I was in the break room and Arlene, the really friendly makeup artist, came up to me. She was holding this collage and told me that LoCo had done similar harm to her...and to many others. Arlene invited me to join the grassroots support group they have for gays and lesbians—apparently they meet after work once a week. She said, 'You're welcome to check it out, Sofia.' I thanked her but had to tell her that I'm not gay. Arlene chuckled and said, 'Yeah, my gaydar was telling me that you weren't, but I thought I'd mention it just in case.'"

Kate gave her an amused look.

"I told Arlene whether I'm gay or straight is beside the point. What those two women are doing is just plain wrong. This type of behavior is unacceptable, not to mention unprofessional." Sofia chalked it up to insecurity: her observation was that people who are unhappy with themselves are the first ones to launch grenades at others. What if she really were a lesbian? Would that justify this juvenile behavior?

"Then let's do something about it. We need to stop LoCo from this kind of nonsense, especially if they're hurting people. Right?" Kate looked straight in Sofia's eyes.

Sofia nodded in agreement. Now they just needed to come up with a plan.

The following week Sofia and Kate put Operation NoMo LoCo into action. After work they waited in the CNBC parking garage like lions stalking their prey. As Lorrie and Cordelia (nattering away as usual) approached their car, Sofia and Kate pounced.

"Hello, ladies," Sofia said as she approached, "we'd like a word with you. About this." She held up the collage.

LoCo took a few steps back with eyes wide until they bumped up against their car. Sofia could swear she saw them trembling.

Kate crossed her arms. "We know you two have been spreading rumors that we are a lesbian couple. First of all, gossiping about your colleagues is unprofessional. Second, you're wrong—neither of us is gay. Basic rule of reporting—get your facts straight."

Lorrie gulped. "Oh, that? That was just a joke. We were having a little harmless fun."

"Harmless?" Kate boomed, her voice echoing in the parking lot. "We do have gay and lesbian colleagues in the office. How do you think your attacks on them have made them feel? You have embarrassed and humiliated people and encroached on their private lives. That is bullying. Why do you two have to be so mean?"

Behind Sofia and Kate a loud rustling noise was audible. Cordelia grabbed Lorrie's arm in terror. They'd brought an army with them. The entire LGBT support group—about sixty people strong—stood arm in arm behind Sofia and Kate.

"All of it was meant to be a joke, huh?" Sofia said sharply. "Do you see anyone here laughing?" She waved her arms in front of the group. "People's personal lives are none of your business. We've had enough of your immature behavior. This stops now. You see all these people around me? Just remember, we're all watching you, so do not mess with anyone again. Got it?"

LoCo clung to each other and Lorrie meekly said, "Uh, we apologize and promise to stop."

Sofia and Kate stepped back, and the two fear-stricken women bolted into their car, burning rubber on their way out. That was the end of the antics from LoCo, much to the relief of so many of their embattled colleagues.

*

That night Sofia got a reprieve. Jasper had wanted to introduce her to his family when his parents were visiting from Carmel, California. Unfortunately, something came up and they had to cancel their trip out east. They were going to try again in a couple of months when Jasper's sister Kathleen would be visiting New York from Switzerland. The pressure was off…for now.

CHAPTER 10

June

SOFIA

Two months passed by quickly and the big dinner with Jasper Frank and his family had arrived. Jasper's sister was in town from Europe and his parents were visiting from California. His brother, who lived in Chicago, was also going to join them. Though nervous about meeting his family, Sofia was eager to learn more about the man she loved. Dinner that Friday evening in June would take place at the River Café in Brooklyn, just across the East River. After wrapping up her regular end-of-week Smashers call, she texted Jasper that she was on her way.

Jasper waited for her at the bar, looking dapper in a black suit, white shirt, and purple tie. Over a glass of wine, they waited for his family to arrive.

Sofia looked around the fancy restaurant filled with mostly older Caucasian patrons and suddenly started to feel uneasy. Jasper seemed to sense her anxiety and launched into an amusing anecdote about his sister. Midstory, Sofia said with some urgency, "Does your family know I'm black?"

Her boyfriend paused, furrowing his brows. "Come to think of it, no. It never occurred to me to mention it, Sofia. Why?"

A wave of panic started to rise up inside of Sofia. "Don't you think it's an important detail for them to know? I mean, are they going to be shocked when they meet me? I don't want a *Guess Who's Coming to*

Dinner scenario." Her shoulders tensed up. Jasper's failure to mention her ethnicity to his family cast a cloak of apprehension over her—was he that unaware of her perspective?

"Don't worry about it, Sofia, it's not a big deal. My family is going to love you, they'd be crazy not to."

"Not a big deal? But being black is an essential part of who I am, Jasper."

"I meant it is not going to be a big deal to my family. Trust me."

"What do they know of me?" Sofia asked.

"I told them you're an amazing person—smart, talented, funny, strong, and beautiful. And I told them I love you." Jasper gazed into her eyes and gently took her hand and kissed it. That small gesture gave her enormous comfort, and the tension in her shoulders started to release its grip.

"I love you, too, Jasper." She leaned closer and kissed him passionately.

"Excuse me, but what kind of behavior is that? And in a public place?" a man's voice said sternly. Sofia looked up to see a thirtysomething black man glaring at them. She froze. Jasper turned to the man.

"Matty, great to see you, man!" Jasper pulled the man close and the they hugged. "Sofia, this is Matthew."

"Hi, Matthew, it's a pleasure to meet you. You're a friend of Jasper's?" Sofia surmised that this was a coincidence his friend was at the restaurant on the same evening.

"Friends? I guess you could call us friends." Matthew had a sly smile on his face.

Sofia was confused. Jasper playfully punched Matthew in the shoulder. "Matthew is my brother, Sofia. Well, technically stepbrother."

"You have a *black* brother?" Sofia blurted in shock. "Are you kidding me?"

"I prefer African-American, actually," Matthew corrected her.

"Yes, Matty's my brother. My mom married Matthew's dad a few years after my father died. His dad was an old college sweetheart of my mother's." He took in Sofia's look of astonishment. "I should probably mention that Matthew's dad—my stepfather—is also African-American, just so you don't say anything indelicate when you meet him," Jasper quipped.

"Okay." For once Sofia was at a loss for words. Now she realized why it didn't occur to Jasper to tell his family that Sofia was black— Jasper came from a mixed-race family, so he was focused not on Sofia's ethnicity, he was focused on her as a person. That was a revelation.

When the diverse Frank family assembled at the restaurant, Sofia felt like they were United Nations delegates gathering for diplomatic talks. His white mother, his African-American stepfather and stepbrother, his sister, and her Japanese husband—what a lovely combination. Jasper's family was intelligent, warm, and loved to laugh.

Over dinner Sofia learned that Jasper's father was a hotel magnate who'd founded Majestic Hotels and Resorts International, a chain of luxury hotels and exclusive vacation spots. After he'd passed away, Jasper and his sister Kathleen had helped run the family business, until Jasper decided to strike out on his own as an entrepreneur. Kathleen was still CEO of the hotel chain.

Jasper regaled his family with the tale of how he and Sofia met during the taxi accident right before her big speech. Sofia teased him about his stealthy trip to Madrid to see her and how he played hard to get. By the time they finished dinner it was clear that Jasper's family adored Sofia, mirroring her sentiments exactly.

*

On the next episode of *Titans Tell All*, Sofia and Kate were particularly excited to welcome entrepreneur Stella Jackson. She was the founder and CEO of Slique, a company that designed and produced stylish jeans for women of all sizes and was beloved by their customers.

Sofia kicked things off. "Stella, thank you so much for joining us on *Titans Tell All*, and welcome. Tell us, how did your company, Slique, come about?"

"It all started one day when I was shopping for new jeans shortly after having my second child. In every store it was as if all the denim makers were designing jeans for the body of a skinny teenage girl—every style was tight around the waist with skinny legs. I was frustrated that I couldn't find a pair of jeans that fit me or flattered my body—I'm a woman of average height who was carrying a few extra pounds." Stella shook her head. She was an attractive woman who probably wore a size eight. "I imagined there were plenty of other women with the same issue, so I decided to design something for us… for real women."

Kate interjected. "It wasn't as if you were starting from scratch. Weren't you an executive with a denim company previously?"

A haunted look came across Stella's face. "Yes, I was the chief operating officer of a denim company that shall remain unnamed, but I left there due to the terrible culture."

"Can you tell us more about your experience there?" Kate asked.

"The company was very successful, but I just couldn't continue working with that CEO. I saw him preying on young, innocent girls and tried everything I could to stop him. He was sexually harassing me and other female employees, so I had to leave that horrible environment."

Sofia shot Kate a knowing look—they'd have to discuss this after the show wrapped. "I see, that sounds challenging. Let's switch gears. Can you tell us, Stella, what's different about Slique denim and why women love your product so much?"

Stella sat up a little straighter. "First of all, we design to the proportions of real women and we have strategically placed panels of stretchy fabric to do things like hold in someone's tummy or lift their rear end; all the while our jeans are super comfortable to wear and move around in. All our jeans are made from four-way-stretch fabric, so they really flex and move with the wearer. And our patented waistband is secure but doesn't bind or squeeze your waist."

"I wear your jeans all the time, Stella, and I have to say they feel great and look fantastic." Sofia smiled. "I feel like I could go hiking in them comfortably!"

"That's exactly how we want our customers to feel, Sofia, like they're free to do just about anything in our jeans. Slique denim is suitable for active pursuits like running around with your kids at the park, and for chic outings like meeting friends at a swanky wine bar." The founder smiled.

They discussed how the business was doing and its plans for growth, and then wrapped up with their Titans Top Ten questions, concluding another engaging program.

*

After the show in the break room Sofia noticed how radiant Kate Frost looked now that she'd recovered fully from her surgery.

"I have to say, Kate, you look fabulous. And that dress is beautiful on you."

Kate blushed. "Thanks, Sof. I have a date tonight with Devinder Jain. Wanted to spruce up a bit." She winked and grinned. "I'm guessing you want to circle back on the issue that Stella Jackson brought up? I noticed you gave me your look."

Sofia was tickled that they were getting to know each other so well. "I figured out that Stella was referring to Charley Voss. Remember when our guest Elle spotted him in the commissary and had a panic attack?"

"I do remember that."

"This is a guy who terrorizes women, Kate. I did a little digging after our program with Elle and it turns out there've been rumors floating around for years about Voss's predatory behavior toward women—apparently it's an open secret in the apparel industry. I'd like to check the situation out a bit more—you know, find out who has been a Voss victim."

Kate bit the end of her pen. "And put a stop to it? Voss is a well-connected, powerful guy, but if he's preying on young women—I'm totally with you on that, Sofia. Let's outline our scoop and pitch it to Randolph."

*

A week later the pair were meeting in Randolph's office to pitch the Voss story to their boss.

Sofia kicked things off. "Randolph, there's an important story that Kate and I would like to work on and wanted to run it by you."

Randolph nodded as he reorganized the binder clips in their bin so they lay neatly.

She continued. "It's come to our attention that the apparel mogul Charley Voss has been sexually harassing women and preying on especially young women who have appeared in Voss ad campaigns over the years. We want to shine the spotlight on him and his predatory actions."

Kate adjusted her glasses. "This is such egregious behavior, Randolph, we want to put a stop to it. Apparently industry insiders know all about Voss's inappropriate actions. It's been an open secret for some time but no one has dared to bring the news to light."

"And how would this tie in to *Titans Tell All*?" Randolph wrinkled his forehead.

"It wouldn't," said Kate. "This would be a special program based on investigative journalism."

He rubbed his chin. "Charley Voss is an extremely powerful man—I don't think you realize how powerful. He's tight with many influential people and celebrities. Just last month he was photographed playing golf with the mayor. If we bring allegations against Voss and they're not airtight, all of us will lose our jobs." He sipped his cup of tea. "Voss has a lot of the media in his back pocket, though not our network," Randolph was quick to add. He looked at them. "Sofia, Kate, do you have people who will go on the record? Women who are willing to share their stories?"

Sofia looked uncertain but Kate jumped in. "We knew you'd ask that question, Randolph. We'll be aggressive about collecting stories from victims and letting them know we're on their side so they will share their experiences publicly." She shot a surreptitious glance at Sofia as if to say, *Just go along with me.*

Their boss looked thoughtful as he wiped clean and then precisely straightened all the pens on his desk. "So you don't have anyone who will go on the record? That's a gaping hole. What I don't want is a half-assed investigation where we make accusations that can't be backed up. We'll be butchered if that happens." He made a slicing motion with his letter opener across his jugular for emphasis. "Look, in no way do I condone Voss's actions, but I think it's a high-risk story to try to tackle. For now, I'd like you two to focus on keeping *Titans Tell All* a success. Let's revisit this idea at a later date."

Sofia's shoulders fell. "Okay, we understand, Randolph."

Outside his office, Sofia turned to Kate. "We didn't have anyone willing to go on the record. That was the big obstacle."

Kate nodded. "I know. But we'll get there."

"But Randolph said we should focus on *Titans.*"

A sly smiled came across Kate's face. "I know. And we'll do that, Sof. But what's stopping us from working on the Voss story, too? Once we get more meat on the bone we can change Randolph's mind."

Sofia chuckled. "If that's the case, then I know a woman from the *Wall Street Journal* who does investigative pieces like this—maybe we can team up with her to cover some of the groundwork."

"Sounds like a plan. Not having permission to do something shouldn't stop us."

GRACE

After the phone-throwing incident, Grace did her best to keep her head down around her boss—literally. Her colleague Jaymee was still in shock about it and was updating Grace on some of Skip's latest antics. By June, Skip had been in the role for seven months; he'd profoundly alienated his executive team and many employees in the company feared him.

"I heard he caused quite a stir at the merchandising meeting with his suggestions to overhaul the product line and change the pricing strategy," Grace whispered.

Jaymee scrunched up her nose. "Skip may have been successful at JMC, but I'm not convinced he can run this business effectively. Honestly, I don't know why they hired him."

Grace shrugged. "This happens all the time, Jaymee. Certain guys get their names known by recruiters. No matter how terrible a job they do, how awful they are to work with, or how crazy their behavior, they continue to get one plum CEO opportunity after another. Meanwhile there are plenty of talented, capable female candidates who are shut out and never get the chance to even be considered. That's why fewer than 4 percent of the CEOs of Fortune 500 companies are female."

"And some of these toxic male CEOs just keep getting jobs they don't deserve? It's so disheartening." Jaymee's gaze dropped to the floor.

"I know. But that's not the worst thing—tomorrow I have to fly with Skip to the London office for our annual check-in...alone. I'm dreading being stuck on a five-hour flight with him. And the throwing range inside a private jet is short."

Grace and Jaymee shared a nervous chuckle.

On Wednesday afternoon Grace showed up at a private airport in New Jersey to travel with Skip Palmer on the corporate jet. It was going to be an uncomfortable trip, but Grace resolved to make the best of it. Skip was still getting accustomed to being a new CEO and was probably extra stressed out.

When Skip entered the lounge, Grace greeted him warmly.

He said a clipped, "Good morning. Let's go."

Grace had brought an issue of *Harvard Business Review* that was focused on how to be a successful CEO. Once they were seated she said, "Skip, I came across this and thought it might interest you." She handed it to him.

"Thank you, Grace. This looks great. By the way, did you get the tickets I wanted?" A special fashion event was being held at the Victoria and Albert Museum, along with the Alexander McQueen fashion show—it was difficult but Grace had managed to snag two of the coveted tickets for her boss. She patted her tote bag. "Got them right here."

"Good." He nodded.

Somehow Grace managed to keep a positive conversation going until Skip checked his email. "Damn it. Colton just resigned. He got a once-in-a-lifetime opportunity to lead a sunglasses business in Hawaii. What a disaster." He tossed off his horn-rimmed glasses and pinched the bridge of his nose. "Now I have no one to run Baby & Kids."

Maybe this was an opportunity for Grace. "Sorry to hear that, Skip. But if you need someone to step in as the interim leader I'd be willing to do it, in addition to my CMO duties. Would that help?"

Skip blinked like a burrowing animal emerging from a dark tunnel into brilliant sunshine. He snorted. "Wow, Grace, you are really aggressive."

The comment hit her like a slap in the face and she sat back stunned. *A statement like that would never be made to a man.* Grace had thought she was solving the problem for her boss by offering to do two jobs for the price of one. What was the issue? "Actually, Skip, I was trying to be helpful. You've got no one in the role now, and I'm willing to lead the business until you make a decision about who you want as the president of Baby & Kids. I'd call that constructive, not aggressive." She'd only worked with Skip for two months, but it seemed like two years to her—each day of navigating her boss's prickly personality was like stepping through a minefield.

"I've already told you, Grace, the only job for you is CMO, and that's final."

Too late, she remembered that her boss didn't like being challenged. Skip forcefully typed out an email on his computer keyboard and then slammed it shut. He turned away and cracked open the *HBR* magazine.

Grace let out a soft sigh. Working with this guy was just so painful. Would they get on any better once Skip saw how well she interacted with the London team, or would he be uncomfortable to learn that she was so highly regarded?

For the remainder of the flight things were pretty quiet. The two of them kept busy with work, reading, and having a light meal until they finally reached their destination. Skip and Grace disembarked and waited in the lounge for their luggage to be brought to them.

He turned to her with a sour look on his face. In a fake, friendly tone he said, "Grace, I don't think this is working out."

"I'm not sure what you mean." Grace didn't have a clue what he was talking about—Skip sounded like a guy trying to break up with his girlfriend and doing a clumsy job of it.

"Oh, I think you know." Skip raised an eyebrow. "This." He spread his hands in front of his body. "I'm afraid we're going to have to part ways, Grace."

"Part ways?" Grace retorted. Was he talking about transportation to the hotel?

The first officer from the jet wheeled up their luggage. Skip kept on talking. "It's clear to me that you don't want the job I have for you—the only job I have for you. Plus, I don't think you've contributed all that much to the business. You did a good job with the CMO role in the past, but frankly, I think you've peaked. I think it's all downhill for you now. So, I'm afraid you're fired, Grace." He gave a self-satisfied smirk.

"Fired?" Grace was indignant. "Wait a second. You recently threw a phone at my head in front of the other executives and now you're firing me?" She laughed. "HR is going to have a field day with that directive, Skip. Also, your comment about me not contributing isn't valid. In fact, your two major initiatives—ordering from the runway and the modular bag—are my ideas, for which you are taking all the credit. I'm not okay with that."

Skip's eyes bored into hers. "I don't have to explain myself to you, Grace. I was a superstar at JMC and plan to attain the same reputation at Palazzo…by implementing great ideas."

"Great ideas that you stole from other people? Is that how you achieved success in the past, Skip?" Grace scoffed. "And oh, by the way, you can't fire me because I quit. But I will not leave without a severance package—I will be in touch with HR about that detail."

Skip's eyes narrowed and he gave her a contemptuous smile. "Well, you no longer have a hotel room, and I canceled all your travel arrangements before we landed. You'll have to find your own way home. Goodbye, Grace." He turned and swiftly walked outside to the waiting limo.

Jerk. Grace stood there with her arms crossed, blood racing, and mind churning. It was already evening in London and she was stranded with no place to stay and no way to get home. She glanced around the luxe lounge, took a deep breath to collect herself, and decided to slow things down. Wheeling her bag off to the side, Grace piled a plate with hors d'oeuvres, poured herself a nice glass of wine, and took a seat in a plush lounge chair.

It was still early in Oregon, so Grace dialed up Vivien to share the news. "We just landed in London and my boss tried to fire me but I quit instead. I had to invoke Rule Zero." Rule Zero was a well-known mandate from the Ceiling Smashers society: Never work with assholes.

"Oh, Grace, what a nightmare. Are you all right?"

"Honestly, I'm a bit shaken up. But I'm also relieved that I won't be working with Skip any longer. What a scumbag, leaving me here stranded." She huffed.

Vivien always managed to find a bright spot. "Grace, you know, this might be a blessing in disguise for you. I mean, you've been saying that you want to run a business, and Skip was clearly not going to let you do that. So maybe this is your chance. The universe has spoken."

Grace paused, holding the wineglass a few inches from her lips. "Wait, Vivi, what do you mean? Find a job running a business with another company? I suppose that's a possibility."

"Actually I had something else in mind. A better solution would be for you to start your own company, Grace. You certainly have the know-how to run a business and create brand cachet. And you have a ton of ideas about baby apparel—as a mom-to-be I'd love to buy the clothes you've been talking about. I think you should go for it!"

What Vivien was saying made sense, but…"But how would I fund it? It's not like I have a pile of cash sitting around to invest in a startup."

"What about your book sales?"

"Ha! Yeah, remind me to take you out for a burger with my last royalty payment." Grace groaned. "Starting a business is a great idea, but I just don't have the capital."

Vivien gave a quick laugh. "Hello? Weren't you recently flying in the helicopter of one of the most successful business magnates in the world, Devinder Jain? On our Smashers call you mentioned that Devinder told you to call him first if you ever needed financial backing for a venture, right? Well, give him a call, Grace!"

Grace slapped the side of her head, nearly spilling her wine. "He did say that. You know, Vivi, that might be the answer. Thanks." Before she ended the call Grace asked how Vivien's pregnancy was going and was glad to hear everything was fine. Grace's brain was already pulsing with ideas for her business.

Since she was in London anyway, Grace decided to spend a few days there to get herself centered and to shop around to generate design ideas for her baby apparel company. Grace took a cab into town, arranging a reasonably priced hotel room on the ride in. As she rummaged through her tote bag, she came across the envelope with the fashion event tickets. With a grin, Grace texted Simone Everett that she was in town and would love to bring her to the Alexander McQueen show as her guest. She also texted Win that she had arrived safely, was extending her stay, and would miss him.

*

Sitting in the front row of the fashion show, the two women had a chance to catch up. "How's your show going?" Grace hugged Simone and asked. "I caught the first episode and you totally rocked it, girl."

Simone beamed. "It's been so much fun, Grace, and I feel strongly about the message of the show. It's all about how a smart woman can solve problems and be a good person but also be a badass." The first episode of Simone's spy-executive TV series had aired in late May with the slate of new programs.

Grace gave the actress a playful punch in the arm. "I must say, you are looking totally buff these days, Simone. I don't think anyone would mess with you."

The actress cast her gaze downward.

"What's the matter?"

Simone shook her head. "Oh, Grace, I know I shouldn't let it bother me, but there's been some really disturbing stuff in the press lately. Some of the tabloids here are asking why an Asian-American actress was cast for the role instead of a Brit. They're also bringing up stuff from my past and questioning my character. I thought I'd put all that behind me. It sucks."

"I saw some of that rubbish—just ignore it, Simone. Surely you realize that some unscrupulous reporters will print anything they want even if there's no basis in fact—even if it harms innocent people. But the thing is, you have integrity. Integrity is about how one relates to oneself. What other people, particularly those who don't know you, think of you is irrelevant. The only person you have to answer to is yourself. Just be your authentic self, that's all you can do."

"I hear you, Grace, and I appreciate those words of wisdom. Also, I'm trying to practice everything you taught me about branding."

Grace put her arm around Simone. "You are your own brand, and oh, by the way, it's up to you to decide what that brand stands for. Take those authentic gems about you that already exist and polish them so they sparkle. When we talk about personal branding, it's not about making you something you're not, it's about making you a better version of what you already are. Ultimately, it's what you stand for that makes you stand out."

Simone looked at her with grateful eyes and gave Grace a hug. "You've been like a big sister to me. I can't tell you how much I cherish your friendship." The two of them looked up and smiled as reporters snapped a photo of them.

Grace whispered, "I also saw the comments Prince Alexander made—he said he thought people were starved to see more diversity on the telly and that you were absolutely brilliant in the role. Alex said he was eager to see more of your show. A prince just stuck up for you—you might want to find a way to thank him." She winked.

The actress gave a shy smile. Then the lights dimmed, the music started pulsing, and the glittering parade of gorgeous clothing creations began.

*

By the end of Grace's visit in London with her impromptu agenda, she felt reinvigorated and was full of ideas for her baby apparel startup. Her plan was to fly home that Sunday and start formulating her business plan and funding request. Over the past forty-eight hours she'd received a deluge of emails—from colleagues fearing that the worst was true and that she was leaving the company. And a particularly opportune email came from the talented designer Laura, who informed Grace that she'd decided to leave Palazzo and was looking for freelance design work. Grace immediately emailed Laura to stay tuned because she had a really interesting opportunity to discuss with her.

She grabbed a free UK newspaper, the *Sunday Times*, from the cart on the jet bridge to read on the plane. When she settled into her coach seat and opened the newspaper she saw the photo of her and Simone Everett in the front row of the Alexander McQueen show—she could just imagine the look on Skip Palmer's face when he saw that picture. She leaned back in her seat with a triumphant smile that remained on her face for the entire flight home.

*

In the month after Grace left the company, she moved at hyper speed. Her business plan for the launch of her baby clothing company was so well received by Devinder Jain that he insisted on being the sole angel investor to help her get her business off the ground. She'd hired Laura to design the product and was figuring out what the business and brand would look like.

The two women were working from Grace's apartment when her

phone rang. It was Vivien. Grace had emailed some early sketches of her clothing line to her friend to take a look, but Vivien had just given birth to a baby girl, so she probably had her hands full. "I'm so glad you called, Vivi! How's baby Lily doing?" The other end of the line was silent. "Vivien?"

*

When the most tragic thing imaginable happened, Vivien let her fiancé, Clay, handle most of the communication, sharing the news with friends and family. But there were a few calls she had to make herself. To her dad, to Coop, and to her Smasher friends. This was one of those calls.

"Oh, Grace, something awful happened."

Grace said, "Hang on, let me go into the bedroom." She heard the sound of a door closing. "What is it, Vivien. Are you okay?"

"Actually, no. Lily—" Vivien's voice croaked. "My baby died."

Grace gasped. "Dear god, no. I can't believe it. I'm so sorry, Vivi. What happened?"

Vivien explained the situation in a weary, weak voice. Every time she told someone it left her trembling with despair. Her baby, Lily, had been born with underdeveloped lungs and died just a few days after being born. Even worse, Clay, at his mother's direction, had deleted all the photos he'd taken of baby Lily. "It's like he just wanted to wipe the memory of her away, Grace. Before the funeral he'd already dismantled the crib, put it back in the box, and returned it to the store." She let out a heavy sigh. "Now I only have one picture of Lily, the one that was sent out with the birth announcement, and I can't stop looking at it. I can't stop thinking about Lily and wondering what her future would have been like." Her voice was low, her grief raw.

"Oh, Vivien, I don't know what to say. Is there anything I can do?"

"This will always be with me, Grace, but I can only hope things get better. How are you doing? Oh, hang on a second…"

Grace heard a muffling sound in the background.

"Sorry, I had to get my laptop. I saw that you had sent me an email asking for my feedback."

*

A panic rose up in Grace. She'd sent the sketches of her baby clothing line to Vivien, but that was the last thing her grieving friend should be looking at now. "No! Vivien, please, don't open the email." She was too late.

Vivien said quietly, "I'm looking at the designs now." Then she fell silent.

"That bad, huh?" Grace made a feeble attempt at a joke. When she heard the sound of Vivien weeping in anguish it felt like someone had stabbed her in the heart. Grace covered her mouth, trying desperately to muffle the sound of her own crying.

She heard Vivien taking a deep breath. "Grace, this...this is wonderful, really. It's exactly what I would have wanted for baby Lily. What are you naming your brand?"

Grace let out a heavy sigh, realizing that the birth of her business coincided with the death of her dear friend's baby. "Twinkle," she choked out in a sob.

*

ANDI

With the verve she'd normally applied to her career, Andi, who was now without a job, embraced her newfound freedom. Since leaving Kaneshiro Bank with a healthy severance she'd dedicated herself to being a more engaged wife and mother. Luca was fully recovered and back to work full time at the Educational Testing Service. He reveled in devising fiendishly difficult test questions for the SAT and GMAT. Andi had been enjoying time with her four-year-old twin boys,

Francesco and Antonio, and learning to cook meals that extended beyond frozen chicken nuggets and baby carrots. While Luca was at work, Andi took her sons on daily adventures around the city.

One sweltering July morning Andi and her sons headed downtown on the subway. She was grateful to get some help from strangers to maneuver her double-wide stroller onto the subway car. Though her sons were able to walk, they'd cover a lot of ground that day, so using the stroller would give them a respite from the long, hot schlep. Andi also felt having her kids strapped in a stroller was a better way to keep them safe on the busy subways. The blast of the air-conditioning in the subway car felt good and Andi took a seat, pulling the stroller closer to her. She wore a sleeveless button-down cotton shirt and shorts with sandals.

At Seventy-Second Street two Hispanic youths got on the train and slouched down in the seats across from Andi. One of the teens pulled out a crinkly cellophane bag of sunflower seeds and offered it to his friend. Together, the two youths sullenly chomped on mouthfuls of sunflower seeds, spitting out the shells onto the floor. Soon the subway floor was covered in slimy puddles of broken shells mixed with saliva. One of the boys spit wet seed shells that landed perilously close to Andi's sandal.

"This is public space, not your personal trash can," Andi snapped. "Would you mind not spitting your seeds on the floor?"

The young man gave her a disdainful look and continued his spitting.

Now Andi was miffed. "That's disgusting. Would you do that in your own home?"

The youth rolled his eyes dramatically and said to his buddy, "Typical. It's always those white folks gettin' on our case and tellin' us what to do." He looked defiantly at Andi.

She leaned over the stroller glaring at the young men. "What makes you think I'm white?" Before the youths could react Andi started speaking in rapid-fire Spanish, admonishing them to set a good example. *"Tengan más respeta por su cultura."* She told them when they acted badly it reflected poorly on all Hispanic people and they should behave in a way that made their mothers proud. *"Comportense."*

Both youths straightened up in their seats and cast guilty gazes at the subway floor. The young man who had spoken so rudely to Andi quietly and painfully swallowed whole the rest of the sunflower seeds bulging in his cheeks. For the remainder of the ride downtown the boys sat there quietly and respectfully. When Andi and her sons got off at their stop in Chelsea, the two young men courteously bid her good day and helped her get the stroller out of the subway car. Andi waited until she walked away before she smiled in amusement.

*

Grace, back from her trip to London, agreed to meet up with Andi at a water park near Chelsea and have some fun with the twins. Coop, who was also not working, promised he'd try to make it over to meet them, as well. These days Vivien and Sofia were the only ones gainfully employed.

As Andi approached the water park, her sons squealed in delight. They shouted, "Aunty Gracie!" when they saw Grace jogging toward them. Grace wore a casual cotton sundress in a pale yellow gingham print and sandals. She scooped up the boys and gave them big hugs and then greeted Andi.

"Okay, my little munchkins, are you ready for some fun? Let's go splash around!" Grace took the twins by the hand and led them into the water park while Andi parked the stroller in the shade. There were huge multicolored whimsical-looking shapes made of a shiny plastic with spouts coming out at various angles, plus an area where sprinklers shot water up from the ground intermittently. Antonio and Francesco splashed, screeched, and had a glorious time running around and cooling off. After some time, Andi and Grace sat on a bench while the boys continued to play in the water and then in the large sand pit nearby.

"Nice to have a break from work, huh?" Grace nudged her. "You enjoying your time off?"

Andi grinned. "Honestly, I didn't know what I was missing. It's been really fun just hanging out with the boys." Her eyes grew dark and the smile fell away. "Grace, I'm just so broken up about Vivien losing her baby. I mean, I can't even imagine…"

A grim expression came over Grace's face. "I know, I'm worried about our girl. She's out there in Portland all alone, and frankly, Clay doesn't seem to be giving her the support she needs. We all want Vivien to succeed at Smart Sports, but what she's had to endure with the terrible culture, and now Lily's death? It's just too much." She shook her head in disgust.

The two women sat in silence for a few minutes. The goofy interaction of Andi's sons made them both smile.

"So, have you thought about what you're going to do next, Andi?"

Andi was quiet for a minute while she considered her response. "Funny that you ask—I have been thinking about it. I've been in private banking for so long and success was always measured by how much money you managed—but I want to do something other than just make my clients rich. I want to do something worthwhile."

"You mean get out of banking completely? But you were so great at it."

Andi shrugged. "Just because you can do something well, it doesn't mean that's the thing you're meant to do. It's like you not wanting to be stuck just doing marketing, Grace." Andi took a minute to tell the boys to share the sand toys. "I want to do something I'm passionate about and where I can have an impact—maybe help build businesses."

The temperature was rising and Grace wiped some perspiration from her forehead. "Andi, I know this might be a touchy subject, but what about getting back into the private equity world? Maybe it's time you went after your white whale."

*

The summer between their first and second year at Wharton had been a pivotal one for Andi. Over one thousand people had applied for a summer internship at the prestigious private equity firm Minch Capital—Andi was one of the few chosen. She knew that having a coveted internship there would basically allow her to write her own ticket for future jobs. Among the twenty interns selected was another classmate and Smasher friend, Courtney Greene.

That summer experience really opened Andi's eyes to the art of deal making and she learned a lot from the talented partners, though the summer interns had limited interaction with Finbar Minch himself. For Andi it was thrilling to research companies and decide which ones to invest in, then help the company founders strategize on how to grow their companies successfully. It was her dream to win a full-time role at the firm.

At the end of the summer Minch Capital threw a posh cocktail party on the top floor of their building to thank their employees and impress summer interns. Murmurs went through the crowd when Finbar appeared, and the interns clamored to get a few precious moments to speak with him and try to make a good impression. This could be their one chance to improve their odds of getting a full-time job at Minch Capital upon graduation.

Andi and Courtney were chatting and comparing notes about their summer experience when another summer intern, Ashley, joined them. She seemed rattled. "You okay, Ashley?" Courtney asked.

"You know, I'd practically kill for a job here, but that guy"—Ashley motioned with her head in Finbar's direction—"just gives me the creeps." She shuddered but looked around cautiously. "I'm going to get another glass of wine." Andi gave Courtney a puzzled look and then they continued their conversation.

After some time Finbar made his way around the room and came to Andi, who by then was standing alone. She was excited to have a conversation with the big boss and brought up all the investment questions she'd kept bottled up over the summer. Finbar was interesting to speak with at first, but soon Andi noticed that he was staring intently at her clothes. She wore a conservative but stylish business suit and a silk blouse with a high crew neck. Andi glanced down—had she spilled something on herself? Hmm, no spill. Finally she realized what was going on—Finbar was ogling her breasts. She tried making eye contact with the financier, but his gaze was glued to her chest. Now she understood Ashley's comment. This was absurd. Here she was trying to have a serious conversation with the guy, and he was leering at her. Andi had just finished her first year at Wharton, during which a TA had sexually harassed her—Finbar's behavior lit the already short fuse on Andi's temper.

When a server came by with a tray of hors d'oeuvres, Andi grabbed a cocktail napkin and opened it up into a rectangle while still trying to have a conversation with Finbar. Taking a pen out of her pocket, she leaned over a side table and drew two widely spaced, parallel arrows pointing upward. Fed up with the boorish behavior, she held the cocktail napkin in front of her chest and said in a loud voice, "Yo, Finbar, I'm up here," with the arrows pointing up toward her face.

The financier looked confused.

"When professionals speak to each other they're supposed to look here"—Andi pointed to her eyes—"not down here." She pointed to the sign in front of her breasts. "I've admired you for many years, Finbar, but this kind of behavior? It's unacceptable. You and your wife are expecting a daughter soon, right? How would you feel if someday her boss looked at her the way you're looking at me?"

Finbar cocked his head to the side and blew out an exasperated breath. "I take it you're not interested in getting a job with my firm, Andi?"

"I'm far more ambitious than that." Andi crumpled the cocktail napkin and handed it to him. Finbar stared at her, his green eyes clear and cool. She walked away.

Her dramatic gesture caught the attention of many eyes in the room, especially the other women. She made her way to the restroom and felt someone steps behind her. Andi spun around and came face-to-face with Linda, a female colleague who'd been with the firm for five years. "Andi, what you did back there...that took guts. So many of the women at the firm have suffered in silence for too long. That ends tonight. I plan on giving Finbar a piece of my mind about his inappropriate behavior. Thank you for being brave enough to take the first step."

Later that night, when the summer interns were out drinking together, the handful of female interns surrounded Andi.

"I'm so glad you did that, Andi," gushed Ashley. "Finbar was eyeing me like a piece of meat, too. It was so creepy."

"His behavior was just gross," Courtney spat.

"Do you really think that was wise, Andi?" said another woman with a frown. "Now you have no shot of getting a job with Minch Capital. After all your hard work over the summer—you're willing to just throw it all away?"

Andi looked directly at her. "If I have to endure some bozo staring at my breasts in order to get a job, it's not worth it. My dignity is worth more than any job." While that was true, it was also a fact that she was walking away from her dream job. She'd been following the career of Finbar Minch for years and this had been her big opportunity...until she'd let her temper get the best of her. Had she just blown it?

"I don't have the guts to do what you did, Andi, but here's to you."

Ashley raised her glass. The others voiced in unison, "To Andi!" as they clinked glasses.

In the fall, when Minch Capital was sending out its few select job offers, Andi's mailbox was empty. Her friend Courtney Greene, however, was one of the lucky ones. On the one hand Andi felt justified in standing up for herself, but on the other hand she knew she'd just lost out big-time.

*

Andi reflected upon Grace's question. "Yeah, I'd love to get back into private equity. I've read that Minch Capital is doing so many exciting deals, but I certainly don't want to put myself into another hostile work environment. Maybe I'll explore other PE firms."

"Haven't you spoken to Courtney about this? Apparently after your summer internship ended the women at the firm had a sit-down with Finbar and voiced their grievances about the way he was treating women. To his credit, he actually listened to them, apologized for his mistakes, and apparently made major changes in his behavior and the culture of the firm. That was ten years ago, Andi—by now it must be a much better place for female professionals."

Andi hadn't heard that information before and blinked up at the scorching sun. "I did not know that. Maybe I should ask Courtney to arrange a meeting for me with Finbar. What do you think?"

"Go for it. The worst he can say is no." Grace elbowed her.

Never one to accept failure, Andi steeled herself to meet the world-renowned financier again and see if they might be able to work together after all. She saw someone coming up the path.

"Hey, Coop, you made it!"

The three friends had a glorious time playing with the twins at the water park, getting lunch at an outdoor café, and simply enjoying their newfound freedom on a brilliant summer day.

*

Later that week Andi, Grace, and Sofia were fulfilling their duty as helpful alumnae by attending a Wharton Women mentoring mixer. Most of the women at the event were current students doing summer internships in the city, eager to get career advice from successful graduates.

A tall Asian woman made a beeline for Andi, who was perusing the refreshment table. "Hello, Andi? My name is Amy Kamimoto. I just spoke with your friend Grace, who mentioned that you worked at Kaneshiro Bank. That's where I'm doing my summer internship, so we have something in common."

Andi smiled at her eager young face. "Nice to meet you, Amy. How's the internship going?"

Cocking her head to one side, Amy seemed deep in thought. "I am very much enjoying the work, but my observation is that the company culture could be more welcoming toward women. I grew up in Japan, so I'm not sure if this bank is similar to other US banks in terms of culture. What was your experience like?"

Andi let out a snort. "I'll give it to you straight, Amy. I came over to Kaneshiro Bank with the Goldman private banking acquisition and my experience was not good. I was sexually harassed by my boss on an ongoing basis. Despite great performance, my pay was cut arbitrarily and my key accounts taken away. Finally, even when I showed video proof of the harassment to the bank's chairman, the decision was made to let my boss remain at the bank. Because the bank didn't seem concerned about my welfare or the welfare of women, I left. End of story."

Amy's face reddened and she covered her mouth with her hand. "Oh, no. I'm so sorry to hear that, Andi. What a loss of talent for the bank." Her look darkened. "May I ask the name of your horrible boss?"

"Lester Labosky." Leaning closer, Andi lowered her voice.

"Whatever you do, Amy, promise me that you'll stay far, far away from that creep."

"I'll do that…and more," Amy said with a determined look in her eye.

*

COOP

The SEC investigation into Hello TelCo and Coop's accounting firm had moved with lightning speed. By the end of April, Coop had found himself on the witness stand testifying about the accounting irregularities he'd unearthed and the cover-up. The fact that he was still wearing his arm sling then had made Coop an even more sympathetic and heroic figure. He found that as he moved about the city, he was easily recognized by people, who gave him smiles and thumbs-up signs.

By the time July rolled around, Coop's arm had healed and he was enjoying his near-celebrity status. He'd spent a sweltering but fun day with Grace, Andi, and her twins and then headed uptown to buy some gourmet food at Zabar's that he'd have for dinner. The store was comfortably chilly inside and crowded with shoppers, the delectable scents wafting through the air. Coop picked out a basketful of tasty items and then got in line to pay. At the checkout stand when he swiped his debit card through the machine it flashed a heart-stopping message: "Insufficient funds." *What?* About six months ago Coop had drained his checking account to write the check for his partner's buy-in. He hadn't yet built up his finances again, and in all the hubbub of the last few months Coop had forgotten he was no longer receiving payments as a partner in the firm. Apparently his balance was now down to zero. Coop groaned. The line of people behind him grumbled and shifted impatiently.

The checkout clerk said dispassionately, "Got another card?"

In fact, he didn't. Coop had gotten in the habit of just carrying around his license, debit card, and cell phone. "Uh, no, sorry, I don't." He looked around desperately. "Should I…should I just put all this stuff back?"

"Come *on*, dude," a guy called out from the line three people back.

"Wait, young man! Aren't you Coop, the whistleblower?" an elderly woman with kind eyes and thick glasses called out to him from the next checkout stand. She picked up her bag and walked over. "Are you having trouble buying groceries, dear?"

Coop turned crimson. "Unfortunately, I am. Seems I'm short on funds."

As the clerk started to void his transaction the elderly woman held up her finger. "No, no, don't worry, I will pay for these." She looked at Coop and smiled. "After what you did to help regular people like me, this is the least I can do for you. I owned stock in Hello TelCo." Before Coop could protest she swiped her card through the machine and paid for his items.

Coop stepped back. "Thank you, ma'am. How can I repay you?"

She waggled a finger. "No repayment necessary. You did the right thing, and I'm pleased and proud to help you. I hope everything works out for you, dear."

Coop thanked her, humbled by this stranger's generosity, and gathered up his grocery bags.

*

When he got home Coop figured a simple transfer from his retirement account would solve the problem. He'd built up a nice nest egg in his 401(k) plan and would just move some money to his checking account and deal with the tax penalty later. After eating dinner he munched on a fruit tart as he sat in front of his personal laptop. Coop made three unsuccessful attempts to transfer funds before finally resorting to calling the help line. Surprisingly, an actual human answered the call.

Coop swallowed the bite of fruit tart and explained that he was having trouble transferring his funds out of his 401(k) account.

"Sir, did you not see the email that went out to all company employees a few days ago?" The customer service woman's voice was slow and sounded anxious.

"No, I didn't," Coop said, sitting back slowly. "I'm no longer an employee so I'm not on the firm's email system. Did I miss something important?" A bad feeling was forming in the pit of his stomach.

"Well, sir, with the SEC charges against the accounting firm, the firm has collapsed and the 401(k) plan has been..."—she paused—"...compromised. There are three parts to the 401(k), all of which were impacted. Contributions that you made to the 401K were being pooled by the company but weren't sent to the plan, so those amounts are null. Any matching contributions by the company are gone since the firm is closing. And because the majority of your holdings in the 401(k) plan were company stock—well, that company stock is now worthless, so that part of your 401(k) plan has no value."

Coop felt panic rising up from his stomach to his brain—the rush of blood was coursing through his head like a crashing wave. "Are you saying that my entire 401(k) is worthless? Gone?"

"Yes, sir. Unfortunately that is the case for many employees. I'm sorry to have to deliver this bad news. Is there anything else I can help you with?"

Coop managed to thank her and hung up the phone in a daze. He rubbed his forehead raw as a full-on freak-out started. *Holy crap, I have no money!* Even worse, he realized that because of his whistleblowing, former colleagues of his were in the same position. He'd had no idea that his actions would cause such repercussions to the innocent employees in the firm. This was a bona fide disaster. The elderly woman in the grocery store had told him he'd done the right thing but it was feeling like anything but.

As terrible as Coop's situation was, it was nothing compared to his friend Vivien, who was still reeling from the death of her baby. She'd recently returned to work at Smart Sports after taking a much-needed two-week break. It was the middle of the day and she was phoning up Coop. Strange.

He did his best to cheer Vivien up. "Sweetie, what you need is a few days in the warm sunshine of Puerto Rico with your dear old friend," Coop told her. He immediately regretted it, his heart pumping in panic. What was he thinking? In his dire financial condition he could barely afford groceries, let alone a trip to Puerto Rico. He breathed a sigh of relief when Vivien suggested a long weekend together sometime in the future. "How are things going at work, Vivi? Oh, how did the interview go?" His friend had been selected as one of the *Wall Street Journal*'s "50 Women to Watch" and she was one of five women selected for an in-depth profile—Coop couldn't have felt prouder of her.

*

Vivien felt a stab of pain and her voice took on a bitter tone as she recounted the story to Coop of how her coworkers Rebecca and Charl had plotted against her. They knew that she'd just lost her baby, yet they had secretly planted a pair of custom-made baby sneakers on the conference table in her office. Their intent was to cause her to fall to pieces in front of the reporter and sabotage her *WSJ* interview.

"For the love of god," Coop huffed, "that woman is a psycho witch from hell. How malicious can a person be? As a new mother, you'd think she'd have some compassion! That's despicable."

Vivien grimaced. "I agree. She's a nightmare." Dealing with these backstabbing people was draining her energy and sapping her spirit. Some were intent on pushing her out of the company and some were among the worst people she'd ever encountered. Vivien had always been a trusting person and assumed people were generally good, but her experience with these folks had her questioning that philosophy.

"How can you work with such awful people?"

"You know, Coop, I've always prided myself on my ability to work with just about anyone," Vivien said, "but even I can't envision the possibility of developing a positive relationship with Rebecca or Charl. Unfortunately, I'm stuck with them for now. Have to make the best of it."

Coop sounded solemn. "You know it will probably only get worse, don't you?"

"You think? Now that Rebecca's given birth to Duncan's only son she thinks her future here is secure no matter what she does. When I took on this role I was just focusing on doing a great job, but I now realize the more important thing to do is to play the game better."

"The whole situation sounds dangerous, Vivi."

"You're telling me. I need to figure out what to do, and fast."

*

Somehow when Coop warned Vivien that things could only get worse, he realized it also applied to his own situation. The stack of bills on his dining room table was piling up—he barely even bothered to check his mailbox. He was starting to rack up credit card debt with its insane interest rates—anathema to someone who'd always practiced a frugal approach to life. Things were getting out of control.

He felt even worse for his friend. It was rough going for her out there in Portland and he wished she'd just come home. As Coop wrapped up the call with Vivien he saw another call coming through. His heart jumped—it was a Washington, DC, area code. Could it be Brad? He answered uncertainly.

*

The call was from a friend of Mrs. Jankowski who was going through a sudden and nasty divorce. Allison Gould had contacted Coop to help her with his forensic accounting skills.

"I'll cover all your expenses, Coop, and pay your standard fee of 5 percent of anything you recover for me. If you can come to DC right away to meet with me, I'd be grateful."

"Of course, Mrs. Gould," Coop said, "I can be there tomorrow. In the meantime, please gather up any hard copies of financial records, and if you can put any electronic records on a flash drive I can get to work right after we meet. Okay?"

The following morning Coop arrived in DC and navigated his way to Allison Gould's home to meet for tea. It was a stately Colonial-style home in the heart of the city with massive white columns at the grand entrance. Mrs. Gould greeted him at the door—she was in her early sixties and slender with gray hair cut in a bob, and casually but elegantly dressed.

"Please excuse the mess," she said as she led him through the immaculate house, passing by the library and the living room with walls adorned with oil paintings. They made their way to the brightly lit solarium in the back, where they sat down. A tea service on a lacquered tray held a steaming pot of tea and gilt-edged cups and saucers of bone china. Tearfully, Mrs. Gould explained her situation, dabbing at her eyes with a lace handkerchief that seemed to appear out of nowhere.

"I was blindsided," said Mrs. Gould. "In fact, my husband and I were planning our retirement in the Caribbean. I was so busy researching islands and real estate. Instead of moving together to a tropical island, my husband has moved on to someone else."

Coop nodded sympathetically. "I'm sorry about your situation, Mrs. Gould. But I'm here to help. Can we go through my list of questions so I can start my investigation of your husband's finances?"

She dabbed at her eyes and answered Coop's questions dutifully. Before he left she handed him a box containing all the information he'd requested on their call. He was glad to help her and could see the look of gratitude and desperation in her pale blue eyes.

Coop's plan was to spend a few days in DC going through all the information Mrs. Gould had provided, doing some analysis, and having a more in-depth meeting with her before heading home to really dig in to the files. Conducting a thorough forensic accounting review would take a couple of months. Mrs. Gould had put Coop up at the Four Seasons Hotel and since he was on an expense account he decided to have a nice dinner (within reason) at the hotel restaurant.

Belly full, Coop took a stroll after dinner in the balmy summer evening. He meandered through Georgetown, looking into shop windows and winding his way through the streets. Down a side street he found a charming little Italian restaurant tucked away behind a garden entrance. It looked so inviting that Coop decided to have a drink at the bar.

He was sitting with his back to the entrance and was about to sip his glass of pinot grigio when a familiar voice made him nearly choke on his drink. There was no mistaking it; it was Brad. Coop turned ever so slightly to look. His ex had entered the restaurant with a blond man and the two walked toward a table in the back. The muscular blond man sat facing Coop's direction while Brad faced the back of the restaurant. The cute blond man had sparkling blue eyes and a smile full of whitened teeth, which he flashed at Brad while reaching over to hold hands with his date. Tearing his eyes away from the couple, Coop rubbed his forehead—so it wasn't that Brad wasn't ready for a relationship, Brad just wasn't ready for a relationship with him. Despite how Brad had treated him, Coop still felt an unimaginable ache in his heart. Why didn't anyone want to be with him? Miserable, he brushed away a tear, left his glass of wine unfinished, and made his way back to the hotel.

It was still early on the West Coast, so Coop dialed up Vivien. "Guess who I just saw?"

Vivien said, "Who?"

Coop snorted. "I'm in DC working for a new client and happened to go into a cute little Italian restaurant. And who should walk in but Brad and his new boyfriend? Can you believe he's already in another relationship?"

"Coop, why do you even care about Brad? He hurt you and was a terrible boyfriend." She let out a sigh. "Anyway, so what if he has a new boyfriend. It's not a competition."

"But it is, Vivi, it's totally a competition! Whoever's the one that doesn't end up alone is the winner. It absolutely is a competition." He couldn't believe he'd actually said that aloud. But Coop was beginning to fret that the dream of having a life partner was slipping away. It seemed like his troubles just continued to mount.

CHAPTER 11

December

ANDI

Today was the big day for Andi. After months of waiting and a couple of postponements, her meeting with Finbar Minch was finally happening that frigid day in early December.

While she rushed around that morning getting her kids ready for school, Andi mentally rehearsed what she was going to say in the meeting. She prepared and packed up lunch and snacks for her sons, bundled them up in warm clothes, and dropped the twins off at their preschool. The icy wind was howling down the city streets and Andi dashed outside again to grab a cab to the midtown offices of Minch Capital.

As Andi entered the building she fully grasped that this was her big chance to go after her white whale, her dream job at Minch Capital— the goal she'd been obsessed with for years. When the elevator doors parted Andi took a deep breath to slow down her racing heart and entered the office. An efficient receptionist took Andi's name and asked her to have a seat in the waiting area. Too nervous to relax, Andi paced in front of the floor-to-ceiling windows, taking in the magnificent windblown view of Central Park.

A young man came out and introduced himself as Finbar's executive assistant, and he led Andi back to the executive's office. He escorted her into the office and asked Andi to take a seat—there were a couple of wing chairs and a sofa around a chrome and marble coffee table. He informed her that Finbar was wrapping up another meeting and would be in shortly. As Andi sat and waited she wondered what kind of reception she'd get from the famous PE firm founder.

For a wealthy financier this office was quite spartan and impersonal—there was an enormous desk with a few manila folders on it with an Aeron chair, a bookshelf stuffed with finance books, a cool modern desk lamp, some artwork on the walls, and a comfortable sitting area. No family photos or anything that would give visitors any details about Finbar Minch. Courtney had mentioned Finbar's "public" office (in which Andi was seated) for meetings and another private corner office that was his real office, which few were allowed to enter.

"Hello, Andi, good to see you." Finbar strode into the office and offered his hand. He was a solidly built man, average height, with brown hair sprinkled with gray and eyes the color of money. Andi thought he looked pretty much the same as the last time she'd seen him with the addition of a few wrinkles around the eyes and a few more pounds in his midsection. "Please, take off your coat."

"Thanks for meeting with me, Finbar." Andi took off her coat and draped it over the arm of the sofa. "How's your daughter doing?"

Finbar laughed. "Which one? I've got five kids now, three girls and two boys."

"Wow, you've been busy. Congratulations. I've got four-year-old twin boys myself." Andi smiled.

"Is that so? Good for you," he said. Then she noticed Finbar glance at her chest and then look away quickly. She ignored it. "So, what do you make of the big announcement?" His bright green eyes sparkled with such mental intensity Andi thought if you could bottle up that energy it would power the entire city for a year.

Andi made it a practice to always check the financial news every morning so she'd be well informed, and she was thankful for that daily habit. Finbar must have been referring to the news that a longtime rival, Sapient Capital, had just purchased one of the oldest retail chains in America. "That was a curious acquisition to me—that retail chain has been struggling for years and I don't see how they can possibly turn things around. But I'm thinking the CEO's rationale for doing it was something else entirely." She looked directly into his eyes.

"How so?"

Again the financier's gaze moved from her eyes to her chest. *Is the same old thing happening? Courtney assured me that Finbar's behavior had changed for the better.* She kept her cool. "I think he did it as a real estate play. There must be at least seventy-five to eighty plum real estate locations for the stores in the fleet. If I were in his shoes I'd set up a separate corporation controlling the real estate and lease the properties back to the retail corporation. Perfectly legal and financially astute—that way even if all the stores tank he's still protected on the upside. Heck, Sapient Capital should make a tidy sum."

Finbar nodded his head and wagged a finger. "Very interesting idea, Andi." She imagined the financial wheels spinning in his mind. "So with eighty locations and the value of the leases over the next five years…let's see, he could see an ROI of 3X."

"More like 3.75X," Andi said, and noted Finbar's nod of approval of her accuracy and quickness with numbers.

"Nice." His eyes dropped down to her chest. Instead of losing her temper Andi asked, "Is everything okay? Is there something unusual about my clothes?"

He rubbed his chin. "Well, um, yes. I wasn't sure if I should say something to you, but you have some kind of goo hanging just there." Finbar pointed.

Indeed, when Andi was making SunButter and jelly sandwiches for the boys she'd somehow gotten a big glob of jelly on her cream-colored blouse. The glob was suspended on her blouse and shaped like the country of Italy. She looked down, horrified, and then let out a laugh in relief. "Oops, grape jelly. Do you have a tissue?"

Finbar chuckled and handed her a box of Kleenex. "So, what have you been up to since Wharton?" Apparently she'd passed his little financial quiz so now they could get to the meat of their conversation.

As she wiped away the grape jelly, Andi explained that she'd joined Goldman Sachs in the private banking division and had spent the last ten years there, until her department was acquired by Kaneshiro Bank. She said she'd recently left. Finbar gave a little shrug. "Too bad you didn't stick it out a little longer. It takes an average of twelve years to make partner at Goldman—you should have waited."

"You're right, it typically does take twelve years—I made partner in seven."

He whistled. "Impressive. I take it you got tired of private banking?"

Andi leaned back. "I'd sum it up by saying that working at Kaneshiro looks good from afar, but it was far from good." She gave a little smirk. "It was time to move on. I want to do something different, help build businesses."

"I have to admit, I was curious to get your request for a meeting. So, what exactly did you want to discuss with me, Andi?"

Andi kept her quivering nerves in check as she spoke. "I've met and advised many female entrepreneurs over the years and have seen how hard it is for them to get private equity capital because they're pitching mainly to men—men who don't always understand their business. I believe that having more women on your team can be an asset for you. I'd like for you to consider hiring me into your firm, Finbar. I brought a copy of my résumé that outlines my accomplishments and shows how I can add value to Minch Capital." She handed him the two-page résumé, which contained highlights of her dollars under management and all the major deals she'd closed.

He was silent as he studied it. After a long pause he took in a deep breath. Finbar looked her in the eye. "Andi, your background is terrific. There's no question you've been tremendously successful. All the people I know in private banking say you're a top performer and a gifted professional." Aha, so he had done some checking on her—was that why he'd postponed their meeting twice? "Now, I could bring you onto the Minch team, have you help identify companies that we should invest in and grow…"

The pace of Andi's heart quickened. Maybe getting a job at Minch Capital would be easier than she thought.

Finbar pulled at his chin. "…but when I really think about it, hiring you doesn't make sense. So, I'm not going to offer you a job with Minch Capital."

Andi sat back in disappointment, her shoulders collapsed in defeat like she'd just lost the 100-meter dash by one-hundredth of a second. Was Finbar still holding a grudge against her for that offense years ago? Guess all that was left for her to do was to thank him for his time and wrap up the meeting. She could sure use a latte—maybe there was a Starbucks nearby. Andi started to reach for her coat.

Finbar leaned forward and continued. "Frankly, hiring you won't maximize your value to me. Instead, here's what I'd like to do. I've been thinking about this for a while—I want to start a PE firm that invests primarily in women-led businesses. You're clearly a leader, Andi. I'd like for you, along with Courtney Greene, who's been a superstar at my firm, to start and lead that business. And I'll stake you."

Andi sat up straight. What? Finbar Minch, one of the most successful PE executives in the world, was telling her that he'd invest in a business that he also wanted her to lead? Her heart was pumping madly and she found herself with her mouth hanging open.

"I don't know what offers you're considering from other PE firms, so if you want to take some time to think about it—"

"No," Andi said. "I mean, no, I don't need to think about it. And yes, I'd love to do it. Thank you, Finbar, really."

"Great, then you and Courtney will be cofounders of the firm and help women entrepreneurs succeed. I'll start you off with a fund of three hundred million dollars to invest, and I want the two of you to raise another two hundred million over the next six to twelve months. You two can work out the details and come back to me with a business plan and investment thesis, and we'll get this thing off the ground. Sound good, Andi?"

She gave a broad smile and gripped his hand, shaking it firmly. "That sounds perfect."

*

A week later Andi and Courtney had their plans laid out for their new PE firm—that was the birth of BC Capital, which stood for "Bold Chicks" Capital. She and Luca were throwing a small holiday party that weekend and Andi couldn't wait to share the news of her women-focused PE firm with her Ceiling Smasher friends. She'd finally harpooned her white whale and she was most definitely in a celebratory mood.

*

GRACE

Twinkle, Grace's baby business, was focused on providing stylish, cute, and functional baby apparel. She had been kicking around the idea for a while to create baby apparel made partially with technical fabrics that were breathable, moisture wicking, and coated to resist stains. Grace was also creating a direct-to-consumer business model (instead of opening retail stores) to minimize her overhead costs and speed getting her brand into the market. She and designer Laura brainstormed and created the product line, researched fabrics, found factories to make samples, and started getting their first season into production for a late spring/early summer launch.

By early December, Grace was getting production samples of the Twinkle clothing line that were to be used for marketing imagery and website assets. She couldn't have been more thrilled. On the second Friday of the month, after Grace had spent most of the day going over design and production details with Laura, she decided to take a break and head to a yoga class. Grace was still experiencing a calming glow from the yoga class when her cell phone rang.

"Hi, darlin', are you on your way over to my place?"

Darn it, she'd nearly forgotten. Win had invited Grace over to meet his publicist.

"Hi Win, yes I'm heading there right now." She wrapped herself up in her long, puffy down coat and dashed into the street to hail a cab to Win's apartment in TriBeCa.

*

Rushing into Win's apartment, Grace greeted him and apologized for being late. Win just smiled and gave her a big hug and kiss, not seeming to notice that she was sticky with sweat from her yoga class. He introduced her to his publicist, a petite woman named Patricia, who was dressed elegantly in designer duds. She was so thin she was almost transparent. "It's a pleasure to meet you, Grace. If you're dating our boy Win you must be something sensational." Patricia gave her a moment to get settled.

Grace sipped a bottle of water that Win handed her. "Good to meet you, too, Patricia." She looked quizzically at her boyfriend, still unsure about why they were meeting.

Win sat on the arm of the sofa next to Grace. "Listen, darlin', we've been dating for well over a year. Sooner or later some sneaky paparazzo is going to snap a picture of us together and I just wanted to get out in front of that."

Nodding, Patricia said, "The moment your picture with Win comes out there's sure to be curiosity about you, so we want to be prepared and control how you'll be described in the press. People will want to know who you are, how you two met, how long you've been dating, and so on." She waved a well-manicured hand.

Grace shrugged. "Okay, I understand."

"Are you an actress or a model, Grace?" Patricia's pen was poised over her notebook and she had a hopeful look.

"Me? No. Far from it." She chuckled. "Actually I did do some modeling back in college to earn money for tuition—catalog work. But that was many years and many pounds ago." Grace laughed.

She jotted down some notes. "Okay, we'll describe you as a former model. Movie stars like Win Wyatt typically date actors or models. That's just the way it is."

Win grimaced and walked to the kitchen to get a bottle of water. "Unfortunately that's true. Not many actors date normal people. By 'normal' I mean someone outside of the industry."

Grace scoffed and directed her comment to Patricia. "Don't you think people would be more interested to see a celebrity dating a regular person—an interesting woman with a professional career?" Then she paused. Perhaps this could work in her favor. "To say I'm a model isn't accurate. I'm a branding expert, author, and entrepreneur, so I'd like to be described as such."

Patricia gave a look of chagrin to Win, which he duly ignored.

"Let's just describe Grace the way she wants," Win said with a tone of finality. "She's launching a baby clothing business called Twinkle this spring, so let's work that tidbit into her description—we can say she's the founder and CEO of Twinkle." He winked at Grace. "Heck might as well leverage the publicity for something useful, right?"

Patricia let out a small sigh and jotted down some notes. "Okay, and how did you two meet?"

Win smiled. "Practicing golf at Chelsea Piers."

The publicist had a slightly horrified look on her face. "Win, darling, I'd much rather say that you met at a charity ball or on vacation in St. Barts—something a little more...glamorous?" Somehow the facts weren't matching up to the exciting narrative his publicist was hoping to create. "How else did you connect? Where was your second meeting?"

"Shopping for towels at Bed Bath & Beyond," Grace stated flatly, shooting a mischievous look at her boyfriend.

Her eyes widened but Patricia said nothing and wrote more notes in her notebook.

Win walked over and placed his hand on her thin shoulder. "It's okay, Patricia, just tell the truth. I think it was a charming way to meet someone." He smiled at Grace, who blushed. "Anyway, this is an exercise to be prepared, just in case."

*

That night Grace and Win were going to dinner at a casual hole-in-the-wall place in the West Village, but on the way they stopped at a nearby holiday party thrown by a friend of his. When they entered the apartment, a third-floor walkup, an attractive young woman rushed up to Win and embraced him. Grace stepped back to give them room and looked at her boyfriend with a raised eyebrow.

Win stepped back and tickled the young woman, who giggled. "Oh, you must be Grace. So excited to meet you! I'm Annika. Win is like my big brother, I just adore him." She gave Grace a welcoming hug.

Grace had to admit the young woman did look familiar. As it turned out Annika had been ten years old when she was cast in a movie with Win called *Countdown* where she played the daughter of a nuclear scientist who gets kidnapped by bad guys. That was the first movie for them both, and they'd bonded and kept up their friendship over the past decade.

"Come on, both of you, I want you to meet my boyfriend." Annika tugged them across the room to introduce them and got them each a drink.

As Win chatted with the boyfriend, Grace sipped her drink and sauntered around the living room. The apartment was modest—not huge in size, but nicely done in muted paint tones with simple, colorful accents. She stopped at a bookshelf that held many framed photos. One of them caught her eye—it was a photo of Annika in a risqué ad for Voss & Co. Grace felt someone move up behind her. Annika.

"I was just looking at this photo—the one of you in Voss Denim."

A pensive look came over the beautiful young woman's face. "Yes, I keep that as a reminder—a reminder to myself to never let anyone take advantage of me again." She paused.

As Annika's story poured out, Grace's horror grew. Annika had been cast in a Voss & Co. ad when she was barely fourteen years old. At the shoot in LA, Charley Voss himself oversaw the details of the ad campaign. On a break when the crew had cleared out, it was just Annika and Voss in the room. He sat beside her and asked if he could touch her luxurious long hair. Annika was baffled by the weird request but since he was the boss she said okay. Voss stroked her hair and pulled her close to him, forcibly kissing her and trying to stick his tongue down her throat. He was groping her when she freed herself and pushed him away, stomping on his boot. Luckily at that moment the photographer returned and Voss quickly left the room. Annika was terrified and didn't know what to do, so she locked herself in the bathroom and called Win, crying. Win was shooting a movie nearby about a futuristic soldier—half man, half machine—and he dropped everything and raced over to the Voss & Co. shoot still in his costume. He tore through the building looking for Annika and checked to make sure she was okay. Then he tracked down Charley Voss, who was relaxing in his office. Win smashed through the door, picked up Voss, and slammed him against a wall. He snarled, "If you ever do anything like that to Annika or another young girl, I will rip out your throat." Then Win went back down to the photo shoot and stood sentry for the rest of the shoot until Annika's mother arrived.

"So you see, I've always felt like Win was my big brother, my protector. I know he'd never let anything bad happen to me." Annika pushed a strand of hair behind her ear. "You've got yourself a keeper there, Grace. He's a really good guy."

"That I know." Grace smiled and put her hand on Annika's shoulder. "Listen, my friend is working on something that may interest you."

*

Grace had to admit that by all standards Andi's Christmas party was looking like a tremendous success. Their closest friends were gathered and Andi was making all the preparations while Luca and the boys entertained their guests. For someone whose only mastery in the kitchen had been pushing the buttons on the microwave, it appeared that Andi had made giant strides.

Grace was in her element explaining her new business to her friends. "Something babies can't do is regulate their temperature. That's why when they're in their cotton onesies and you pick them up they're always hot and sweaty on their backsides."

Luca remarked, "I remember that with the boys when they were infants."

"Right. So my Twinkle baby clothing is breathable and moisture wicking so babies stay dry and comfortable with some technical fabrics in key temperature zones. Vivien helped me source the material—it actually feels like cotton." She gave a nod of thanks to her friend. "Also I'm using a special stain-resistant coating, so you can just crumple up the clothing and the stain turns into a powder, which you can just shake out or brush off—it's really cool."

Andi brought in another platter of enticing appetizers and set it down. "That sounds amazing, Grace. I remember when the boys were starting to eat solid food—carrot puree—and it stained everything orange. It was impossible to get it off their clothes, remember that, Luca? Kind of weird that no baby clothing company even offers orange bibs. That seems like a no-brainer."

"I know, that's an easy fix." Grace laughed. "We'll have some orange bibs in the line in addition to patterned bibs that mask any stains. We're doing a direct-to-consumer model and will offer a subscription service, so moms can register their babies on our Twinkle site and every three months they'll receive a regular bundle of new clothes appropriate for their baby's age and stage of development. For example, when their baby starts crawling we have pants and leggings with reinforced knees. We're shooting a couple of videos in January that will explain how the product works and also the subscription service, which I think would make a great gift."

"The gifting idea is terrific. You should market that to the AARP crowd—lots of grandparents looking for gifts for their grandkids," Vivien suggested with enthusiasm.

Grace knew how difficult it must be for her friend to talk about anything baby related, having lost her newborn daughter, Lily. That was five months ago, but the pain was still evident just under the surface. She reached over and squeezed Vivien's hand in support.

Vivien's fiancé, Clay, rubbed her shoulders.

"I'm working on getting all the pieces in place so by the time the product is produced we can get the whole business launched—probably in May or June." Grace rubbed her hands with glee.

Grace mingled and chatted with everyone and was surprised when Sofia's boyfriend, Jasper, pulled her aside. "You're clearly a creative genius, Grace, and I'm working on an idea that could use your ingenuity."

"Really?" Grace was intrigued.

Jasper looked around and saw Sofia approaching. She'd apparently taken a call in one of the bedrooms and didn't look pleased. "Can I get your phone number and we can talk about it sometime in the future? Please don't mention it to Sofia, okay?"

She nodded in agreement. Then Grace suddenly remembered the Voss tidbit she was going to share with Sofia. "Actually, I need to discuss something with Sofia that's work related—would you mind giving us a minute?"

Grace pulled Sofia aside. "Got something to share with you, Sofi. Something that might be useful to your work."

"What is it, Grace?"

"Win and I were at a party recently and I met a young actress who told me a pretty wild story about Charley Voss. Aren't you investigating him?"

"Yes, go on." As Grace was sharing the story she noticed Jasper signaling Sofia to come join him. Sofia waved him off a little rudely. Grace wrapped up her story and then Sofia walked away to text her colleague Kate.

With everyone gathered in the living room, Sofia finally joined them and sat on the sofa next to Jasper, who took Sofia's hand and kissed it, saying something softly to her.

An irritated scowl on her face, Sofia said, "What I want is more champagne. Would you mind getting me a glass, please?"

Jasper did as requested but Grace could see the hurt look on his face as he walked over to the bar. Sofia had been happier with Jasper than Grace had ever seen her friend—she hoped Sofia wouldn't throw away this wonderful relationship.

*

SOFIA

Sofia had to admit she was exhausted. In addition to working on two different CNBC programs, she and Kate Frost were investigating Charley Voss. The weekend, which should have been a chance to chill, was a whirlwind of social activities. After her Friday Smashers get together, Jasper had taken Sofia out for sushi and a movie and they'd had a wonderful time together. She felt like they were getting along great and that he really got her.

373

On Saturday night Sofia and Jasper attended a Christmas party at Andi's home. Apparently during her work hiatus Andi had taken several cooking classes, and for the party she'd magically whipped up delicious appetizers and a hearty buffet dinner. Luca and the boys kept their guests occupied with games like Jenga and Trouble. It was heartwarming to see Andi's family interacting in a goofy, natural way, everyone healthy and happy.

Her Smasher friends were gathered together and Sofia felt giddy to be surrounded by them. Grace was there without Win, who was visiting family in Michigan. Vivien was home for the holidays and attending the party with Clay. And Coop rounded out the group with his lively personality. Everyone was joking around, playing with the boys, and drinking and eating with abandon.

Sofia was able to grab a few minutes alone with Vivien. "How are you, Vivi? I know you're doing great things at Smart Sports, but my god, what you've been through." The struggles that Vivien had faced since moving to Portland, Oregon, had been monumental.

Vivien leaned against the wall and looked upward. "At one point recently I really felt like I'd reached my limit, you know? I called my dad and told him I was ready to pack it in and come home."

That comment made Sofia's eyes grow wide—she'd never known Vivien to be anything but determined and successful. Once her friend set her mind to do something, you could count on her to achieve it and do it in style—that was pure Vivien. "What did he say?"

"He said that tragedy and hardship are a test of courage." Doing her best imitation of her father, Vivien continued, "'If you meet that test bravely, you'll leave it bigger than it found you and that conquering spirit will always be within you. But giving up—what would that accomplish? You will have thrown away your dream and all your hard work. You will have failed yourself, and that's something I know you'd never want to live with.'" Vivien's expression turned fierce. "My dad said 'You might run away from a place or an experience, but you can never run away from yourself?' Man, he just knows me too well."

Sofia laughed lightly. "Yep, that sounds like classic Dr. Lee wisdom telling you not to give up. I bet he also told you, 'Be great and be good.' That's my favorite saying of his."

Antonio came over and pulled Vivien away to play with him and his brother, Francesco.

Jasper came from behind and put his arms around Sofia's waist. "This is great, isn't it, Sofia? Being surrounded by family, friends, and little ones during the holidays. I could definitely see us doing this someday." He nuzzled her neck. His comment was jarring given her somber mood, and she pulled away from him.

Just then Sofia's phone buzzed. It was a text from Kate Frost, asking her to call her urgently. She excused herself to one of the bedrooms and phoned her colleague.

"Sorry to bother you on a Saturday night, Sofia, but we have a situation." There was tension in Kate's voice.

"What kind of situation?"

Kate let out a sigh. "We've been FOC'd."

"Huh? What does that mean?"

"Looks like two of our CEO guests for this week's *Titans Tell All* program have abruptly pulled out. They're FOCs, Friends of Charley's. Even though we've kept our Voss investigation under wraps, Voss has heard rumblings that we're asking questions about him and he doesn't like it. He's using his influence to try and quash our investigation."

Sofia grunted. "And Voss's friends are taking his side and canceling their appearances on our show. Lovely." They had interviewed a few of Voss's victims so far, but no one was willing to go on the record. Everyone seemed fearful of the career repercussions of challenging such a powerful and well-connected man. Without someone willing to share their story publicly, they had zilch.

"Yeah. You should also check your voice mail at work. I got a weird anonymous message warning me to stop trying to dig up dirt on a particular businessman. And I also got an email from one of Voss's attorneys basically telling us to cease and desist." Kate cleared her throat. "That's not all. Randolph has asked to see the both of us first thing on Monday morning—I think we're going to get an earful from him."

"Yikes, not good. If we could only come up with something concrete before then. Well, thanks for the call, Kate, let's chat tomorrow night to prep for the discussion with the big boss." Before heading back into the living room to join the others, Sofia checked her email on her phone. She, too, had gotten a meeting request (more like a court summons) from Randolph for Monday morning and a stern message from a Voss attorney. Also, the organizers of a conference had sent her an email to regretfully inform her that her speaking engagement in February had been canceled—Voss & Co. was one of the conference sponsors. Symmetrical knots formed in her shoulders, and Sofia's festive mood vanished.

When she reentered the living room, Grace pulled her aside. "I wanted to share something with you, Sofi. Something that might be useful to your work."

Sofia focused her full attention on her friend. "What is it, Grace?"

"Win and I were at a party recently and I met a young actress who told me a pretty wild story about Charley Voss. Aren't you investigating him?"

"Yes, go on." As Grace was sharing the story, a smiling Jasper signaled Sofia to come join him. She waved him off. What she was hearing was meaningful. She and Grace spoke a while longer and then Sofia took another minute to text Kate an update. Finally, she rejoined the rest of her friends and sat on the sofa next to Jasper.

He took her hand and kissed it. Then he gestured toward Andi and her family. "Sofia, don't you want all this?"

Sofia scowled. In the last twenty minutes she'd learned of major problems with her show, her boss, and her investigation, and a canceled speaking engagement on top of it all. A vortex of stress and frustration was building inside her chest like a tornado—and now Jasper was bringing up marriage and kids? She said coolly, "What I want is more champagne. Would you mind getting me a glass, please?" Admittedly, her tone was harsher than she'd intended, but her head was pounding.

Jasper did as requested.

*

Soon enough it was time to leave. On the walk back home, Jasper, still in a sentimental mood, threw out hints about marriage like a fly-fisherman casting out his line. Sofia snapped, "Jasper, please. Would you give it a rest? I can't deal with this right now."

He stopped walking and drew back with a darkened, hurt expression.

They walked home in silence, and instead of coming up, Jasper said good night in the lobby of Sofia's building. For an instant she felt guilty about the way she'd treated Jasper that night, but she would just call him the next day and figure out a way to make it up to him. Sofia barely had enough energy to brush her teeth and wash her face, then crash into bed. She was asleep before her head hit her silk pillowcase.

When she awoke the next morning, Sofia reached for her cell phone and switched it on. She'd gotten a text from Jasper—what a sweetheart, he was probably saying good morning and checking in on her. She read his message. *Trouble with our tech team in India. Need to head out there today to work with our engineers for a week or so. We'll catch up when I'm back.* It was the most businesslike message she'd ever received from him—Sofia's heart went cold.

The following week Sofia didn't hear a peep from Jasper—no texts, no voice mails. The couple of texts she sent went unanswered. Sofia wondered if she'd screwed things up irreparably.

*

"Boys, sit up straight and eat over your plates." Andi admonished Francesco and Antonio while Luca cut up and divided the remainder of the pancakes and French toast for the twins. Sofia had joined Andi and her family for their ritual of Sunday brunch at Sarabeth's Kitchen, not far from their Upper West Side apartment. The five of them were seated in the back of the restaurant at the family's favorite table.

Sofia made a goofy face at the twins, making them giggle. "The pancakes here are delish, aren't they?" she said, catching Andi's glance, to encourage the boys to eat.

The boys nodded vigorously and stuffed their faces with food. "More bacon, please, Mama," Francesco said in a sweet voice.

Sofia had to admit, Andi's sons were just as delectable as the yummy food, with their short haircuts, adorable Sunday outfits, big shiny eyes, and enthusiastic smiles. Maybe Jasper was onto something here. She mentally replayed their last abbreviated conversation about marriage as she casually scanned the restaurant. Andi was talking about her plans for the PE firm she was starting with fellow Smasher Courtney Greene when something caught Sofia's eye.

A guy way in the front at a corner table looked a lot like Jasper. Hang on; she realized, it was Jasper. And he was having lunch with an attractive woman. Okay, not to worry, could be work related. But then Sofia saw something peculiar—Jasper took the woman's hand and peered at it, and then back up at the woman, deeply engrossed in their conversation. Why was he holding her hand and who was this woman? Sofia tried keeping the conversation going with Andi but she suddenly felt her back stiffen up. She'd impatiently brushed off Jasper's attempt to discuss marriage, so was he exploring other options now? She'd always assumed they were dating exclusively but in truth they'd never discussed not seeing other people. Jasper and the woman were deeply engaged in conversation, and he was writing something down and the woman was nodding and smiling. What was going on?

"You okay, Sof? You have kind of a weird expression on your face," Andi asked.

Sofia snapped back to attention. "I'm fine, just fine. Guess I'm not used to having heavy brunches these days." Her insides were churning, and when she stole another glance up at Jasper she saw that he was already gone, and so was the woman.

*

Troubled by what she'd seen at lunch, Sofia phoned up Grace to get her perspective. She blurted, "I saw Jasper having lunch with another woman today and he was holding her hand. Is he cheating on me?"

"Oh, Sofia, don't be silly. When we were at Andi's party it was plain to see that you guys are crazy about each other. He was probably having lunch with an old friend. Anyway, Jasper doesn't strike me as the kind of guy who would cheat on his girl."

"It's just that he tried bringing up the topic of marriage after we left Andi's party and—well, I basically shut him down. Then a week later I see him having a meal with an attractive woman while I thought he was out of town." Her voice sounded as tense as her nerves.

"You love him, right, Sofia? Then give Jasper the benefit of the doubt. Why don't you just ask him about the lunch thing and see how he responds. You'll be able to tell if something weird is going on. Just trust your gut."

*

Not one to let something sit for too long Sofia decided to ring up Jasper. "Welcome home, I missed you, sweet pea."

He sounded distracted but said, "Thanks, Sofia, that's nice to hear."

She heard a loud zipper sound in the background. Was he packing or unpacking? Attempting to sound casual, Sofia said, "I didn't know you were back already. I was having brunch today with Andi and her family and thought I saw you out of the corner of my eye. Were you at Sarabeth's?"

Jasper grunted. "Huh? Oh, yeah, I had a meeting."

"Oh. Someone from work?" Her tone was hopeful.

"Let's just say it's someone I may do some business with," Jasper responded cryptically. "Anyway, I'm rushing to the airport now, Sofia. Not sure when I'll be back."

Sofia was crestfallen. She'd been hoping to spend some time with him to try to make amends and win him back. "Where are you going, Jasper?"

His voice dropped to nearly a whisper. "I just got a call that my mom has had a massive stroke. I'm flying out to California to be with her and help out. Listen, my car is waiting to take me to the airport so I need to get going. My sister and I are having a conference call with my mom's doctor on my way to the airport. I'll be in touch as soon as I can, Sofia."

There was no time for further conversation. Sofia expressed her concern about Jasper's mother. She was saying "I love you" but Jasper was racing out the door and hung up the phone prematurely. Had she just lost the man that she now realized she couldn't be without?

*

COOP

Normally the lead-up to the holidays was the time of year Coop anticipated most—he loved spending Christmas with his large family and giving special presents to each of his many nieces and nephews. But he was strapped for cash and unsure if he should even show up for his family's big celebration.

He'd spent most of the summer working hard on Allison Gould's case and wrapped up his findings by mid-September. Armed with the new financial information, Mrs. Gould and her divorce attorney went into court feeling confident. Coop couldn't realistically expect any payment until after her divorce settlement came through, so for him it was a waiting game. Meanwhile his debts were still piling up. But for tonight he was going to relax at Andi's holiday party, have a few cocktails, and try to enjoy the festivities.

"What do you mean you may not make it home for Christmas?" Vivien threw her hands up in the air. "You've got to spend the holiday with your family, Coop."

*

Vivien and her dad had enjoyed several Christmases with the Coopers, and for her it was one of the social highlights of the year. The Cooper family was warm, funny, and welcoming. Every year a different Cooper sibling hosted Christmas Eve dinner and afterward Santa (usually Coop in a costume) showed up with a bulging sack of gifts. There was a frenzy of squeals and excited chatter as giftwrap was ripped open by every member of the family, although the kids had to reserve four gifts each to open on Christmas morning. Vivien had told Coop many times how much she loved hanging out with his family, especially during the holidays.

Coop gobbled down some bacon-wrapped dates. "The problem is, I don't have money to buy gifts for everyone and I can't show up empty handed."

Vivien imagined it must have killed Coop to admit that—he was the oldest of nine kids and always put pressure on himself to be the most successful and the most generous to his nieces and nephews. She spoke softly. "I'm happy to give you the money you need, Coop."

He shook his head vigorously. "God no, Vivi, I can't take a handout. But thanks for the offer."

She tried to think of what could help his situation. "Maybe you can suggest to your mom that everyone does a Secret Santa gift for each of the adults and a limit of two small gifts per child? I remember her saying that your family spends way too much money on Christmas gifts, anyway."

Coop cocked his head. "That's not a bad idea. I'll give her a call tomorrow."

Vivien's fiancé, Clay, came over to join them on the sofa. "How goes it, Coop?" Clay was impossibly handsome but sometimes could be a bit cold. She knew Coop didn't care for him all that much and Clay wasn't completely comfortable with her gay friend. "How are you going to parlay your newfound fame as a whistleblower?" The SEC investigation had concluded with the collapse of the telecom client and Coop's accounting firm, and multiple parties had been sent to jail. Now there was no way another accounting firm would hire Coop—what was her friend going to do next? From the sound of things he needed to get on a more solid financial footing and soon.

Coop kind of ignored the question. "I've been doing some occasional accounting work for private clients. Mainly divorcées who are being cheated out of a fair financial settlement. Actually, I've been enjoying the work. I'm kind of like an accounting Columbo, if you will. It's quite fascinating, the schemes some people concoct to hide assets—you wouldn't believe some of the financial shenanigans I've seen so far!" Coop chuckled. "At any rate, I do feel like I am making a positive difference in people's lives."

"I can imagine," said Clay, trying to stifle a yawn. "I'm going to grab some more grub." He got up and went over to the buffet table.

Accounting had never been Vivien's favorite subject at Wharton, and she gave Coop a look.

As if he were reading her mind he said, "Listen, I know you think accounting is boring, Vivi, but I love it. Especially forensic accounting—it's such a challenge and so fascinating…to me."

"Then why not start your own firm, Coop?"

"What, and go head-to-head with the mammoth accounting firms?

I don't think I could do that. They offer so many services it would be hard to compete against them."

"You don't have to. Just keep doing what you're already doing—helping divorcées. You can specialize. Think about your mom's situation and how you came through for her. There must be a lot of women in that situation and you could be a tremendous help to them."

"That's true," Coop said slowly. You could almost hear the gears in his brain clicking.

Vivien poked her friend in the ribs. "You could turn that into a business, Coop. You've built up a reputation as a do-gooder. Use that as leverage." She looked at him and tilted her chin up. "With a US divorce rate of around 50 percent, I'd think there'd be a big potential client base."

"Know what? That's a terrific idea, Vivi. That way I can still use my accounting skills. But how would I get it off the ground and market it?"

"Grace, can you come here a sec?" Vivien called across the room to Grace, who was in a corner wrapping up a conversation with Sofia. She turned to Coop. "Your friend is a renowned branding expert—ask her for some help. And she's also starting up a business, so I'm sure she can share some tips with you."

A look of confidence came across Coop's face and she could see his resolve starting to gel. Vivien was happy to see her friend finally take control of his career.

"Cool. I think it would be great to do something that I care about and has a positive impact."

"I know it's been rough lately, Coop, but better days are ahead for you. I just know it." Vivien leaned over and gave him a hug.

By the time Grace came over to join them they were ready to brainstorm on ideas for Coop's business. Vivien breathed a sigh of relief—things were starting to look up for Coop.

Back at home in New Jersey for Christmas, Coop was reveling in the family merriment around the large dining room table. Alma Jankowski was dining with them, and she was effusive about how much help and expertise he'd provided to her. Coop swelled with pride and a bit of embarrassment at the praise Mrs. Jankowski showered upon him in front of his siblings and his parents.

"Gary," she said, turning to Coop, "I know of a few dozen other women in the same situation I was in, women looking for the kind of help you offer." Since her longtime boss had recently retired, Mrs. Jankowski was no longer an executive assistant and had more free time on her hands. The fact that she could refer clients to Coop was a godsend.

"Well, Mrs. Jankowski, it just so happens that I've decided to start my own forensic accounting business to help divorcées get financial fairness in their settlements. So I'm looking for new clients and your referrals are appreciated." A thunderbolt struck Coop. "Wait a minute, I have a great idea. Why don't you work as my business manager? You can help with the administration of the business and new client acquisition."

Alma Jankowski practically jumped up from her seat. "Gary, I'd be pleased and proud to work with you." They chatted about some preliminary details as they dug into their meal. Coop mentioned that he'd be able to pay her after the business was started up and running with a regular income stream. "Don't you worry about that, dear. I'd just like to do something useful with my time and keep my brain engaged." She patted his cheek.

With Mrs. Jankowski helping him and Grace guiding him on his marketing, Coop was putting all the components in place to start his own business. It was like a riding a roller coaster—thrilling and terrifying at the same time. He sat back and thought of the words of George Bernard Shaw, *The people who get on in this world are the people who get up and look for the circumstances they want, and, if they can't find them, make them.* It felt good to have his future in his own hands for the first time.

*

Because of Coop's dire financial situation, he'd had to put his gym membership on hold. So on a chilly December morning a couple of days after Christmas, he decided to go for a run to clear his head and plan for his business launch. Wearing extra layers and a thin wool hat, Coop worked up a good pace on the running path along the West Side Highway. The cold air that invaded his lungs actually felt refreshing after a while, and by the time he'd made it back down the path near Chelsea he was feeling invigorated.

Coop was doing his post-run stretching when he noticed a cute runner sitting on a bench tying his sneakers. The guy had a forlorn look on his face like a stray, lost puppy. Coop said a simple hello and somehow that opened the door. The cute runner said he'd just moved from Philadelphia and this was his first time running on the path, so Coop asked him some questions and made a couple of recommendations on the best running route. When Coop happened to mention that he went to graduate school in Philly, their convivial chat continued, with Coop doing extra stretches and the cute runner, named Dean, tying and untying his shoes to extend their chat. It was getting colder by the minute and Coop finally, reluctantly, started to say goodbye.

"Coop, would you like to get together for dinner tonight? The city seems pretty quiet and I'd love to have some company." Dean smiled hopefully.

Here was a nice, normal, good-looking gay man asking Coop out—it was a miracle. But Coop's thoughts immediately snapped back to his financial picture—he simply could not afford to eat out these days.

"That sounds great, Dean, but I'm not sure I can do dinner tonight," Coop said noncommittally.

Dean looked disappointed and he stood up. "Okay, let's trade numbers anyway. If you free up for dinner just let me know." He asked for Coop's number and texted him his. With a flirtatious grin he said, "Hope to see you soon!" Then he took off running.

*

Coop jogged back home and wrestled internally with turning Dean down for dinner. He seemed like such a nice, friendly guy. But he had to be cautious about his spending—his credit card debt was already out of control. Resignedly Coop checked his mailbox and grabbed the stack of envelopes—probably bills and collection notices that he didn't want to open in the lobby and risk the prying eyes of neighbors.

Inside his apartment, Coop threw the stack of mail on the counter and one item caught his eye—a registered envelope. This could be either be very good or very bad. Holding his breath, he tore it open and saw it was a check from his client Allison Gould—a check for 5 percent of the three million dollars he'd recovered for her, a check for one hundred fifty grand! Coop felt like he'd just won the lottery and let out a whoop of victory, arms raised over his head.

He grabbed his phone and typed out a text. *Dean, it's Coop. Looks like I can do dinner after all. Give me a call later.*

*

Since Vivien had to head back to Portland on the second of January, she took advantage of her remaining time in the city and got together with Coop one last time. Late afternoon on New Year's Day they sat on the sofa in Coop's living room gabbing comfortably like old times and sipping wine.

"So, I met someone." Coop threw out a hook, his blue eyes twinkling.

"What? That's great!" Vivien swatted him on the arm, then straightened up and set her wineglass down on the coffee table. "Tell me everything—how'd you meet, what's he like?"

Coop proceeded to share every detail about how he'd met Dean, who was an architect. He'd just moved to NYC from Philly. They'd gone out for dinner and Coop had thoroughly enjoyed it. "We're going out for a second date this weekend, Vivi. If all goes well we might go running together, too."

"I'm excited for you, Coop." Her heart lifted at the prospect of Coop's finally finding a life partner. "I just want you to be happy with someone who is as wonderful as you are."

"Oh, well," Coop scoffed, "that might be difficult. I am pretty wonderful."

They giggled and beamed at each other.

Vivien checked her watch. "Oh, I have to meet Clay for dinner soon. I wish I could hang out with you some more. Keep me posted on Dean, he sounds promising."

As he sat back on the sofa Coop's eyes drifted upward and he sighed. "I still fantasize about finding a partner and eventually opening up a quaint bed-and-breakfast in Vermont." He blushed and gave a little laugh. "Who knows where this will lead, Vivi, but it sure is nice to dream."

PART FOUR

CHAPTER 12

May

COOP

It truly was amazing to Coop how quickly money could disappear. Back in December he'd received a check for one hundred fifty thousand dollars from Mrs. Gould—what he thought was a small fortune at that time. He'd used those funds to pay off his mountain of credit card debt, his outstanding mortgage payments, and all his outstanding bills. Coop had also spent a good chunk of the money on starting his forensic accounting business.

With Grace's help Coop had gotten the key components of his brand and marketing sorted out. Plus she'd advised him on all the administrative tasks of starting a business, and Coop hired a website designer and spent money on a graphic designer to come up with a logo for his business. This was the birth of Coop's forensic accounting firm targeted toward divorcées—it was called Figures. The tagline was *Figures Forensic Accounting Services: Let us help you uncover the difference between what you're getting and what you deserve.*

By May, Coop's business had officially opened its doors—the only thing he needed now was more clients. He'd been so consumed with getting the business set up, he hadn't focused as much on client acquisition. Keenly aware that he had limited income and his checking account was dwindling down to its last two thousand dollars, Coop's nerves were raw. Perhaps he didn't have the temperament to run his own business? The thought of potentially racking up more credit card debt made Coop break out in hives.

*

As Coop headed home from a relaxing run with his boyfriend Dean, the gorgeous spring day lifted his spirits. Dean was preparing dinner for them that night and had hurried off to the farmers' market and grocery store. Coop glanced at his phone. While they were running he'd gotten another call from Patrick Ellis. The SEC investigation and trial requiring Coop to serve as a whistleblower witness had taken a lot out of him, as evidenced by a few more gray hairs in his bathroom mirror reflection. Patrick had already called twice earlier in the past week and he'd neglected to return the calls. Coop felt a pang of guilt and reluctantly dialed Patrick's number.

"How are you, Coop?" Patrick's voice sounded bright.

"I'm okay, Patrick. How's it going?" Coop was dreading another request to provide information or appear in court.

"All good. Listen, Coop, I have to meet with you. Official business. Can we get together for drinks on Thursday when I'm in town?"

Coop hesitated in silence.

"It's really important that I see you, Coop." Patrick sounded resolute.

With a sigh Coop agreed and they made plans for when and where to meet.

*

A few days later Coop found himself seated in the Monkey Bar in midtown waiting to meet Patrick for a cocktail—it was the same place they'd met when they started the conversation about the accounting scandal. Coop was casually dressed in jeans and an oxford shirt. A lively crowd of men in suits and some businesswomen stood around engaged in energetic conversation over a couple of after-work drinks.

392

Coop sat sipping a chilled vodka martini with a whimsical plastic monkey hanging off the rim of the glass—the monkey's impish smile seemed to be taunting him.

Patrick rushed into the bar, greeted Coop, and ordered a martini. He waited to start speaking to Coop until the efficient bartender poured his drink and he took the first sip. Patrick held the liquid in his mouth for a moment and swallowed it down with a huge smile, like a man lost in the Sahara desert for days finally taking his first sip of water.

Coop wondered why Patrick seemed in such a happy mood.

Patrick raised his glass. "Bad people were doing illegal things and they were found out and held accountable—no better outcome than that, eh? Here's to you, Coop." They clinked glasses.

"Thanks, Patrick. I'm glad the guilty people were brought to justice."

Patrick leaned closer. "We just wrapped up all the financial details of the case last month. Looks like we'll be able to recover a tidy sum for the investors who were the victims of fraud. Before I forget, this is for you, Coop." He took a legal-size envelope from his inside jacket pocket, placed it on the gleaming wooden bar, and slid it toward Coop.

"What is this?"

"You'll see. Just open it." Patrick's eyes lit up.

Coop picked up the envelope and slid his thumb under the flap, working the envelope open. Inside was a government-issued check... for five million dollars. And Coop's name was on it. He stammered, "Wh-what is this? Is this some kind of joke, Patrick?"

Patrick gave him a playful punch in the arm. "Coop, it's your whistleblower award—standard practice in these cases. The award is typically 10 percent of the monetary sanctions collected in the investigatory process, and since we recovered fifty million dollars to return to shareholders, you get this check for five million dollars." Coop sat there with his mouth open and his eyes wide. "Not too shabby, eh? I've been trying to get ahold of you so I could give this to you. I'd think that being without a job since—"

"Oh my god, oh my god," Coop murmured breathlessly. "You mean I get to keep this? I had no idea about a whistleblower award."

"That first day we met at the SEC offices I know we overwhelmed you with a lot of paperwork, my friend, but on one of the forms there was a box you checked that said if you qualified for a whistleblower award you'd take it. So take it. You deserve it."

In that instant it was like a glorious light came shining down from the heavens, which sent Coop's spirit soaring into the stratosphere. This was incredible. He'd been worried about money for longer than he could remember and now he finally had the one thing he'd thought was unattainable…financial security. Coop felt like he could breathe for the first time in ages. Tearfully, Coop thanked his friend. "I'd say this calls for another round, on me!"

*

Most folks who came into a sudden fortune would go out and purchase a couple of big-ticket items, like a new car or a yacht. But not Coop. He was prudent and methodical in his allocation of the big check. First, he paid off his mortgage so he wouldn't have to worry about it ever again. Second, he opened an investment account for retirement and selected a diversified portfolio. Next he started a college fund for each of his nieces and nephews. And he set aside some money in a savings account that was dedicated for Christmas spending. He also finally ordered that Herman Miller sectional sofa he'd been eyeing for some time. The last thing Coop did, uncharacteristically, was head to Nordstrom (not Nordstrom Rack) for the day, where he gave a personal shopper a budget of ten thousand dollars and bought himself an entirely new wardrobe—that was his big splurge.

*

Coop could hardly wait for dinner that evening. Vivien was in town for a Ceiling Smashers dinner, so on her free night Coop was going to introduce her to Dean. They were all going to Coop and Vivien's favorite Italian spot, called Pasticcio. Coop wore one of his snazzy new outfits.

Dean was already sitting at the table when Coop arrived at the restaurant and was greeted by the host and his wife. He gave Dean a quick kiss and sat down gushing about his friend Vivien. "She's my best friend in the world, I'm so excited that you're going to meet her, luv."

His boyfriend's eyes were a little glassy and he nodded as he gulped down a glass of water.

When Vivien arrived she got hugs from the restaurant owners and then rushed over to give Coop a big hug. "Congrats on the whistleblower award—I'm thrilled for you," she whispered in his ear. She was the only one whom Coop had dared to share the news with about his windfall. She turned to Dean and smiled. "I'm so glad to finally meet you, Dean. Sounds like you've been making Coop very happy for the past five months."

Dean stood up to shake hands and as he reached across the table he knocked over a small crystal vase with flowers. He was clearly on edge, perhaps feeling like he needed to win Vivien's approval in order to continue dating Coop.

When the table was restored to its original dry state, the three of them sat down, ordered drinks, and had some small talk. Dean's forehead was glistening with beads of sweat and he was gulping down glass after glass of water. Soon he had to excuse himself to use the restroom. Coop felt a little embarrassed about how nervously Dean was acting.

*

Vivien relished the opportunity to spend time with her dear friend Coop and meet his boyfriend. Dean was evidently very nervous to meet her. In fact, he'd drunk the entire carafe of water and had just left the table to use the restroom. Dean was a clean-cut, attractive guy of medium build—a bit stockier than Coop—with thick dark hair, brown eyes, and a wholesomeness about him. When Dean was out of earshot Vivien leaned over to her friend. "He's cute, Coop! And he seems really nice. How are things going?"

Her friend smiled. "Dean's really great. Smart, successful, cute, interesting, nice. He's very sweet to me, but…"

Vivien looked at her friend quizzically as she took a sip of her wine.

"You know, Dean is very…steady. We get along well. In fact, we rarely even argue. I just wonder if there's enough…passion in the relationship." Coop wrinkled his brow a bit.

This set off warning bells to Vivien. It seemed like Coop had something good—she hoped he wouldn't discard it like an article of clothing he felt was out of vogue. He had just purged his entire closet but that didn't mean he should purge Dean, too. "By 'passion' do you mean 'drama,' Coop? Didn't you have your fill of that with Brad?" She raised an eyebrow. "Maybe you're just not used to dating a really nice, normal guy. I think he's perfect for you, my friend."

Dean returned, and over shared appetizers of baked clams, beef carpaccio, and arugula salad, the three of them chatted and got more comfortable. It seemed like Dean was finally starting to relax by the time their entrées arrived. While Coop was Vivien's dearest friend, he did have his quirks, but Dean seemed so taken with him that he embraced any of Coop's irksome habits as endearing. Dean was telling a funny and complimentary story about Coop and toward the end of it Coop swatted him on the arm. "Uh, I don't know why you enjoy telling that story so much," he snapped.

Dean looked a little wounded. It was not like Coop to be that snippy. Coop gave Vivien a furtive look. "Oh, please excuse me." He jumped up. "I forgot this restaurant only takes cash so I need to run down to the ATM quickly. I'll be right back. Vivi, wait for me to order dessert, okay?" The two friends had arranged it so Vivien could speak with Dean alone to get to know him better. Coop wanted to get her unvarnished opinion. He dashed out the door.

"So, how are things with Coop going?" she asked cautiously.

"Coop is amazing, he really is. It's a gift to date someone who is funny, smart, adorable, and has his act together. Someone who knows what he wants." Dean grinned. "I'm just enjoying being with him." He confided, "Truth be told, my last relationship had a lot of ups and downs, so I appreciate Coop's maturity."

"All I can say is that you have wonderful taste in men. Coop is one of the people I admire most," said Vivien. "What do you mean about your last relationship having lots of ups and downs?"

Dean gave her the lowdown. He'd been with his partner, a successful plastic surgeon, for over ten years, and in the last few years of their relationship Dean was pushing for them to get married. His boyfriend was very hesitant about making a long-term commitment and it was the source of many arguments and much drama. Ultimately, Dean realized they weren't going to move forward so he finally made the difficult decision to break up with the guy. It was heart-wrenching for both of them to separate their lives and friendships after so many years together. That was the main reason that Dean had moved to NYC from Philadelphia at the end of last year.

Vivien shook her head. "I'm sorry, Dean, that sounds tough."

His look darkened. "It was. I still miss Jesse. I don't know if I'll ever fully recover from the breakup." Dean sat back a gave a little smile. "But being with Coop has been such a joy—and a refreshing change. Did you know that when he retires Coop wants to open up a little bed-and-breakfast in Vermont? We've been talking about it and he wants me to design it, isn't that sweet?"

She let out a little laugh. "Yes, I know all about Coop's big Vermont dreams. But here's the thing—he hates waking up early, so I honestly don't know if running a bed-and-breakfast is in the cards for him. He's way too cranky in the mornings."

Dean leaned closer. "That's true, he's a bit grumpy in the mornings. I try to steer clear of him until he's had a few sips of his Diet Coke. I usually busy myself making breakfast for us both so he has time to wake up gradually." He chuckled. "Anyway, I think the brunt of running a B & B would fall on my shoulders since Coop will be relying upon me to whip up eggs Benedict and blueberry pancakes for our guests."

Here was a great guy who clearly adored her best friend. "Listen, Dean, I can see that you love Coop and you guys seem terrific together. I just hope you'll be patient with him—Coop isn't accustomed to being with someone who treats him the way he deserves to be treated, with kindness and respect."

*

Cash in hand, Coop came into the restaurant and returned to the table. Dean and Vivien seemed deep in conversation. Trying to get caught up, he asked, "What are you guys talking about?"

His best friend and his boyfriend looked up at him and smiled.

"Oh, we were just discussing dessert options," Vivien said with a sly look.

The three of them ordered another round of drinks and a couple of desserts to share. While Dean was ordering a cappuccino from the waiter, Coop leaned over and hugged his friend. He said softly, "Vivi, I'm so happy right now."

"You deserve it, Coop," she whispered back.

With a flourish, Coop signaled for the check and proclaimed that he was treating them to dinner. He had much to celebrate.

*

SOFIA

The day after Andi's holiday party, Sofia and Kate got on a video call with Annika and enlisted her support in encouraging other women to go on the record with their stories. By Monday morning, just in time for their meeting with Randolph, Sofia and Kate had something concrete to share with their boss. They were half expecting Randolph to chastise them for working on the investigation without his express consent. Instead he said, "I think you two need to get the rest of the story together. And quickly." He wagged a finger. "But make damn sure you're thorough. I want this story to be airtight."

Sofia said, "Will do, Randolph. We're also partnering with an investigative journalist from the *Wall Street Journal* who's working on the story from a different angle. She's looking into some questionable financial practices going on at Voss's denim company and how the company culture has facilitated the malfeasance. She's gotten the download from us and we're coordinating on a multipronged launch of this story."

"This will be big, Randolph," Kate added.

"Good. Well, then why are you two still sitting here in my office? Go get him." Uncharacteristically, Randolph winked and gave half a smile.

*

The two women walked down the hall back to Kate's office and she swiftly shut the door. She stood in front of Sofia with stick-straight legs and jiggled her arms excitedly, hands flapping around like fluttering birds.

"What's going on, Kate? Are you all right?" Sofia asked, worried that Kate was having some kind of seizure.

"We need to wrap up this investigation before June."

Sofia knotted her brow. "Okay, that's doable. But why the June deadline?"

Kate leaned over and squeezed both of Sofia's shoulders, bringing her face within inches. "This is top secret news because we haven't announced it yet. I got engaged over Christmas, Sofia. Devinder proposed to me and we're getting married in June…in India!" She unlocked her desk drawer and pulled out a Cartier ring box. Inside was an enormous emerald-cut diamond set in platinum with two baguettes.

"Oh my gosh, that's fantastic news, Kate. Jeez, that diamond is the size of a bread plate!" Sofia gave her friend a heartfelt hug and then stepped back. "I couldn't be happier for you."

*

Over the past five months the three reporters had worked tirelessly getting all the details of their story on Charley Voss. A major victory was that they had twelve women willing to go public with their stories. All the while Kate had been in the throes of wedding planning and often solicited Sofia's advice on wedding details.

By early May their story was about to break in a coordinated fashion. But the final requirement from Randolph before they could release the story was to get another side of the story…from Charley Voss himself.

"We have to let him know the story we're about to publish and give him a chance to provide his comments. He should know what the allegations are from these twelve women." Randolph sounded firm.

Kate cocked her head. "We've tried contacting Voss for comment multiple times, but he's shut us down. For months we've gotten threats from his lawyers and Voss has thrown up a ton of roadblocks to prevent us from making this story public."

"He's also contacted some of his victims and threatened to sue them for slander if they share their stories. These women are afraid of being tied up in court and financially wiped out, and having their careers destroyed by Voss. Do you really think a guy like that is going to cooperate with us?"

"He will if he wants his side of things to be known," Randolph said.

He added, "You say he's been denying all allegations—well, now's his chance to share his perspective."

Sofia gulped. It was clear that their boss wouldn't let them proceed without doing this final task but her shoulders were in a vise grip of tension just thinking about it.

*

Two days later the three reporters found themselves in neutral territory for the meeting. Sofia, Kate, and the *WSJ* reporter, Hyun Park, had declined to go to Voss's office and give him the upper hand. He would not agree to come to the CNBC or *WSJ* offices, so they were conducting their clandestine meeting in a conference room of a midtown hotel. Before the three women entered the room Kate pulled Sofia and Hyun aside. "Voss is a classic bully. We cannot let him intimidate us in there. Right?"

Sofia and Hyun nodded, and they entered the nondescript conference room and sat on one side of the large table. Opposite them sat Charley Voss and two of his attorneys plus a hulking, dark-haired man wearing sunglasses who did not identify himself. The guy was probably Voss's bodyguard and could easily have been a former Mossad agent.

In person Charley Voss was not what Sofia expected. From all the victims' accounts Sofia was well aware of Voss's predatory behavior— he was a monster who used his power and physicality to abuse unsuspecting women. But the man sitting across from her appeared benign and relaxed, and was youthful looking. Charley Voss had dark wavy hair and was tall and slender. He wore a tight T-shirt under a blazer with Voss jeans and designer sneakers. Perhaps the most off-putting aspect was that he was smiling and playing with a shiny metal fidget spinner encrusted with diamonds. He held the spinner between his thumb and index finger and flicked it with the other hand so it spun smoothly on its ball bearings.

Sofia and Hyun each pulled out their notebooks and pens while Kate took out a micro digital recording device. As Kate was taking a folder of notes out of her bag, a small personal pink Taser tumbled out—she hastily stuffed it back in her bag and said, "For when I'm running in Central Park." She shot a sideways look at Sofia, who figured that Kate had done that on purpose, probably as a subtle warning to Voss and his team. Kate asked Voss for permission to record the meeting and he looked at his lawyers and then nodded.

The conversation started off with Sofia, Kate, and Hyun giving the highlights of their coverage. Voss's lawyers asked for the names of the women involved and took copious notes. Upon hearing the first few names, Voss chuckled.

"Oh, I get it. These women were very young when they worked with me—they're probably just confused about the situation or they're remembering it incorrectly. This is all just a trivial misunderstanding." Voss spoke in a surprisingly high voice, but his tone was smooth like that of a diamond district jeweler trying to charm them into buying an overpriced bracelet.

Sofia pursed her lips. "We have more victims who have come forward, actually. Twelve to be exact. Why don't we share the specifics of each story, and you can respond to or refute them."

As Sofia and Kate took turns methodically unveiling each of the twelve cases and providing all the lurid details of the events, Voss's eyes widened. His smile disappeared but he continued to spin his ornate toy. "I don't recall that," Voss said in response to nearly every account. Hyun went over the financial irregularities with Voss & Co. that she had been investigating and, again, Voss claimed to have no knowledge.

After about forty minutes, Sofia realized they weren't getting any noteworthy comments from Voss. He spun his toy and shifted in his seat, looking impatient. "Look, just email a copy of your story to my lawyers." He nodded at one of them, who pushed a business card across the table. "They'll get back to you with our comments."

"We'll need your comments by five o'clock today. This story goes to print for tomorrow's *Wall Street Journal*, and our program is airing tomorrow evening. Prime time. Live," Kate stated.

Voss's eyes flashed. "Listen, I know the CEO of Dow Jones, and I play in a weekly poker game with a board director of Comcast, which owns NBCUniversal, which owns CNBC. That means I'm tight with the guys who own the three of you. I could kill this story if I wanted to, but you know what? It doesn't matter. No one is going to care about a few women complaining about me. I'm above all of this." He flicked the spinner for emphasis, ignoring the worried looks from his lawyers. Voss glanced at his chunky, costly watch and motioned to his lawyers that the meeting was over. The burly bodyguard silently got up and left with the two lawyers. Sofia, Kate, and Hyun gathered their belongings.

When Voss reached the door he turned back and said in a menacing whisper, "Just remember, I always win. These women who are trying to take me down? They're about to learn a very costly lesson. I'm gonna make them pay. I always win."

Voss gave a snort and exited the room. Hyun stood frozen. Sofia, wide-eyed, looked over at Kate, who had a funny look in her eyes. She pushed aside her notes, under which rested the digital recording device, which was still on. Kate picked it up and switched it off. "Voss must have forgotten I was recording the meeting because I just got that. All of it."

"And we can use it, right?" Sofia asked. "We got his permission to record."

"Sure can."

*

Early the next morning the Voss story appeared on the front page of the *Wall Street Journal* with Hyun Park's byline shared with Sofia and Kate. It detailed some of the apparel mogul's antics and the questionable financial dealings of his company. Simultaneously, a teaser video was released on social media that Sofia and Kate had put together in which each of Charley Voss's victims shared a snippet of their horrendous experiences—put to the soundtrack of Phil Collins's "In the Air Tonight."

That night Voss's twelve victims were featured in a special live broadcast hosted by Sofia and Kate where they conducted an in-depth interview with all the women together. Several women remembered being offered a beverage by Voss and then feeling dizzy. It appeared that he'd drugged some of these women to facilitate his predatory actions. Among the women on the special program were the young actress Annika, the model turned entrepreneur Elle, and the Slique Denim CEO, Stella. When Sofia and Kate played back Voss's recorded quote about winning from their meeting, it created a strong visceral reaction in his victims. They concluded the special program with a message from each of the twelve women to Voss with the headline "It's never okay..."

*

Sofia and Kate's exposé was the top story of the week, the month, and possibly even the year. The media was abuzz and someone coined it the N-O movement, which stood for "Never Okay," from the victims' quotes. The video of the twelve women went viral and the special program hosted by Sofia and Kate had the highest ratings of any show in CNBC's history. Even Randolph made a point of stopping by to tell Kate and Sofia, "Good work."

Sofia felt good about breaking the story despite the voice mail bomb she and Kate had received from Voss. He'd left an expletive-filled message complaining that the post-meeting comments he'd made should have been off the record and shouldn't have been used in their story. She learned that Voss had also contacted Randolph to complain and their boss had told him he backed his reporters and they were running the story.

What Sofia could not have predicted was that once the story broke, scores more victims would come forward to share their stories of Voss encounters on social media. The victim count escalated to over forty women. Soon the district attorney announced he was conducting an investigation into Charley Voss, and they seized his passport. It looked like Voss was finally going to have to answer for his actions. FOC's, or Friends of Charley, started to distance themselves from the powerful businessman. It was clear that the bad behavior by this prominent man would no longer tolerated or swept under the carpet. The N-O Movement was unstoppable.

Sofia was jubilant about the success of their story and felt like a true warrior. The ability to make an impact and help others was why she'd entered the field of journalism in the first place—this was what it was all about.

*

While Sofia's spirit was soaring from her work success, she couldn't help but feel an emptiness inside. Jasper was still on the West Coast working from his Silicon Valley office while caring for his mother, whose recovery from a stroke was coming along slowly. Sofia felt a hole in her soul. And all the discussions she was having with an over-the-moon Kate Frost about her wedding details only drove home to Sofia that marriage was something she did want after all.

"Grace, it's killing me," Sofia admitted to her friend as they did a power walk along the High Line, an elevated park created on a former NYC railroad spur. It was early on a Saturday morning in May and the cool, comfortable weather made their exercise even more refreshing

"What are you talking about, Sofi?"

Sofia slowed her pace. "Jasper's been working from the West Coast since the New Year— we've hardly had a chance to talk much and I haven't seen him in ages. I…I think I've lost him, Grace." She stopped and looked up, trying to prevent her eyes from tearing up. "You know, I've been so closed off to marriage all these years but right around the time Jasper left is when I realized something."

Her friend stopped walking. "What's that?"

"The headline is that I can see myself marrying Jasper and spending the rest of my life with him. Happily." Sofia revealed her big, dark secret. "You know the moment that I knew? We were at the movies the night before Andi's Christmas party. You know how they have the bulk candy bins, the kind where you scoop out what you want? Well, I was getting drinks for us and Jasper got some Junior Mints and gummy bears, my favorite. As we were walking into the theater I reached into the gummy bear bag and ate one. I went, 'Yuck, this one is orange flavored. I don't like the orange or green ones, only the red and white ones.' Jasper told me to go ahead to our seats. He came in a few minutes later handing me a bag. 'What's this?' I asked, unable to see in the dark theater. He said, 'They're my special Sofia gummy bears. I hand-selected them for you—there's only red and white ones in the bag.' In that instant I knew that Jasper was the one. Can you believe it, Grace? I finally feel ready for marriage but then I blow it."

Grace put her hand on her friend's shoulder. "What do you mean you 'blow it?'"

"At Andi's party I was super stressed out about work and the Voss investigation and I didn't treat Jasper very well. Then on the walk home he started to bring up the topic of marriage—which I should have been elated about—but I had a massive stress headache and told him I couldn't discuss it. I was pretty short with him, Grace. Ugh, what have I done? Maybe he's just given up on me and moved on to another woman. If that's the case I'll never forgive myself."

Sofia could have sworn she caught the briefest little smile on

Grace's face and her friend turned away for a minute. "So you think things are over between you and Jasper?"

"Yes. Well, I hope not. I don't know. I understand that he needs to be with his mother now, but but I haven't seen him in forever." Sofia was practically wailing. "What can I do?"

"Sofia, why don't you call him and find out when Jasper is coming home? Maybe the two of you can have a heart-to-heart chat and sort things out. I think he needs to know how you feel."

*

GRACE

Grace, using all the self-control she could muster, could not allow her friend Sofia to see her reaction. They were getting some exercise along the High Line park on a weekend morning and Sofia was lamenting about losing Jasper, afraid that things might be over between them.

The funny part of it that Grace couldn't let on to Sofia was that Jasper had called Grace the previous week to get her opinion on how he should propose to Sofia. These two lovebirds were clearly getting their signals crossed and it was comical.

*

"Here's my idea, Grace," Jasper had started enthusiastically. "I was thinking about taking Sofia to a Yankees ballgame and during the seventh-inning stretch"—his voice was rising with excitement—"I'll pull out the ring box, kneel down, and then 'Sofia, will you marry me?' will flash up on the jumbotron so the whole stadium can see it. Can you imagine everyone cheering for us when Sofia accepts my proposal?"

Grace hesitated. "Um, no, Jasper. I really can't imagine that. Sofia has always preferred keeping her private life just that—private. Getting a marriage proposal in front of thousands of strangers would be for Sofia on par with being bound and submerged into a tank of ravenous piranhas. No, our girl would want something a little more intimate. And oh, by the way, Sofia isn't as crazy about baseball as you are. Sorry, Jasper, I think you're going to need to come up with something else."

"Oh." He sounded crestfallen. "That was my big idea. Now I've got nothing."

She tried to reassure him. "Not to worry. Let me talk to her a little and give it some thought. I'm sure we can come up with something that's special and meaningful to you both. All right?"

"Sure, Grace, thanks for your help. And for keeping this on the QT."

*

When Grace got home after their power walk together during which she'd heard Sofia's story about the gummy bears, she picked up the phone. "Jasper, I think I've got the perfect way for you to propose, and it involves gummy bears."

*

Grace's baby business, Twinkle, had just launched in May and over the past week or so she was in a constant state of agitation and surveillance about her startup. The product line looked great, the videos explaining the product features were up on the website, their branding and marketing was adorable. Now they just needed customers. One afternoon her phone rang and when she saw it was Devinder Jain calling a jolt of panic shot through her veins. He was the major investor in her business and was probably wondering how well—or not—it was going.

"Hello, Devinder. How are you?"

"Wonderful, couldn't be better. How are things with you, Grace?"

She swallowed. "Well, thank you. The business went live a week ago. Initial traffic to the website has been good, but we need to build up our customer base and generate more sales. But I have lots of ideas to accomplish that."

"Please, continue," he said.

"We're using a multipronged approach. First, we've sent out some product to key influencers, basically gifts for their newborn babies. I'm hoping that in the coming months that will turn into some collateral we can use to build the business—getting photos on Instagram, in magazines, product reviews, or quotes from the influencers that we can use on our website. Second, I've reached out to several key magazines to get on their 'best baby gifts' lists. Third, we've partnered with some other baby brands and created a 'Hello World!' baby basket of items and promotions for new parents—those will be distributed in maternity wards in hospitals in twenty key cities over the next three to six months. And lastly, we're working on a viral marketing campaign where we feature a super-cute baby talking about the problems—"

"A talking baby?"

"It'll be dubbed."

"Of course! Silly me. Go on."

"So she's talking about the problems of being a baby and how the comfortable and functional Twinkle baby clothes solve her problems. So the baby is appealing to her mom and dad to buy Twinkle apparel for her."

Devinder let out a laugh. "Grace, that sounds perfect. I hear some concern in your voice and I want to tell you not to worry. It took years for the businesses I started to make money, so I certainly don't expect you to turn a profit in a matter of weeks. I have confidence you'll make it a success over time. Anyway, that wasn't the reason I was calling you."

Grace took a seat and relaxed a little. "It wasn't?" What else could he want to discuss?

"I have some big news. Kate Frost and I are getting married. We are planning to have a June wedding in India, and of course, you are invited. Since you were the one who arranged our introduction, it is only fitting that you should be there to take part in the celebration. Your friend Sofia will also be attending. It promises to be a fantastic time, Grace."

This was unexpected. "How wonderful, Devinder, I'm so happy for you and Kate! Of course it would be my honor to attend your wedding."

"Excellent, then I'll have my assistant make all your travel arrangements. She'll reach out to you in the next day or two. Okay?"

"I can't wait."

*

Taking a short break from work, Grace had just finished a late afternoon vinyasa class and left the yoga studio. Still moist with perspiration, she stopped by a bodega to pick up a cold drink and upon exiting nearly collided with a well-dressed woman. "Shelby! Great to see you." It was her old friend from Palazzo, wearing her signature red high-heeled boots and black capris pants. Shelby worked in merchandising in the women's business.

Shelby lowered her oversized sunglasses and peered over them. "Hello, Grace, good to see you, too." She scrutinized Grace's sweaty outfit and started to walk away before Grace stopped her.

"How are you, Shelby? How are things at work?"

Shelby turned back and waved a hand of darkly polished fingernails in the air. "All good. How about you. Are you working these days?"

"I've started my own baby clothing business called Twinkle," Grace replied. "Just launched it, as a matter of fact." This was strange. Grace had considered Shelby to be a good friend from work, but since she'd left the company she hadn't heard a peep from her. Many friends from work had held a goodbye party for Grace

410

at a wine bar near the office and she had to admit it stung a little that Shelby hadn't even shown up for it. Even some colleagues from the London office had flown over to attend. "I've missed our chats, Shelby. Maybe we can catch up over coffee sometime?"

Shelby wrinkled her nose and whipped off her sunglasses. "No, thanks, Grace. Now that you're not at the company anymore, there's really no point."

Grace took a step back, shocked. "No point?"

"Why would there be? Plus you and Skip didn't get on well, so any contact I have with you could only have negative political ramifications for me." Shelby donned her sunglasses.

The words were harsh to hear and caught Grace off guard. Her first instinct was to tell Shelby she was being a jerk, but she was still feeling Zen from the yoga class and did something else entirely. "You know what, Shelby? Thank you for being so direct and sparing me the effort of trying to maintain a friendship that you don't value."

With a shrug Shelby said her final words before walking away. "Good luck with your venture, Grace. It's amazing how many startups don't make it, but kudos to you for trying anyway."

Grace stood there, arms crossed, and harrumphed. She'd show them all that she could make her business a success.

*

"I can't believe you're going so far away, Win. I'm going to miss you!" Grace was snuggling with Win in a VIP lounge at JFK airport. An airline representative would be coming by in a few minutes to escort Win to his flight just before it took off.

Win gave her a long, comforting hug. "Darlin', I'm going to miss you, too. Maybe you can come visit me in New Zealand on the set?"

That wasn't likely. Grace was heads-down working on Twinkle and exhausting every creative ounce in her body to boost sales. The last thing she had time for was to fly halfway across the world to sit and watch Win filming his latest movie, an epic adapted from a book series. Still, she said, "Maybe. Or you can come back here during a break in the shooting. I guess it's only a few weeks until we meet up in India for Devinder and Kate's wedding—you're still going to be my plus-one, right?"

"Wouldn't miss it, darlin'. Don't worry, we'll figure out a way to see each other before too much time passes." He smiled and then kissed her.

The airline representative came over and said it was time to head to the gate. They embraced one last time and after a quick kiss, Win was escorted down the stairs. Grace watched from a window and saw Win open the door to a waiting black Audi sedan. He blew a kiss to Grace and then got into the car. Grace's eyes followed the car as it was expertly maneuvered across the tarmac to the airplane that was transporting Win far away.

*

A few weeks later Grace found herself again in the arms of her man Win. Grace had flown with Sofia to India and Win had taken a flight from his shoot in New Zealand to attend the gorgeous and opulent wedding of Devinder and Kate. The ceremony was being held at the magnificent Umaid Bhawan Palace in Jodhpur. The bride and groom had asked their guests to leave their cell phones in their rooms so no one could leak photos, but their wedding was covered by professional photographers. Kate and Devinder were planning to sell photos of their wedding to different media outlets and donate the proceeds to charity.

During the reception Grace and Win were twirling together on the dance floor and all smiles while a photographer snapped pictures of the dazzling couple. For Grace it was a joyous celebration and a welcome respite from worrying twenty-four/seven about Twinkle. These days she was waking up at four o'clock in the morning consumed with how to generate more sales for her business. Grace remembered the comment from her former friend Shelby about how so many startups fail—would Twinkle be included in that set?

*

ANDI

Andi and her BC Capital business partner Courtney were attending a huge retail conference called ShopTalk in Las Vegas. One of the conference highlights was a half day where retail startups would pitch to an audience of private equity and venture capital investors. Pitch day was the main draw for Andi and Courtney. Each startup had fifteen minutes to share their business model, talk about progress, and try to drum up interest from the audience in investing in their company. As Andi had looked around she'd noted that the audience comprised mostly men.

During a break in the presentations over coffee and pastries, Andi and Courtney heard some guys talking about the startup concepts they found preposterous—an organic baby food delivery company, a natural skincare company, a chain of women-only workout centers, a company making biometric sports bras, and an online personal shopping business. "Wacky," "silly," and "frivolous" were descriptors that Andi had heard the men use as they ridiculed these startups. The problem was that these guys were wrong—they just didn't get it. Those were the exact companies that were high on BC Capital's list.

The two women ran into different men they knew from the industry and a couple of clever ones tried to pry some information out of them.

"Courtney, Andi, how goes it? See anything that interests you?"

"Hello, ladies, which of the companies appealed to you?"

"What do you think looks promising?"

Clearly the guys were trying to get intel on companies that BC

Capital was gravitating toward, hoping to get in on those deals. But Andi and Courtney kept their cards close to their vests and were noncommittal in their responses to those questions. Some of the guys were people they'd want to partner up with, but they wanted to get deals with their target companies first.

The presentations were followed by a lavish cocktail party in the main ballroom. Huge crystal chandeliers hung from the ceiling and a bar lit with a soft blue lights was stationed at either end of the room. Servers walked around with trays of appetizers and there were two large stations chock-full of cheese plates, fruit, and a variety of hors d'oeuvres. Andi and Courtney walked into the dimly lit room and Andi nudged her friend. "Check it out."

Suspended from the ceiling in a large swath of white silky fabric that was wrapped around her midsection was a scantily clad, gorgeous woman who hung upside down and poured champagne. Champagne flutes were lined up on a table and the guest would have to walk over to the floating woman to be served. There was a striking man in a similar getup just across the room.

Courtney shook her head and chuckled. "Only in Vegas, huh?"

Andi and Courtney got a drink at the bar and then methodically went down their list of top picks. They were going to use this time to seek out those startup founders, mostly women, who by then were dejected from trying in vain to convince the men to invest in a business they simply didn't understand or appreciate. It was the right strategy, because by the time Andi and Courtney circled around to these founders they were desperate for attention and eager to make a deal exchanging equity for capital. In less than forty minutes BC Capital had signed up every one of their top picks for a meeting and potential investment.

Andi was waiting in line at the bar when a man in front of her, drinks in hand, turned to make his way back out to the ballroom. He glanced at her and then quickly walked away. Myron Burry, the snake she'd worked with at Kaneshiro Bank. She hadn't seen him or even thought about him for over a year. He was clearly ignoring her.

"Myron!" she called out sharply.

He flinched and then turned slowly with a sheepish look. "Oh, Andi. Hello."

Shocked to see him, Andi said, "What on earth are you doing here, Myron?"

"I'm looking at joining a PE firm, so they invited me to the conference as part of the interview process. Well, gotta go." Myron scurried away, sheltering the drinks like a rat protecting a morsel of cheese that it intended to keep for itself. Was he still at Kaneshiro or had they finally wised up and canned him? Andi watched him go and saw him deliver the drinks to a couple of guys. The last thing she wished for was to encounter Myron in yet another business sector.

*

To celebrate out of view of the founders and other PE folks that night, Andi and Courtney went to another hotel far down the strip and had a "chillaxing" dinner with cocktails and a nice bottle of red wine. BC Capital had three hundred million dollars from Finbar Minch, and they'd worked hard to raise another two hundred million and were closing in on the magic number. They'd been on the hunt for women-led companies to invest in and were finding that most were startups and smaller businesses. This conference was ripe hunting grounds for them.

After dinner the two of them made their way back to the hotel, and as they passed the bar some of the female founders they'd agreed to potentially invest in were celebrating. The founders insisted that Andi and Courtney join them at the concert that was being sponsored by the conference—Justin Timberlake was the featured singer. Reluctantly, they followed along to the private club at the top of one of the hotels—a black venue with large industrial metal accents resembling a dungeon.

There, they rocked out to the tunes, enjoyed a great performance, and did a few too many tequila shots.

Andi barely remembered getting back to her hotel room sometime in the wee hours of the morning and essentially passed out as soon as she walked in the door.

*

The morning after that wild night, with a little sleep and a rehydrating shower, Andi felt revived and made plans to meet Courtney for breakfast in the hotel restaurant. Courtney, with her dark, glowing skin and sparkling brown eyes, looked surprisingly peppy and fully recovered from their wild night out—perhaps Andi was just out of practice now that she was a mom who typically was asleep by ten p.m.

"Okay, so by my count we will have one hundred million dollars of our capital invested in eight companies, plus we'll reserve another hundred and fifty million for additional investment in those companies to fund their growth," Courtney said, plunging into the business discussion. She was a bright woman, great with numbers, and seemed to have a limitless supply of energy—that was probably why Finbar thought so highly of her.

Andi hadn't even had her coffee yet and held up her hand. "Courtney, for god's sake, I'm still trying to get over last night's festivities. Will you please let me have a few sips of coffee before we start talking numbers? I drank more last night than I have in the past two months!"

Courtney let out a throaty laugh and pushed a plate of scones toward Andi. "Here, have one of these, you need to get your blood sugar back up."

Once Andi felt the caffeine start kicking in she was ready for a meaty conversation. "So with five hundred million total to invest we still have two hundred fifty million left to spend. What are we going to do with that?"

"One thing's for sure, we've got to find a woman-led business that is of significant size. Before we left for Vegas, Finbar told me he was counting on us closing a major deal before the end of the year, so we've got less than six months to do it. I know we've had this on our radar since we started the firm, but the clock is ticking, Andi."

Andi ruminated for a moment—Finbar Minch had given her this huge opportunity and a lot of capital to start their firm. If they ended the year with hundreds of millions of dollars just sitting unused, they would be eviscerated. Worse, Finbar might conclude that the idea of a women-focused PE firm was a bad one. The mere thought made her heart drop down to the floor. The air-conditioning in the hotel was frigid, and as Andi shivered she wrapped her hands around her coffee mug. "You're right. We've just got to keep plugging away until we find a large enough company with a female CEO. But the reality is there just aren't a lot of big companies led by women. Who knew it would be this difficult?"

Courtney checked her watch and got up. "You want to head over to the conference? There are some interesting speakers on the agenda."

"I'll catch up with you after the first session, Courtney. I want to swing by Starbucks for another coffee to warm up."

After breakfast Andi walked over to the large Starbucks adjacent to the hotel to sit and have an overpriced, heavily caloric, and highly caffeinated drink. She just wanted a calm environment away from the noise of the slot machines that assaulted her ears from every corner of the hotel's lobby. She plopped herself down in an overstuffed chair in close proximity to two men who were obviously having a work meeting. From their discussion on a potential investment it sounded like they were also in the PE business. Andi's ears perked up at what she heard next.

"So, what did you think of the guy we interviewed yesterday? Myron was supposedly a superstar in Kaneshiro's private banking department."

"Mmm-hmm. Obviously he was a key person there. Some of the deals he brought in"—the second guy ticked off some major deals although they were actually deals that Andi had put together and closed—"were primo. Really strong stuff."

"I think he'd make a good addition to Sapient Capital, don't you?"

"Yup, I give the thumbs-up on Myron. Let's make him an offer."

Andi nearly choked on her drink. Sapient Capital was a dominant player and a rival of Minch Capital. So that's who Myron was interviewing with? She put on a mask of bored indifference as the two men picked up their things, walked past her, and left the Starbucks. So she'd be potentially competing against Myron Burry? That didn't bother her—heck, Andi welcomed the opportunity to crush a cockroach like Myron…with pleasure.

CHAPTER 13

September

SOFIA

After attending the wedding of Devinder Jain and Kate Frost, it seemed that Sofia couldn't escape her thoughts about marriage. But all was quiet on the Jasper Frank front.

She decided to take Grace's advice to call Jasper.

"Hi, Jasper, how are you? How's your mom doing?"

Jasper said, "I've missed hearing your voice, Sofia. I'm actually at the medical clinic with my mom and stepdad. Her recovery is going really well. How are you?"

She let out a breath of relief. "Oh, I'm so relieved to hear that, Jasper. I've been doing okay, but I really miss you." She was hoping to hear him say he missed her, too.

"I saw your story on Voss—that was groundbreaking, Sofi. I'm so proud of you. That was some crackerjack reporting."

"Thanks." Sofia's throat felt parched, but she plunged in. "Listen, I want you to know how much you mean to me, how much I love you, and how difficult it's been to be without you. Our separation has made me realize how much I want you in my life. In fact, I can't imagine a future without you, Jasper."

There was silence on the other end for a moment. Then, to her great relief, Jasper said, "It makes me happy to hear you say that, Sofia. You know, I'm actually flying back to New York tomorrow afternoon."

"What? Oh, that's great. Why don't we meet for dinner at that cute French restaurant we like?" Sofia immediately started making plans for a romantic evening.

He hesitated. "Um, I think it would be better to meet at your apartment. I have something I'd like to discuss with you."

Was this something good or an impending disaster? Was he breaking up with her? Was that why he didn't want to meet in a public place, so she wouldn't cause a scene?

For the entire next day, Sofia's shoulders were knotted up with tension. She was so distracted at work, trying to anticipate her conversation with Jasper that night.

*

When Sofia's doorbell rang that warm September evening she ran to it and then stopped short, taking a deep breath to calm her nerves. She threw open the door and Jasper stood there smiling with his soft brown eyes twinkling. They embraced like old times, and it comforted Sofia in so profound a way it was impossible to put into words. "I missed you terribly," she murmured into his suit jacket.

"That's good to hear, Sofia." Jasper stepped back and pulled something from his pocket. "Here, I brought you something." He handed her a clear cellophane bag full of gummy bears. An unusual gift after being apart for so long. "Take a look."

Jasper had picked out only the red and white gummy bears, her favorites. "Aww, how thoughtful, Jasper. Only my favorites. Thank you," she said cautiously. Was this a positive sign or a parting gift?

"Come, let's sit together." He led her into the living room and sat down on the sofa.

Sofia clutched the bag of candy like it was a life preserver. Was Jasper about to tell her that he'd decided to move on? Would he tell her there was another woman? She was so trepidatious she remained silent.

"I know we've been apart for a while, Sofia, but I've been doing a lot of thinking while we were separated. After Andi's Christmas party, I was fishing around trying to gauge your interest in marriage." His eyes bored straight into hers and Sofia tried to keep a placid look on her face, while inside she was cringing when she remembered how sharply she'd treated Jasper that night.

She drew in a breath. "About that, Jasper, I apologize for—"

"Please, Sofia, let me finish. This is important."

Sofia nodded but was ready to burst into tears.

"I was wrong to do that," Jasper said. "You're a strong, smart woman who knows what she wants out of life. And this is a situation that requires decisiveness." Jasper looked at her and saw that Sofia's face was ashen. "Please, open the bag of candy, Sofia."

She dutifully complied and untied the red satin ribbon and opened the bag.

"Look inside."

Nestled within the red and white gummy bears was something glistening. Sofia gasped and covered her mouth, tilting the bag toward Jasper to show him the surprise she'd discovered inside. He reached in and drew out the prize and then knelt before her holding the magnificent platinum and diamond ring in his fingers. It was a sparkly round diamond surrounded by a ring of channel-set diamonds with small diamonds set along the band. Magnificent. If Sofia could have chosen any ring in the world this would have been the one.

"Sofia, my love. Marry me. I can't imagine my life without you as my partner, my mate, my wife. I've realized that you're the only one for me. Please, say—"

"YES!" Sofia shrieked, stunned. "A thousand times yes. I will marry you, Jasper." She threw her arms around him and they kissed deeply. Jasper slipped the engagement ring onto her finger, and tears of joy streamed down Sofia's face as she laughed. Still stunned, she said, "But, I'm confused. Who was that woman you were having brunch with at Sarabeth's?"

Jasper rubbed his chin. "Oh, her? She's the jewelry designer I hired to create your engagement ring, Sof. And your friend Grace was a big help in coming up with the perfect way to propose—she said you told her about the gummy bears that I picked for you and how that was when you knew you were destined to be with me." A mischievous grin spread across his handsome, happy face.

"I can't imagine a more perfect proposal, Jasper. I love you so much."

They embraced, popped open a bottle of champagne, and over a scrumptious dinner of takeout food talked about the glorious future that lay ahead of them.

*

The next evening, during cocktail hour at the Royalton Hotel, surrounded by her Smasher friends plus Coop and Courtney Greene, Andi's PE partner, Sofia couldn't have felt happier. Although the opposite was true for Vivien, who was back in town for a speaking engagement at *Fortune's* Most Powerful Women Summit, which had occurred the day before.

What an ordeal the past months had been for Vivien. While she'd accomplished the impossible, the new CEO, Duncan Doric, had abruptly fired her a week ago for no reason. To make matters worse, Vivien had admitted onstage at the *Fortune* conference in front of thousands of people that she'd been fired. She looked and sounded miserable. In fact, Sofia had never seen her friend achieve anything but success after success, so it was painful to hear everything she'd endured. But they needed to help Vivien. Courtney and Andi were trying to convince her to look at opportunities to run a PE-backed company.

Sofia, who had been quiet so far, said, "Courtney's right, Vivi, you should get to know the private equity world. Your talents would be appreciated and well compensated there." She lifted her glass to take a sip of her cocktail.

"Hang on, what's that, Sofi?" Vivien's jaw dropped. "That bling."

Everyone's eyes moved to Sofia's left hand, where a huge diamond ring sat.

Sofia gave a sheepish smile and announced, "Jasper and I got engaged."

Her friends whooped and cheered, firing off questions to Sofia. Vivien ordered a bottle of champagne to celebrate.

"The wedding's going to be in early December." Sofia paused for effect. "In Paris." She leaned over to Grace and said, "By the way, I appreciate your help in the proposal department."

Grace waved her hand. "Do you know that your guy was going to propose to you at a Yankees game via Jumbotron? I nixed that one."

Sofia let out a sigh. "Thank god. If Jasper had proposed to me that way he might have gotten a different response," she joked. "But the way he did it was absolutely perfect, thanks to you."

*

ANDI

Andi and Courtney sat and stared at the phone on the conference room table, willing it to ring.

"We've got to close this deal, Andi." Courtney tapped her pen anxiously on the table.

Andi nodded and gulped.

The two of them had been relentless in their search for a female-led company to invest in—one that was sizable enough to deploy the two hundred fifty million dollars they were itching to put to work. After much searching they came across a fast-growing company in the women's apparel space. The company provided virtual stylists for customers and sent them a box every month of fashionable clothing and accessories. The founder was looking for new capital to help them build out their business and expand internationally.

Unfortunately for BC Capital, due to the success of this business, there were a few other PE firms willing to pony up the money to help them grow.

Andi and Courtney had courted the founder and thought they'd gotten on well and shared the same philosophy about how to take the company forward. Now they were waiting for a call from her to learn if they were ready to move ahead with BC Capital as investors.

The piercing sound of the phone ringing jolted Andi. Courtney grabbed it before the second ring.

"Hello? This is Courtney." She held the receiver to her ear and listened. It wasn't a very long or very two-way conversation. "I see. Are you sure? Well, keep in touch and let us know how we might help you in the future." She hung up the phone and smacked her hand down onto the table.

"I take it we didn't get it?" Andi asked.

Courtney shook her head. "Nope. Sapient Capital did. She said she wanted to go with a firm with a longer track record."

In the back of her mind Andi wondered if Myron Burry had been on the team that had stolen this deal away from them.

"What a disappointment. I liked the founder and I really like the space. We'll just have to find another great business to invest in, Andi." Courtney was never one to stay down for long.

Just then the phone rang again and the caller ID said Minch Capital.

They looked at each other with wide eyes. Andi pushed the speakerphone button on the phone and said hello. As they suspected, Finbar Minch was on the other end.

"So the apparel subscription deal is dead, huh?" Finbar stated in a flat, serious tone like a weary police officer interrogating yet another common criminal. How could he have gotten the news that quickly? Had he bugged their offices or something? As if he'd read their minds, Finbar explained, "I just got a gloating email from the CEO of Sapient

Capital. I don't like being bested by that SOB. Let's not allow that to happen again, all right?"

Andi and Courtney replied in the affirmative and exchanged nervous glances. They'd been working diligently to find a significant woman-led business, but there were so few.

"What else have you got on the docket? You're running out of time, ladies."

"We're looking into some other promising options, Finbar," Courtney replied smoothly.

"Well find one. And close it." Finbar's severe tone indicated he would not accept failure from BC Capital. "Don't make me regret giving you this chance." He said goodbye and hung up.

Andi let out a puff of air. "What promising options, Courtney? We've got nada. Zippo."

Her friend gave her a steely look. "Then we're just going to have to figure something out, right?"

It was getting late. Andi checked her watch. "I'd better get going. I'm supposed to meet Grace, Sofia, and Coop for drinks at the Royalton. Plus Vivien is in town for a speaking engagement and after all the tough stuff she's been through we wanted to get together and support her. Why don't you join us, Courtney?"

"Sure, I'll swing by in a little while. I want to noodle on our options a little more."

As Andi left the BC Capital offices she took another look at their logo on the closed door. Their other investments were doing well, but the quandary was they had boatloads of money to invest and nothing to invest it in. *Are we going to survive or is Finbar going to pull the plug on us?* Her heart was racing.

*

Andi held the cold drink in her hands and nearly drank it down in one gulp. She sat back enjoying the strong air-conditioning at the stylish

Royalton Hotel cocktail lounge. It was a hot, sticky day in September and being in a comfortable environment with soft jazz music playing felt like a sanctuary after BC Capital's soul-crushing business loss. Courtney had joined them and asked Vivien how she was doing. As Andi listened to her friend recount the low points of her experience as an executive at Smart Sports, she realized that Vivien had toughed it out and stayed strong despite everything. She deserved some major props.

Andi nudged her. "You kicked ass, Vivi. You got fantastic results. You were the first female president in the industry and achieved success in record time."

"Yeah, but I never imagined I could be fired while doing a 'fantastic' job." Vivien shook her head and sipped her drink. "Well, at least now you guys can't say I've never failed at anything." She laughed bitterly.

Grace put her arm around Vivien's shoulders. "You should be proud of what you accomplished, no matter how things turned out or how unfairly they treated you. This is just a setback."

The appetizers arrived and Coop popped one in his mouth. "Don't let it get to you, Vivi. People get fired every day for totally random reasons. We'll just find you another business to run, that's all. Next."

Vivien looked at her friends with a grateful expression.

"I'd love to go back to running my old division, just not as part of Smart Sports anymore," Vivien sighed. "To have my team back and to lead the business the way I see fit—that would be perfect."

Hang on a second, what did she just say? Could the salvation of BC Capital come from her friend Vivien?

"Hey, that's an interesting idea." Courtney's brown eyes sparkled, indicating her brain was revving up. "Are you proposing doing a corporate carve-out of the Women's Apparel business from the company? Would the board go for that? What size deal could that be potentially?"

Andi and Courtney exchanged a knowing glance.

"That could be very intriguing," Andi murmured, "very intriguing."

"Guys, I was just thinking out loud," Vivien said, "or dreaming is more like it. I don't think the CEO would be up for it."

This was an opportunity they should explore further with Vivien. But in the meantime, it might help to get her friend comfortable with the private equity world. They offered to make some introductions.

*

Later that night at dinner the four Smashers plus Coop talked about everything under the sun, including the topic of success.

Grace sighed. "To me, success would be generating enough sales to prove that my baby clothing ideas are on track. It's been four months and so far we haven't gotten the traction I was expecting."

The others nodded sympathetically, especially Coop, who was also starting a business.

"Just give it some time, Grace. I know it will work," Vivien said.

"What about you, Vivi, how will you know when you've made it?" asked Andi.

"Oh that's easy. Two ways. First, I'd define success as having control over my career and calling my own shots." Vivien's eyes lit up. "And second, when Hugh Jackman asks me for my autograph!"

They all laughed and then Sofia spoke. "You know, I used to always look at success as being at the top of my game, doing my job well, and having an impact. But I realize there's no true success without personal happiness, too. Love is a critical ingredient to success in life."

"Sounds like Jasper is the one, Sofi." Vivien smiled.

"Yes, Vivi. Just like you have Clay. Isn't true love grand?" Sofia held her champagne glass up to her friend.

Andi was silent, but a profound feeling had taken hold of her. She reflected upon the struggles that she and Luca had faced over the past two years and how they'd pulled together as a team and dealt with everything. As she thought tenderly of Luca and how their relationship continued to grow and improve, she pinpointed the emotion she was experiencing...gratitude. She raised her glass. "Here's to true love," Andi said with a look of sincerity in her eyes.

The five friends smiled at each other, toasted to true love, and finished one last glass of wine for the evening.

*

GRACE

This was just like caring for a newborn. Grace was staying up late to take care of many details, waking up in the wee hours of the morning to get a jump on things, and was spending every moment obsessing over her baby...in this case, Twinkle. She was experiencing the stresses typical of a startup CEO. While Twinkle's sales of baby clothing had picked up a bit lately, the performance was not at the level that Grace had planned or hoped.

There should have been a perfect storm of marketing efforts coming together to impact the business: the viral talking baby campaign, the hospital gift baskets cosponsored with other brands, and the videos showing how the product was unique. Grace and her now team of seven were waiting for a big bang from all that marketing activity. But even with Grace's expertise, she was learning that it was tough to get a new business and a new brand off the ground. She pored over every aspect of the business. Was there a problem with the product? The aesthetics? The merchandising strategy? The price points? Or was it just a matter of waiting for the brand to become better known? This was a conundrum that Grace was intent on solving, and quickly.

At least she'd have one evening to relax and take a break from it all with her Smasher friends. Grace checked her watch and closed her laptop.

*

It was so great to be together again with Vivien, Coop, Andi, and Sofia. And their Smasher friend Courtney, who was working at BC Capital with Andi, had also stopped by to join them. It was painful to hear about Vivien being recently fired for no good reason and despite everything she had achieved.

When Sofia revealed that she and Jasper had gotten engaged, Grace couldn't stop smiling. She was thrilled for Sofia and just relieved that all the unnecessary drama between those lovebirds was put to rest.

*

Afterward, at dinner with Vivien, Sofia, Andi, and Coop, the conversation meandered all over the place, but Grace finally had a chance to talk about her boyfriend Win Wyatt.

"How is it, dating a movie star?" Coop asked, eyes wide.

"Honestly, Win is a great guy. He's smart, down-to-earth, funny, and has a good heart. We get along really well." Grace paused.

Vivien said, "I'm sensing a 'but' coming, Grace. Am I right?"

She laughed. "I just don't know if I could handle all the celebrity strangeness that comes with his job. People gawking at him all the time, photographers snapping his picture, weird stories being written in the tabloids—there's just no privacy. I'm glad we've been keeping our relationship under wraps, but sooner or later it's going to come out." Grace grimaced.

"Grace, if anyone can handle the celebrity lifestyle I'm sure you can. Heck, when they start snapping your photo I'd take the opportunity to advertise Twinkle, get some free publicity for your business!" Vivien nudged her with her elbow.

Andi perked up. "Totally, Grace, you should do that. Remember Sandy from our class who started Swanky Sips?" Their Wharton classmate had started a high-end sparkling water company right out of B-school and years later sold to Coca-Cola for a fortune. "Sandy told me that whenever she went out she'd carry a bottle of Swanky

SHAZ KAHNG

Sips and when she was eating in a restaurant she'd turn the bottle so the label was facing outwards, so everyone could see it. She took every opportunity to show off her brand."

That got Grace thinking. Maybe as a gift with purchase for first-time customers she'd make up a canvas tote bag with the Twinkle name and logo featured prominently. She'd also make sure to carry it around with her. She could also make up T-shirts for her team and give them as prizes to their customers. "You know what, I am going to do just that!"

Late that night when Grace got home she combed the internet for personalized canvas totes and T-shirts and placed her order.

*

A couple of weeks later, Grace was leaving her office to pick up some lunch at a nearby falafel place. As had become a habit recently, she carried her Twinkle tote bag everywhere. Someone from across the street called out, "Over here! Look here!" As she wove through the other pedestrians, Grace turned to look and heard the furious clicking sound of a camera shutter. The other New Yorkers on the street were as puzzled as she was and Grace shrugged, rounded the corner, and started to think about her lunch order.

A few days passed and Grace forgot about the incident until she got a text from Andi. *Hey, Grace, I was just in the grocery store and you're on the cover of the tabloids—check it out!*

It was a sunny Saturday morning and Grace donned sunglasses and a ball cap with her blond hair pulled back into a ponytail. Head down, she walked swiftly out of her building and made a beeline to the closest market. After grabbing some roasted almonds and fruit, she proceeded to the checkout stand and there she was…the headline on two tabloid newspapers was "Win Wyatt's Mystery Woman—Who Is Grace King?" and "Grace King Is Win Wyatt's New Love." There was the picture of her leaving her office with the Twinkle tote on her shoulder. Grace was both shocked and a little tickled.

She grabbed the tabloids and laid them on the conveyer belt, paid in cash, and tore back to her place. In the privacy of her apartment she read that people were buzzing about Win Wyatt's dating not a supermodel but a marketing executive and founder of a baby clothing business named Twinkle. They wrote that Grace had an undergraduate degree in mechanical engineering from Northwestern and an MBA from Wharton. The fact that such a huge celebrity was dating a "normal" person was big news. People were dying to know more about her, how she'd met Win, how long they'd been dating, etc. Another picture caught her eye—it was a photo of her and Win dancing together at Devinder and Kate's wedding.

Grace read over the articles a second time and then her phone buzzed. A text from Devinder. *Grace, we released the photo of you and Win at our wedding—thought a little attention could help Twinkle. Hope you don't mind.* That devil. Devinder was becoming as skilled at PR as Grace these days. She chuckled. Win would be home later today on a break from shooting and she'd have to show him the tabloids. Maybe she should meet him at the airport carrying her Twinkle tote bag and give him a proper welcome.

*

On Sunday morning after a leisurely breakfast, Grace and Win were canoodling on the sofa and discussing how they'd like to spend their time together during the two-week break from his movie shoot. As she got up to pour them each another cup of coffee, Grace noticed that her phone was buzzing like crazy. She saw that in the past fifteen minutes she'd received five text messages and three phone calls. Suddenly on high alert, she scrolled through the messages. The young woman in charge of her website had been calling and texting. Grace dialed her up. "Hi, Zinia, what's up?"

"Grace, the website has crashed. I'm working on fixing it now, but the past twenty-four hours have been crazy."

"What do you mean, Zinia?"

"Traffic to the Twinkle website increased about 1,000 percent in the past twenty-four hours; that's what made it crash. Also, there's a big issue that the merchandising team wants to speak with you about."

Grace, still in her pajamas, stood frozen at her kitchen counter. *Oh god, what else has gone wrong?* She did her best to remain calm and steady her voice. "Okay, can you tell me what the merchandising issue is?"

Zinia guffawed in disbelief. "We're out of product, Grace. As of this morning we're sold out of everything."

"Everything?" she repeated incredulously. "You mean there's no more product on the site at all? Where did all the traffic come from?"

"Looks like a large number were from new parents who received the hospital baskets we distributed. I also checked YouTube and the number of hits we've gotten for our talking baby video and product videos has grown exponentially over the past week, so I think we have buyers who watched our videos. All the marketing programs seem to have kicked in at the same time, Grace. After doing some analysis on the site, I noticed that the traffic coming from organic search is also incredibly high—apparently a lot of folks are typing in 'Twinkle' on their search engines."

The perfect storm of marketing efforts had finally hit—plus the bump in traffic from people seeing Grace and Win's photo had surely helped. "This is awesome!" Grace let out a whoop. "Let's get a message on the home page saying that due to high demand we've sold out but will be back in stock shortly. We should ask people to sign up for our mailing list and we'll let them know when our styles are back in stock."

"Got it, Grace. I'm on it." Zinia sounded ready to jump into action.

"I'll connect with the merchandising team and production team and get more inventory on the site quickly." Grace said goodbye and hung up the phone.

She turned and saw Win's bright blue eyes peering over the sofa at her curiously. "Everything all right, darlin'?"

Grace beamed. "Everything is awesome. Twinkle is taking off! Looks like I've actually got a business."

*

COOP

The clever marketing Coop had done with Grace's help for his firm Figures Forensic Accounting Services was kicking in. In fact, his client roster was growing so much he had to hire four accountants to help him. One client, an actress in her fifties who was splitting from her CEO husband, would surely put him on the map since hers was such a high-profile divorce.

*

The night before he'd had a fun evening of cocktails at the Royalton with his friends, followed by dinner. He awoke feeling a bit dehydrated from all the alcohol. Coop smacked his lips and tried to swallow to soothe his parched throat. He yawned and stretched out in his bed while the morning sun entered through the slits in the venetian blinds.

Coop rolled over and turned on his cell phone, which was sitting on his nightstand. There was a text from Vivien. *Please meet me for breakfast this morning. Really need to talk.* That didn't sound good. He texted her back to figure out a place and time and then hurried to take a quick shower.

*

When Vivien arrived at the diner at ten a.m. sharp she was surprised to find the perpetually tardy Coop already seated at a corner table. The remaining one-third of his Diet Coke was further evidence of his early arrival. Coop looked up and with joy in his expression waved to his friend. He gave Vivien a big squeeze of a hug.

Vivien had had a rough night and probably looked like she'd been through the wringer. She sat down at the table and placed her hands on top of the menu.

Coop glanced down at her left hand and sucked in a sudden gasp—he'd probably noticed that her hand was devoid of her engagement ring—and then tried to cover it up as a fake cough. Coop would never make it as a CIA operative.

The two friends discussed what type of food they were going to order until Coop seemed like he could stand it no longer.

"Vivi, I'm sorry, but the suspense is killing me. What's going on?"

"Clay and I broke off our engagement last night."

"Oh my god! I noticed you weren't wearing the ring. What happened, sweetie?"

Vivien struggled to find the right words but ended up blurting, "Clay's been cheating on me...with his ex, Elizabeth Atwood. And they're engaged."

"No! How could he?" Coop reached over and put his hand on her arm.

The force of Coop's reaction broke down the wall of composure that Vivien was struggling to maintain. Tears spilled down her cheeks.

"That's not all, Coop," she choked out. "Clay has gotten Elizabeth pregnant. She's expecting his baby. I went to his place last night after our dinner and found all of this out."

"Oh, Vivi, I'm so sorry. It's all... it's like a soap opera," replied an astounded Coop. "What a colossal idiot. Clay has you—wonderful you—and he goes and makes a complete mess of things. I don't understand that boy."

"I loved him and I trusted him and he cheated on me and proposed to someone else while he was engaged to me, Coop. I'm so angry with him for doing it, and angry with myself for not knowing any better." Vivien blew her nose and then shook her head in disgust.

As she spoke a pain that had eaten away at her soul for months like leprosy suddenly dissolved. It was right after baby Lily's death that she'd come to the realization that Clay wasn't the one for her. But with so much chaos going on in her life, she'd ignored her instincts and stayed with her fiancé. Yes, she was hurting right now, but at least she was free. Vivien envisioned what marriage with Clay might have looked like, and she felt certain she'd have a much happier future without him.

"I hate Clay for hurting you," Coop said through gritted teeth as he wiped away his tears. "And I have a confession to make, sweetie. I never really liked Clay, so I'm kind of glad he's out of the picture." He shrugged apologetically.

"Oh, Coop." Vivien chuckled. "In the future I'll make sure you approve of my boyfriend before I get engaged, how's that?"

He gave her a nod. "So what are you going to do with the ring?"

"I'm going to sell it and give the money to charities. Clay always talked about our civic duty to help those less fortunate, but I never saw him donate any of his family's money to a good cause. So, I'll do it for him." She winked. "At least something good will come out of this fiasco."

Coop gave her a long, adoring look. "You know, Vivi, I think Eleanor Roosevelt said it best…"

Vivien waited for another one of Coop's quotes.

"'A woman is like a tea bag. You never know how strong she is until she gets into hot water.' And you are one incredibly strong woman, Vivi."

*

Coop was still reeling over the news about Vivien's broken engagement, but he also felt relieved that she was rid of the guy. He knew she could find someone much better than Clayton Finch to take on as her life partner.

He was also feeling a little guilty that things were going so well for him in the relationship department. He and his boyfriend Dean were spending virtually all of their free time together and talking about plans for the future. Coop finally felt like he'd found "the one." In fact, he was so sure of it that he was going to bring Dean home for a big family barbecue and introduce him to everyone. It would be the first time Coop had ever brought a boyfriend home to meet his family and he was simply over the moon about it.

*

The day before the family barbecue Coop received a cryptic text from Dean. *Please come to my place after you finish work—have to talk with you.* It was reminiscent of the message Vivien had sent him and for a moment it sent Coop off kilter. But he scoffed and figured that Dean was just nervous about meeting Coop's large family and probably wanted to make sure he had all the names of his siblings in order. He responded, *Okay, luv, see you soon.*

He showed up at Dean's apartment, a modern and well-kept two-bedroom apartment on the Upper East Side. When Coop walked in he noticed a packed rolling bag waiting in the front foyer.

"Hi luv," Coop gave his boyfriend a kiss and a hug. "I'm so happy to see you."

Dean looked wan. "Hi, Coop. Do you want something to drink?"

"Maybe a glass of water, please."

Coop followed Dean into the kitchen, where his boyfriend took a tall glass out of the cabinet and handed it to Coop, sans water. He seemed incredibly distracted.

"Is everything all right?" Coop asked.

Dean exhaled with puffed out cheeks and then said, "Let's sit down for a minute." He motioned toward the living room and Coop went ahead and sat down on the sofa, still holding the empty glass. Dean sat down and then immediately stood up again. He paced the space in the living room in front of the sofa. "Coop, I want you to know that I love you and I really care about you. These past nine months with you have been some of the happiest of my life." A bad feeling started to form in the pit of Coop's stomach. He was waiting for the "but." And then it came.

"But I can't go with you to meet your family."

Coop nodded. "Okay, luv. Do you think it's too soon to meet my family?"

"No, it's not that. It's something else entirely. Something I never expected to happen. Coop, I don't know how to tell you this..." Dean looked around as if he were trying to pull an explanation out of the air like a magician producing a dove from a puff of smoke. "I'm engaged."

The shock of that statement hit Coop like a punch that knocked the breath out of his body. The glass slipped out of his hand, smashing onto the floor. "Oh, I'm sorry. Wait, what did you say, Dean?"

Dean ignored the glass shards on the floor. "I'm engaged, Coop. You know my ex and I had been together for over ten years, but Jesse didn't want to get married—that's why we broke up and I moved here from Philadelphia. I thought things were over between us. But he showed up here yesterday and we spent hours talking about our relationship. Jesse told me he'd never felt such a void in his life until the day I left and every day since we've been apart. He said he couldn't live without me and had been a fool to let me go." With a pained look on his face Dean slowly sat down on the sofa next to Coop. "At the end of our discussion Jesse got down on one knee and proposed to me with this." Dean's left hand sported a beautiful titanium band with a thin black carbon strip in the middle. "He had this custom-designed for me. Can you believe that fool? He goes and spends a fortune on a custom-designed ring without even knowing if I'd say yes." Dean wagged his head from side to side.

"But you did say yes, didn't you?" Coop whispered. His body was shaking with despair.

Dean put his hand on Coop's knee. "I did. As much as I love you, Coop, I searched my heart and realized that I still love Jesse. And I can't just throw away the ten wonderful years we had together, the life we built together. Ending my relationship with you is one of the most difficult things I've ever done, because I think you're an amazing person. I've enjoyed every minute we've been together. But I just know that Jesse is 'the one' for me. I'm so sorry about this, Coop." Dean's eyes were misty with emotion. "I never wanted to hurt you."

Coop sat in a stupor as the tears started to flow. The news lacerated his heart like a scalpel slashing the organ into shreds. His relationship with Dean had been going so beautifully. Dean was supposed to be his person, his life partner. How could everything change so suddenly? This was the last thing he'd ever expected to hear. Coop dropped his head in his hands and said in a muffled voice, "Goodbye, Vermont."

CHAPTER 14

December

GRACE

By early December, life couldn't have been better for Grace. Twinkle had really taken off and she had a thriving business with a buzzed-about brand. Even her main investor, Devinder, was in awe of how well things were going. Grace made sure her Twinkle team had everything in order to keep the business running smoothly before she took off to the airport for her flight to Paris.

Win couldn't make it to Sofia's wedding in France from his shoot in New Zealand, but he and Grace were going to rendezvous in the Australian outback to celebrate Christmas together in a few weeks. By then the movie Win was filming would be wrapping up. Grace couldn't wait for some alone time with her boyfriend away from the photographers who had been hounding her for the past few months.

*

As Grace headed to the airport with Sofia, Andi, and Coop, the four of them gabbed excitedly about the wedding festivities. Vivien would fly to NYC from Portland and was meeting them at the airport so they could make the flight to Paris together. Grace's phone was buzzing, and not recognizing the number, she let it roll to voice mail.

After the four of them checked in, delighted that Sofia had managed to get them all upgraded to first class, Grace took a minute to check her voice mail while they were in the long security line. She nearly dropped her phone in shock when she heard the voice on the message.

"Grace, my dear, it's your friend Shelby! I just wanted to congratulate you on the success of the Twinkle business—sounds like it's going gangbusters. I just knew you'd make it a winner. Things at Palazzo are great and we're all so proud of you here. I miss you—you know, we should really get together for drinks soon or maybe do a double date with Win Wyatt and my boyfriend. Oh, and Skip Palmer sends his best regards. By the way, I don't know if you know this but I am now heading up merchandising for the Baby & Kids business. We've run into some business issues lately and since you're now an expert in the space I thought you could help us out. I need you to call me back before end of day. Okay? Bye now."

That was too much. There wasn't a single "please" or "thank you" in Shelby's request. What nerve. *Shelby's going to be waiting a long, long time for that return phone call.*

*

Reunited with Vivien, the Smashers and Coop boarded the plane and accepted the glass of champagne offered to each of them. Grace was seated next to Andi, while Vivien was in front of them and Coop across the aisle from Vivien. Sofia came back to clink champagne glasses and Grace toasted her friends.

She sat back mulling over the recent events in her life and reflecting on how unpredictable events could have such a dramatic impact. Grace had randomly met movie star Win Wyatt while practicing golf at Chelsea Piers and now they were happily dating. She'd written a successful book on branding called *Rise: Six Steps to Resuscitate Your Brand After a Fiasco*. As one brand case study for her book, Grace had helped Flip Style get back on track and turn their business around. The other rebranding case study was focused on getting Simone

Everett's personal brand and career back on track, and now Simone was starring in a hit TV series. When Grace's plans to run the Baby & Kids business at Palazzo were obliterated by CEO Skip Palmer, she'd arisen from the ashes and launched her own baby business, Twinkle, which was growing extremely well.

Grace was grateful for all her good fortune. She recalled the last thing Skip Palmer had said to her: "You did a good job with the CMO role in the past, but frankly, I think you've peaked. I think it's all downhill for you now." *Nope, Skip old boy, I'm still rising.* She let out a brief chuckle and looked around at her Smasher friends. *Yes,* she thought, *we're all still rising.*

*

ANDI

Andi was grabbing some snacks in an airport shop near their gate when she heard someone call her name. She turned to see a tall Asian woman waving at her. Amy Kamimoto.

"Andi, so nice to see you again. Remember we met at the Wharton mentoring event?" Amy said with a big smile.

"Yes, of course, Amy. How are you? How did your internship at Kaneshiro Bank turn out?"

Amy looked pensive. "It was a good experience. And also an opportunity to make some big changes."

"Changes?" Andi was puzzled. Her confusion only increased when she saw the man standing behind Amy...Chairman Okubo.

"Hello, Andi. So good to see you. I'd like to catch up with you sometime soon." Chairman Okubo smiled warmly and shook her hand. "Amy, our flight leaves shortly so I need to check on our gate. I'll be right back. Excuse me."

Andi stood there baffled.

"Let me explain. My father"—Amy gestured to Chairman Okubo,

who was walking away— "had me work as a summer intern so I could see firsthand how the US bank was run and what the culture was like. I was kind of working undercover as his eyes and ears."

"But, your last name...," Andi murmured.

Amy laughed, covering her mouth. "Yes, I used my mother's maiden name so I wouldn't be known to anyone at the bank. Clever, eh? Anyway, based on what I reported back to my father, he made some major changes. My father was disgusted with how your situation was handled. A new CEO was installed recently, and it will please you to know that Lester Labosky has been fired." She nodded at Andi's wide-eyed expression. "Now Kaneshiro Bank is a much safer place for women. Perhaps you'll consider returning to the bank?"

So Lester had finally gotten the boot? His favorite expression was *I always get what I want.* Well, maybe he hadn't gotten what he wanted, but it sure looked like he'd gotten what he deserved.

Andi let out a little laugh at the thought. "I think my banking days are over, Amy. But, I started a PE firm, so perhaps you'll consider joining my firm when you graduate from Wharton."

They agreed to keep in touch and parted ways.

*

On the plane Andi sat back in her seat and let out a deep sigh. It felt like the last few months had been a whirlwind. The corporate carve-out of the Smart Sports women's apparel business hadn't happened. But Malcolm Smart, a cofounder of Smart Sports, had backed a plan to take the company private with the help of outside capital from BC Capital and Gaius Capital. The icing on the cake was that he required that Vivien Lee take on the role of CEO of Smart Sports—a ceiling-smashing event worthy of note. As part of the deal, Andi would have a seat on the board to actively manage their investment. Andi was proud of her friend and knew that Vivien would make a phenomenal CEO—in fact, her money was on it. All of that made their boss, Finbar, feel reinvigorated about his support of BC Capital.

But perhaps the most significant change in Andi's life was that she had finally learned to appreciate her husband, Luca, and recognize how wonderful he was. They were really in synch—working as teammates, enjoying their family life, and growing their love for each other.

*

Grace, who was sitting in the airplane seat next to Andi, said, "When is Luca coming to Paris?"

Andi smiled. "Well, I unveiled a big surprise for Luca. He's a *futbol* fanatic, so after Sofia's wedding we are going to the World Cup with the twins and Luca's parents. I was able to get tickets for all of us to go to the soccer games in Germany. He is so stoked!"

"That's awesome, Andi. Very thoughtful of you."

"Luca and his parents are taking the boys to their hometown of Venice, and while his parents look after Francesco and Antonio he will meet me in Paris for Sofia's wedding. Then we'll all rendezvous in Germany for the World Cup. It's going to be amazing."

Grace smiled at her and then looked up.

Sofia was standing in the aisle clinking champagne glasses with her friends. "Ladies, and Coop, here's to true love."

"Hang on a second," Andi interjected. "I need to revise my statement." Her friends gave her a puzzled look. "Remember when I said that the secret to true love is simply finding someone you can live with and someone who can live with you?" She gave a sideways look at Grace, who had added that last part. "Well, I was wrong. The secret to true love is finding someone you can't live without." She toasted to each of her dear friends and to Luca, who was always in her heart.

Much later in the flight, when the hubbub of a celebrity, Hugh Jackman, sitting next to Vivien on the flight had died down, Andi reflected on Vivien's definition of success: "First, I'd define success as having control over my career and calling my own shots." Vivien would be getting that chance as the Smart Sports CEO. "And second, when Hugh Jackman asks me for my autograph!"

As if on cue, Andi heard Hugh asking Vivien for her autograph. She couldn't help herself—she gave the back of Vivien's seat a playful kick and laughed, snorting champagne out of her nose.

*

SOFIA

On the one hand, Sofia couldn't believe that this was actually happening—she was on a flight to Paris with her friends for her wedding to Jasper Frank. On the other hand, she couldn't wait for it to be over so she could begin her life with him.

Jasper was flying to the wedding location from Carmel, California, where his parents lived. His mother had recovered from her stroke but Jasper wasn't taking any chances and wanted to make sure his parents arrived safely in France for their ceremony. Sofia didn't mind; it just showed what a kind and thoughtful man she was about to marry.

They'd had a number of long talks about their life together and Sofia had finally realized that being with someone—marrying someone— didn't mean giving up her career or her dreams. In fact, if anything Jasper was pushing her to do more in her career, especially after she and Kate Frost broke the story of Charley Voss's victimizing so many women. The good news was that Voss had been fired from his CEO role at Voss & Co. and arrested, and was having to atone for all his dark deeds. Sofia felt proud of her work and that she was able to help other women—that was what a true Ceiling Smasher did.

*

Sofia walked back a couple of rows to where her friends were seated, and they toasted with full champagne glasses and a ping that was the sound of celebration. She listened to what Andi had to say about true love, and she couldn't have agreed more—Sofia couldn't possibly imagine a life without Jasper in it.

Coop was looking a bit distracted, so Sofia sat on the armrest of his seat for a chat. Speaking in French, she said, "How are you doing these days, Coop?" It had been a few months since his boyfriend Dean had abruptly ended things by getting engaged to his ex-boyfriend. Coop's eyes—usually sparkling with merriment—still held a clouded look of sadness.

He patted her arm. "I'm fine, Sof, thanks for asking. I just never imagined that finding love would be so difficult. Anyway, I'm just so happy for you. And Jasper."

"Can you believe it? Me, getting married? Who'd have thought."

Her previous aversion to marriage was no secret and the two of them laughed.

Sofia felt happiness radiating through her body and she only wanted the same for Coop. "I just wanted to tell you not to lose hope, Coop. I mean, Jasper and I met because of a taxi accident—how random is that? You just never know how you'll find your soul mate or how he'll find you. Right?"

Coop looked around and noticed the cute guy sitting next to him. Continuing their conversation in French, he said, "That's true, Sofia. For example, take this cute guy sitting next to me. If he's single, can whip up a soufflé, and can discuss the best exchange-traded funds, then he'd be perfect for me."

Giggling, they both stole a glance at Coop's cute seat mate, who didn't react to their comments. Probably only spoke English. The flight attendant asked the passengers to take their seats, so Sofia bid adieu to Coop for a little while.

Sofia took her seat and closed her eyes, imaging a wonderful future with Jasper. For the first time in what seemed like forever, a powerful sense of possibility grabbed hold of her. She felt the delicious anticipation that she was about to embark on a journey whose outcome she could not predict...and she wouldn't have wanted it any other way.

*

COOP

"I don't know, Vivi. Maybe I'm just destined to live a solitary life." Those had been Coop's sober words to his best friend, Vivien, a few days ago. "But I just want to feel that spark with someone. Is that too much to ask?"

"You will, Coop, you will. Anyway, we're both single now, so you'd better dance with me at Sofia's wedding."

Though he was still devastated about the breakup with Dean a few months ago, Coop thought things weren't all bad. In fact, the other areas of his life were going great. He'd started up his own forensic accounting firm and was getting more clients than he could handle. The work was enjoyable and he really felt like he was helping people. And for the first time in his life his finances were in such good shape that Coop even allowed himself to relax a little.

*

Sitting in first class on a flight to Paris to attend Sofia's wedding, Coop was surrounded by his dear friends. What could be better than that? He noticed Vivien's *Fortune* magazine and started...his friend's face was on the front cover!

"Let me see that, Vivi!" He practically grabbed it out of her hands. Coop intently read the story about her new CEO role. He was so proud of his friend. Sipping his champagne, Coop continued flipping through the magazine until he came to another familiar face that made him scowl. Felix Culo, his old nemesis, was appearing in court wearing an orange jumpsuit and handcuffs. It was the sentencing hearing, and Felix had tears streaming down his face at the announcement of his fate. This was the guy who'd had no qualms about screwing over many innocent people. *Karma, baby.*

Coop closed the magazine, and when he looked up he did a double take. He nearly fell out of his seat when Hugh Jackman walked down the aisle and took the seat next to Vivien. Sofia came back, and the five friends toasted to true love.

Coop felt a pang in his heart.

Sofia, who spoke five languages fluently, sat on the armrest of Coop's seat excitedly conversing with him in French until the flight attendant announced that they were preparing to leave and needed everyone in their seats. Coop wrapped up his conversation with Sofia and made what he thought was a pretty witty comment about the cute, unsuspecting guy sitting next to him. She gave him a wink and headed back to her seat.

Coop picked up the amenities kit on the shelf in front of him, unzipped it, and had started to examine it when he heard an unfamiliar voice speaking in French.

"By the way, the cute guy's name is Rafael, and thank you for the compliment." Apparently his seat mate did speak French. Oops.

Coop turned crimson. "Duh, I should have figured that on a flight to Paris there would be other French speakers. Sorry about that, Rafael. My name is Coop." They shook hands, and Coop almost pulled his away in surprise—Rafael had a serious callus at the base of his index finger.

"Well, my knowledge of ETFs is somewhat limited, but the soufflé part of your request I can handle since I'm a chef." Rafael gave an impish grin. "Perhaps when you are in Paris you can come visit my restaurant?"

Coop perked up. A cute guy and gourmet food—now, that sounded like an appetizing combination.

Sparks began to fly.

Vivien looked over at Coop, who was deep in conversation with the guy sitting beside him—she could swear that Coop was full-on flirting and it made her smile.

So much had happened over the past couple of years, especially in recent months. What each of them had accomplished was nothing short of remarkable.

Coop, who was taking a pause from his conversation with his seat mate, leaned over toward her. Gesturing to their friends and their posh first-class seats, he raised his champagne glass and said, "Isn't this the best, Vivi?"

Vivien let out a sigh. "It sure is, Coop. In the words of Oscar Wilde, 'I have the simplest of tastes, I am always satisfied with the best.' Here's to best friends and the many marvelous adventures ahead of us."

ACKNOWLEDGEMENTS:

I'd like to thank the many people who in different ways helped to bring this story to life:

My readers, who provide that spark of inspiration that keeps me writing. Your ardent enthusiasm, positivity, and support are greatly appreciated.

My daughters, Gemma and Zoe, for their abundant energy and ideas, and for making me smile every day.

My husband, Bill Diotte, for his steadfast support and encouragement, and for his big heart.

My family, especially my sister, Kathy Kahng, and my sisters-in-law, Kathy Agnew, Elaine Sauve, and Jane Yacko for being great examples of brains, determination, and grace.

My network of Wharton and Cornell alumni and the many amazing women leaders I've known.

My friends, especially Gina Barge and Ed & Glenda Spangler for always being so supportive. Also thanks to John Olson and Syd for their delightful companionship.

My beta readers, especially Michael Pogozelski, Suzie Ivelich, and Christine Chen for all their time, effort, and detailed feedback.

My fantastic team of editors and designers who helped shape the book into something special.

$\sim$

ABOUT THE AUTHOR

Shaz Kahng is a serial Board Director and CEO with a track record of achieving goals previously thought impossible. In her quest to become a CEO, Shaz has been a scientist, a consulting partner, an e-commerce expert, and a brand and marketing strategist. Over the course of her career she has encountered many unique and unbelievable business situations, some of which have made their way into her books. She is a graduate of Cornell University and The Wharton School.

An adventurous spirit, Shaz is also a certified rescue SCUBA diver, certified skydiver, dancer, fitness enthusiast, golfer, and is studying Tae Kwon Do. She is the mother of twin girls and lives with her family in Connecticut.

Stay up to date with Shaz and the *Ceiling Smashers* series via her website:
ceilingsmashers.com

SMASHERS SYNCHED: QUESTIONS & TOPICS FOR READING GROUP DISCUSSION

1. What did you like best about this book?
2. What aspects of the story could you most relate to and why?
3. Which character and associated plot line resonated with you most?
4. Each character goes through some major changes and shifts in direction in their professional lives- what has been the biggest change you've made in your career? Please share your experiences.
5. Throughout the story, each character has to work with a new colleague and win them over. Who do you think handled that interaction most effectively? Have you had to deal with a difficult colleague and what did you do?
6. In the book each character deals with a myriad of challenges, both personally and professionally? What stood out to you?
7. One of the themes in this book was the bond between women. What aspect of that subject resonated with you?
8. Which character in the book would you most like to meet and have dinner with? What would be an interesting topic of conversation?
9. What's your favorite quote from the book and why?
10. If you could ask the author one question about the book what would it be?

Made in the USA
Middletown, DE
06 April 2021

36387055R00274